Critical Writings by the English Romantics

英国浪漫主义者诗论

Edited by Yuan Xianjun
袁宪军———编

海峡出版发行集团 | 福建教育出版社

图书在版编目（CIP）数据

英国浪漫主义者诗论／袁宪军编. —福州：福建教育出版社，2021.11
 ISBN 978-7-5334-7706-6

Ⅰ.①英… Ⅱ.①袁… Ⅲ.①浪漫主义－诗歌研究－英国 Ⅳ.①I567.072

中国版本图书馆 CIP 数据核字（2017）第 079991 号

Critical Writings by the English Romantics
英国浪漫主义者诗论
袁宪军　编

出版发行	福建教育出版社 （福州市梦山路 27 号　邮编：350025　网址：www.fep.com.cn） 编辑部电话：010-62027445 发行部电话：010-62024258　0591-87115073）
出 版 人	江金辉
印　　刷	福建新华联合印务集团有限公司 （福州市晋安区后屿路 6 号　邮编：350014）
开　　本	890 毫米×1240 毫米　1/32
印　　张	9.875
字　　数	150 千字
插　　页	2
版　　次	2021 年 11 月第 1 版　2021 年 11 月第 1 次印刷
书　　号	ISBN 978-7-5334-7706-6
定　　价	45.00 元

如发现本书印装质量问题，请向本社出版科（电话：0591-83726019）调换。

Contents

Preface 1

William Blake 5
   A Vision of the Last Judgment 5
   The Ancient Britons 19
   On Homer's Poetry 24

William Wordsworth 26
   Preface to *Lyrical Ballads, with Pastoral and Other Poems* (1802) 26
   Preface to *Poems* (1815) 50
   Essay, Supplementary to the Preface (1815) 66

Samuel Taylor Coleridge 93
   BIOGRAPHIA LITERARIA (1817) 93
      CHAPTER XII 93
      CHAPTER XIII 123
      CHAPTER XIV 131
      CHAPTER XV 138
      CHAPTER XVII 145
      CHAPTER XVIII 159
   On the Principles of Genial Criticism (Essay Third) 182
      Agreeable 182

    Beautiful 183
    Recapitulation 187

Thomas Love Peacock 192
    The Four Ages of Poetry (1820) 192

Percy Bysshe Shelley 207
    A Defence of Poetry 207

John Keats 239
    Letters 239
        To Benjamin Bailey, 22nd November 1817 239
        To George and Tom Keats, 21st December 1817 ... 242
        To John Hamilton Reynolds, 3rd Februrary 1818 ... 242
        To John Hamilton Reynolds, 19th February 1818 ... 248
        To James Augustus Hessey, 9th October 1818 250
        To Richard Woodhouse, 27th October 1818 251
        To George and Georgiana Keats, 16th December 1818 ... 253
        To George and Georgiana Keats, 19th March 1819 ... 254
        To Percy Bysshe Shelley, 16th August 1820 256

William Hazlitt 258
    The Spirit of the Age or Contemporary Portraits 258
        Mr Coleridge 258
        Sir Walter Scott 269
        Lord Byron 281
        Mr Southey 293
        Mr Wordsworth 302

Preface

The collection in a single volume of the critical and theoretical writings by the English Romantics that will provide material for the reader interested in Romanticism to have a reasonably thorough course of readings is accumulated mainly with the consideration that the survival of the spirit of the Romantic Age might be plausibly a promotive agency in our cultivation of a sound and elevated society and that the way of critical and creative thinking of the English Romantics might spur the 'spontaneous overflow of powerful feelings' in our young people's endeavour and attempt in their enterprise, business, and daily life. The tenor of the critical writings collected here are, though being focused upon and not confined to Romantics' theoretical speculation of poetry and criticism of poetic compositions, with their attachment to emancipation, freedom, imagination, intuition, perception, etc, elucidated elaborately and effectively here and there in their writings. A conscious observation of the contemporary society, a unfettered and steadfast contemplation of self in relation to others, and a sustained looking to nature and to the light of their own genius, is perhaps exactly what we want in the development of our world, both material and intellectual. In short, the cultivation of a noble mind which prevails throughout the writings of the English Romantics, I hope, will help to strengthen and broaden the power of criticism with an aim at seeing 'the object as in itself it really is' and freeing us from remaining in 'a sphere where alone narrow and relative conceptions have any worth and validity,'[①] thus being of referential assistance to the establishment of a spirit of the age at present.

The selection of the essays in this volume abides by the general supposition maintained by critics at large. Thus William Blake, William Wordsworth, Sam-

---

[①] Matthew Arnold, *The Function of Criticism at the Present Time* (1864).

uel Taylor Coleridge, Percy Bysshe Shelley and John Keats are the leading figures whose critical ideas have been acknowledged and commented world-widely ever since their writings were published, and they have been included in an impressive variety of collections and selections concerning Romanticism. In this volume I make no attempt to change the ordinance. However, I could not completely restrain myself from a personal preference though I know that objectivity is always the principle in any of this kind of sellections. Therefore there must be some writings or passages carrying a certain weight of importance not included in this volume, but that does not mean that the reader would not have the opportunity of acquiring a general understanding of the organic whole of the critical thought of the Romantic(s). Of course, there is a great difference in the handling of the particular writer. For example, I do not include Blake's 'Annotations to Reynolds' Discourses' and 'Marginalia,' which are usually taken as the basic enunciation of Blake's critical thought and are thus preferred by other editors. Here the major consideration is that, as in the other writers in this volume, the whole text is provided as long as possible since the context is crucial in our understanding of the principal concepts and ideas of the Romantics (and thus the complete chapters rather than extracts are offered from Coleridge's *Biographia Literaria* and Keats's letters). But we will not lose Blake's opinions on the principal subjects of the age. I include here Wordsworth's 'Essay, Supplementary to the Preface' and 'Preface to *Poems*' in addition to the 'Preface to *Lyrical Ballads*,' so that the reader may discern the minute changes as well as the development of his theoretical thinking. Love Peacock's 'The Four Ages of Poetry' and Shelley's 'A Defence of Poetry' are as usual put together in order that the reader sees clearly the contrary speculations with regard to Romantic poetry. One thing out of the reader's expectations is perhaps the inclusion of the passages from William Hazlitt's *The Spirit of the Age*, the aim of which is for the modern reader to get a glimpse of the critical portraits of English Romantics by one of their contemporaries.

I will not supply anything like an introduction or a headnote for each part since I would rather the reader resort to his/her own judgment, not the preoccupation of the editor, for what 'itself it really is.' And neither will I provide footnotes unless I believe compulsary—the footnotes only brush aside the obstacles that hinder the reader's understanding.

I am, of course, indebted to many people who have contributed in one way or another to the completion of a series of books published and to be published in Fujian Education Press, among which this is one. Special thanks go to Jiang Hua, whithout whose timely and effective help the series would never come into being.

Yuan Xianjun

William Blake

A Vision of the Last Judgment

THE LAST Judgment: when all those are Cast away who trouble Religion with Questions concerning Good & Evil or Eating of the Tree of those Knowledges or Reasonings which hinder the Vision of God turning all into a Consuming fire. When Imagination, Art & Science & all Intellectual Gifts all the Gifts, all the Holy Ghost, are lookd upon as of no use & only Contention remains to Man, then the Last Judgment begins, & its Vision is seen by the Imaginative Eye of Every one according to the situation he holds.

The Last Judgment is not Fable or Allegory, but Vision. Fable or Allegory are a totally distinct & inferior kind of Poetry. Vision or Imagination is a Representation of what Eternally Exists, Really & Unchangeably. Fable or Allegory is Formd by the Daughters of Memory. Imagination is Surrounded by the daughters of Inspiration, who in the aggregate are calld Jerusalem. Fable is Allegory, but what Critics call The Fable is Vision itself. The Hebrew Bible & the Gospel of Jesus are not Allegory but Eternal Vision or Imagination of All that Exists. Note here that Fable or Allegory is seldom without some Vision. *Pilgrim's Progress* is full of it, the Greek Poets the same; but Allegory & Vision ought to be known as Two Distinct Things, & so calld for the Sake of Eternal Life. Plato has made Socrates say that Poets & Prophets do not Know or Understand what they write or Utter; this is a most Pernicious Falshood. If they do not, pray is an inferior Kind to be call'd Knowing? Plato confutes himself.

The Last Judgment is one of these Stupendous Visions. I have represented it as I saw it; to different People it appears differently as every thing else does;

for tho on Earth things seem Permanent, they are less permanent than a Shadow, as we all know too well.

The Nature of Visionary Fancy, or Imagination, is very little Known & the Eternal nature & permanence of its ever Existent Images is considerd as less permanent than the things of Vegetative & Generative Nature; yet the Oak dies as well as the Lettuce, but Its Eternal Image & Individuality never dies, but renews by its seed; just so the Imaginative Image returns to the seed of Contemplative Thought. The Writings of the Prophets illustrate these conceptions of the Visionary Fancy by their various sublime & Divine Images as seen in the Worlds of Vision.

[...] when they Assert that Jupiter usurped the Throne of his Father Saturn & brought on an Iron Age & Begat on Mnemosyne or Memory. The Greek Muses which are not Inspiration as the Bible is. Reality was Forgot & the Vanities of Time & Space only Rememberd & calld Reality. Such is the Mighty difference between Allegoric Fable & Spiritual Mystery. Let it here be Noted that the Greek Fables originated in Spiritual Mystery & Real Vision, which are lost & clouded in Fable & Alegory, while the Hebrew Bible & the Greek Gospel are Genuine, Preservd by the Saviour's Mercy. The Nature of my Work is Visionary or Imaginative; it is an Endeavour to Restore what the Ancients calld the Golden Age.

This world of Imagination is the World of Eternity; it is the Divine bosom into which we shall all go after the death of the Vegetated body. This World of Imagination is Infinite & Eternal, whereas the world of Generation or Vegetation is Finite & Temporal. There Exist in that Eternal World the Permanent Realities of Every Thing which we see are reflected in this Vegetable Glass of Nature. All Things are comprehended in their Eternal Forms in the Divine body of the Saviour, the True Vine of Eternity, The Human Imagination, who appeard to Me as Coming to Judgment among his Saints & throwing off the Temporal that the Eternal might be Establishd; around him were seen the Images of Existences according to a certain order suited to my Imaginative Eye.

Here follows the description of the Picture. Query the Above ought to follow the description.

Jesus seated between the Two Pillars, Jachin & Boaz with the Word of Divine Revelation on his Knees & on each side the four & twenty Elders sitting in Judgment; the Heavens opening around him by unfolding the clouds around his throne. The Old H[eaven] & old Earth are passing away & the N[ew] H[eaven] & N[ew] Earth descending as a Scroll. The Just arise on his right & the wicked on his Left hand. A Sea of fire Issues from before the Throne. Adam & Eve appear first before the Judgment Seat; in humiliation Abel surrounded by Innocents & Cain with the flint in his hand with which he slew his brother falling with the head downward. From the Cloud on which Eve stands Satan is seen falling headlong wound round by the tail of the serpent whose bulk naild to the Cross, round which he wreathes is falling into the Abyss. Sin is also represented as a female bound in one of the Serpents folds surrounded by her fiends. Death is Chaind to the Cross & Time falls together with death dragged down by a Demon crownd with Laurel; another demon with a Key has the charge of Sin & is dragging her down by the hair; beside them a figure is seen scaled with iron scales from head to feet, precipitating himself into the Abyss with the Sword & Balances; he is Og King of Bashan—

On the Right Beneath the Cloud on which Abel kneels is Abraham with Sarah & Isaac, & also Hagar & Ishmael. Abel kneels on a bloody Cloud, descriptive of those Churches, before the flood that they were filld with blood & fire & vapour of smoke, even till Abrahams time the vapour & heat was not Extinguishd. These States Exist now. Man Passes on, but States remain for Ever; he passes thro them like a traveller, who may as well suppose that the places he has passed thro exist no more, as a Man may suppose that the States he has passd thro exist no more. Every Thing is Eternal.

In Eternity one Thing never Changes into another Thing. Each Identity is Eternal; consequently Apuleius's *Golden Ass* & Ovid's *Metamorphosis* & others of the like kind are Fable, yet they contain Vision in a Sublime degree, being derived from real Vision in More Ancient Writings. Lot's Wife being Changed into Pillar of Salt alludes to the Mortal Body being renderd a Permanent Statue, but not Changed or Transformed into Another Identity while it retains its own Individuality. A Man can never become Ass nor Horse; some are born with shapes of Men, who may be both; but Eternal Identity is one thing & Corporeal Vegetation is another thing. Changing Water into Wine by Jesus & into Blood by Moses relates to Vegetable Nature also.

 Beneath Ishmael is Mahomet & on the left beneath the falling figure of Cain is Moses casting his tables of stone into the Deeps. It ought to be understood that the Persons, Moses & Abraham, are not here meant, but the States Signified by those Names, the Individuals being representatives or Visions of those States as they were reveald to Mortal Man in the Series of Divine Revelations as they are written in the Bible; these various States I have seen in my Imagination when distant they appear as One Man, but as you approach they appear Multitudes of Nations. Abraham hovers above his posterity which appear as Multitudes of Children ascending from the Earth surrounded by Stars as it was said. As the Stars of Heaven for Multitude Jacob & his Twelve Sons hover beneath the feet of Abraham & recieve their children from the Earth. I have seen when at a distance Multitudes of Men in Harmony appear like a single Infant sometimes in the Arms of a Female.

 But to proceed with the description of those on the Left hand. Beneath the Cloud on which Moses kneels is two figures, a Male & Female chaind together by the feet; they represent those who perishd by the flood. Beneath them a multitude of their associates are seen falling headlong. By the side of them is a Mighty fiend with a Book in his hand which is Shut. He represents the person namd in Isaiah (XXII. c & 20. V.) Eliakim the Son of Hilkiah; he drags Satan down headlong he is crownd with oak & has by the side of the Scaled figure representing Og. King of Bashan is a Figure with a Basket emptiing out the vanities of Riches & Worldly Honours. He is Araunah the Jebusite, master of the threshing floor; above him are two figures elevated on a Cloud representing the Pharisees who plead their own Righteousness before the throne. They are weighed down by two fiends. Beneath the Man with the Basket are three fiery fiends with grey beards & scourges of fire; they represent Cruel Laws; they scourge a groupe of figures down into the Deeps. Beneath them are various figures in attitudes of contention representing various States of Misery which alas every one on Earth is liable to enter into & against which we should all watch.

The Ladies will be pleasd to see that I have represented the Furies by Three Men & not by three Women. It is not because I think the Ancients wrong, but they will be pleasd to remember that mine is Vision & not Fable. The Spectator may suppose them Clergymen in the Pulpit, Scourging Sin instead of Forgiving it.

The Earth beneath these falling Groupes of figures is rocky & burning and seems as if convulsd by Earthquakes; a Great City on fire is seen in the Distance; the Armies are fleeing upon the Mountains. On the foreground hell is opened & many figures are descending into it down stone steps & beside a Gate beneath a rock howling & lamenting where Sin & Death are to be closed Eternally by that Fiend who carries the Key in one hand & drags them down with the other. On the rock & above the Gate a fiend with wings urges the wicked onwards with fiery darts; he represents the Assyrian, is Hazael the Syrian, who drives abroad all those who rebell against their Saviour; beneath the steps Babylon represented by a King crowned Grasping his Sword & his Scepter; he is just awakend out of his Grave; around him are other Kingdoms arising to Judgment, represented in this Picture as Single Personages according to the descriptions in the Prophets. The Figure dragging up a Woman by her hair represents the Inquisition as do those contending on the sides of the Pit & in Particular the Man Strangling two Women represents a Cruel Church.

Two persons, one in Purple the other in Scarlet, are descending down the Steps into the Pit; these are Caiphas & Pilate, Two States where all those reside who Calumniate & Murder under Pretence of Holiness & Justice. Caiphas has a Blue Flame like a Miter on his head; Pilate has bloody hands that never can be cleansed; the Females behind them represent the Females belonging to such States who are under perpetual terrors & vain dreams, plots & secret deceit. Those figures that descend into the Flames before Caiphas & Pilate are Judas & those of his Class. Achitophel is also here with the cord in his hand.

Between the Figures of Adam & Eve appears a fiery Gulph descending from the sea of fire. Before the throne in this Cataract Four Angels descend headlong with four trumpets to awake the Dead. Beneath these is the Seat of the Harlot namd Mystery in the Revelations. She is siezed by Two Beings, each with three heads; they Represent Vegetative Existence. As it is written in Revelations they strip her naked & burn her with fire; it represents the Eternal Consummation of Vegetable Life & Death with its Lusts. The wreathed Torches in their hands represents Eternal Fire which is the fire of Generation or Vegetation; it is an Eternal Consummation. Those who are blessed with Imaginative Vision see This Eternal Female & tremble at what others fear not while they despise & laugh at what others fear. Her Kings & Councellors & Warriors descend in Flames Lamenting & looking upon her in astonishment & Terror. & Hell is opend beneath her Seat on the Left hand. Beneath her feet is a flaming Cavern in which is seen the Great Red Dragon with Seven heads & ten Horns he has; Satan's book of Accusations lying on the rock open before him; he is bound in chains by Two strong demons; they are Gog & Magog, who have been compelld to subdue their Master Ezekiel (XXXVIIIc 8v) with their Hammer & Tongs about to new Create the Seven Headed Kingdoms. The Graves beneath are opend & the Dead awake & obey the call of the Trumpet; those on the Right hand awake in joy; those on the Left in Horror. Beneath the Dragon's Cavern a Skeleton begins to Animate starting into life at the Trumpets sound while the Wicked contend with each other on the brink of perdition. On tho Right a Youthful couple are awaked by their Children; an Aged patriarch is awakd by his aged wife. He is Albion, our Ancestor, patriarch of the Atlantic Continent, whose History Preceded that of the Hebrews & in whose Sleep, or Chaos, Creation began; his Emanation or Wife is Jerusalem, who is about to be recievd like the Bride of the [Lamb]; at their head the Aged Woman is Brittannia, the Wife of Albion: Jerusalem is their Daughter. Little Infants creep out of the flowery mould into the Green fields of the blessed who in various joyful companies embrace & ascend to meet Eternity.

 The Persons who ascend to Meet the Lord, coming in the Clouds with power & great Glory, are representations of those States described in the Bible under the Names of the Fathers before & after the Flood. Noah is seen in the Midst of these, Canopied by a Rainbow, on his right hand Shem & on his Left Japhet; these three Persons represent Poetry, Painting & Music, the three Powers in Man of conversing with Paradise, which the flood did not Sweep away.

Above Noah is the Church Universal, represented by a Woman Surrounded by Infants. There is such a State in Eternity; it is composed of the Innocent, civilized Heathen & the Uncivilized Savage, who having not the Law do by Nature the things contain in the Law. This State appears like a Female crownd with Stars driven into the Wilderness. She has the Moon under her feet. The Aged Figure with Wings having a writing tablet & taking account of the numbers who arise is That Angel of the Divine Presence mentiond in Exodus (XIVc 19v) & in other Places; this Angel is frequently calld by the Name of Jehovah, Elohim, The I am of the Oaks of Albion.

Around Noah & beneath him are various figures Risen into the Air; among these are Three Females representing those who are not of the dead but of those found Alive at the Last Judgment. They appear to be innocently gay & thoughtless, not being among the Condemnd because ignorant of crime in the midst of a corrupted Age. The Virgin Mary was of this Class. A Mother Meets her numerous Family in the Arms of their Father; these are representations of the Greek, Learned & Wise, as also of those of other Nations, such as Egypt & Babylon in which were multitudes who shall meet the Lord coming in the Clouds.

The Children of Abraham or Hebrew Churchare represented as a Stream of Light, Figures on which are seen Stars somewhat like the Milky way; they ascend from the Earth where Figures kneel Embracing above the Graves & Represent Religion or Civilized Life, such as it is in the Christian Church who are the Offspring of the Hebrew.

Just above the graves & above the spot where the Infants creep out of the Ground Stand two, a Man & Woman; these are the Primitive Christians. The two Figures in purifying flames by the side of the Dragon's cavern represents the Latter state of the Church when on the verge of Perdition yet protected by a Flaming Sword. Multitudes are seen ascending from the Green fields of the blessed, in which a Gothic Church is representative of true Art Calld Gothic in All Ages by those who follow the Fashion, as that is calld which is without Shape or Fashion. On the right hand of Noah, a Woman with Children represents the State Calld Laban the Syrian. It is the Remains of Civilization in the State from whence Abraham was taken. Also On the right hand of Noah, A Female descends to meet her Lover or Husband representative of that Love calld Friendship, which Looks for no other heaven than their Beloved & in him sees all reflected as in a Glass of Eternal Diamond.

On the right hand of these rise the Diffident & Humble, & on their left a solitary Woman with her infant; these are caught up by three aged Men who appear as suddenly emerging from the blue sky for their help. These three Aged Men represent Divine Providence as opposd to & distinct from Divine vengeance represented by three Aged men on the side of the Picture among the Wicked with scourges of fire.

If the Spectator could Enter into these Images in his Imagination, approaching them on the Fiery Chariot of his Contemplative Thought, if he could Enter into Noah's Rainbow or into his bosom or could make a Friend & Companion of one of these Images of wonder, which always intreats him to leave mortal things, as he must know, then would he arise from his Grave, then would he meet the Lord in the Air, & then he would be happy.

General Knowledge is Remote Knowledge; it is in Particulars that Wisdom consists & Happiness too. Both in Art & in Life, General Masses are as Much Art as a Pasteboard Man is Human. Every Man has Eyes, Nose & Mouth; this Every Idiot knows, but he who enters into & discriminates most minutely the Manners & Intentions, the Characters in all their branches, is the alone Wise or Sensible Man, & on this discrimination All Art is founded. I intreat then that the Spectator will attend to the Hands & Feet to the Lineaments of the Countenances; they are all descriptive of Character, & not a line is drawn without intention & that most discriminate & particular. As Poetry admits not a Letter that is Insignificant, so Painting admits not a Grain of Sand or a Blade of Grass Insignificant, much less an Insignificant Blur or Mark.

Above the Head of Noah is Seth [as] this State [is] calld. Seth is Male & Female in a higher state of Happiness & wisdom than Noah, being nearer [to] the State of Innocence beneath; the feet of Seth two figures represent the two Seasons of Spring & Autumn. While beneath the feet of Noah Four Seasons represent the Changed State made by the flood.

By the side of Seth is Elijah. He comprehends all the Prophetic Characters he is seen on his fiery Chariot bowing before the throne of the Saviour. In like manner, The figures of Seth & his wife Comprehends the Fathers before the flood & their Generations; when seen remote, they appear as One Man. A little below Seth on his right are Two Figures, a Male & Female, with numerous Children; these represent those who were not in the Line of the Church & yet were Saved from among the Antediluvians who Perished. Between Seth & these a female figure with the back turnd represents the Solitary State of those who previous to the Flood walked with God.

All these arise toward the opening Cloud before the Throne led onward by triumphant Groupes of Infants. & the Morning Stars sang together. Between Seth & Elijah three Female Figures crownd with Garlands Represent Learning & Science which accompanied Adam out of Eden.

The Cloud that opens rolling apart before the throne & before the New Heaven, & the New Earth is Composed of Various Groupes of Figures, particularly the Four Living Creatures mentiond in Revelations as Surrounding the Throne. These I suppose to have the chief agency in removing the old heavens & the old Earth to make way for the New Heaven & the New Earth to descend from the throne of God & of the Lamb. That Living Creature on the Left of the Throne Gives to the Seven Angels the Seven Vials of the wrath of God, with which they hovering over the Deeps. Beneath pour out upon the wicked their Plagues; the Other Living Creatures are descending with a Shout & with the Sound of the Trumpet Directing the Combats in the upper Elements. In the two Corners of the Picture on the Left hand Apollyon is foild before the Sword of Michael, & on the Right the Two Witnesses are subduing their Enemies. On the Cloud are opend the Books of Remembrance of Life & of Death before that of Life. On the Right some figures bow in humiliation before that of Death; on the left the Pharisees are pleading their own Righteousness; the one Shines with beams of Light, the other utters Lightnings & tempests.

A Last Judgment is Necessary because Fools flourish. Nations Flourish under Wise Rulers & are depressd under foolish Rulers. It is the same with Individuals as Nations: works of Art can only be produc'd in Perfection where the Man is either in Affluence or is Above the Care of it. Poverty is the Fool's Rod, which at last is turn'd on his own back.

This is A Last Judgment, when Men of Real Art Govern & Pretenders Fall. Some People & not a few Artists have asserted that the Painter of this Picture would not have done so well if he had been properly Encouragd. Let those who think so reflect on the State of Nations under Poverty & their incapability of Art; tho Art is Above Either, the Argument is better for Affluence than Poverty; & tho he would not have been a greater Artist, yet he would have produc'd Greater works of Art in proportion to his means. A Last Judgment is not for the purpose of making Bad Men better, but for the Purpose of hindering them from opressing the Good with Poverty & Pain by means of Such Vile Arguments & Insinuations.

Around the Throne Heaven is opend & the Nature of Eternal Things Displayd, All Springing from the Divine Humanity. All beams from him Because as he himself has said, All dwells in him. He is the Bread & the Wine; he is the Water of Life. Accordingly on Each Side of the opening Heaven appears an Apostle: that on the Right Represents Baptism; that on the Left Represents the Lord's Supper.

All Life consists of these Two: Throwing off Error & Knaves from our company continually & recieving Truth or Wise Men into our Company Continually. He who is out of the Church & opposes it is no less an Agent of Religion than he who is in it: to be an Error & to be Cast out is a part of God's Design. No man can Embrace True Art till he has Explord & Cast out False Art (such is the Nature of Mortal Things), or he will be himself Cast out by those who have Already Embraced True Art. Thus My Picture is a History of Art & Science, the Foundation of Society, Which is Humanity itself.

What are all the Gifts of the Spirit but Mental Gifts? Whenever any Individual Rejects Error & Embraces Truth, a Last Judgment passes upon that Individual.

Over the Head of the Saviour & Redeemer The Holy Spirit like a Dove is surrounded by a blue Heaven in which are the two Cherubim that bowd over the Ark, for here the temple is opend in Heaven & the Ark of the Covenant is as a Dove of Peace. The Curtains are drawn apart, Christ having rent the Veil. The

Candlestick & the Table of Shew bread appear on Each side a Glorification of Angels with Harps surround the Dove.

The Temple stands on the Mount of God; from it flows on each side the River of Life on whose banks Grows the tree of Life, among whose branches temples & Pinnacles, tents & pavilions, Gardens & Groves Display Paradise with its Inhabitants walking up & down in Conversations concerning Mental Delights. Here they are no longer talking of what is Good & Evil or of what is Right or Wrong & puzzling themselves in Satan's Labyrinth, But are Conversing with Eternal Realities as they Exist in the Human Imagination. We are in a World of Generation & death & this world we must cast off if we would be Painters Such as Rafael, Mich Angelo & the Ancient Sculptors. If we do not cast off this world, we shall be only Venetian Painters who will be cast off & Lost from Art.

Jesus is surrounded by Beams of Glory in which are seen all around him Infants emanating from him; these represent the Eternal Births of Intellect from the divine Humanity. A Rainbow surrounds the throne & the Glory in which youthful Nuptials recieve the infants in their hands. In Eternity Woman is the Emanation of Man; she has No Will of her own. There is no such thing in eternity as a Female Will.

On the Side next [to] Baptism are seen those calld in the Bible Nursing Fathers & Nursing Mothers; they have Crowns. The Spectator may suppose them to be the good Kings & Queens of England; they represent Education. On the Side next [to] the Lord's Supper, The Holy Family consisting of Mary, Joseph, John the Baptist, Zacharias & Elizabeth recieving the Bread & Wine among other Spirits of the Just made perfect. Beneath these a Cloud of Women & Children are taken up fleeing from the rolling Cloud, which separates the Wicked from the Seats of Bliss. These represent those who tho willing were too weak to Reject Error without the Assistance & Countenance of those Already in the Truth, for a Man Can only Reject Error by the Advice of a Friend or by the Immediate Inspiration of God. It is for this Reason among many others that I have put the Lord's Supper on the Left hand of the Picture. Throne for it appears so at the Last Judgment for a Protection.

Many suppose that before the Creation All was Solitude & Chaos. This is the most pernicious Idea that can enter the Mind, as it takes away all sublimity from the Bible & Limits All Existence to Creation & to Chaos, To the Time & Space fixed by the Corporeal Vegetative Eye, & leaves the Man who entertains such an Idea the habitation of Unbelieving Demons. Eternity Exists, and All things in Eternity Independent of Creation which was an act of Mercy.

I have represented those who are in Eternity by some in a Cloud within the Rainbow that Surrounds the Throne; they merely appear as in a Cloud when any thing of Creation, Redemption or Judgment are the Subjects of Contemplation, tho their Whole Contemplation is Concerning these things. The Reason they so appear is The Humiliation of the Reasoning & Doubting Selfhood, & the Giving all up to Inspiration. By this it will be seen that I do not consider either the Just or the Wicked to be in a Supreme State, but to be every one of them States of the Sleep which the Soul may fall into in its Deadly Dreams of Good & Evil when it leaves Paradise following the Serpent.

The Greeks represent Chronos or Time as a very Aged Man; this is Fable, but the Real Vision of Time is in Eternal Youth. I have, however, somewhat accomodated my Figure of Time to the Common opinion, as I myself am also infected with it & my Vision is also infected, & I see Time Aged—alas, too much so.

Allegories are things that Relate to Moral Virtues. Moral Virtues do not Exist; they are Allegories & dissimulations. But Time & Space are Real Beings, a Male & a Female: Time is a Man, Space is a Woman, & her Masculine Portion is Death.

The Combats of Good & Evil is Eating of the Tree of Knowledge. The Combats of Truth & Error is Eating of the Tree of Life. These are not only Universal, but Particular. Each are Personified. There is not an Error but it has a Man for its Agent; that is, it is a Man.. There is not a Truth but it has also a Man. Good & Evil are Qualities in Every Man, whether a Good or Evil Man. These are Enemies & destroy one another by every Means in their power, both of deceit & of open Violence. The Deist & the Christian are but the Results of these Opposing Natures. Many are Deists who would in certain Circumstances have been Christians in outward appearance. Voltaire was one of this number; he was as intolerant as an Inquisitor. Manners make the Man, not Habits. It is the same in Art: by their Works ye shall know them; the Knave who is Converted to Deism & the Knave who is Converted to Christianity is still a Knave, but he himself will not know it, tho Every body else does. Christ comes as he came at first to deliver those who were bound under the Knave, not to deliver the Knave. He Comes to Deliver Man, the Accused & not Satan, the Accuser. We do not find any where that Satan is Accused of Sin; he is only accused of Unbelief & thereby drawing Man into Sin that he may accuse him. Such is the Last Judgment—a Deliverance from Satan's Accusation. Satan thinks that Sin is displeasing to God; he ought to know that Nothing is displeasing to God but Unbelief & Eating of the Tree of Knowledge of Good & Evil.

Men are admitted into Heaven not because they have curbed & governd their Passions, or have No Passions, but because they have Cultivated their Understandings. The Treasures of Heaven are not Negations of Passion, but Realities of Intellect, from which All the Passions Emanate Uncurbed in their Eternal Glory. The Fool shall not enter into Heaven let him be ever so Holy. Holiness is not The Price of Enterance into Heaven. Those who are cast out are All Those who, having no Passions of their own because No Intellect, Have spent their lives in Curbing & Governing other People's by the Various arts of Poverty & Cruelty of all kinds. Wo, Wo, Wo to you Hypocrites! Even Murder, the Courts of Justice, more merciful than the Church, are compelld to allow, is not done in Passion, but in Cool Blooded Design & Intention.

The Modern Church Crucifies Christ with the Head Downwards.

Many Persons, such as Paine & Voltaire, with some of the Ancient Greeks, say: 'we will not Converse concerning Good & Evil; we will live in Paradise & Liberty.' You may do so in Spirit, but not in the Mortal Body as you pretend, till after the Last Judgment; for in Paradise they have no Corporeal & Mortal Body—that originated with the Fall & was calld Death & cannot be removed but by a Last judgment. While we are in the world of Mortality we Must Suffer. The Whole Creation Groans to be deliverd. There will always be as many Hypocrites born as Honest Men, & they will always have superior

Power in Mortal Things. You cannot have Liberty in this World without what you call Moral Virtue, & you cannot have Moral Virtue without the Slavery of that half of the Human Race who hate what you call Moral Virtue.

The Nature of Hatred & Envy & of All the Mischiefs in the World are here depicted. No one Envies or Hates one of his Own Party; even the devils love one another in their Way; they torment one another for other reasons than Hate or Envy; these are only employd against the Just. Neither can Seth Envy Noah, or Elijah Envy Abraham, but they may both of them Envy the Success of Satan or of Og or Molech. The Horse never Envies the Peacock, nor the Sheep the Goat, but they Envy a Rival in Life & Existence whose ways & means exceed their own, let him be of what Class of Animals he will; a Dog will envy a Cat who is pamperd at the expense of his comfort, as I have often seen. The Bible never tells us that Devils torment one another thro Envy; it is thro this that they torment the Just—but for what do they torment one another? I answer: For the Coercive Laws of Hell, Moral Hypocrisy. They torment a Hypocrite when he is discovered; they Punish a Failure in the tormentor who has sufferd the Subject of his torture to Escape.

In Hell all is Self Righteousness; there is no such thing there as Forgiveness of Sin; he who does Forgive Sin is Crucified as an Abettor of Criminals, & he who performs Works of Mercy in Any shape whatever is punishd &, if possible, destroyd, not thro Envy or Hatred or Malice, but thro Self Righteousness that thinks it does God service, which God is Satan. They do not Envy one another: They contemn & despise one another.

Forgiveness of Sin is only at the Judgment Seat of Jesus the Saviour, where the Accuser is cast out, not because he Sins but because he torments the Just & makes them do what he condemns as Sin & what he knows is opposite to their own Identity.

It is not because Angels are Holier than Men or Devils that makes them Angels, but because they do not Expect Holiness from one another, but from God only.

The Player is a liar when he Says: 'Angels are happier than Man because they are better.' Angels are happier than Men & Devils because they are not always Prying after Good & Evil in One Another & eating the Tree of Knowledge for Satan's Gratification.

Thinking as I do that the Creator of this World is a very Cruel Being, & being a Worshipper of Christ, I cannot help saying: 'The Son, O how unlike the Father!' First God Almighty comes with a Thump on the Head. Then Jesus Christ comes with a balm to heal it.

The Last Judgment is an Overwhelming of Bad Art & Science. Mental Things are alone Real; what is Calld Corporeal, Nobody Knows of its Dwelling Place: it is in Fallacy, & its Existence an Imposture. Where is the Existence Out of Mind or Thought? Where is it but in the Mind of a Fool! Some People flatter themselves that there will be No Last Judgment & that Bad Art will be adopted & mixed with Good Art, That Error or Experiment will make a Part of Truth, & they Boast that it is its Foundation. These People flatter themselves. I will not Flatter them! Error is Created. Truth is Eternal. Error, or Creation, will be Burned Up, & then, & not till then, Truth or Eternity will appear. It is Burnt up the Moment Men cease to behold it.

I assert for My self that I do not behold the Outward Creation & that to me it is hindrance & not Action; it is as the Dirt upon my feet, No part of Me. What it will be Questiond, 'When the Sun rises, do you not see a round Disk of fire somewhat like a Guinea?' O no, no, I see an Innumerable company of the Heavenly host crying 'Holy, Holy, Holy is the Lord God Almighty.' I question not my Corporeal or Vegetative Eye any more than I would Question a Window concerning a Sight: I look thro it & not with it.

The Ancient Britons

IN THE last battle of King Arthur, only three Britons escaped; these were the Strongest Man, the Beautifullest Man and the Ugliest Man: these three marched through the field unsubdued, as gods, and the sun of Britain set, but shall arise again with tenfold splendour when Arthur shall awake from sleep, and resume his Dominion over Earth and Ocean.

The three classes of Men, who are represented by the most Beautiful, the most Strong, and the most Ugly, could not be represented by any historical facts but those of our own country, the Ancient Britons, without violating costume. The Britons (say historians) were Naked Civilized Men, learned, studious, abstruse in thought and contemplation; naked, simple, plain in their Acts and Manners; wiser than after-ages. They were overwhelmed by brutal arms, all but a small remnant; Strength, Beauty and Ugliness escaped the wreck, and remain forever unsubdued, age after age.

The British antiquities are now on the artist's hands; all his Visionary Contemplations, relating to his own country and its Ancient Glory, when it was, as it again shall be, the source of learning and Inspiration. Arthur was a name for the Constellation Arcturus, or Boötes, the Keeper of the North Pole. And all the fables of Arthur and his Round Table; of the Warlike Naked Britons; of Merlin; of Arthur's conquest of the whole World; of his death, or sleep, and promise to return again; of the Druid monuments or temple; of the pavement of Watling Street; of London stone, of the carvens in Cornwall, Wales, Derbyshire, and Scotland; of the Giants of Ireland and Britain; of the Elemental Beings called by us the general name of Fairies; and of these three who escaped, namely Beauty, Strength, and Ugliness. Mr B[1] has in his hands poems of the highest antiquity: Adam was a Druid, and Noah; also Abraham was called to succeed the Druidical Age, which began to turn Allegoric and Mental signification into Corporeal Command, whereby Human sacrifice would have depopulated the Earth. All these things are written in Eden. The artist is an inhabitant of the Happy Country; and if everything goes on as it has begun, the World of Vegetation and Generation may expect to be opened again to Heaven, through Eden, as it was in the Beginning.

The Strong Man represents the Human Sublime. The Beautiful Man represents the Human Pathetic, which was in the wars of Eden divided into Male and Female. The Ugly Man represents the Human Reason. They were originally one Man, who was fourfold; he was self-divided, and his real Humanity slain on

---

[1] Blake is probably referring to himself and his own prophetic poems—editor's note.

the stems of Generation, and the form of the fourth was like the Son of God. How he became divided is a subject of great Sublimity and Pathos. The artist has written it under Inspiration, and will, if God please, publish it; it is voluminous, and contains the ancient history of Britain, and the world of Satan and of Adam.

In the meantime he has painted this picture, which supposes that in the Reign of that British prince, who lived in the fifth century, there were remains of those naked Heroes in the Welsh Mountains; they are there now, Gray saw them in the person of his bard on Snowdon; there they dwell in Naked Simplicity; Happy is he who can see and converse with them above the shadows of Generation and Death. The giant Albion, was Patriarch of the Atlantic; he is the Atlas of the Greeks, one of those the Greeks called Titans. The stories of Arthur are the Acts of Albion applied to a prince of the fifth centruy, who conquered Europe, and held the Empire of the World in the dark age, which the Romans never again recovered. In this picture, believing with Milton the ancient British history, Mr B has done as all the Ancients did, and as all the Moderns who were worthy of Fame, given the historical fact in its Poetical vigor so as it always happens, and not in that dull way that some istorians pretend, who, being weakly organozed themselves, cannot see either Miracle or Prodigy; all is to them a dull round of Probabilities and Possibilities; but the hitory of all times and places is nothing else but Improbabilities; what we should say was impossible if we did not See it always before our Eyes.

The Antiquities of every nation under Heaven, is no less Sacred than that of the Jews. They are the same thing, as Jacob Bryant and all antiquaries have proved. How other Antiquities came to be neglected and disbelieved, while those of the Jews are collected and arranged, is an inquiry worthy both of the Antiquarian and the Divine. All had originally one Language, and one Religion: this was the Religion of Jesus, the everlasting Gospel. Antiquity preaches the Gospel of Jesus. The reasoning historian, turner and twister of causes and consequences, such as Hume, Gibbon, and Voltaire, cannot with all their artifice turn or twist one Fact or disarrange self-evident Action and Reality. Reasons and opinions concerning Acts are not history. Acts themselves alone are History, and these are neither the exclusive property of Hume, Gribbon, nor Votaire, Echard, Rapin, Plutarch, nor Herodotus. Tell me the acts, O historian, and leave me to reason upon them as I please; away with your Reasoning and your Rubbish! All that is not Action is not worth reading. Tell me the what; I do not want you to tell me the Why, and the How; I can find that out Myself, as well as you can, and I will not be fooled by you into Opinion, that you please to impose, to disbelieve what you think Improbable or Impossible. His opinions, who does not see Spiritual Agency, is not worth any Man's reading; he who rejects a Fact because it is impossible. His opinions, who does not see Spiritual Agency, is not worth any man's reading; he who rejects a Fact because it is improbable, must reject all History and retain Doubts only.

It has been said to the Artist, 'take the *Apollo* for the model of your Beautiful Man, and the *Hercules* for your Strong Man, and the *Dancing Fawn* for your Ugly Man.' Now he comes to his trial. He knows that what he does is not inferior to the Grandest Antiques. Superior they cannot be, for Human Power cannot go beyond either what he does, or what they have done; it is the Gift of God, it is Inspiration and Vision. He had resolved to emulate those precious remains of Anriquity; he has done so and the result you behold; his ideas of Strengh and Beauty have not been greatly different. Poetry as it exists now on earth, in various remains of ancient Authors, Music as it exists in old Tunes or Melodies, Painting and Sculpture as it exists in the remains of Antiquity and in the works of more Modern Genius, is Inspiration, and cannot be surpassed; it is perfect and Eternal. Milton, Shakespeare, Michelangelo, Raphael, the finest specimens, of ancient Sculpture and Painting and Architecture, Gothic, Grecian, Hindu and Egyptian, are the extent of the human Mind. The Human Mind cannot go beyond the gift of God, the Holy Ghost. To suppose that Art can go beyong the finest Specimens of art that are now in the World, is not knowing what Art is; it is being blind to the gifts of the Spirit.

It will be necessary for the Painter to say something concerning his Ideas of Beauty, Strength and Ugliness.

The Beauty that is annexed and appended to Folly, is a lamentable accident and error of the Mortal and perishing Life; it does but seldom happen; but with this unnatural mixture the Sublime Artist can have nothing to do; it is fit for the Burlesque. The Beauty proper for Sublime Art is Lineaments, or Forms and features that are capable of being the receptacles of Intellect; accordingly the painter has given in his Beautiful man, his own idea of Intellectual Beauty. The face and limbs that deviates or alters least, from Infancy to Old age, is the face and limbs of greatest Beauty and Perfection.

The Ugly, likewise, when accompanied and annexed to Imbecility and Disease, is a subject for burlesque and not for Historical Grandeur; the artist has imagined his Ugly man, one approaching to the beast in Features and Form, his forehead small, without frontals; his jaws large; his nose high on the ridge, and narrow; his chest, and the stamina of his make, comparatively little, and his joints and his extremities large; his eyes, with scarce any whites, narrow and cunning, and everything tending toward what is truly Ugly, the incapability of Intellect.

The Artist has considered his Strong Man as a receptacle of Wisdom, a sublime energizer; his Features and limbs do not spindle out into length without Strength, nor are they too large and unwieldy for his Brain and Bosom. Strength consists in accumulation of Power to the principal seat, and from thence a regular gradation and subordination; Strength is compactness, not extent nor bulk.

The Strong Man acts from conscious Superiority, and marches on in fearless dependence on the Divine Decrees, raging with the inspiration of a Prophetic Mind. The Beautiful Man acts from duty and anxious Solicitude for the fates of those for whom he combats. The Ugly Man acts from love of carnage, and delight in the savage barbarities of war, rushing with sportive Precipitation into the very teeth of the affrighted enemy.

The Roman soldiers rolled together in a heap before them: 'Like the rolling thing before the Whirlwind'; each show a different Character, and a different Expression of Fear, or Revenge, or Envy, or blank Horror, or Amazement, or devout Wonder and unresisting Awe.

The dead and the dying Britons, naked, mingled with armed Romans, strew the field beneath. Among these the last of the Bards who were capable of attending warlike deeds is seen Falling, outstretched among the Dead and the Dying, singing to his harp in the Pains of Death.

Distant among the mountains are Druid temples, similar to Stonehenge. The Sun sets behind the mountains bloody with the Day of Battle.

The flush of Health in flesh exposed to the Open Air, nourished by the spirits of Forests and Floods in that ancient happy period, which History has recorded, cannot be like the sickly daubs of Titan or Rubens. Where will the copier of Nature, as it now is, find a civilized man, who has been accustomed to go Naked? Imagination only can furnish us with Colouring appropriate, such as is found in the frescoes of Raphael and Michelangelo: the disposition of Forms always direct colouring in works of True Art. As to a modern Man, stripped from his load of clothing, he is like a dead corpse. Hence Rubens, Titian, Correggio and all of that class, are like leather and chalk; their Men are like leather, and their Women like chalk, for the disposition of their Forms will not admit of grand colouring; in Mr B's Britons the blood is seen to circulate in their Limbs; he defies competition in colouring.

On Homer's Poetry

EVERY poem must necessarily be a perfect Unity, but why Homer's is peculiarly so, I cannot tell: he has told the story of Bellerophon & omitted the Judgement of Paris, which is not only a part, but a principal part, of Homer's subject.

But when a Work has Unity, it is as much in a Part as in the Whole; the torso is as much a Unity as the *Laocoön*.

As Unity is the cloak of folly, so Goodness is the cloak of knavery. Those who will have Unity exclusively in Homer come out with a Moral like a sting in the tail. Aristotle says Characters are either Good or Bad: now Goodness or Badness has nothing to do with Character: an Apple tree, a Pear tree, a Horse, a Lion, are Characters; but a Good Apple tree or a Bad is an Apple tree still; a Horse is not more a Lion for being a Bad Horse. That is its Character: its Goodness or Badness is another consideration.

It is the same with the Moral of a whole Poem as with the Moral Goodness of its parts. Unity & morality, are secondary considerations & belong to Philosophy & not to Poetry, to Exception & not to Rule, to Accident & not to Substance. The Ancients called it eating of the tree of good & evil.

The Classics, It is the classics! & not Goths nor Monks, that Desolate Europe with Wars.

William Wordsworth

Preface to *Lyrical Ballads, with Pastoral and Other Poems* (1802)

THE FIRST volume of these Poems has already been submitted to general perusal. It was published, as an experiment, which, I hoped, might be of some use to ascertain, how far, by fitting to metrical arrangement a selection of the real language of men in a state of vivid sensation, that sort of pleasure and that quantity of pleasure may be imparted, which a Poet may rationally endeavour to impart.

    I had formed no very inaccurate estimate of the probable effect of those Poems: I flattered myself that they who should be pleased with them would read them with more than common pleasure: and, on the other hand, I was well aware, that by those who should dislike them they would be read with more than common dislike. The result has differed from my expectation in this only, that I have pleased a greater number, than I ventured to hope I should please.

    For the sake of variety, and from a consciousness of my own weakness, I was induced to request the assistance of a Friend, who furnished me with the Poems of the ANCIENT MARINER, the FOSTER-MOTHER'S TALE, the NIGHTINGALE, and the Poem entitled LOVE. I should not, however, have requested this assistance, had I not believed that the Poems of my Friend would in great measure have the same tendency as my own, and that, though there would be found a differnece, there would be found no discordance in the colours of our style; as our opinions on the subject of poetry do almost entirely coincide.

    Several of my Friends are anxious for the success of these Poems from a belief, that, if the views with which they were composed were indeed realized, a class of Poetry would be produced, well adapted to interest mankind permanently, and not unimportant in the multiplicity, and in the quality of its moral relations: and on this account they have advised me to prefix a systematic defence of the theory, upon which the poems were written. But I was unwilling to undertake the task, because I knew that on this occasion the Reader would look coldly upon my arguments, since I might be suspected of having been principally influenced by the selfish and foolish hope of reasoning him into an approbation of these particular Poems: and I was still more unwilling to undertake the task, because, adequately to display my opinions, and fully to enforce my arguments, would require a space wholly disproportionate to the nature of a preface. For to treat the subject with the clearness and coherence, of which I believe it susceptible, it would be necessary to give a full account of the present state of the public taste in this country, and to determine how far this taste is healthy or depraved; which, again, would not be determined, without pointing out in what manner language and the human mind act and re-act on each other, and without retracing the revolutions, not of literature alone, but likewise of society itself. I have therefore altogether declined to enter regularly upon this defence; yet I am sensible, that there would be something like impropriety in abruptly obtruding upon the Public, without a few words of introduction, Poems so materially different from those upon which general approbation is at present bestowed.

It is supposed, that by the act of writing in verse an Author makes a formal engagement that he will gratify certain known habits of association; that he not only thus apprises the Reader that certain classes of ideas and expressions will be found in his book, but that others will be carefully excluded. This exponent or symbol held forth by metrical language must in different eras of literature have excited very different expectations: for example, in the age of Catullus, Terence and Lucretius, and that of Statius or Claudian; and in our own country, in the age of Shakespeare and Beaumont and Fletcher, and that of Donne and Cowley, or Dryden, or Pope. I will not take upon me to determine the exact import of the promise which by the act of writing in verse an Author, in the present day, makes to his Reader; but I am certain, it will appear to many persons that I have not fulfilled the terms of an engagement thus voluntarily contracted. They who have been accustomed to the gaudiness and inane phraseology of many modern writers, if they persist in reading this book to its conclusion, will, no doubt, frequently have to struggle with feelings of strangeness and awkwardness: they will look round for poetry, and will be induced to inquire by what species of courtesy these attempts can be permitted to assume that title. I hope therefore the Reader will not censure me, if I attempt to state what I have proposed to myself to perform; and also, (as far as the limits of a preface will permit) to explain some of the chief reasons which have determined me in the choice of my purpose: that at least he may be spared any unpleasant feeling of disappointment, and that myself may be protected from one of the most dishonourable accusation[s] which can be brought against an Author, namely, that of an indolence which prevents him from endeavouring to ascertain what is his duty, or, when his duty is ascertained, prevents him from performing it.

The principal object, then, which I proposed to myself in these Poems was to choose incidents and situations from common life, and to relate or describe them, throughout, as far as was possible, in a selection of language really used by men; and, at the same time, to throw over them a certain colouring of imagination, whereby ordinary things should be presented to the mind in an unusual way; and, further, and above all, to make these incidents and situations interesting by tracing in them, truly though not ostentatiously, the primary laws of our nature: chiefly, as far as regards the manner in which we associate ideas in a state of excitement. Low and rustic life was generally chosen, because in that condition, the essential passions of the heart find a better soil in which they can attain their maturity, are less under restraint, and speak a plainer and more emphatic language; because in that condition of life our elementary feelings coexist in a state of greater simplicity, and, consequently, may be more accurately contemplated, and more forcibly communicated; because the manners of rural life germinate from those elementary feelings, and, from the necessary character of rural occupations, are more easily comprehended, and are more durable; and, lastly, because in that condition the passions of men are incorporated with the beautiful and permanent forms of nature. The language, too, of these men has been adopted (purified indeed from what appear to be its real defects, from all lasting and rational causes of dislike or disgust) because such men hourly communicate with the best objects from which the best part of language is originally derived; and because, from their rank in society and the sameness and narrow circle of their intercourse, being less under the influence of social vanity, they convey their feelings and notions in simple and unelaborated expressions. Accordingly, such a language, arising out of repeated experience and regular feelings, is a more permanent, and a far more philosophical language, than that which is frequently substituted for it by Poets, who think that they are conferring honour upon themselves and their art, in proportion as they separate themselves from the sympathies of men, and indulge in arbitrary and capricious habits of expression, in order to furnish food for fickle tastes, and fickle appetites, of their own creation.①

I cannot, however, be insensible to the present outcry against the triviality and meanness, both of thought and language, which some of my contemporaries have occasionally introduced into their metrical compositions; and I acknowledge that this defect, where it exists, is more dishonourable to the Writer's own character than false refinement or arbitrary innovation, though I should contend at the same time that it is far less pernicious in the sum of its consequences. From such verses the Poems in these volumes will be found distinguished at least by one mark of difference, that each of them has a worthy *purpose*. Not that I mean to say, that I always began to write with a distinct purpose formerly conceived; but I believe that my habits of meditation have so formed my feelings, as that my descriptions of such objects as strongly excite those feelings, will be found to carry along with them a *purpose*. If in this opinion I am mistaken, I can have little right to the name of a Poet. For all good poetry is the spontaneous overflow of powerful feelings: but though this be true, Poems to which any value can be attached, were never produced on any variety of subjects but by a man, who being possessed of more than usual organic sensibility, had also thought long and

---

① It is worth while here to observe that the affecting parts of Chaucer are almost always expressed in language pure and universally intelligible even to this day.

deeply. For our continued influxes of feeling are modified and directed by our thoughts, which are indeed the representatives of all our past feelings; and, as by contemplating the relation of these general representatives to each other, we discover what is really important to men, so, by the repetition and continuance of this act, our feelings will be connected with important subjects, till at length, if we be originally possessed of much sensibility, such habits of mind will be produced, that, by obeying blindly and mechanically the impulses of those habits, we shall describe objects, and utter sentiments, of such a nature and in such connexion with each other, that the understanding of the being to whom we address ourselves, if he be in a healthful state of association, must necessarily be in some degree enlightened, and his affections ameliorated.

I have said that each of these poems has a purpose. I have also informed my Reader what this purpose will be found principally to be: namely, to illustrate the manner in which our feelings and ideas are associated in a state of excitement. But, speaking in language somewhat more appropriate, it is to follow the fluxes and refluxes of the mind when agitated by the great and simple affections of our nature. This object I have endeavoured in these short essays to attain by various means; by tracing the maternal passion through many of its more subtle windings, as in the poems of the IDIOT BOY and the MAD MOTHER; by accompanying the last struggles of a human being, at the approach of death, cleaving in solitude to life and society, as in the Poem of the FORSAKEN INDIAN; by showing, as in the Stanzas entitled WE ARE SEVEN, the perplexity and obscurity which in childhood attend our notion of death, or by displaying the strength of fraternal, or to speak more philosophically, of moral attachment when early associated with the great and beautiful objects of nature, as in THE BROTHERS; or as in the Incident of SIMON LEE, by placing my Reader in the way of receiving from ordinary moral sensations another and more salutary impression than we are accustomed to receive from them. It has also been part of my general purposes to attempt to sketch characters under the influence of less impassioned feelings, as in the TWO APRIL MOrnINGS, THE FOUNTAIN, THE OLD MAN TRAVELLING, THE TWO THIEVES, &c. characters of which the elements are simple, belonging rather to nature than to manners, such as exist now, and will probably always exist, and which from their constitution may be distinctly and profitably contemplated. I will not abuse the indulgence of my Reader by dwelling longer upon this subject; but it is proper that I should mention one other circumstance which distinguishes these Poems from the popular Poetry of the day; it is this, that the feeling therein developed gives importance to the action and situation, and not the action and situation to the feeling. My meaning will be rendered perfectly intelligible by referring my Reader to the Poems entiled POOR SUSAN and the CHILDLESS FATHER, particularly to the last Stanza of the latter Poem.

I will not suffer a sense of false modesty to prevent me from asserting, that I point my Reader's attention to this mark of distinction, far less for the sake of these particular Poems than from the general importance of the subject. The subject is indeed important! For the human mind is capable of being excited without the application of gross and violent stimulants; and he must have a very faint perception of its beauty and dignity who does not know this, and who does not further know, that one being is elevated above another, in proportion as he possesses this capability. It has therefore appeared to me, that to endeavour to produce or enlarge this capability is one of the best services in which, at any period, a Writer can be engaged; but this service, excellent at all times, is especially so at the present day. For a multitude of causes, unknown to former times, are now acting with a combined force to blunt the discriminating powers of the mind, and, unfitting it for all voluntary exertion to reduce it to a state of almost savage torpor. The most effective of these causes are the great national events which are daily taking place, and the encreasing accumulation of men in cities, where the uniformity of their occupations produces a craving for extraordinary incident, which the rapid communication of intelligence hourly gratifies. To this tendency of life and manners the literature and theatrical exhibitions of the country have conformed themselves. The invaluable works of our elder writers, I had almost said the works of Shakespeare and Milton, are driven into neglect by frantic novels, sickly and stupid German Tragedies, and deluges of idle and extravagant stories in verse. —When I think upon this degrading thirst after outrageous stimulation, I am almost ashamed to have spoken of the feeble effort with which I have endeavoured to counteract it; and, reflecting upon the magnitude of the general evil, I should be oppressed with no dishonourable melancholy, had I not a deep impression of certain inherent and indestructible qualities of the human mind, and likewise of certain powers in the great and permanent objects that act upon it, which are equally inherent and indestructible; and did I not further add to this impression a belief, that the time is approaching when the evil will be systematically opposed, by men of greater powers, and with far more distinguished success.

Having dwelt thus long on the subjects and aim of these Poems, I shall request the Reader's permission to apprize him of a few circumstances relating to their *style*, in order, among other reasons, that he may not censure me for not having performed what I never attempted. The Reader will find that personifications of abstract ideas rarely occur in these volumes; and are utterly rejected, as an ordinary device to elevate the style, and raise it above prose. I have proposed to myself to imitate, and, as far as possible, to adopt the very language of men; and assuredly such personifications do not make any natural or regular part of that language. They are, indeed, a figure of speech occasionally prompted by passion, and I have made use of them as such; but I have endeavoured utterly to reject them as a mechanical device of style, or as a family language which Writers in metre seem to lay claim to by prescription. I have wished to keep the Reader in the company of flesh and blood, persuaded that by so doing I shall interest him. I am, however, well aware that others who pursue a different track will interest him likewise; I do not interfere with their claim, I only wish to prefer a claim of my own. There will also be found in these volumes little of what is usually called poetic diction; I have taken as much pains to avoid it as others ordinarily take to produce it; this I have done for the reason already alleged, to bring my language near to the language of men; and further, because the pleasure which I have proposed to myself to impart is of a kind very different from that which is supposed by many persons to be the proper object of poetry. I do not know how, without being culpably particular, I can give my Reader a more exact notion of the style in which I wished these poems to be written than by informing him that I have at all times endeavoured to look steadily at my subject; consequently, I hope that there is in these Poems little falsehood of description, and that my ideas are expressed in language fitted to their respective importance. Something must have been gained by this practice, as it is friendly to one property of all good poetry, namely, good sense; but it has necessarily cut me off from a large portion of phrases and figures of speech which from father to son have long been regarded as the common inheritance of Poets. I have also thought it expedient to restrict myself still further, having abstained from the use of many expressions, in themselves proper and beautiful, but which have been foolishly repeated by bad Poets, till such feelings of disgust are connected with them as it is scarcely possible by any art of association to overpower.

If in a Poem there should be found a series of lines, or even a single line, in which the language, though naturally arranged, and according to the strict laws of metre, does not differ from that of prose, there is a numerous class of critics, who, when they stumble upon these prosaisms, as they call them, imagine that they have made a notable discovery, and exult over the Poet as over a man ignorant of his own profession. Now these men would establish a canon of criticism which the Reader will conclude he must utterly reject, if he wishes to be pleased with these volumes. And it would be a most easy task to prove to him, that not only the language of a large portion of every good poem, even of the most elevated character, must necessarily, except with reference to the metre, in no respect differ from that of good prose, but likewise that some of the most interesting parts of the best poems will be found to be strictly the language of prose, when prose is well written. The truth of this assertion might be demonstrated by innumerable passages from almost all the poetical writings, even of Milton himself. I have not space for much quotation; but, to illustrate the subject in a general manner, I will here adduce a short composition of Gray, who was at the head of those who, by their reasonings, have attempted to widen the space of separation betwixt Prose and Metrical composition, and was more than any other man curiously elaborate in the structure of his own poetic diction.

> In vain to me the smiling mornings shine,
> And reddening Phœbus lifts his golden fire:
> The birds in vain their amorous descant join,
> Or cheerful fields resume their green attire.
> These ears, alas! for other notes repine;
> *A different object do these eyes require;*
> *My lonely anguish melts no heart but mine;*
> *And in my breast the imperfect joys expire;*
> Yet morning smiles the busy race to cheer,
> And new-born pleasure brings to happier men;
> The fields to all their wonted tribute bear;
> To warm their little loves the birds complain.
> *I fruitless mourn to him that cannot hear,*
> *And weep the more because I weep in vain.*

It will easily be perceived, that the only part of this Sonnet which is of any value is the lines printed in Italics: it is equally obvious, that, except in the rhyme, and in the use of the single word ' fruitless' for fruitlessly, which is so far a defect, the language of these lines does in no respect differ from that of prose.

By the foregoing quotation it has been shown that the language of Prose may yet be well adapted to Poetry; and it was previously asserted that a large portion of the language of every good poem can in no respect differ from that of good Prose. I will go further. I do not doubt that it may be safely affirmed, that there neither is, nor can be, any essential difference between the language of prose and metrical composition. We are fond of tracing the resemblance between Poetry and Painting, and, accordingly, we call them Sisters: but where shall we find bonds of connexion sufficiently strict to typify the affinity betwixt metrical and prose composition? They both speak by and to the same organs; the bodies in which both of them are clothed may be said to be of the same substance, their affections are kindred, and almost identical, not necessarily differing even in degree; Poetry① sheds no tears 'such as Angels weep,' but natural and human tears; she can boast of no celestial choir that distinguishes her vital juices from those of prose; the same human blood circulates through the veins of them both.

If it be affirmed that rhyme and metrical arrangement of themselves constitute a distinction which overturns what I have been saying on the strict affinity of metrical language with that of prose, and paves the way for other artificial distinctions which the mind voluntarily admits, I answer that the language of such Poetry as I am recommending is, as far as is possible, a selection of the language really spoken by men; that this selection, wherever it is made with true taste and feeling, will of itself form a distinction far greater than would at first be imagined, and will entirely separate the composition from the vulgarity and meanness of ordinary life; and, if metre be superadded thereto, I believe that a dissimilitude will be produced altogether sufficient for the gratification of a rational mind. What other distinction would we have? Whence is it to come? And where is it to exist? Not, surely, where the Poet speaks through the mouths of his characters: it cannot be necessary here, either for elevation of style, or any of its supposed ornaments; for, if the Poet's subject be judiciously chosen, it will naturally, and upon fit occasion, lead him to passions the language of which, if selected truly and judiciously, must necessarily be dignified and variegated, and alive with metaphors and figures. I forbear to speak of an incongruity which would shock the intelligent Reader, should the Poet interweave any foreign splendour of his own with that which the passion naturally suggests: it is sufficient to say that such addition is unnecessary. And, surely, it is more probable that those passages, which with propriety abound with metaphors and figures, will have their due effect, if, upon other occasions where the passions are of a

---

① I here use the word 'Poetry' (though against my own judgement) as opposed to the word Prose, and synonymous with metrical composition. But much confusion has been introduced into criticism by this contradistinction of Poetry and Prose, instead of the more philosophical one of Poetry and Matter of Fact, or Science. The only strict antithesis to Prose is Metre; nor is this, in truth, a *strict* antithesis, because lines and passages of metre so naturally occur in writing prose, that it would be scarcely possible to avoid them, even were it desirable.

milder character, the style also be subdued and temperate.

But, as the pleasure which I hope to give by the Poems now presented to the Reader must depend entirely on just notions upon this subject, and, as it is in itself of high importance to our taste and moral feelings, I cannot content myself with these detached remarks. And if, in what I am about to say, it shall appear to some that my labour is unnecessary, and that I am like a man fighting a battle without enemies, I would remind such persons that, whatever may be the language outwardly holden by men, a practical faith in the opinions which I am wishing to establish is almost unknown. If my conclusions are admitted, and carried as far as they must be carried if admitted at all, our judgements concerning the works of the greatest Poets both ancient and modern will be far different from what they are at present, both when we praise, and when we censure: and our moral feelings influencing and influenced by these judgements will, I believe, be corrected and purified.

Taking up the subject, then, upon general grounds, let me ask, what is meant by the word Poet? What is a Poet? To whom does he address himself? And what language is to be expected from him? He is a man speaking to men: a man, it is true, endowed with more lively sensibility, more enthusiasm and tenderness, who has a greater knowledge of human nature, and a more comprehensive soul, than are supposed to be common among mankind; a man pleased with his own passions and volitions, and who rejoices more than other men in the spirit of life that is in him; delighting to contemplate similar volitions and passions as manifested in the goings-on of the Universe, and habitually impelled to create them where he does not find them. To these qualities he has added a disposition to be affected more than other men by absent things as if they were present; an ability of conjuring up in himself passions, which are indeed far from being the same as those produced by real events, yet (especially in those parts of the general sympathy which are pleasing and delightful) do more nearly resemble the passions produced by real events, than anything which, from the motions of their own minds merely, other men are accustomed to feel in themselves; whence, and from practice, he has acquired a greater readiness and power in expressing what he thinks and feels, and especially those thoughts and feelings which, by his own choice, or from the structure of his own mind, arise in him without immediate external excitement.

But, whatever portion of this faculty we may suppose even the greatest Poet to possess, there cannot be a doubt that the language which it will suggest to him, must, in liveliness and truth, fall short of that which is uttered by men in real life, under the actual pressure of those passions, certain shadows of which the Poet thus produces, or feels to be produced, in himself. However exalted a notion we would wish to cherish of the character of a Poet, it is obvious, that while he describes and imitates passions, his situation is altogether slavish and mechanical, compared with the freedom and power of real and substantial action and suffering. So that it will be the wish of the Poet to bring his feelings near to those of the persons whose feelings he describes, nay, for short spaces of time perhaps, to let himself slip into an entire delusion, and even confound and identify his own feelings with theirs; modifying only the language which is thus suggested to him, by a consideration that he describes for a particular purpose, that of giving pleasure. Here, then, he will apply the principle of selection on which I have so much insisted, namely, that of selection; on this he will depend for removing what would otherwise be painful or disgusting in the passion; he will feel that there is no necessity to trick out or to elevate nature: and, the more industriously he applies this principle, the deeper will be his faith that no words, which his fancy or imagination can suggest, will be to be compared with those which are the emanations of reality and truth.

But it may be said by those who do not object to the general spirit of these remarks, that, as it is impossible for the Poet to produce upon all occasions language as exquisitely fitted for the passion as that which the real passion itself suggests, it is proper that he should consider himself as in the situation of a translator, who deems himself justified when he substitutes excellencies of another kind for those which are unattainable by him; and endeavours occasionally to surpass his original, in order to make some amends for the general inferiority to which he feels that he must submit. But this would be to encourage idleness and unmanly despair. Further, it is the language of men who speak of what they do not understand; who talk of Poetry as of a matter of amusement and idle pleasure; who will converse with us as gravely about a *taste* for Poetry, as they express it, as if it were a thing as indifferent as a taste for Rope-dancing, or Frontiniac or Sherry. Aristotle, I have been told, hath said, that Poetry is the most philosophic of all writing: it is so: its object is truth, not individual and local, but general, and operative; not standing upon external testimony, but carried alive into the heart by passion; truth which is its own testimony, which gives strength and divinity to the tribunal to which it appeals, and receives them from the same tribunal. Poetry is the image of man and nature. The obstacles which stand in the way of the fidelity of the Biographer and Historian, and of their consequent utility, are incalculably greater than those which are to be encountered by the Poet who has an adequate notion of the dignity of his art. The Poet writes under one restriction only, namely, the necessity of giving immediate pleasure to a human Being possessed of that information which may be expected from him, not as a lawyer, a physician, a mariner, an astronomer, or a natural philosopher, but as a Man. Except this one restriction, there is no object standing between the Poet and the image of things; between this, and the Biographer and Historian, there are a thousand.

Nor let this necessity of producing immediate pleasure be considered as a degradation of the Poet's art. It is far otherwise. It is an acknowledgement of the beauty of the universe, an acknowledgement the more sincere, because it is not formal, but indirect; it is a task light and easy to him who looks at the world in the spirit of love: further, it is a homage paid to the native and naked dignity of man, to the grand elementary principle of pleasure, by which he knows, and feels, and lives, and moves. We have no sympathy but what is propagated by pleasure: I would not be misunderstood; but wherever we sympathize with pain it will be found that the sympathy is produced and carried on by subtle combinations with pleasure. We have no knowledge, that is, no general principles drawn from the contemplation of particular facts, but what has been built up by pleasure, and exists in us by pleasure alone. The Man of science, the Chemist and Mathematician, whatever difficulties and disgusts they may have had to struggle with, know and feel this. However painful may be the objects with which the Anatomist's knowledge is connected, he feels that his knowledge is pleasure;

and where he has no pleasure he has no knowledge. What then does the Poet? He considers man and the objects that surround him as acting and re-acting upon each other, so as to produce an infinite complexity of pain and pleasure; he considers man in his own nature and in his ordinary life as contemplating this with a certain quantity of immediate knowledge, with certain convictions, intuitions, and deductions which by habit become of the nature of intuitions; he considers him as looking upon this complex scene of ideas and sensations, and finding every where objects that immediately excite in him sympathies which, from the necessities of his nature, are accompanied by an overbalance of enjoyment.

To this knowledge which all men carry about with them, and to these sympathies in which without any other discipline than that of our daily life we are fitted to take delight, the Poet principally directs his attention. He considers man and nature as essentially adapted to each other, and the mind of man as naturally the mirror of the fairest and most interesting properties of nature. And thus the Poet, prompted by this feeling of pleasure which accompanies him through the whole course of his studies, converses with general nature with affections akin to those, which, through labour and length of time, the Man of Science has raised up in himself, by conversing with those particular parts of nature which are the objects of his studies. The knowledge both of the Poet and the Man of Science is pleasure; but the knowledge of the one cleaves to us as a necessary part of our existence, our natural and unalienable inheritance; the other is a personal and individual acquisition, slow to come to us, and by no habitual and direct sympathy connecting us with our fellow-beings. The Man of Science seeks truth as a remote and unknown benefactor; he cherishes and loves it in his solitude: the Poet, singing a song in which all human beings join with him, rejoices in the presence of truth as our visible friend and hourly companion. Poetry is the breath and finer spirit of all knowledge; it is the impassioned expression which is in the countenance of all Science. Emphatically may it be said of the Poet, as Shakespeare hath said of man, 'that he looks before and after.' He is the rock of defence for human nature; an upholder and preserver, carrying every where with him relationship and love. In spite of difference of soil and climate, of language and manners, of laws and customs, in spite of things silently gone out of mind and things violently destroyed, the Poet binds together by passion and knowledge the vast empire of human society, as it is spread over the whole earth, and over all time. The objects of the Poet's thoughts are every where; though the eyes and senses of man are, it is true, his favourite guides, yet he will follow wheresoever he can find an atmosphere of sensation in which to move his wings. Poetry is the first and last of all knowledge—it is as immortal as the heart of man. If the labours of Men of Science should ever create any material revolution, direct or indirect, in our condition, and in the impressions which we habitually receive, the Poet will sleep then no more than at present, but he will be ready to follow the steps of the Man of Science, not only in those general indirect effects, but he will be at his side, carrying sensation into the midst of the objects of the Science itself. The remotest discoveries of the Chemist, the Botanist, or Mineralogist, will be as proper objects of the Poet's art as any upon which it can be employed, if the time should ever come when these things shall be familiar to us, and the relations under which they are contemplated by the followers of these respective Sciences shall be manifestly and palpably material to us as enjoying and suffering beings. If the time should ever come when what is now called Science, thus familiarized to men, shall be ready to put on, as it were, a form of flesh and blood, the Poet will lend his divine spirit to aid the transfiguration, and will welcome the Being thus produced, as a dear and genuine inmate of the household of man. —It is not, then, to be supposed that any one, who holds that sublime notion of Poetry which I have attempted to convey, will break in upon the sanctity and truth of his pictures by transitory and accidental ornaments, and endeavour to excite admiration of himself by arts, the necessity of which must manifestly depend upon the assumed meanness of his subject.

What I have thus far said applies to Poetry in general; but especially to those parts of composition where the Poet speaks through the mouths of his characters; and upon this point it appears to have such weight that I will conclude, there are few persons of good sense, who would not allow that the dramatic parts of composition are defective, in proportion as they deviate from the real language of nature, and are coloured by a diction of the Poet's own, either peculiar to him as an individual Poet, or belonging simply to Poets in general; to a body of men who, from the circumstance of their compositions being in metre, it is expected will employ a particular language.

It is not, then, in the dramatic parts of composition that we look for this distinction of language; but still it may be proper and necessary where the Poet speaks to us in his own person and character. To this I answer by referring my Reader to the description before given of a Poet. Among the qualities which I have enumerated as principally conducing to form a Poet, is implied nothing differing in kind from other men, but only in degree. The sum of what I have there said is, that the Poet is chiefly distinguished from other men by a greater promptness to think and feel without immediate external excitement, and a greater power in expressing such thoughts and feelings as are produced in him in that manner. But these passions and thoughts and feelings are the general passions and thoughts and feelings of men. And with what are they connected? Undoubtedly with our moral sentiments and animal sensations, and with the causes which excite these; with the operations of the elements and the appearances of the visible universe; with storm and sun-shine, with the revolutions of the seasons, with cold and heat, with loss of friends and kindred, with injuries and resentments, gratitude and hope, with fear and sorrow. These, and the like, are the sensations and objects which the Poet describes, as they are the sensations of other men, and the objects which interest them. The Poet thinks and feels in the spirit of the passions of men. How, then, can his language differ in any material degree from that of all other men who feel vividly and see clearly? It might be *proved* that it is impossible. But supposing that this were not the case, the Poet might then be allowed to use a peculiar language when expressing his feelings for his own gratification, or that of men like himself. But Poets do not write for Poets alone, but for men. Unless therefore we are advocates for that admiration which depends upon ignorance, and that pleasure which arises from hearing what we do not understand, the Poet must descend from this supposed height; and, in order to excite rational sympathy, he must express himself as other men express themselves. To this it may be added, that while he is only selecting from the real language of men, or, which amounts to the same thing, composing accurately in the spirit of such selection, he is treading upon safe ground, and we know what we are to expect from him. Our feelings are the same with respect to metre; for, as it may be proper to remind the Reader, the distinction of metre is regular and uniform, and not like that which is produced by what is usually called poetic diction, arbitrary, and subject to infinite caprices upon which no calculation whatever can be made. In the one case, the Reader is utterly at the mercy of the Poet respecting what imagery or diction he may choose to connect with the passion, whereas, in the other, the metre obeys certain laws, to which the Poet and Reader both willingly submit because they are certain, and because no interference is made by them with the passion but such as the concurring testimony of ages has shown to heighten and improve the pleasure which co-exists with it.

It will now be proper to answer an obvious question, namely, Why, professing these opinions, have I written in verse? To this, in addition to such answer as is included in what I have already said, I reply, in the first place, because, however I may have restricted myself, there is still left open to me what confessedly constitutes the most valuable object of all writing, whether in prose or verse, the great and universal passions of men, the most general and interesting of their occupations, and the entire world of nature, from which I am at liberty to supply myself with endless combinations of forms and imagery. Now, supposing for a moment that whatever is interesting in these objects may be as vividly described in prose, why am I to be condemned, if to such description I have endeavoured to superadd the charm which, by the consent of all nations, is acknowledged to exist in metrical language? To this, by such as are yet unconvinced by what I have already said, it may be answered, that a very small part of the pleasure given by Poetry depends upon the metre, and that it is injudicious to write in metre, unless it be accompanied with the other artificial distinctions of style with which metre is usually accompanied, and that, by such deviation more will be lost from the shock which will thereby be given to the Reader's associations, than will be counterbalanced by any pleasure which he can derive from the general power of numbers. In answer to those who still contend for the necessity of accompanying metre with certain appropriate colours of style in order to the accomplishment of its appropriate end, and who also, in my opinion, greatly underrate the power of metre in itself, it might perhaps, as far as relates to these Poems, have been almost sufficient to observe, that poems are extant, written upon more humble subjects, and in a more naked and simple style than I have aimed at, which poems have continued to give pleasure from generation to generation. Now, if nakedness and simplicity be a defect, the fact here mentioned affords a strong presumption that poems somewhat less naked and simple are capable of affording pleasure at the present day; and, what I wish *chiefly* to attempt, at present, was to justify myself for having written under the impression of this belief.

But I might point out various causes why, when the style is manly, and the subject of some importance, words metrically arranged will long continue to impart such a pleasure to mankind as he who is sensible of the extent of that pleasure will be desirous to impart. The end of Poetry is to produce excitement in co-existence with an overbalance of pleasure. Now, by the supposition, excitement is an unusual and irregular state of the mind; ideas and feelings do not in that state succeed each other in accustomed order. But, if the words by which this excitement is produced are in themselves powerful, or the images and feelings have an undue proportion of pain connected with them, there is some danger that the excitement may be carried beyond its proper bounds. Now the co-presence of something regular, something to which the mind has been accustomed in various moods and in a less excited state, cannot but have great efficacy in tempering and restraining the passion by an intertexture of ordinary feeling, and of feeling not strictly and necessarily connected with the passion. This is unquestionably true, and hence, though the opinion will at first appear paradoxical, from the tendency of metre to divest language in a certain degree of its reality, and thus to throw a sort of half-consciousness of unsubstantial existence over the whole composition, there can be little doubt but that more pathetic situations and sentiments, that is, those which have a greater proportion of pain connected with them, may be endured in metrical composition, especially in rhyme, than in prose. The metre of the old Ballads is very artless; yet they contain many passages which would illustrate this opinion, and, I hope, if the following Poems be attentively perused, similar instances will be found in them. This opinion may be further illustrated by appealing to the Reader's own experience of the reluctance with which he comes to the re-perusal of the distressful parts of Clarissa Harlowe, or the Gamester. While Shakespeare's writings, in the most pathetic scenes, never act upon us as pathetic beyond the bounds of pleasure—an effect which, in a much greater degree than might at first be imagined, is to be ascribed to small, but continual and regular impulses of pleasurable surprise from the metrical arrangement. —On the other hand (what it must be allowed will much more frequently happen) if the Poet's words should be incommensurate with the passion, and inadequate to raise the Reader to a height of desirable excitement, then (unless the Poet's choice of his metre has been grossly injudicious) in the feelings of pleasure which the Reader has been accustomed to connect with metre in general, and in the feeling, whether cheerful or melancholy, which he has been accustomed to connect with that particular movement of metre, there will be found something which will greatly contribute to impart passion to the words, and to effect the complex end which the Poet proposes to himself.

If I had undertaken a systematic defence of the theory upon which these poems are written, it would have been my duty to develop the various causes upon which the pleasure received from metrical language depends. Among the chief of these causes is to be reckoned a principle which must be well known to those who have made any of the Arts the object of accurate reflection; I mean the pleasure which the mind derives from the perception of similitude in dissimilitude. This principle is the great spring of the activity of our minds, and their chief feeder. From this principle the direction of the sexual appetite, and all the passions connected with it, take their origin: it is the life of our ordinary conversation; and upon the accuracy with which similitude in dissimilitude, and dissimilitude in similitude are perceived, depend our taste and our moral feelings. It would not be a useless employment to have applied this principle to the consideration of metre, and to have shown that metre is hence enabled to afford much pleasure, and to have pointed out in what manner that pleasure is produced. But my limits will not permit me to enter upon this subject, and I must content myself with a general summary.

I have said that poetry is the spontaneous overflow of powerful feelings: it takes its origin from emotion recollected in tranquillity: the emotion is contemplated till by a species of reaction the tranquillity disappears, and an emotion, kindred to that which was before the subject of contemplation, is gradually produced, and does itself actually exist in the mind. In this mood successful composition generally begins, and in a mood similar to this it is carried on; but the emotion, of whatever kind, and in whatever degree, from various causes is qualified by various pleasures, so that in describing any passions whatsoever, which are voluntarily described, the mind will upon the whole be in a state of enjoyment. Now, if Nature be thus cautious in preserving in a state of enjoyment a being so employed, the Poet ought to profit by the lesson thus held forth to him, and ought especially to take care, that whatever passions he communicates to his Reader, those passions, if his Reader's mind be sound and vigorous, should always be accompanied with an overbalance of pleasure. Now the music of harmonious metrical language, the sense of difficulty overcome, and the blind association of pleasure which has been previously received from works of rhyme or metre of the same or similar construction, an indistinct perception perpetually renewed of language closely resembling that of real life, and yet, in the circumstance of metre, differing from it so widely, all these imperceptibly make up a complex feeling of delight, which is of the most important use in tempering the painful feeling which will always be found intermingled with powerful descriptions of the deeper passions. This effect is always produced in pathetic and impassioned poetry; while, in lighter compositions, the ease and gracefulness with which the Poet manages his numbers are themselves confessedly a principal source of the gratification of the Reader. I might perhaps include all which it is *necessary* to say upon this subject by affirming, what few persons will deny, that, of two descriptions, either of passions, manners, or characters, each of them equally well executed, the one in prose and the other in verse, the verse will be read a hundred times where the prose is read once. We see that Pope, by the power of verse alone, has contrived to render the plainest common sense interesting, and even frequently to invest it with the appearance of passion. In consequence of these convictions I related in metre the Tale of GOODY BLAKE

AND HARRY GILL, which is one of the rudest of this collection. I wished to draw attention to the truth, that the power of the human imagination is sufficient to produce such changes even in our physical nature as might almost appear miraculous. The truth is an important one; the fact (for it is a *fact*) is a valuable illustration of it. And I have satisfaction of knowing that it has been communicated to many hundreds of people who would never have heard of it, had it not been narrated as a Ballad, and in a more impressive metre than is usual in Ballads.

Having thus explained a few of my reasons why I have written in verse, and why I have chosen subjects from common life, and endeavoured to bring my language near to the real language of men, if I have been too minute in pleading my own cause, I have at the same time been treating a subject of general interest; and it is for this reason that I request the Reader's permission to add a few words with reference solely to these particular poems, and to some defects which will probably be found in them. I am sensible that my associations must have sometimes been particular instead of general, and that, consequently, giving to things a false importance, sometimes from diseased impulse I may have written upon unworthy subjects; but I am less apprehensive on this account, than that my language may frequently have suffered from those arbitrary connexions of feelings and ideas with particular words and phrases, from which no man can altogether protect himself. Hence I have no doubt, that, in some instances, feelings even of the ludicrous may be given to my Readers by expressions which appeared to me tender and pathetic. Such faulty expressions, were I convinced they were faulty at present, and that they must necessarily continue to be so, I would willingly take all reasonable pains to correct. But it is dangerous to make these alterations on the simple authority of a few individuals, or even of certain classes of men; for where the understanding of an Author is not convinced, or his feelings altered, this cannot be done without great injury to himself: for his own feelings are his stay and support, and, if he sets them aside in one instance, he may be induced to repeat this act till his mind loses all confidence in itself, and become utterly debilitated. To this it may be added, that the Reader ought never to forget that he is himself exposed to the same errors as the Poet, and perhaps in a much greater degree: for there can be no presumption in saying, that it is not probable he will be so well acquainted with the various stages of meaning through which words have passed, or with the fickleness or stability of the relations of particular ideas to each other; and, above all, since he is so much less interested in the subject, he may decide lightly and carelessly.

Long as I have detained my Reader, I hope he will permit me to caution him against a mode of false criticism which has been applied to Poetry in which the language closely resembles that of life and nature. Such verses have been triumphed over in parodies of which Dr. Johnson's stanza is a fair specimen.

> 'I put my hat upon my head,
> And walk'd into the Strand,
> And there I met another man
> Whose hat was in his hand.'

Immediately under these lines I will place one of the most justly admired stanzas of the '*Babes* in the Wood.'

> 'These pretty Babes with hand in hand
> Went wandering up and down;
> But never more they saw the Man
> Approaching from the Town.'

In both these stanzas the words, and the order of the words, in no respect differ from the most unimpassioned conversation. There are words in both, for example, 'the Strand,' and 'the Town,' connected with none but the most familiar ideas; yet the one stanza we admit as admirable, and the other as a fair example of the superlatively contemptible. Whence arises this difference? Not from the metre, not from the language, not from the order of the words; but the *matter* expressed in Dr. Johnson's stanza is contemptible. The proper method of treating trivial and simple verses, to which Dr. Johnson's stanza would be a fair parallelism, is not to say, This is a bad kind of poetry, or This is not poetry; but This wants sense; it is neither interesting in itself nor can *lead* to anything interesting; the images neither originate in that sane state of feeling which arises out of thought, nor can excite thought or feeling in the Reader. This is the only sensible manner of dealing with such verses. Why trouble yourself about the species till you have previously decided upon the genus? Why take pains to prove that an ape is not a Newton, when it is self-evident that he is not a man?

I have one request of my Reader, which is, that in judging these Poems he would decide by his own feelings genuinely, and not by reflection upon what will probably be the judgement of others. How common is it to hear a person say, 'I myself do not object to this style of composition, or this or that expression, but to such and such classes of people it will appear mean or ludicrous.' This mode of criticism, so destructive of all sound unadulterated judgement, is almost universal: I have therefore to request, that the Reader would abide independently by his own feelings, and that if he finds himself affected he would not suffer such conjectures to interfere with his pleasure.

If an Author by any single composition has impressed us with respect for his talents, it is useful to consider this as affording a presumption, that on other occasions where we have been displeased, he nevertheless may not have written ill or absurdly; and, further, to give him so much credit for this one composition as may induce us to review what has displeased us with more care than we should otherwise have bestowed upon it. This is not only an act of justice, but, in our decisions upon poetry especially, may conduce in a high degree to the improvement of our own taste: for an *accurate* taste in poetry, and in all the other arts, as Sir Joshua Reynolds has observed, is an *acquired* talent, which can only be produced by thought, and a long continued intercourse with the best models of composition. This is mentioned, not with so ridiculous a purpose as to prevent the most inexperienced Reader from judging for himself, (I have already said that I wish him to judge for himself;) but merely to temper the rashness of decision, and to suggest, that, if Poetry be a subject on which much time has not been bestowed, the judgement may be erroneous; and that in many cases it necessarily will be so.

I know that nothing would have so effectually contributed to further the end which I have in view, as to have shewn of what kind the pleasure is, and how that pleasure is produced, which is confessedly produced by metrical composition essentially different from that which I have here endeavoured to recommend: for the Reader will say that he has been pleased by such composition; and what can I do more for him? The power of any art is limited; and he will suspect, that, if I propose to furnish him with new friends, it is only upon condition of his abandoning his old friends. Besides, as I have said, the Reader is himself conscious of the pleasure which he has received from such composition, composition to which he has peculiarly attached the endearing name of Poetry; and all men feel an habitual gratitude, and something of an honourable bigotry for the objects which have long continued to please them; we not only wish to be pleased, but to be pleased in that particular way in which we have been accustomed to be pleased. There is a host of arguments in these feelings; and I should be the less able to combat them successfully, as I am willing to allow, that, in order entirely to enjoy the Poetry which I am recommending, it would be necessary to give up much of what is ordinarily enjoyed. But, would my limits have permitted me to point out how this pleasure is produced, I might have removed many obstacles, and assisted my Reader in perceiving that the powers of language are not so limited as he may suppose; and that it is possible for poetry to give other enjoyments, of a purer, more lasting, and more exquisite nature. This part of the subject has not been altogether neglected; but it has been less my present aim to prove, that the interest excited by some other kinds of poetry is less vivid, and less worthy of the nobler powers of the mind, than to offer reasons for presuming, that, if the object which I have proposed to myself were adequately attained, a species of poetry would be produced, which is genuine poetry; in its nature well adapted to interest mankind permanently, and likewise important in the multiplicity and quality of its moral relations.

From what has been said, and from a perusal of the Poems, the Reader will be able clearly to perceive the object which I had proposed to myself: he will determine how far I have attained this object; and, what is a much more important question, whether it be worth attaining: and upon the decision of these two questions will rest my claim to the approbation of the Public.

Preface to *Poems* (1815)

THE OBSERVATIONS prefixed to that portion of these Volumes, which was published many years ago, under the title of 'Lyrical Ballads,' have so little of a special application to the greater part, perhaps, of this collection, as subsequently enlarged and diversified, that they could not with any propriety stand as an Introduction to it. Not deeming it, however, expedient to suppress that exposition, slight and imperfect as it is, of the feelings which had determined the choice of the subjects, and the principles which had regulated the composition of those Pieces, I have transferred it to the end of the second Volume, to be attended to, or not, at the pleasure of the Reader.

In the Preface to that part of 'The Recluse,' lately published under the title of 'The Excursion,' I have alluded to a meditated arrangement of my minor Poems, which should assist the attentive Reader in perceiving their connection with each other, and also their subordination to that Work. I shall here say a few words explanatory of this arrangement, as carried into effect in the present Volumes.

The powers requisite for the production of poetry are, first, those of observation and description, i. e. the ability to observe with accuracy things as they are in themselves, and with fidelity to describe them, unmodified by any passion or feeling existing in the mind of the Describer: whether the things depicted be actually present to the senses, or have a place only in the memory. This power, though indispensable to a Poet, is one which he employs only in submission to necessity, and never for a continuance of time; as its exercise supposes all the higher qualities of the mind to be passive, and in a state of subjection to external objects, much in the same way as a Translator or Engraver ought to be to his original. 2ndly, Sensibility, —which, the more exquisite it is, the wider will be the range of a Poet's perceptions; and the more will he be incited to observe objects, both as they exist in themselves and as re-acted upon by his own mind. (The distinction between poetic and human sensibility has been marked in the character of the Poet delineated in the original preface, before-mentioned). 3rdly, Reflection, —which makes the Poet acquainted with the value of actions, images, thoughts, and feelings; and assists the sensibility in perceiving their connexion with each other. 4thly, Imagination and Fancy, —to modify, to create, and to associate. 5thly, Invention, —by which characters are composed out of materials supplied by observation; whether of the Poet's own heart and mind, or of external life and nature; and such incidents and situations produced as are most impressive to the imagination, and most fitted to do justice to the characters, sentiments, and passions, which the Poet undertakes to illustrate. And, lastly, Judgement, —to decide how and where, and in what degree, each of these faculties ought to be exerted; so that the less shall not be sacrificed to the greater; nor the greater, slighting the less, arrogate, to its own injury, more than its due. By judgement, also, is determined what are the laws and appropriate graces of every species of composition.

The materials of Poetry, by these powers collected and produced, are cast, by means of various moulds, into divers forms. The moulds may be enumerated, and the forms specified, in the following order. 1st, the Narrative, —including the Epopœia, the Historic Poem, the Tale, the Romance, the Mock-heroic, and, if the spirit of Homer will tolerate such neighbourhood, that dear production of ourdays, the metrical Novel. Of this Class, the distinguishing mark, is, that the Narrator, however liberally his speaking agents be introduced, is himself the source from which everything primarily flows. Epic Poets, in order that their mode of composition may accord with the elevation of their subject, represent themselves as singing from the inspiration of the Muse, Arma virumque *cano*; but this is a fiction, in modern times, of slight value: The Iliad or the Paradise Lost would gain little in our estimation by being chanted. The other poets who belong to this class are commonly content to *tell* their tale; —so that of the whole it may be affirmed that they neither require nor reject the accompaniment of music.

2ndly, The Dramatic, —consisting of Tragedy, Historic Drama, Comedy, and Masque; in which the poet does not appear at all in his own person, and where the whole action is carried on by speech and dialogue of the agents; music being admitted only incidentally and rarely. The Opera may be placed here, inasmuch as it proceeds by dialogue; though depending, to the degree that it does, upon music, it has a strong claim to be ranked with the Lyrical. The characteristic and impassioned Epistle, of which Ovid and Pope have given examples, considered as a species of monodrama, may, without impropriety, be placed in this class.

3rdly, The Lyrical, —containing the Hymn, the Ode, the Elegy, the Song, and the Ballad; in all which, for the production of their *full* effect, an accompaniment of music is indispensable.

4thly, The Idyllium, —descriptive chiefly either of the processes and appearances of external nature, as the 'Seasons' of Thomson; or of characters, manners, and sentiments, as are Shenstone's Schoolmistress, The Cotter's Saturday Night of Burns, The Twa Dogs of the same Author; or of these in conjunction with the appearances of Nature, as most of the pieces of Theocritus, the Allegro and Penseroso of Milton, Beattie's Minstrel, Goldsmith's 'Deserted Village.' The Epitaph, the Inscription, the Sonnet, most of the epistles of poets writing in their own persons, and all loco-descriptive poetry, belonging to this class.

5thly, Didactic, —the principal object of which is direct instruction; as the Poem of Lucretius, the Georgics of Virgil, 'The Fleece' of Dyer, Mason's 'English Garden,' &c.

And, lastly, philosophical satire, like that of Horace and Juvenal; personal and occasional Satire rarely comprehending sufficient of the general in the individual to be dignified with the name of poetry.

Out of the three last has been constructed a composite species, of which Young's Night Thoughts and Cowper's Task are excellent examples.

It is deducible from the above, that poems, apparently miscellaneous, may with propriety be arranged with reference to the powers of mind *predominant* in the production of them; or to the mould in which they are cast; or, lastly, to the subjects to which they relate. From each of these considerations, the following Poems have been divided into classes; which, that the work may more obviously correspond with the course of human life, and for the sake of exhibiting in it the three requisites of a legitimate whole, a beginning, a middle, and an end, have been also arranged, as far as it was possible, according to an order of time, commencing with Childhood, and terminating with Old Age, Death, and Immortality. My guiding wish was, that the small pieces of which these volumes consist, thus discriminated, might be regarded under a two-fold view; as composing an entire work within themselves, and as adjuncts to the philosophical Poem, 'The Recluse.' This arrangement has long presented itself habitually to my own mind. Nevertheless, I should have preferred to scatter the contents of these volumes at random, if I had been persuaded that, by the plan adopted, any thing material would be taken from the natural effect of the pieces, individually, on the mind of the unreflecting Reader. I trust there is a sufficient variety in each class to prevent this; while, for him who reads with reflection, the arrangement will serve as a commentary unostentatiously directing his attention to my purposes, both particular and general. But, as I wish to guard against the possibility of misleading by this classification, it is proper first to remind the Reader, that certain poems are placed according to the powers of mind, in the Author's conception, predominant in the production of them; *predominant*, which implies the exertion of other faculties in less degree. Where there is more imagination than fancy in a poem it is placed under the head of imagination, and vice versa. Both the above Classes might without impropriety have been enlarged from that consisting of 'Poems founded on the Affections;' as might this latter from those, and from the class 'Proceeding from Sentiment and Reflection.' The most striking characteristics of each piece, mutual illustration, variety, and proportion, have governed me throughout.

It may be proper in this place to state, that the Extracts in the 2nd Class entilted 'Juvenile Pieces,' are in many palces altered from the printed copy, chiefly by omission and compression. The slight alterations of another kind were for the most part made not long after the publication of the Poems from which the Extracts are taken. These Extracts seem to have a tiltle to be placed here as they were the productions of youth, and represent implicitly some of the features of a youthful mind, at a time when images of nature supplied to it the place of thought, sentiment, and almost of action; or, as it will be found expressed, of a state of mind when

> 'the sounding cataract
> Haunted me like a passion: the tall rock,
> The mountain, and the deep and gloomy wood,
> Their colours and their forms, were then to me
> An appetite; a feeling and a love,
> That had no need of a remoter charm,
> By thought supplied, nor any interest
> Unborrowed from the eye' —

I will own that I was much at a loss what to select of these descriptions; and perhaps it would have been better either to have reprinted the whole, or suppressed what I have given.

None of the other Classes, except those of Fancy and Imagination, require any particular notice. But a remark of general application may be made. All Poets, except the dramatic, have been in the practice of feigning that their works were composed to the music of the harp or lyre: with what degree of affectation this has been done in modern times, I leave to the judicious to determine. For my own part, I have not been disposed to violate probability so far, or to make such a large demand upon the Reader's charity. Some of these pieces are essentially lyrical; and, therefore, cannot have their due force without a supposed musical accompaniment; but, in much the greatest part, as a substitute for the classic lyre or romantic harp, I require nothing more than an animated or impassioned recitation, adapted to the subject. Poems, however humble in their kind, if they be good in that kind, cannot read themselves; the law of long syllable and-short must not be so inflexible—the letter of metre must not be so impassive to the spirit of versification—as to deprive the Reader of all voluntary power to modulate, in subordination to the sense, the music of the poem; —in the same manner as his mind is left at liberty, and even summoned, to act upon its thoughts and images. But, though the accompaniment of a musical instrument be frequently dispensed with, the true Poet does not therefore abandon his privilege distinct from that of the mere Proseman;

> 'He murmurs near the running brooks
> A music sweeter than their own.'

I come now to the consideration of the words Fancy and Imagination, as employed in the classification of the following Poems. 'A man,' says an intelligent Author, 'has "imagination," in proportion as he can distinctly copy in idea the impressions of sense: it is the faculty which *images* within the mind the phenomena of sensation. A man has fancy in proportion as he can call up, connect, or associate, at pleasure, those internal images (φαυταξειν is to cause to appear) so as to complete ideal representations of absent objects. Imagination is the power of depicting, and fancy of evoking and combining. The imagination is formed by patient observation; the fancy by a voluntary activity in shifting the scenery of the mind. The more accurate the imagination, the more safely may a painter, or a poet, undertake a delineation, or a description, without the presence of the objects to be characterized. The more versatile the fancy, the more original and striking will be the decorations produced.' —*British Synonyms discriminated, by W. Taylor.*

Is not this as if a man should undertake to supply an account of a building, and be so intent upon what he had discovered of the foundation as to conclude his task without once looking up at the superstructure? Here, as in other instances throughout the volume, the judicious Author's mind is enthralled by Etymology; he takes up the original word as his guide, his conductor, his escort, and too often does not perceive how soon he becomes its prisoner, without liberty to tread in any path but that to which it confines him. It is not easy to find out how imagination, thus explained, differs from distinct remembrance of images; or fancy from quick and vivid recollection of them: each is nothing more than a mode of memory. If the two words bear the above meaning, and no other, what term is left to designate that Faculty of which the Poet is 'all compact'; he whose eyes glances from earth to heaven, whose spiritual attributes body-forth what his pen is prompt in turning to shape; or what is left to characterize fancy, as insinuating herself into the heart of objects with creative activity? —Imagination, in the sense of the word as giving title to a Class of the following Poems, has no reference to images that are merely a faithful copy, existing in the mind, of absent external objects; but is a word of higher import, denoting operations of the mind upon those objects, and processes of creation or of composition, governed by certain fixed laws. I proceed to illustrate my meaning by instances. A parrot *hangs* from the wires of his cage by his beak or by his claws; or a monkey from the bough of a tree by his paws or his tail. Each creature does so literally and actually. In the first Eclogue of Virgil, the Shepherd, thinking of the time when he is to take leave of his Farm, thus addresses his Goats:

> 'Non ego vos posthac viridi projectus in antro
> Dumosa *pendere* procul de rupe videbo,'
> —'half way up
> *Hangs* one who gathers samphire,

is the well-known expression of Shakespeare, delineating an ordinary image upon the cliffs of Dover. In these two instances is a slight exertion of the faculty which I denominate imagination, in the use of one word: neither the goats nor the samphire-gatherer do literally hang, as does the parrot or the monkey; but, presenting to the senses something of such an appearance, the mind in its activity, for its own gratification, contemplates them as hanging.

> 'As when far off at Sea a Fleet descried
> *Hangs* in the clouds, by equinoctial winds
> Close sailing from Bengala or the isles
> Of Ternate or Tidore, whence Merchants bring
> Their spicy drugs; they on the trading flood
> Through the wide Ethiopian to the Cape
> Ply, stemming nightly toward the Pole; so seemed
> Far off the flying Fiend.'

Here is the full strength of the imagination involved in the word, *hangs*, and exerted upon the whole image: First, the Fleet, an aggregate of many Ships, is represented as one mighty Person, whose track, we know and feel, is upon the waters; but, taking advantage of its appearance to the senses, the Poet dares to represent it as *hanging in the clouds*, both for the gratification of the mind in contemplating the image itself, and in reference to the motion and appearance of the sublime objects to which it is compared.

From images of sight we will pass to those of sound:

'Over his own sweet voice the Stock-dove *broods*';

of the same bird,

'His voice was *buried* among trees,
Yet to be come at by the breeze';

'Oh, Cuckoo! shall I call thee *Bird*,
Or but a wandering *Voice*?'

The stock-dove is said to *coo*, a sound well imitating the note of the bird; but, by the intervention of the metaphor *broods*, the affections are called in by the imagination to assist in marking the manner in which the bird reiterates and prolongs her soft note, as if herself delighting to listen to it, and participating of a still and quiet satisfaction, like that which may be supposed inseparable from the continuous process of incubation. 'His voice was buried among trees,' a metaphor expressing the love of *seclusion* by which this Bird is marked; and characterizing its note as not partaking of the shrill and the piercing, and therefore more easily deadened by the intervening shade; yet a note so peculiar and withal so pleasing, that the breeze, gifted with that love of the sound which the Poet feels, penetrates the shades in which it is entombed, and conveys it to the ear of the listener.

Shall I call thee Bird,
Or but a wandering Voice?

This concise interrogation characterizes the seeming ubiquity of the voice of the Cuckoo, and dispossesses the creature almost of a corporeal existence; the Imagination being tempted to this exertion of her power by a consciousness in the memory that the Cuckoo is almost perpetually heared throughout the season of Spring, but seldom becomes an object of sight.

Thus far of images independent of each other, and immediately endowed by the mind with properties that do not inhere in them, upon an incitement from properties and qualities the existence of which is inherent and obvious. These processes of imagination are carried on either by conferring additional properties upon an object, or abstracting from it some of those which it actually possesses, and thus enabling it to react upon the mind which hath performed the process, like a new existence.

I pass from the Imagination acting upon an individual image to a consideration of the same faculty employed upon images in a conjunction by which they modify each other. The Reader has already had a fine instance before him in the passage quoted from Virgil, where the apparently perilous situation of the Goat, hanging upon the shaggy precipice, is contrasted with that of the Shepherd, contemplating it from the seclusion of the Cavern in which he lies stretched at ease and in security. Take these images separately, and how unaffecting the picture compared with that produced by their being thus connected with, and opposed to, each other!

> 'As a huge Stone is sometimes seen to lie
> Couched on the bald top of an eminence,
> Wonder to all who do the same espy
> By what means it could thither come, and whence;
> So that it seems a thing endued with sense,
> Like a Sea-beast crawled forth, which on a shelf
> Of rock or sand reposeth, there to sun himself.
>
> Such seemed this Man; not all alive or dead,
> Nor all asleep, in his extreme old age.
> Motionless as a cloud the old Man stood,

> That heareth not the loud winds when they call,
> And moveth altogether if it move at all.'

In these images, the conferring, the abstracting, and the modifying powers of the Imagination, immediately and mediately acting, are all brought into conjunction. The Stone is endowed with something of the power of life to approximate it to the Sea-beast; and the Sea-beast stripped of some of its vital qualities to assimilate it to the stone; which intermediate image is thus treated for the purpose of bringing the original image, that of the stone, to a nearer resemblance to the figure and condition of the aged Man; who is divested of so much of the indications of life and motion as to bring him to the point where the two objects unite and coalesce in just comparison. After what has been said, the image of the Cloud need not be commented upon.

Thus far of an endowing or modifying power: but the Imagination also shapes and creates; and how? By innumerable processes; and in none does it more delight than in that of consolidating numbers into unity, and dissolving and separating unity into number, —alternations proceeding from, and governed by, a sublime consciousness of the soul in her own mighty and almost divine powers. Recur to the passage already cited from Milton. When the compact Fleet, as one Person, has been introduced 'sailing from Bengala,' 'They,' i. e. the 'Merchants,' representing the Fleet resolved into a Multitude of Ships, 'ply' their voyage towards the extremities of the earth: 'So' (referring to the word 'As' in the commencement) 'seemed the flying Fiend'; the image of his Person acting to recombine the multitude of Ships into one body, —the point from which the comparison set out. 'So seemed,' and to whom seemed? To the heavenly Muse who dictates the poem, to the eye of the Poet's mind, and to that of the Reader, present at one moment in the wide Ethiopian, and the next in the solitudes, then first broken in upon, of the infernal regions!

> Modo me Thebis, modo ponit Athenis.

Hear again this mighty Poet, —speaking of the Messiah going forth to expel from Heaven the rebellious Angels,

> Attended by ten thousand, thousand Saints
> He onward came: far off his coming shone, —

the retinue of Saints, and the Person of the Messiah himself, lost almost and merged in the splendour of that indefinite abstraction, 'His coming!'

As I do not mean here to treat this subject further than to throw some light upon the present Volumes, and especially upon one division of them, I shall spare myself and the Reader the trouble of considering the Imagination as it deals with thoughts and sentiments, as it regulates the composition of characters, and determines the course of actions: I will not consider it (more than I have already done by implication) as that power which, in the language of one of my most esteemed Friends, 'draws all things to one; which makes things animate or inanimate, beings with their attributes, subjects with their accessories, take one colour and serve to one effect.' ① The grand store-house of enthusiastic and meditative Imagination, of poetical, as contradistinguished from human and dramatic Imagination, is the prophetic and lyrical parts of the holy Scriptures, and the works of Milton; to which I cannot forbear to add to those of Spenser. I select these writers in preference to those of ancient Greece and Rome because the anthropomorphitism of the Pagan religion subjected the minds of the greatest poets in those countries too much to the bondage of definite form; from which the Hebrews were preserved by their abhorrence of idolatry. This abhorrence was almost as strong in our great epic Poet, both from circumstances of his life, and from the consitution of his mind. However imbued the surface might be with classical literature, he was a Hebrew in soul; and all things tended in him towards the sublime. Spenser, of a gentler nature, maintained his freedom by aid of his allegorical spirit, at one time inciting him to create persons out of abstractions; and, at another, by a superior effort of genius, to give the universality and permanence of abstractions to his human beings, by means of attributes and em-

---

① Charles Lamb upon the genius of Hogarth.

blems that belong to the highest moral truths and the purest sensations, —of which his character of Una is a glorious example. Of the human and dramatic Imagination the works of Shakespeare are an inexhaustible source.

> 'I tax not you, ye Elements, with unkindness,
> I never gave you Kingdoms, called you Daughters.'

And if, bearing in mind the many Poets distinguished by this prime quality, whose names I omit to mention; yet justified by recollection of the insults which the ignorant, the incapable, and the presumptuous, have heaped upon these and my other writings, I may be permitted to anticipate the judgment of posterity upon myself, I shall declare (censurable, I grant, if the notoriety of the fact above stated does not justify me) that I have given in these unfavourable times evidence of exertions of this faculty upon its worthiest objects, the external universe, the moral and religious sentiments of Man, his natural affections, and his acquired passions; which have the same ennobling tendency as the productions of men, in this kind, worthy to be holden in undying remembrance.

I dismiss this subject with observing—that, in the series of Poems placed under the head of Imagination, I have begun with one of the earliest processes of Nature in the development of this faculty. Guided by one of my own primary consciousnesses, I have represented a commutation and transfer of internal feelings, co-operating with external accidents to plant, for immortality, images of sound and sight, in the celestial soil of the Imagination. The Boy, there introduced, is listening, with something of a feverish and restless anxiety, for the recurrence of the riotous sounds which he had previously excited, and, at the moment when the intenseness of his mind is beginning to remit, he is surprised into a perception of the solemn and tranquillizing images which the Poem describes. —The Poems next in succession exhibit the faculty exerting itself upon various objects of external universe; then follow others, where it is employed upon feelings, characters, and actions; and the Class is concluded with imaginative pictures of moral, political, and religious sentiments.

To the mode in which Fancy has already been characterized as the power of evoking and combining, or, as my friend Mr. Coleridge has styled it, 'the aggregative and associative power,' my objection is only that the definition is too general. To aggregate and to associate, to evoke and to combine, belong as well to the Imagination as to the Fancy; but either the materials evoked and combined are different; or they are brought together under a different law, and for a different purpose. Fancy does not require that the materials which she makes use of should be susceptible of change in their constitution, from her touch; and, where they admit of modification, it is enough for her purpose if it be slight, limited and evanescent. Directly the reverse of these, are the desires and demands of the Imagination. She recoils from every thing but the plastic, the pliant, and the indefinite. She leaves it to Fancy to describe Queen Mab as coming,

> 'In shape no bigger than an agate stone
> On the fore-finger of an Alderman.'

Having to speak of stature, she does not tell you that her gigantic Angel was as tall as Pompey's pillar; much less that he was twelve cubits, or twelve hundred cubits high; or that his dimensions equalled those of Teneriffe or Atlas; —because these, and if they were a million times as high, it would be the same, are bounded: The expression is, 'His stature reached the sky!' the illimitable firmament! —When the Imagination frames a comparison, if it does not strike on the first presentation, a sense of the truth of the likeness, from the moment that it is perceived, grows—and continues to grow—upon the mind; the resemblance depending less upon outline of form and feature, than upon expression and effect; less upon casual and outstanding, than upon inherent and internal, properties: —moreover, the images invariably modify each other. —The law under which the processes of Fancy are carried on is as capricious as the accidents of things, and the effects are surprising, playful, ludicrous, amusing, tender, or pathetic, as the objects happen to be appositely produced or fortunately combined. Fancy depends upon the rapidity and profusion with which she scatters her thoughts and images, trusting that their number, and the felicity with which they are linked together, will make amends for the want of individual value: or she prides herself upon the curious subtilty and the successful elaboration with which she can detect their lurking affinities. If she can win you over to her purpose, and impart to you her feelings, she cares not how unstable or transitory may be her influence, knowing that it will not be out of her power to resume it upon an apt occasion. But the Imagination is conscious of an indestructible dominion; —the Soul may fall away from it, not being able to sustain its grandeur; but, if once felt and acknowledged, by no act of any other faculty of the mind can it be relaxed, impaired, or diminished. —Fancy is given to quicken and to beguile the temporal part of our Nature, Imagination to incite and to support the eternal. — Yet is it not the less true that Fancy, as she is an active, is also, under her own laws and in her own spirit, a creative faculty? In what manner Fancy ambitiously aims at a rivalship with the Imagination, and Imagination stoops to work with the materials of Fancy, might be illustrated from the compositions of all eloquent writers, whether in prose or verse; and chiefly from those of our own Country. Scarcely a page of the impassioned parts of Bishop Taylor's Works can be opened that shall not afford examples. —Referring the Reader to those inestimable Volumes, I will content myself with placing a conceit (ascribed to Lord Chesterfield) in contrast with a passage from the Paradise Lost:

'The dews of the evening most carefully shun,
They are the tears of the sky for the loss of the Sun.'

After the transgression of Adam, Milton, with other appearances of sympathizing Nature, thus marks the immediate consequence,

'Sky lowered, and muttering thunder, some sad drops
Wept at completion of the mortal sin.'

The associating link is the same in each instance; —dew and rain, not distinguishable from the liquid substance of tears, are employed as indications of sorrow. A flash of surprise is the effect in the former case, a flash of surprise, and nothing more; for the nature of things does not sustain the combination. In the latter, the effects from the act, of which there is this immediate consequence and visible sign, are so momentous that the mind acknowledges the justice and reasonableness of the sympathy in Nature so manifested; and the sky weeps drops of water as if with human eyes, as 'Earth had, before, trembled from her entrails, and Nature given a second groan.'

Awe-stricken as I am by contemplating the operations of the mind of this truly divine Poet, I scarcely dare venture to add that 'An address to an Infant,' which the Reader will find under the Class of Fancy in the present Volumes, exhibits something of this communion and interchange of instruments and functions between the two powers; and is, accordingly, placed last in the class, as a preparation for that of Imagination which follows.

Finally, I will refer to Cotton's 'Ode upon Winter,' an admirable composition though stained with some peculiarities of the age in which he lived, for a general illustration of the characteristics of Fancy. The middle part of this ode contains a most lively description of the entrance of Winter, with his retinue, as 'A palsied King,' and yet a military Monarch, —advancing for conquest with his Army; the several bodies of which, and their arms and equipments, are described with a rapidity of detail, and a profusion of fanciful comparisons, which indicate on the part of the Poet extreme activity of intellect, and a correspondent hurry of delightful feeling. Winter retires from the foe into his fortress, where

> 'a magazine
> Of sovereign juice is cellared in.
> Liquor that will the siege maintain
> Should Phoebus ne'er return again.'

Though myself a water-drinker, I cannot resist the pleasure of transcribing what follows, as an instance still more happy of Fancy employed in the treatment of feeling than, in its preceding passages, the Poem supplies of her management of forms.

'Tis that, that gives the Poet rage,
And thaws the gelly'd blood of Age;
Matures the Young, restores the Old,
And makes the fainting Coward bold.

It lays the careful head to rest,
Calms palpitations in the breast,
Renders our lives' misfortune sweet;
...

Then let the chill Scirocco blow,
And gird us round with hills of snow,
Or else go whistle to the shore,
And make the hollow mountains roar.

Whilst we together jovial sit
Careless, and crown'd with mirth and wit;
Where, though bleak winds confine us home,
Our fancies round the world shall roam.

We'll think of all the Friends we know,
And drink to all worth drinking to;
When having drunk all thine and mine,
We rather shall want healths than wine.

But where Friends fail us, we'll supply
Our friendships with our charity;
Men that remote in sorrows live,
Shall by our lusty Brimmers thrive.

We'll drink the Wanting into Wealth,
And those that languish into health,
The Afflicted into joy; th' Opprest
Into security and rest.

The Worthy in disgrace shall find

Favour return again more kind,
And in restraint who stifled lie,
Shall taste the air of liberty.

The Brave shall triumph in success,
The Lover shall have Mistresses,
Poor unregarded Virtue, praise,
And the neglected Poet, Bays.

Thus shall our healths do others good,
Whilst we ourselves do all we would;
For, freed from envy and from care,
What would we be but what we are?'

It remains that I should express my regret at the neseccity of separating my compositions from some beautiful Poems of Mr. Coleridge, with which they have been long associated in publication. The feelings, with which that joint pubication was made, have been gratified; its end is answered, and the time is come when considerations of general propriety dictate the separation. Three short pieces, (now first published) are the work of a Female Friend; the the Reader, to whom they may be acceptable, is indebted to me for his pleasure; if any one regard them with dislike, or be disposed to condemn them, let the censure fall upon him, who, trusting in his own sense of their merit and their fitness for the place which they occupy, *extorted* them from the Authoress.

When I sate down to write this preface it was my intention to have made it more comprehensive; but as all that I deem necessary is expressed, I will here detain the reader no longer: —what I have further to remark shall be inserted, by way of interlude, at the close of this Volume.

Essay, Supplementary to the Preface (1815)

BY THIS time, I trust that the judicious Reader, who has now first become acquainted with these poems, is persuaded that a very senseless outcry has been raised against them and their Author. —Casually, and very rarely only, do I see any periodical publication, except a daily newspaper; but I am not wholly unacquainted with the spirit in which my most active and persevering Adversaries have maintained their hostility; not with the impudent falsehoods and base artifices to which they have had recourse. These, as implying a consciousness on their parts that attacks honestly and fairly conducted would be unavailing, could not but have been regarded by me with triumph; had they been accompanied with such display of talents and information as might give weight to the opinions of the Writers, whether favourable or unfavourable. But the ignorance of those who have chosen to stand forth as my enemies, as far as I am acquainted with their enmity, has unfortunately been still more gross than their disingenuousness, and their incompetence more flagrant than their malice. The effect in the eyes of the discerning is indeed ludicrous; yet, contemptible as such men are, in return for the forced compliment paid me by their long-continued notice (which, as I have appeared so rarely before the public, no one can say has been solicited) I entreat them to spare themselves. The lash, which they are aiming at my productions, does, in fact, only fall on phantoms of their own brain; which, I grant, I am innocently instrumental in raising. —By what fatality the orb of my genius (for genius none of them seem to deny me) acts upon these men like the moon upon a certain description of patients, it would be irksome to inquire; nor would it consist with the respect which I owe myself to take further notice of opponents whom I internally despise.

With the young, of both sexes, Poetry is, like love, a passion; but, for much the greater part of those who have been proud of its power over their minds, a necessity soon arises of breaking the pleasing bondage; or it relaxes of itself; — the thoughts being occupied in domestic cares, or the time engrossed by business. Poetry then becomes only an occasional recreation; while to those whose existence passes away in a course of fashionable pleasure, it is a species of luxurious amusement. —In middle and declining age, a scattered number of serious persons resort to poetry, as to religion, for a protection against the pressure of trivial employments, and as a consolation for the afflictions of life. And lastly, there are many, who, having been enamoured of this art, in their youth, have found leisure, after youth was spent, to cultivate general literature; in which poetry has continued to be comprehended *as a study.*

Into the above Classes the Readers of poetry may be divided; Critics abound in them all; but from the last only can opinions be collected of absolute value, and worthy to be depended upon, as prophetic of the destiny of a new work. The young, who in nothing can escape delusion, are especially subject to it in their intercourse with poetry. The cause, not so obvious as the fact is unquestionable, is the same as that from which erroneous judgements in this art, in the minds of men of all ages, chiefly proceed; but upon Youth it operates with peculiar force. The appropriate business of poetry (which, nevertheless, if genuine, is as permanent as pure science), her appropriate employment, her privilege and her *duty*, is to treat of things not as they *are*, but as they *appear*, not as they exist in themselves, but as they *seem* to exist to the *senses* and to the *passions*. What a world of delusion does this acknowledged obligation prepare for the inexperienced! what temptations to go astray are here held forth for them whose thoughts have been little disciplined by the understanding, and whose feelings revolt from the sway of reason! —When a juvenile Reader is in the height of his rapture with some vicious passage, should experience throw in doubts, or common-sense suggest suspicions, a lurking consciousness that the realities of the Muse are but shows, and that her liveliest excitements are raised by transient shocks of conflicting feeling and successive assemblages of contradictory thoughts—is ever at hand to justify extravagance, and to sanction absurdity. But, it may be asked, as these illusions are unavoidable, and no doubt eminently useful to the mind as a process, what good can be gained by making observations, the tendency of which is to diminish the confidence of youth in its feelings, and thus to abridge its innocent and even profitable pleasures? The reproach implied in the question could not be warded off, if Youth were incapable of being delighted with what is truly excellent; or if these errors always terminated of themselves in due season. But, with the majority, though their force be abated, they continue through life. Moreover, the fire of youth is too vivacious an element to be extinguished or damped by a philosophical remark; and, while there is no danger that what has been said will be injurious or painful to the ardent and the confident, it may prove beneficial to those who, being enthusiastic, are, at the same time, modest and ingenuous. The intimation may unite with their own misgivings to regulate their sensibility, and to bring in, sooner than it would otherwise have arrived, a more discreet and sound judgement.

If it should excite wonder that men of ability, in later life, whose understandings have been rendered acute by practice in affairs, should be so easily and so far imposed upon when they happen to take up a new work in verse, this appears to be the cause; —that, having discontinued their attention to poetry, whatever progress may have been made in other departments of knowledge, they have not, as to this art, advanced in true discernment beyond the age of youth. If then a new poem fall in their way, whose attractions are of that kind which would have enraptured them during the heat of youth, the judgement not being improved to a degree that they shall be disgusted, they are dazzled; and prize and cherish the faults for having had power to make the present time vanish before them, and to throw the mind back, as by enchantment, into the happiest season of life. As they read, powers seem to be revived, passions are regenerated, and pleasures restored. The Book was probably taken up after an escape from the burthen of business, and with a wish to forget the world, and all its vexations and anxieties. Having obtained this wish, and so much more, it is natural that they should make report as they have felt.

If Men of mature age, through want of practice, be thus easily beguiled into admiration of absurdities, extravagances, and misplaced ornaments, thinking it proper that their understandings should enjoy a holiday, while they are unbending their minds with verse, it may be expected that such Readers will resemble their former selves also in strength of prejudice, and an inaptitude to be moved by the unostentatious beauties of a pure style. In the higher poetry, an enlightened Critic chiefly looks for a reflection of the wisdom of the heart and the grandeur of the imagination. Wherever these appear, simplicity accompanies them; Magnificence herself, when legitimate, depending upon a simplicity of her own, to regulate her ornaments. But it is a well-known property of human nature that our estimates are ever governed by comparisons, of which we are conscious with various degrees of distinctness. Is it not, then, inevitable (confining these observations to the effects of style merely) that an eye, accustomed to the glaring hues of diction by which such Readers are caught and excited, will for the most part be rather repelled than attracted by an original Work the colouring of which is disposed according to a pure and refined scheme of harmony? It is in the fine arts as in the affairs of life, no man can *serve* (i. e. obey with zeal and fidelity) two Masters.

As Poetry is most just to its own divine origin when it administers the comforts and breathes the spirit of religion, they who have learned to perceive this truth, and who betake themselves to reading verse for sacred purposes, must be preserved from numerous illusions to which the two Classes of Readers, whom we have been considering, are liable. But, as the mind grows serious from the weight of life, the range of its passions is contracted accordingly; and its sympathies become so exclusive, that many species of high excellence wholly escape, or but languidly excite, its notice. Besides, Men who read from religious or moral inclinations, even when the subject is of that kind which they approve, are beset with misconceptions and mistakes peculiar to themselves. Attaching so much importance to the truths which interest them, they are prone to overrate the Authors by whom those truths are expressed and enforced. They come prepared to impart so much passion to the Poet's language, that they remain unconscious how little, in fact, they receive from it. And, on the other hand, religious faith is to him who holds it so momentous a thing, and error appears to be attended with such tremendous consequences, that, if opinions touching upon religion occur which the Reader condemns, he not only cannot sympathize with them however animated the expression, but there is, for the most part, an end put to all satisfaction and enjoyment. Love, if it before existed, is converted into dislike; and the heart of the Reader is set against the Author and his book. —to these excesses, they, who from their professions ought to be the most guarded against them, are perhaps the most liable; I mean those sects whose religion, being from the calculating understanding, is cold and formal. For when Christianity, the religion of humility, is founded upon the proudest faculty of our nature, what can be expected but contradictions? Accordingly, believers of this cast are at one time contemptuous; at another, being troubled, as they are and must be with inward misgivings, they are jealous and suspicious; —and at all seasons, they are under temptation to supply, by the heat with which they defend their tenets, the animation which is wanting to the constitution of the religion itself.

Faith was given to man that his affections, detached from the treasures of time, might be inclined to settle upon those of eternity; —the elevation of his nature, which this habit produces on earth, being to him a presumptive evidence of a future state of existence; and giving him a title to partake of its holiness. The religious man values what he sees chiefly as an 'imperfect shadowing forth' of what he is incapable of seeing. The concerns of religion refer to indefinite objects, and are too weighty for the mind to support them without relieving itself by resting a great part of the burthen upon words and symbols. The commerce between Man and his Maker cannot be carried on but by a process where much is represented in little, and the infinite Being accommodates himself to a finite capacity. In all this may be perceived the affinity between religion and poetry; between religion—making up the deficiencies of reason by faith, and poetry—passionate for the instruction of reason; between religion—whose element is infinitude, and whose ultimate trust is the supreme of things, submitting herself to circumscription and reconciled to substitutions; and poetry—ethereal and transcendent, yet incapable to sustain her existence without sensuous incarnation. In this community of nature may be perceived also the lurking incitements of kindred error; —so that we shall find that no poetry has been more subject to distortion, than that species the argument and scope of which is religious; and no lovers of the art have gone farther astray than the pious and the devout.

Whither then shall we turn for that union of qualifications which must necessarily exist before the decisions of a critic can be of absolute value? For a mind at once poetical and philosophical; for a critic whose affections are as free and kindly as the spirit of society, and whose understanding is severe as that of dispassionate government? Where are we to look for that initiatory composure of mind which no selfishness can disturb? For a natural sensibility that has been tutored into correctness without losing anything of its quickness; and for active faculties, capable of answering the demands which an Author of original imagination shall make upon them, —associated with a judgement that cannot be duped into admiration by aught that is unworthy of it? —Among those and those only, who, never having suffered their youthful love of poetry to remit much of its force, have applied, to the consideration of the laws of this art, the best power of their understandings. At the same time it must be observed—that, as this Class comprehends the only judgements which are trust-worthy, so does it include the most erroneous and perverse. For to be mis-taught is worse than to be untaught; and no perverseness equals that which is supported by systems, no errors are so difficult to root out as those which the understanding has pledged its credit to uphold. In this Class are contained Censors, who, if they be pleased with what is good, are pleased with it only by imperfect glimpses, and upon false principles; who, should they generalize rightly, to a certain point, are sure to suffer for it in the end; —who, if they stumble upon a sound rule, are fettered by misapplying it, or by straining it too far; being incapable of perceiving when it ought to yield to one of higher order. In it are found critics too petulant to be passive to a genuine Poet, and too feeble to grapple with him; Men, who take upon them to report of the course which he holds whom they are utterly unable to accompany, —confounded if he turn quick upon the wing, dismayed if he soar steadily into 'the region'; —Men of palsied imaginations and indurated hearts; in whose minds all healthy action is languid, —who, therefore, feed as the many direct them, or with the many, are greedy after vicious provocatives; —Judges, whose censure is auspicious, and whose praise ominous! In this Class meet together the two extremes of best and worst.

    The observations presented in the foregoing series, are of too ungracious a nature to have been made without reluctance; and, were it only on this account I would invite the reader to try them by the test of comprehensive experience. If the number of judges who can be confidently relied upon be in reality so small, it ought to follow that partial notice only, or neglect, perhaps long continued, or attention wholly inadequate to their merits—must have been the fate of most works in the higher departments of poetry; and that, on the other hand, numerous productions have blazed into popularity, and have passed away, leaving scarcely a trace behind them: —it will be, further, found that when Authors have at length raised themselves into general admiration and maintained their ground, errors and prejudices have prevailed concerning their genius and their works, which the few who are conscious of those errors and prejudices would deplore; if they were not recompensed by perceiving that there are select Spirits for whom it is ordained that their fame shall be in the world an existence like that of Virtue, which owes its being to the struggles it makes, and its vigour to the enemies whom it provokes; —a vivacious quality ever doomed to meet with opposition, and still triumphing over it; and, from the nature of its dominion, incapable of being brought to the sad conclusion of Alexander, when he wept that there were no more worlds for him to conquer.

Let us take a hasty retrospect of the poetical literature of this Country for the greater part of the last two Centuries, and see if the facts correspond with these inferences.

Who is there that now reads the Creation of Dubartas? Yet all Europe once resounded with his praise; he was caressed by Kings; and, when his Poem was translated into our language, the Faery Queen faded before it. The name of Spenser, whose genius is of a higher order than even that of Ariosto, is at this day scarcely known beyond the limits of the British Isles. And, if the value of his works is to be estimated from the attention now paid to them by his Countrymen, compared with that which they bestow on those of some other writers, it must be pronounced small indeed.

> 'The laurel, meed of mighty *Conquerors*
> And Poets *sage*' —

are his own words; but his wisdom has, in this particular, been his worst enemy; while, its opposite, whether in the shape of folly or madness, has been their best friend. But he was a great power, and bears a high name: the laurel has been awarded to him.

A Dramatic Author, if he write for the Stage, must adapt himself to the taste of the Audience, or they will not endure him; accordingly the mighty genius of Shakespeare was listened to. The People were delighted; but I am not sufficiently versed in Stage antiquities to determine whether they did not flock as eagerly to the representation of many pieces of contemporary Authors, wholly undeserving to appear upon the same boards. Had there been a formal contest for superiority among dramatic Writers, that Shakespeare, like his predecessors Sophocles and Euripides, would have often been subject to the mortification of seeing the prize adjudged to sorry competitors, becomes too probable when we reflect that the Admirers of Settle and Shadwell were, in a later age, as numerous, and reckoned as respectable in point of talent as those of Dryden. At all events, that Shakespeare stooped to accommodate himself to the People, is sufficiently apparent; and one of the most striking proofs of his almost omnipotent genius is, that he could turn to such glorious purpose those materials which the prepossessions of the age compelled him to make use of. Yet even this marvellous skill appears not to have been enough to prevent his rivals from having some advantage over him in public estimation; else how can we account for passages and scenes that exist in his works, unless upon a supposition that some of the grossest of them, a fact which in my own mind I have no doubt of, were foisted in by the Players, for the gratification of the many?

But that his Works, whatever might be their reception upon the stage, made but little impression upon the ruling Intellects of the time, may be inferred from the fact that Lord Bacon, in his multifarious writings, nowhere either quotes or alludes to him.[1] His dramatic excellence enabled him to resume possession of the stage after the Restoration; but Dryden tells us that in his time two of of Beaumont's and Fletcher's Plays were acted for one of Shakespeare's. And so faint and limited was the perception of the poetic beauties of his dramas in the time of Pope, that, in his Edition of the Plays, with a view of rendering to the general Reader a necessary service, he printed between inverted commas those passages which he thought most worthy of notice.

At this day, the French Critics have abated nothing of their aversion to this

---

[1] The learned Hakewill (a 3d edition of whose book bears date 1635) writing to refute the error 'touching Nature's perpetual and universal decay', cites triumphantly the names of Ariosto, Tasso, Bartas, and Spenser, as instances that poetic genius had not degenerated; but he makes no mention of Shakespeare.

darling of our Nation: 'the English with their Bouffon de Shakespeare' is as familiar an expression among them as in the time of Voltaire. Baron Grimm is the only French writer who seems to have perceived his infinite superiority to the first names of the French Theatre; an advantage which the Parisian Critic owed to his German blood and German education. The most enlightened Italians, though well acquainted with our language, are wholly incompetent to measure the proportions of Shakespeare. The Germans only, of foreign nations, are approaching towards a knowledge and feeling of what he is. In some respects they have acquired a superiority over the fellow countrymen of the Poet: for among us it is a current, I might say, an established opinion that Shakespeare is justly praised when he is pronounced to be 'a wild irregular genius, in whom great faults are compensated by great beauties. ' How long may it be before this misconception passes away, and it becomes universally acknowledged that the judgement of Shakespeare in the selection of his materials, and in the manner in which he has made them, heterogeneous as they often are, constitute a unity of their own, and contribute all to one great end, is not less admirable than his imagination, his invention, and his intuitive knowledge of human Nature!

There is extant a small Volume of miscellaneous Poems in which Shakespeare expresses his own feelings in his own Person. It is not difficult to conceive that the Editor, George Steevens, should have been insensible to the beauties of one portion of that Volume, the Sonnets; though there is not a part of the writings of this Poet where is found in an equal compass a greater number of exquisite feelings felicitously expressed. But, from regard to the Critic's own credit, he would not have ventured to talk of an[1] act of parliament not being strong enough to compel the perusal of these, or any production of Shakespeare, if he had not known that the people of England were ignorant of the treasures contained in those little pieces; and if he had not, moreover, shared the too common propensity of human nature to exult over a supposed fall into the mire of a genius

---

[1] This flippant insensibility was publicly reprehended by Mr. Coleridge in a course of Lectures upon Poetry given by him at the Royal Institution. For the various merits of thought and language in Shakespeare's Sonnets, see Numbers 27, 29, 30, 32, 33, 54, 64, 66, 68, 73, 76, 86, 91, 92, 93, 97, 98, 105, 107, 108, 109, 111, 113, 114, 116, 117, 129, and many others.

whom he had been compelled to regard with admiration, as an inmate of the celestial regions, —'there sitting where he durst not soar.'

Nine years before the death of Shakespeare, Milton was born; and early in life he published several small poems, which, though on their first appearance they were praised by a few of the judicious, were afterwards neglected to that degree that Pope, in his youth, could pilfer from them without danger of detection. —Whether these poems are at this day justly appreciated I will not undertake to decide: nor would it imply a severe reflection upon the mass of Readers to suppose the contrary; seeing that a Man of the acknowledged genius of Voss, the German Poet, could suffer their spirit to evaporate; and could change their character, as is done in the translation made by him of the most popular of these pieces. At all events it is certain that these Poems of Milton are now much read, and loudly praised; yet were they little heard of till more than 150 years after their publication; and of the Sonnets, Dr. Johnson, as appears from Boswell's Life of him, was in the habit of thinking and speaking as contemptuously as Stevens wrote upon those of Shakespeare.

About the time when the Pindaric Odes of Cowley and his imitators, and the productions of that class of curious thinkers whom Dr. Johnson has strangely styled Metaphysical Poets, were beginning to lose something of that extravagant admiration which they had excited, the Paradise Lost made its appearance. 'Fit audience find though few,' was the petition addressed by the Poet to his inspiring Muse. I have said elsewhere that he gained more than he asked; this I believe to be true; but Dr. Johnson has fallen into a gross mistake when he attempts to prove, by the sale of the work, that Milton's Countrymen were '*just* to it' upon its first appearance. Thirteen hundred Copies were sold in two years; an uncommon example, he asserts, of the prevalence of genius in opposition to so much recent enmity as Milton's public conduct had excited. But be it remembered that, if Milton's political and religious opinions, and the manner in which he announced them, had raised him many enemies, they had procured him numerous friends; who, as all personal danger was passed away at the time of publication, would be eager to procure the master-work of a man whom they revered, and whom they would be proud of praising. The demand did not immediately increase; 'for,' says Dr. Johnson, 'many more Readers' (he means Persons in the habit of reading poetry) 'than were supplied at first the Nation did not afford.' How careless must a writer be who can make this assertion in the face of so many existing title-pages to belie it! Turning to my own shelves, I find the folio of Cowley, 7th edition, 1681. A book near it is Flatman's Poems, 4th Edition, 1686; Waller, 5th Edition, same date. The Poems of Norris of Bemerton not long after went, I believe, through nine Editions. What further demand there might be for these works I do not know; but I well remember, that 25 Years ago, the Booksellers' stalls in London swarmed with the folios of Cowley. This is not mentioned in disparagement of that able writer and amiable man; but merely to shew—that, if Milton's works were not more read, it was not because readers did not exist at the time. Only 3000 copies of the Paradise Lost sold in 11 Years; and the Nation, says Dr. Johnson, had been satisfied from 1623 to 1664, that is, 41 Years, with only two Editions of the Works of Shakespeare; which probably did not together make 1000 Copies; facts adduced by the critic to prove the 'paucity of Readers.'—There were readers in multitudes; but their money went for other purposes, as their admiration was fixed elsewhere. We are authorized, then, to affirm that the reception of the Paradise Lost, and the slow progress of its fame, are proofs as striking as can be desired that the positions which I am attempting to establish are not erroneous. —① How amusing to shape to one's self such a critique as a Wit of Charles's days, or a Lord of the Miscellanies, or trading Journalist of King William's time, would have brought forth, if he had set his faculties industriously to work upon this Poem, everywhere impregnated with *original* excellence!

So strange indeed are the obliquities of admiration, that they whose opinions are much influenced by authority will often be tempted to think that there

---

① Hughes is express upon this subject; in his dedication of Spenser's Works to Lord Somers he writes thus: 'It was your Lordship's encouraging a beautiful Edition of Paradise Lost that first brought that incomparable Poem to be generally known and esteemed.'

are no fixed principles in human nature for this art to rest upon.[1] I have been honoured by being permitted to peruse in MS. a tract composed between the period of the Revolution and the close of that Century. It is the Work of an English Peer of high accomplishments, its object to form the character and direct the studies of his son. Perhaps nowhere does a more beautiful treatise of the kind exist. The good sense and wisdom of the thoughts, the delicacy of the feelings, and the charm of the style, are, throughout, equally conspicuous. Yet the Author, selecting among the Poets of his own country those whom he deems most worthy of his son's perusal, particularizes only Lord Rochester, Sir John Denham, and Cowley. Writing about the same time, Shaftesbury, an author at present unjustly depreciated, describes the English Muses as only yet lisping in their Cradles.

The arts by which Pope, soon afterwards, contrived to procure to himself a more general and a higher reputation than perhaps any English Poet ever attained during his life-time, are known to the judicious. And as well known is it to them, that the undue exertion of those arts, is the cause why Pope has for some time held a rank in literature, to which, if he had not been seduced by an over-love of immediate popularity, and had confided more in his native genius, he never could have descended. He bewitched the nation by his melody, and dazzled it by his polished style, and was himself blinded by his own success. Having wandered from humanity in his Eclogues with boyish inexperience, the praise, which these compositions obtained, tempted him into a belief that Nature was not to be trusted, at least in pastoral Poetry. To prove this by example, he put his friend Gay upon writing those Eclogues which their Author intended to be burlesque. The Instigator of the work, and his Admirers, could perceive in them nothing but what was ridiculous. Nevertheless, though these Poems contain some detestable passages, the effect, as Dr. Johnson well observes, 'of reality and truth became conspicuous even when the intention was to show them grovelling and degrading.' These Pastorals, ludicrous to such as prided them-

---

[1] This opinion seems actually to have been entertained by Adam Smith, the worst critic, David Hume not excepted, that Scotland, a soil to which this sort of weed seems natural, has produced.

selves upon their refinement, in spite of those disgusting passages, 'became popular, and were read with delight as just representations of rural manners and occupations.'

Something less than 60 years after the publication of the Paradise Lost appeared Thomson's Winter; which was speedily followed by his other Seasons. It is a work of inspiration; much of it is written from himself, and nobly from himself. How was it received? 'It was no sooner read,' says one of his contemporary Biographers, 'than universally admired: those only excepted who had not been used to feel, or to look for anything in poetry, beyond a *point* of satirical or epigrammatic wit, a smart *antithesis* richly trimmed with rhyme, or the softness of an *elegiac* complaint. To such his manly classical spirit could not readily commend itself; till, after a more attentive perusal, they had got the better of their prejudices, and either acquired or affected a truer taste. A few others stood aloof, merely because they had long before fixed the articles of their poetical creed, and resigned themselves to an absolute despair of ever seeing anything new and original. These were somewhat mortified to find their notions disturbed by the appearance of a poet, who seemed to owe nothing but to nature and his own genius. But, in a short time, the applause became unanimous; every one wondering how so many pictures, and pictures so familiar, should have moved them but faintly to what they felt in his descriptions. His digressions too, the overflowings of a tender benevolent heart, charmed the reader no less; leaving him in doubt, whether he should more admire the Poet or love the Man.'

This case appears to bear strongly against us: —but we must distinguish between wonder and legitimate admiration. The subject of the work is the changes produced in the appearances of nature by the revolution of the year: and, by undertaking to write in verse, Thomson pledged himself to treat his subject as became a Poet. Now, it is remarkable that, excepting a passage or two in the Windsor Forest of Pope, and some delightful pictures in the Poems of Lady Winchelsea, the poetry of the period intervening between the publication of the Paradise Lost and the Seasons does not contain a single new image of external nature; and scarcely presents a familiar one from which it can be inferred that the eye of the Poet has been steadily fixed upon his object, much less that his feelings had urged him to work upon it in the spirit of genuine imagination. To what a low state knowledge of the most obvious and important phenomena had sunk, is evident from the style in which Dryden has executed a description of Night in one of his Tragedies, and Pope his translation of the celebrated moonlight scene in the Iliad. A blind man, in the habit of attending accurately to descriptions casually dropped from the lips of those around him, might easily depict these appearances with more truth. Dryden's lines are vague, bombastic, and senseless;[1] those of Pope, though he had Homer to guide him, are throughout false and contradictory. The verses of Dryden, once highly celebrated, are forgotten; those of Pope still retain their hold upon public estimation, —nay, there is not a passage of descriptive poetry, which at this day finds so many and such ardent admirers. Strange to think of an Enthusiast, as may have been the case with thousands, reciting those verses under the cope of a moonlight sky, without having his raptures in the least disturbed by a suspicion of their absurdity. —If these two distinguished Writers could habitually think that the visible universe was of so little consequence to a Poet, that it was scarcely necessary for him to cast his eyes upon it, we may be assured that those passages of the elder poets which faithfully and poetically describe the phenomena of nature, were not at that time holden in much estimation, and that there was little accurate attention paid to those appearances.

Wonder is the natural product of Ignorance; and as the soil was *in such good condition* at the time of the publication of the Seasons, the crop was doubtless abundant. Neither individuals nor nations become corrupt all at once, nor are they enlightened in a moment. Thomson was an inspired Poet, but he could not work miracles; in cases where the art of seeing had in some degree been

---

[1] CORTES, *alone, in a night-gown.*
All things are hush'd as Nature's self lay dead;
The mountains seem to nod their drowsy head:
The little Birds in dreams their songs repeat,
And sleeping Flowers beneath the Night-dew sweat:
Even Lust and Envy sleep; yet Love denies
Rest to my soul, and slumber to my eyes.

Dryden's Indian Emperor.

learned, the teacher would further the proficiency of his pupils, but he could do little *more*; though so far does vanity assist men in acts of self-deception that many would often fancy they recognized a likeness when they knew nothing of the original. Having shown that much of what his Biographer deemed genuine admiration must in fact have been blind wonderment, —how is the rest to be accounted for? —Thomson was fortunate in the very title of his Poem, which seemed to bring it home to the prepared sympathies of every one: in the next place, notwithstanding his high powers, he writes a vicious style; and his false ornaments are exactly of that kind which would be most likely to strike the undiscerning. He likewise abounds with sentimental common-places, that from the manner in which they were brought forward bore an imposing air of novelty. In any well-used Copy of the Seasons the Book generally opens of itself with the rhapsody on love, or with one of the stories (perhaps Damon and Musidora); these also are prominent in our Collections of Extracts; and are the parts of his Works which, after all, were probably most efficient in first recommending the Author to general notice. Pope, repaying praises which he had received, and wishing to extol him to the highest, only styles him 'an elegant and philosophical Poet'; nor are we able to collect any unquestionable proofs that the true characteristics of Thomson's genius as an imaginative poet were perceived, till the elder Warton, almost 40 Years after the publication of the Seasons, pointed them out by a note in his Essay on the life and writings of Pope. In the Castle of Indolence (of which Gray speaks so coldly) these characteristics were almost as conspicuously displayed, and in verse more harmonious and diction more pure. Yet that fine Poem was neglected on its appearance, and is at this day the delight only of a few!

When Thomson died, Collins breathed forth his regrets in an Elegiac Poem, in which he pronounces a poetical curse upon *him* who should regard with insensibility the place where the Poet's remains were deposited. The Poems of the mourner himself have now passed through innumerable editions, and are universally known; but if, when Collins died, the same kind of imprecation had been pronounced by a surviving admirer, small is the number whom it would not have comprehended. The notice which his poems attained during his life-time was so small, and of course the sale so insignificant, that not long before his death he deemed it right to repay to the Bookseller the sum which he had advanced for them, and threw the Edition into the fire.

Next in importance to the Seasons of Thomson, though a considerable distance from that work in order of time, come the Reliques of Ancient English Poetry; collected, new-modelled, and in many instances (if such a contradiction in terms may be used) composed, by the Editor, Dr. Percy. This work did not steal silently into the world, as is evident from the number of legendary tales, which appeared not long after its publication; and which were modelled, as the Authors persuaded themselves, after the old Ballad. The Compilation was however ill-suited to the then existing taste of City society; and Dr. Johnson, mid the little senate to which he gave laws, was not sparing in his exertions to make it an object of contempt. The Critic triumphed, the legendary imitators were deservedly disregarded, and, as undeservedly, their ill-imitated models sank, in this Country, into temporary neglect; while Burger, and other able Writers of Germany, were translating, or imitating, these Reliques, and composing, with the aid of inspiration thence derived, Poems, which are the delight of the German nation. Dr. Percy was so abashed by the ridicule flung upon his labours from the ignorance and insensibility of the Persons with whom he lived, that, though while he was writing under a mask he had not wanted resolution to follow his genius into the regions of true simplicity and genuine pathos, (as is evinced by the exquisite ballad of Sir Cauline and by many other pieces) yet, when he appeared in his own person and character as a poetical writer, he adopted, as in the tale of the Hermit of Warkworth, a diction scarcely in any one of its features distinguishable from the vague, the glossy, and unfeeling language of his day. I mention this remarkable fact with regret, esteeming the genius of Dr. Percy in this kind of writing superior to that of any other man by whom, in modern times, it has been cultivated. That even Burger (to whom Klopstock gave, in my hearing, a commendation which he denied to Goethe and Schiller, pronouncing him to be a genuine Poet, and one of the few among the Germans whose works would last) had not the fine sensibility of Percy, might be shown from many passages, in which he has deserted his original only to go astray. For example,

> Now daye was gone, and night was come,
> And all were fast asleepe,
> All, save the Lady Emmeline,
> Who sate in her bowre to weepe:
>
> And soone she heard her true Love's voice
> Low whispering at the walle,
> Awake, awake, my dear Ladye,
> 'Tis I thy true-love call.

Which is thus tricked out and dilated,

> Als nun die Nacht Gebirg' und Thal
> Vermummt in Rabenschatten,
> Und Hochburgs Lampen über-all
> Schon ausgeflimmert hatten,
> Und alles tief entschlafen war;
> Doch nur das Fräulein immerdar,
> Voll Fieberangst, noch wachte,
> Und seinen Ritter dachte:
> Da horch! Ein süsser Liebeston
> Kam leis empor geflogen.
> 'Ho, Trudchen, ho! Da bin ich schon!
> Frisch auf! Dich angezogen!'

But from humble ballads we must ascend to heroics.

All hail Macpherson! hail to thee, Sire of Ossian! The Phantom was begotten by the snug embrace of an impudent Highlander upon a cloud of tradition—it travelled southward, where it was greeted with acclamation, and the thin Consistence took its course through Europe, upon the breath of popular applause. The Editor of the 'Reliques' had indirectly preferred a claim to the praise of invention by not concealing that his supplementary labours were considerable: how selfish his conduct, contrasted with that of the disinterested Gael, who, like Lear, gives his kingdom away, and is content to become a pensioner upon his own issue for a beggarly pittance! —Open this far-famed Book! —I have done so at random, and the beginning of the 'Epic Poem Temora,' in 8 Books, presents itself. 'The blue waves of Ullin roll in light. The green hills are covered with day. Trees shake their dusky heads in the breeze. Grey torrents pour their noisy streams. Two green hills with aged oaks surround a narrow plain. The blue course of a stream is there. On its banks stood Cairbar of Atha. His spear supports the king; the red eyes of his fear are sad. Cormac rises on his soul with all his ghastly wounds.' Precious memorandums from the pocket-book of the blind Ossian!

If it be unbecoming, as I acknowledge that for the most part it is, to speak disrespectufully of Works that have enjoyed for a length of time a widely-spread reputation, without at the same time producing irrefragable proofs of their unworthiness, let me be forgiven upon this occasion. —Having had the good fortune to be born and reared in a mountainous Country, from my very childhood I have felt the falsehood that pervades the volumes imposed upon the World under the name of Ossian. From what I saw with my own eyes, I knew that the imagery was spurious. In nature everything is distinct, yet nothing defined into absolute independent singleness. In Macpherson's work it is exactly the reverse; everything (that is not stolen) is in this manner defined, insulated, dislocated, deadened, —yet nothing distinct. It will always be so when words are substituted for things. To say that the characters never could exist, that the manners are impossible, and that a dream has more substance than the whole state of society, as there depicted, is doing nothing more than pronouncing a censure which Macpherson defied; when, with the steeps of Morven before his eyes, he could talk so familiarly of his Car-borne heroes; — Of Morven, which, if one may judge from its appearance at the distance of a few miles, contains scarcely an acre of ground sufficiently accommodating for a sledge to be trailed along its surface. —Mr. Malcolm Laing has ably shewn that the diction of this pretended translation is a motley assemblage from all quarters; but he is so fond of making out parallel passages as to call poor Macpherson to account for his '*ands*' and his '*buts!*' and he has weakened his argument by conducting it as if he thought that every striking resemblance was a *conscious* plagiarism. It is enough that the coincidences are too remarkable for its being probable or possible that they could arise in different minds without communication between them. Now as the Translators of the Bible, and Shakespeare, Milton, and Pope, could not be indebted to Macpherson, it follows that he must have owed his fine feathers to them; unless we are prepared gravely to assert, with Madame de Stael, that many of the characteristic beauties of our most celebrated English Poets, are derived from the ancient Fingallian; in which case the modern translator would have been but giving back to Ossian his own. —It is consistent that Lucien Buonaparte, who could censure Milton for having surrounded Satan in the infernal regions with courtly and regal splendour, should pronounce the modern Ossian to be the glory of Scotland; —a Country that has produced a Dunbar, a Buchanan, a Thomson, and a Burns! These opinions are of ill omen for the Epic ambition of him who has given them to the world.

Yet, much as those pretended treasures of antiquity have been admired, they have been wholly uninfluential upon the literature of the Country. No succeeding Writer appears to have caught from them a ray of inspiration; no Author, in the least distinguished, has ventured formally to imitate them—except the Boy, Chatterton, on their first appearance. He had perceived, from the successful trials which he himself had made in literary forgery, how few critics were able to distinguish between a real ancient medal and a counterfeit of modern manufacture; and he set himself to the work of filling a Magazine with *Saxon Poems*, —counterparts of those of Ossian, as like his as one of his misty stars is to another. This incapability to amalgamate with the literature of the Island is, in my estimation, a decisive proof that the book is essentially unnatural; nor should I require any other to demonstrate it to be a forgery, audacious as worthless. — Contrast, in this respect, the effect of Macpherson's publication with the Reliques of Percy, so unassuming, so modest in their pretensions! —I have already stated how much Germany is indebted to this latter work; and for our own Country, its poetry has been absolutely redeemed by it. I do not think that there is an able writer in verse of the present day who would not be proud to acknowledge his obligations to the Reliques; I know that it is so with my friends; and, for myself, I am happy in this occasion to make a public avowal of my own.

Dr Johnson, more fortunate in his contempt of the labours of Macpherson than those of his modest friend, was solicited not long after to furnish Prefaces biographical and critical for the works of some of the most eminent English Poets. The Booksellers took upon themselves to make the collection; they referred probably to the most popular miscellanies, and, unquestionably, to their Books of accounts; and decided upon the claim of Authors to be admitted into a body of the most Eminent, from the familiarity of their names with the readers of that day, and by the profits, which, from the sale of his works, each had brought and was bringing to the Trade. The Editor was allowed a limited exercise of discretion, and the Authors whom he recommended are scarcely to be mentioned without a smile. We open the volume of Prefatory Lives, and to our astonishment the *first* name we find is that of Cowley! —What is become of the Morning-star of English Poetry? Where is the bright Elizabethan Constellation? Or, if Names be more acceptable than images, where is the ever-to-be-honoured Chaucer? where is Spenser? where Sidney? and, lastly where he, whose rights as a Poet, contradistinguished from those which he is universally allowed to possess as a Dramatist, we have vindicated, where Shakespeare? —These, and a multitude of others not unworthy to be placed near them, their contemporaries and successors, we have *not*. But in their stead, we have (could better be expected when precedence was to be settled by an abstract of reputation at any given period made as in this case before us?) Roscommon, and Stepney, and Phillips, and Walsh, and Smith, and Duke, and King, and Spratt—Halifax, Granville, Sheffield, Congreve, Broome, and other reputed Magnates; Writers in metre utterly worthless and useless, except for occasions like the present, when their productions are referred to as evidence what a small quantity of brain is necessary to procure a considerable stock of admiration, provided the aspirant will accommodate himself to the likings and fashions of his day.

As I do not mean to bring down this retrospect to our own times, it may with propriety be closed at the era of this distinguished event. From the literature of other ages and countries, proofs equally cogent might have been adduced, that the opinions announced in the former part of this Essay are founded upon truth. It was not an agreeable office, nor a prudent undertaking, to declare them; but their importance seemed to render it a duty. It may still be asked, where lies the particular relation of what has been said to these Volumes? —The question will be easily answered by the discerning Reader who is old enough to remember the taste that prevailed when some of these Poems were first published, 17 years ago; who has also observed to what degree the Poetry of this Island has since that period been coloured by them; and who is further aware of the unremitting hostility with which, upon some principle or other, they have each and all been opposed. A sketch of my own notion of the constitution of Fame has been given; and, as far as concerns myself, I have cause to be satisfied. The love, the admiration, the indifference, the slight, the aversion, and even the contempt, with which these Poems have been received, knowing, as I do, the source within my own mind, from which they have proceeded, and the labour and pains, which, when labour and pains appeared needful, have been bestowed upon them, — must all, if I think consistently, be received as pledges and tokens, bearing the same general impression though widely different in value; —they are all proofs that for the present time I have not laboured in vain; and afford assurances, more or less authentic, that the products of my industry will endure.

If there be one conclusion more forcibly pressed upon us than another by the review which has been given of the fortunes and fate of Poetical Works, it is this, —that every Author, as far as he is great and at the same time *original*, has had the task of *creating* the taste by which he is to be enjoyed: so has it been, so will it continue to be. This remark was long since made to me by the philosophical Friend for the separation of whose Poems from my own I have previously expressed my regret. The predecessors of an original Genius of a high order will have smoothed the way for all that he has in common with them; — and much he will have in common; but, for what is peculiarly his own, he will be called upon to clear and often to shape his own road: —he will be in the condition of Hannibal among the Alps.

And where lies the real difficulty of creating that taste by which a truly original Poet is to be relished? Is it in breaking the bonds of custom, in overcoming the prejudices of false refinement, and displacing the aversions of inexperience? Or, if he labour for an object which here and elsewhere I have proposed to myself, does it consist in divesting the Reader of the pride that induces him to dwell upon those points wherein Men differ from each other, to the exclusion of those in which all Men are alike, or the same; and in making him ashamed of the vanity that renders him insensible of the appropriate excellence which civil arrangements, less unjust than might appear, and Nature illimitable in her bounty, have conferred on Men who stand below him in the scale of society? Finally, does it lie in establishing that dominion over the spirits of Readers by which they are to be humbled and humanized, in order that they may be purified and exalted?

If these ends are to be attained by the mere communication of *knowledge*, it does *not* lie here. —TASTE, I would remind the Reader, like IMAGINATION, is a word which has been forced to extend its services far beyond the point to which philosophy would have confined them. It is a metaphor, taken from a *passive* sense of the human body, and transferred to things which are in their essence *not* passive, —to intellectual *acts* and *operations*. The word, imagination, has been overstrained, from impulses honourable to mankind, to meet the demands of the faculty which is perhaps the noblest of our nature. In the instance of taste, the process has been reversed; and from the prevalence of dispositions at once injurious and discreditable, —being no other than that selfishness which is the child of apathy, —which, as Nations decline in productive and creative power, makes them value themselves upon a presumed refinement of judging. Poverty of language is the primary cause of the use which we make of the word, imagination; but the word, taste, has been stretched to the sense which it bears in modern Europe by habits of self-conceit, inducing that inversion in the order of things whereby a passive faculty is made paramount among the faculties conversant with the fine arts. Proportion and congruity, the requisite knowledge being supposed, are subjects upon which taste may be trusted; it is competent to this office; —for in its intercourse with these the mind is *passive*, and is affected painfully or pleasurably as by an instinct. But the profound and the exquisite in feeling, the lofty and universal in thought and imagination; or in ordinary language the pathetic and the sublime; —are neither of them, accurately speaking, objects of a faculty which could ever without a sinking in the spirit of Nations have been designated by the metaphor—*Taste*. And why? Because without the exertion of a co-operating *power* in the mind of the Reader, there can be no adequate sympathy with either of these emotions: without this auxiliary impulse elevated or profound passion cannot exist.

Passion, it must be observed, is derived from a word which signifies *suffering*; but the connexion which suffering has with effort, with exertion, and *action*, is immediate and inseparable. How strikingly is this property of human nature exhibited by the fact, that, in popular language, to be in a passion, is to be angry! —But,

> 'Anger in hasty *words* or *blows*
> Itself discharges on its foes.'

To be moved, then, by a passion, is to be excited, often to external, and always to internal, effort; whether for the continuance and strengthening of the passion, or for its suppression, accordingly as the course which it takes may be painful or pleasurable. If the latter, the soul must contribute to its support, or it never becomes vivid, —and soon languishes, and dies. And this brings us to the point. If every great Poet with whose writings men are familiar, in the highest exercise of his genius, before he can be thoroughly enjoyed, has to call forth and to communicate *power*, this service, in a still greater degree, falls upon an original Writer, at his first appearance in the world. —Of genius the only proof is, the act of doing well what is worthy to be done, and what was never done before: Of genius, in the fine arts, the only infallible sign is the widening the sphere of human sensibility, for the delight, honour, and benefit of human nature. Genius is the introduction of a new element into the intellectual universe: or, if that be not allowed, it is the application of powers to objects on which they had not before been exercised, or the employment of them in such a manner as to produce effects hitherto unknown. What is all this but an advance, or a conquest, made by the soul of the Poet? Is it to be supposed that the Reader can make progress of this kind, like an Indian Prince or General—stretched on his Palanquin, and borne by his Slaves? No; he is invigorated and inspired by his Leader, in order that he may exert himself; for he cannot proceed in quiescence, he cannot be carried like a dead weight. Therefore to create taste is to call forth and bestow power, of which knowledge is the effect; and *there* lies the true difficulty.

As the pathetic participates of an *animal* sensation, it might seem—that, if the springs of this emotion were genuine, all men, possessed of competent knowledge of the facts and circumstances, would be instantaneously affected. And, doubtless, in the works of every true Poet will be found passages of that species of excellence, which is proved by effects immediate and universal. But there are emotions of the pathetic that are simple and direct, and others—that are complex and revolutionary; some—to which the heart yields with gentleness, others, —against which it struggles with pride: these varieties are infinite as the combinations of circumstance and the constitutions of character. Remember, also, that the medium through which, in poetry, the heart is to be affected—is language; a thing subject to endless fluctuations and arbitrary associations. The genius of the Poet melts these down for his purpose; but they retain their shape and quality to him who is not capable of exerting, within his own mind, a corresponding energy. There is also a meditative, as well as a human, pathos; an enthusiastic, as well as an ordinary, sorrow; a sadness that has its seat in the depths of reason, to which the mind cannot sink gently of itself—but to which it must descend by treading the steps of thought. And for the sublime, —if we consider what are the cares that occupy the passing day, and how remote is the practice and the course of life from the sources of sublimity, in the soul of Man, can it be wondered that there is little existing preparation for a Poet charged with a new mission to extend its kingdom, and to augment and spread its enjoyments?

Away, then, with the senseless iteration of the word, *popular,* applied to new works in Poetry, as if there were no test of excellence in this first of the fine arts but that all Men should run after its productions, as if urged by an appetite, or constrained by a spell! —The qualities of writing best fitted for eager reception are either such as startle the world into attention by their audacity and extravagance; or they are chiefly of a superficial kind, lying upon the surfaces of manners; or arising out of a selection and arrangement of incidents, by which the mind is kept upon the stretch of curiosity, and the fancy amused without the trouble of thought. But in everything which is to send the soul into herself, to be admonished of her weakness or to be made conscious of her power; —wherever life and nature are described as operated upon by the creative or abstracting virtue of the imagination; wherever the instinctive wisdom of antiquity and her heroic passions uniting, in the heart of the Poet, with the meditative wisdom of later ages, have produced that accord of sublimated humanity, which is at once a history of the remote past and a prophetic enunciation of the remotest future, *there*, the Poet must reconcile himself for a season to few and scattered hearers. —Grand thoughts, (and Shakespeare must often have sighed over this truth) as they are most naturally and most fitly conceived in solitude, so can they not be brought forth in the midst of plaudits without some violation of their sanctity. Go to a silent exhibition of the productions of the Sister Art, and be convinced that the qualities which dazzle at first sight, and kindle the admiration of the multitude, are essentially different from those by which permanent influence is secured. Let us not shrink from following up these principles as far as they will carry us, and conclude with observing—that there never has been a period, and perhaps never will be, in which vicious poetry, of some kind or other, has not excited more zealous admiration, and been far more generally read, than good; but this advantage attends the good, that the *individual*, as well as the species, survives from age to age: whereas, of the depraved, though the species be immortal, the individual quickly *perishes*; the object of present admiration vanishes, being supplanted by some other as easily produced; which, though no better, brings with it at least the irritation of novelty, —with adaptation, more or less skilful, to the changing humours of the majority of those who are most at leisure to regard poetical works when they first solicit their attention.

    Is it the result of the whole that, in the opinion of the Writer, the judgement of the People is not to be respected? The thought is most injurious; and could the charge be brought against him, he would repel it with indignation. The People have already been justified, and their eulogium pronounced by implication, when it was said, above—that, of *good* poetry, the *individual*, as well as the species, *survives*. And how does it survive but through the People? what preserves it but their intellect and their wisdom?

> '—Past and future, are the wings
> On whose support, harmoniously conjoined,
> Move the great Spirit of human knowledge—'
>
> MS.

The voice that issues from this Spirit, is that Vox populi which the Deity inspires. Foolish must he be who can mistake for this a local acclamation, or a transitory outcry—transitory though it be for years, local though from a Nation. Still more lamentable is his error, who can believe that there is anything of divine infallibility in the clamour of that small though loud portion of the community, ever governed by factitious influence, which, under the name of the PUBLIC, passes itself, upon the unthinking, for the PEOPLE. Towards the Public, the Writer hopes that he feels as much deference as it is entitled to: but to the People, philosophically characterized, and to the embodied spirit of their knowledge, so far as it exists and moves, at the present, faithfully supported by its two wings, the past and the future, his devout respect, his reverence, is due. He offers it willingly and readily; and, this done, takes leave of his Readers, by assuring them—that, if he were not persuaded that the Contents of these Volumes, and the Work to which they are subsidiary, evince something of the 'Vision and the Faculty divine'; and that, both in words and things, they will operate in their degree, to extend the domain of sensibility for the delight, the honour, and the benefit of human nature, notwithstanding the many happy hours which he has employed in their composition, and the manifold comforts and enjoyments they have procured to him, he would not, if a wish could do it, save them from immediate destruction; —from becoming at this moment, to the world, as a thing that had never been.

Samuel Taylor Coleridge

BIOGRAPHIA LITERARIA (1817)

CHAPTER XII

A chapter of requests and premonitions concerning the perusal or omission of the chapter that follows.

IN THE perusal of philosophical works I have been greatly benefited by a resolve, which, in the antithetic form and with the allowed quaintness of an adage or maxim, I have been accustomed to word thus: 'until you understand a writer's ignorance, presume yourself ignorant of his understanding. ' This golden rule of mine does, I own, resemble those of Pythagoras in its obscurity rather than in its depth. If however the reader will permit me to be my own Hierocles, I trust, that he will find its meaning fully explained by the following instances. I have now before me a treatise of a religious fanatic, full of dreams and super natural experiences. I see clearly the writer's grounds, and their hollowness. I have a complete insight into the causes, which through the medium of his body has acted on his mind; and by application of received and ascertained laws I can satisfactorily explain to my own reason all the strange incidents, which the writer records of himself. And this I can do without suspecting him of any intentional falsehood. As when in broad daylight a man tracks the steps of a traveller, who had lost his way in a fog or by a treacherous moonshine, even so, and with the same tranquil sense of certainty, can I follow the traces of this bewildered visionary. I understand his ignorance.

On the other hand, I have been reperusing with the best energies of my mind the TIMAEUS of Plato. Whatever I comprehend, impresses me with a reverential sense of the author's genius; but there is a considerable portion of the work, to which I can attach no consistent meaning. In other treatises of the same philosopher, intended for the average comprehensions of men, I have been delighted with the masterly good sense, with the perspicuity of the language, and the aptness of the inductions. I recollect likewise, that numerous passages in this author, which I thoroughly comprehend, were formerly no less unintelligible to me, than the passages now in question. It would, I am aware, be quite fashionable to dismiss them at once as Platonic jargon. But this I cannot do with satisfaction to my own mind, because I have sought in vain for causes adequate to the solution of the assumed inconsistency. I have no insight into the possibility of a man so eminently wise, using words with such half-meanings to himself, as must perforce pass into no-meaning to his readers. When in addition to the motives thus suggested by my own reason, I bring into distinct remembrance the number and the series of great men, who after long and zealous study of these works had joined in honouring the name of Plato with epithets, that almost transcend humanity, I feel, that a contemptuous verdict on my part might argue want of modesty, but would hardly be received by the judicious, as evidence of superior penetration. Therefore, utterly baffled in all my attempts to understand the ignorance of Plato, I conclude myself ignorant of his understanding.

In lieu of the various requests which the anxiety of authorship addresses to the unknown reader, I advance but this one; that he will either pass over the following chapter altogether, or read the whole connectedly. The fairest part of the most beautiful body will appear deformed and monstrous, if dissevered from its place in the organic whole. Nay, on delicate subjects, where a seemingly trifling difference of more or less may constitute a difference in kind, even a faithful display of the main and supporting ideas, if yet they are separated from the forms by which they are at once clothed and modified, may perchance present a skeleton indeed; but a skeleton to alarm and deter. Though I might find numerous precedents, I shall not desire the reader to strip his mind of all prejudices, nor to keep all prior systems out of view during his examination of the present. For in truth, such requests appear to me not much unlike the advice given to hypochondriacal patients in Dr. Buchan's Domestic Medicine; *videlicet* [namely], to preserve themselves uniformly tranquil and in good spirits. Till I had discovered the art of destroying the memory *a parte post* [from behind], without injury to its future operations, and without detriment to the judgment, I should suppress the request as premature; and therefore, however much I may wish to be read with an unprejudiced mind, I do not presume to state it as a necessary condition.

The extent of my daring is to suggest one criterion, by which it may be rationally conjectured beforehand, whether or no a reader would lose his time, and perhaps his temper, in the perusal of this, or any other treatise constructed on similar principles. But it would be cruelly misinterpreted, as implying the least disrespect either for the moral or intellectual qualities of the individuals thereby precluded. The criterion is this: if a man receives as fundamental facts, and therefore of course indemonstrable and incapable of further analysis, the general notions of matter, spirit, soul, body, action, passiveness, time, space, cause and effect, consciousness, perception, memory and habit; if he feels his mind completely at rest concerning all these, and is satisfied, if only he can analyse all other notions into some one or more of these supposed elements with plausible subordination and apt arrangement: to such a mind I would as courteously as possible convey the hint, that for him the chapter was not written.

Vir bonus es, doctus, prudens; ast *haud tibi spiro.*[1]

For these terms do in truth include all the difficulties, which the human mind can propose for solution. Taking them therefore in mass, and unexamined, it required only a decent apprenticeship in logic, to draw forth their contents in all forms and colours, as the professors of legerdemain at our village fairs pull

---

[1] 'You are a good man, learned, prudent; but I do not blow for you' *(trans. by H. J. Jackson)—editor's note.*

out ribbon after ribbon from their mouths. And not more difficult is it to reduce them back again to their different genera. But though this analysis is highly useful in rendering our knowledge more distinct, it does not really add to it. It does not increase, though it gives us a greater mastery over, the wealth which we before possessed. For forensic purposes, for all the established professions of society, this is sufficient. But for philosophy in its highest sense as the science of ultimate truths, and therefore *scientia scientiarum* [the science of sciences], this mere analysis of terms is preparative only, though as a preparative discipline indispensable.

Still less dare a favourable perusal be anticipated from the proselytes of that compendious philosophy, which talking of mind but thinking of brick and mortar, or other images equally abstracted from body, contrives a theory of spirit by nicknaming matter, and in a few hours can qualify its dullest disciples to explain the *omne scibile* [everything knowable] by reducing all things to impressions, ideas, and sensations.

But it is time to tell the truth; though it requires some courage to avow it in an age and country, in which disquisitions on all subjects, not privileged to adopt technical terms or scientific symbols, must be addressed to the Public. I say then, that it is neither possible nor necessary for all men, nor for many, to be philosophers. There is a philosophic (and inasmuch as it is actualized by an effort of freedom, an artificial) consciousness, which lies beneath or (as it were) behind the spontaneous consciousness natural to all reflecting beings. As the elder Romans distinguished their northern provinces into Cis-Alpine and Trans-Alpine, so may we divide all the objects of human knowledge into those on this side, and those on the other side of the spontaneous consciousness; *citra et trans conscientiam communem*. The latter is exclusively the domain of pure philosophy, which is therefore properly entitled *transcendental,* in order to discriminate it at once, both from mere reflection and representation on the one hand, and on the other from those flights of lawless speculation which, abandoned by all distinct consciousness, because transgressing the bounds and purposes of our intellectual faculties, are justly condemned, as *transcendent*.① The first range of hills, that encircles the scanty vale of human life, is the horizon for the majority of its inhabitants. On its ridges the common sun is born and departs. From them

---

① This distinction between transcendental and transcendent is observed by our elder divines and philosophors, whenever they express themselves scholastically. Dr. Johnson indeed has confounded the two words; but his own authorities do not bear him out. Of this celebrated dictionary I will venture to remark once for all, that I should suspect the man of a morose disposition who should speak of it without respect and gratitude as a most instructive and entertaining book, and hitherto, unfortunately, an indispensable book; but I confess, that I should be surprised at hearing from a philosophic and thorough scholar any but very qualified praises of it, as a dictionary. I am not now alluding to the number of genuine words omitted; for this is (and perhaps to a greater extent) true, as Mr. Wakefield has noticed, of our best Greek lexicans, and this too after the successive labours of so many giants in learning. I refer at present both to omissions and commissions of a more important nature. What thses are, me saltem judice [at least in my opinion], will be stated at full in The Friend, republished and completed.

    I had never heard of the correspondence between Wakefield and Fox till I saw the account of it this morning (16th September 1815) in the Monthly Review, I was not a little gratified at finding, that Mr. Wakefield had proposed to himself nearly the same plan for a Greek and English Dictionary, which I had formed, and began to execute, now ten years ago. but far, far more grieved am I, that he did not live to complete it. I cannot but think it a subject of most serious regret, that the same heavy expenditure, which is now employing in the republication of Stephanus augmented, had not been applied to a new lexican on a more philosophical plan, with the English, German, and French synonyms as well as Latin. In almost every instance the precise individual meaming might be given in an English or German word; whereas in Latin we must too often be contented with a mere general and inclusive term. How indeed can it be otherwise, when we attempt to render the most copious language of the world, the most admirable for the fineness of its distinctions, into one of the poorest and most vague languages? Especially, when we reflect on the comparative number of the works, still extant, written, while the Greek and Latin were living languages. Were I asked, what I deemed the greatest and most unmixed benefit, which a wealthy individual, or an association of wealthy individuals, could bestow on their country and on mankind, I should not hesitate to answer, 'a philosophical English dictionary; with the Greek, Latin, Germam, French, Spanish and Italian synonyms, and with correspondent indexes.' That the learned languages might thereby be acquired, better, in half the time, is but a part, and not the most important part, of the advantages which would accrue from such a work. O! if it should be permitted by providence, that without detriment to freedom and independence our Government might be enabled to become more than a committee for war and revenue! There was a time, when everything was to be done by Government. Have we not flown off to the contrary extreme?

the stars rise, and touching them they vanish. By the many, even this range, the natural limit and bulwark of the vale, is but imperfectly known. Its higher ascents are too often hidden by mists and clouds from uncultivated swamps, which few have courage or curiosity to penetrate. To the multitude below these vapours appear, now as the dark haunts of terrific agents, on which none may intrude with impunity; and now all aglow, with colours not their own, they are gazed at as the splendid palaces of happiness and power. But in all ages there have been a few, who measuring and sounding the rivers of the vale at the feet of their furthest inaccessible falls have learned, that the sources must be far higher and far inward; a few, who even in the level streams have detected elements, which neither the vale itself nor the surrounding mountains contained or could supply. How and whence to these thoughts, these strong probabilities, the ascertaining vision, the intuitive knowledge may finally supervene, can be learnt only by the fact. I might oppose to the question the words with which Plotinus① supposes Nature to answer a similar difficulty. 'Should any one interrogate her, how she works, if graciously she vouchsafe to listen and speak, she will reply, it behoves thee not to disquiet me with interrogatories, but to understand in silence, even as I am silent, and work without words. '

Likewise in the fifth book of the fifth Ennead, speaking of the highest and intuitive knowledge as distinguished from the discursive, or in the language of Wordsworth

---

① Ennead, iii. 1. 8. c. 3. The force of the Greek συνιέναι is imperfectly expressed by 'understand'; our own idiomatic phrase 'to go along with me' comes nearest to it. The passage, that follows, full of profound sense, appears to me evidently corrupt; and in fact no writer more wants, better deserves, or is less likely to obtain a new and more correct edition. — τἰοὖν συνιέναι; οτι τό γενόμενον εστι θεαμα εμον, σιωπησις (mallem, [I should prefer] θεαμα, εμου σιωπωσης,) και φυσει γενομενον θεωρημα και μοι γενομενη εκ θεωρίας της ωδι, την φυσιν εχειν φιλοθεαμονα υπαρχει (mallem, και μοι ης γενομενη εκ θεωρίας αυτης ωδις). 'What then are we to understand? That whatever is produced is an intuition, I silent; and that, which is thus generated, is by its nature a theorem, or form of contemplative nature.' So Synesius: Ωδιsιερα, Αρρητε, γονα [sacred travail, ineffable generation]. The after compason of the process of the *natura naturans* [naturing nature] with that of the geometrician is drawn from the very heart of philosophy.

The vision and the faculty divine;

he says: 'it is not lawful to enquire from whence it sprang, as if it were a thing subject to place and motion, for it neither approached hither, nor again departs from hence to some other place; but it either appears to us or it does not appear. So that we ought not to pursue it with a view of detecting its secret source, but to watch in quiet till it suddenly shines upon us; preparing ourselves for the blessed spectacle as the eye waits patiently for the rising sun. ' They and they only can acquire the philosophic imagination, the sacred power of self-intuition, who within themselves can interpret and understand the symbol, that the wings of the air-sylph are forming within the skin of the caterpillar; those only, who feel in their own spirits the same instinct, which impels the chrysalis of the horned fly to leave room in its involucrum for antenna, yet to come. They know and feel, that the potential works in them, even as the actual works on them! In short, all the organs of sense are framed for a corresponding world of sense; and we have it. All the organs of spirit are framed for a correspondent world of spirit: though the latter organs are not developed in all alike. But they exist in all, and their first appearance discloses itself in the moral being. How else could it be, that even worldlings, not wholly debased, will contemplate the man of simple and disinterested goodness with contradictory feelings of pity and respect? 'Poor man! he is not made for this world. ' Oh! herein they utter a prophecy of universal fulfilment; for man must either rise or sink.

It is the essential mark of the true philosopher to rest satisfied with no imperfect light, as long as the impossibility of attaining a fuller knowledge has not been demonstrated. That the common consciousness itself will furnish proofs by its own direction, that it is connected with master currents below the surface, I shall merely assume as a postulate *pro tempore* [for the time being]. This having been granted, though but in expectation of the argument, I can safely deduce from it the equal truth of my former assertion, that philosophy cannot be intelligible to all, even of the most learned and cultivated classes. A system, the first principle of which it is to render the mind intuitive of the spiritual in man (i. e. of that which lies on the other side of our natural consciousness) must needs have a great obscurity for those, who have never disciplined and strengthened this ulterior consciousness. It must in truth be a land of darkness, a perfect Anti-

Goshen, for men to whom the noblest treasures of their own being are reported only through the imperfect translation of lifeless and sightless motions. Perhaps, in great part, through words which are but the shadows of notions; even as the notional understanding itself is but the shadowy abstraction of living and actual truth. On the immediate, which dwells in every man, and on the original intuition, or absolute affirmation of it, (which is likewise in every man, but does not in every man rise into consciousness) all the certainty of our knowledge depends; and this becomes intelligible to no man by the ministry of mere words from without. The medium, by which spirits understand each other, is not the surrounding air; but the freedom which they possess in common, as the common ethereal element of their being, the tremulous reciprocations of which propagate themselves even to the inmost of the soul. Where the spirit of a man is not filled with the consciousness of freedom (were it only from its restlessness, as of one still struggling in bondage) all spiritual intercourse is interrupted, not only with others, but even with himself. No wonder then, that he remains incomprehensible to himself as well as to others. No wonder, that, in the fearful desert of his consciousness, he wearies himself out with empty words, to which no friendly echo answers, either from his own heart, or the heart of a fellow being; or bewilders himself in the pursuit of notional phantoms, the mere refractions from unseen and distant truths through the distorting medium of his own unenlivened and stagnant understanding! To remain unintelligible to such a mind, exclaims Schelling on a like occasion, is honour and a good name before God and man.

The history of philosophy (the same writer observes) contains instances of systems, which for successive generations have remained enigmatic. Such he deems the system of Leibnitz, whom another writer (rashly I think, and invidiously) extols as the only philosopher, who was himself deeply convinced of his own doctrines. As hitherto interpreted, however, they have not produced the effect, which Leibnitz himself, in a most instructive passage, describes as the criterion of a true philosophy; namely, that it would at once explain and collect the fragments of truth scattered through systems apparently the most incongruous. The truth, says he, is diffused more widely than is commonly believed; but it is often painted, yet oftener masked, and is sometimes mutilated and sometimes, alas! in close alliance with mischievous errors. The deeper, however, we penetrate into the ground of things, the more truth we discover in the doctrines of the greater number of the philosophical sects. The want of substantial reality in the objects of the senses, according to the sceptics; the harmonies or numbers, the prototypes and ideas, to which the Pythagoreans and Platonists reduced all things: the One and All of Parmenides and Plotinus, without Spinozism;① the necessary connection of things according to the Stoics, reconcilable with the

---

① This is happily effected in three lines by Synesius, in his Fourth Hymn:

Εν και Παντα [One and All]—(taken by itself) is Spinozism.

Εν δ' 'Απαντων [One of All]—a mere *anima Mundi* [World-spirit]

Εν τε προ παντων [One before All]—is mechanical Theism.

But unite all three, and the result is the Theism of Saint Paul and Christianaity.

Synesius was censured for his doctrine of the Pre-existence of the Soul; but never, that I can find, arraigned or deemed heretical for his Pantheism, though neither Giordano Bruno, or Jacob Behmen ever avowed it more broadly.

Μυστας δε Noos,
Τα τε και τα λεγει,
Βυθον αρρητον
Αμφιχορευων.
Συ το τικτον εφυs,
Συ το τικτομενον.
Συ το φωτιξιον,
Συ το λαμπομενον.
Συ το φαινομενον,
Συ το κρυπτομενουs
Ιδιαιs αυγαιs.
'Εν και παντα,
'Εν καθ' εαυτο,
Και δια παντων.

[The mind initiated in the mysteries says such and such things, moving in harmony the while round Thy awful abysm. Thou art the Generator, Thou the Generated; Thou the Light that shineth, Thou the Illumined; Thou what is revealed, Thou that which is hidden in thine own beams; The One and All, The One Self-contained and dispersed through all things. (*The Collected Works of Samuel Taylor Coleridge*)]

Pantheism is therefore not necessarily irreligious or heretical, though it may be taught a-theistically. Thus Spinoza would agree with Synesius in calling God Φυσιs εν Νοεροιs, the Nature in Intelligence; but he could not subscribe to the proceeding Νουs και Νοεροs, i. e. Himself Intelligence and Intelligent.

In this biographical sketch of my literary life I may be excuted, if I mention here, I had translated the eight Hymns of Synesius from the Greek into English Anacreontics before my 15th year.

spontaneity of the other schools; the vital-philosophy of the Cabbalists and Hermetists, who assumed the universality of sensation; the substantial forms and entelechies of Aristotle and the schoolmen, together with the mechanical solution of all particular phaenomena according to Democritus and the recent philosophers—all these we shall find united in one perspective central point, which shows regularity and a coincidence of all the parts in the very object, which from every other point of view must appear confused and distorted. The spirit of sectarianism has been hitherto our fault, and the cause of our failures. We have imprisoned our own conceptions by the lines, which we have drawn, in order to exclude the conceptions of others. J'ai trouvé que la plupart des Sectes ont raison dans une bonne partie de ce qu'elles avancent, mais non pas tant en ce qu'elles nient①.

A system, which aims to deduce the memory with all the other functions of intelligence, must of course place its first position from beyond the memory, and anterior to it, otherwise the principle of solution would be itself a part of the problem to be solved. Such a position therefore must, in the first instance be demanded, and the first question will be, by what right is it demanded? On this account I think it expedient to make some preliminary remarks on the introduction of Postulates in philosophy. The word postulate is borrowed from the science of mathematics. (See Schell. abhandl. zur Erläuter. des id. der. Wissenschaftslehre.) In geometry the primary construction is not demonstrated, but postulated. This first and most simple construction in space is the point in motion, or the line. Whether the point is moved in one and the same direction, or whether its direction is continually changed, remains as yet undetermined. But if the direction of the point have been determined, it is either by a point without it, and then there arises the straight line which incloses no space; or the direction of the point is not determined by a point without it, and then it must flow back again on itself, that is, there arises a cyclical line, which does enclose a space. If the straight line be assumed as the positive, the cyclical is then the negation

---

① 'I have found that most sects are right in much that they affirm, but not so much so in what they deny'—editor's note.

of the straight. It is a line, which at no point strikes out into the straight, but changes its direction continuously. But if the primary line be conceived as undetermined, and the straight line as determined throughout, then the cyclical is the third compounded of both. It is at once undetermined and determined; undetermined through any point without, and determined through itself. Geometry therefore supplies philosophy with the example of a primary intuition, from which every science that lays claim to evidence must take its commencement. The mathematician does not begin with a demonstrable proposition, but with an intuition, a practical idea.

But here an important distinction presents itself. Philosophy is employed on objects of the inner sense, and cannot, like geometry, appropriate to every construction a correspondent outward intuition. Nevertheless, philosophy, if it is to arrive at evidence, must proceed from the most original construction, and the question then is, what is the most original construction or first productive act for the inner sense. The answer to this question depends on the direction which is given to the inner sense. But in philosophy the inner sense cannot have its direction determined by an outward object. To the original construction of the line I can be compelled by a line drawn before me on the slate or on sand. The stroke thus drawn is indeed not the line itself, but only the image or picture of the line. It is not from it, that we first learn to know the line; but, on the contrary, we bring this stroke to the original line generated by the act of the imagination; otherwise we could not define it as without breadth or thickness. Still however this stroke is the sensuous image of the original or ideal line, and an efficient mean to excite every imagination to the intuition of it.

It is demanded then, whether there be found any means in philosophy to determine the direction of the inner sense, as in mathematics it is determinable by its specific image or outward picture. Now the inner sense has its direction determined for the greater part only by an act of freedom. One man's consciousness extends only to the pleasant or unpleasant sensations caused in him by external impressions; another enlarges his inner sense to a consciousness of forms and quantity; a third in addition to the image is conscious of the conception or notion of the thing; a fourth attains to a notion of his notions—he reflects on his own reflections; and thus we may say without impropriety, that the one possesses more or less inner sense, than the other. This more or less betrays already, that philosophy in its first principles must have a practical or moral, as well as a theoretical or speculative side. This difference in degree does not exist in the mathematics. Socrates in Plato shows, that an ignorant slave may be brought to understand and of himself to solve the most difficult geometrical problem. Socrates drew the figures for the slave in the sand. The disciples of the critical philosophy could likewise (as was indeed actually done by La Forge and some other followers of Descartes) represent the origin of our representations in copperplates; but no one has yet attempted it, and it would be utterly useless. To an Esquimaux or New Zealander our most popular philosophy would be wholly unintelligible. The sense, the inward organ, for it is not yet born in him. So is there many a one among us, yes, and some who think themselves philosophers too, to whom the philosophic organ is entirely wanting. To such a man philosophy is a mere play of words and notions, like a theory of music to the deaf, or like the geometry of light to the blind. The connection of the parts and their logical dependencies may be seen and remembered; but the whole is groundless and hollow, unsustained by living contact, unaccompanied with any realizing intuition which exists by and in the act that affirms its existence, which is known, because it is, and is, because it is known. The words of Plotinus, in the assumed person of Nature, hold true of the philosophic energy. Το θεωρουν μου θεωρημα ποιει, ωσπερ οι Γεωμετραι θεωρουντες γραφουσιν. Αλλ' εμου μη γραφουσης, θεωρουσης δε, υφισηανται αι των σωματων γραμμαι. With me the act of contemplation makes the thing contemplated, as the geometricians contemplating describe lines correspondent; but I not describing lines, but simply contemplating, the representative forms of things rise up into existence.

The postulate of philosophy and at the same time the test of philosophic capacity, is no other than the heaven-descended Know thyself! (*E caelo descendit,* Γνωθι σεαυτον [It came down from heaven, Know thyself]). And this at once practically and speculatively. For as philosophy is neither a science of the reason or understanding only, nor merely a science of morals, but the science of being altogether, its primary ground can be neither merely speculative nor merely practical, but both in one. All knowledge rests on the coincidence of an object with a subject. (My readers have been warned in a former chapter that, for their convenience as well as the writer's, the term, subject, is used by me in its scholastic sense as equivalent to mind or sentient being, and as the necessary correlative of object or *quicquid objicitur menti* [whatever is cast before the mind].) For we can *know* that only which is true: and the truth is universally placed in the coincidence of the thought with the thing, of the representation with the object represented.

Now the sum of all that is merely objective, we will henceforth call nature, confining the term to its passive and material sense, as comprising all the phenomena by which its existence is made known to us. On the other hand the sum of all that is subjective, we may comprehend in the name of the self or intelligence. Both conceptions are in necessary antithesis. Intelligence is conceived of as exclusively representative, nature as exclusively represented; the one as conscious, the other as without consciousness. Now in all acts of positive knowledge there is required a reciprocal concurrence of both, namely of the conscious being, and of that which is in itself unconscious. Our problem is to explain this concurrence, its possibility and its necessity.

During the act of knowledge itself, the objective and subjective are so instantly united, that we cannot determine to which of the two the priority belongs. There is here no first, and no second; both are coinstantaneous and one. While I am attempting to explain this intimate coalition, I must suppose it dissolved. I must necessarily set out from the one, to which therefore I give hypothetical antecedence, in order to arrive at the other. But as there are but two factors or elements in the problem, subject and object, and as it is left indeterminate from which of them I should commence, there are two cases equally possible.

1. EITHER THE OBJECTIVE IS TAKEN AS THE FIRST, AND THEN WE HAVE TO ACCOUNT FOR THE SUPERVENTION OF THE SUBJECTIVE, WHICH COALESCES WITH IT.

The notion of the subjective is not contained in the notion of the objective. On the contrary they mutually exclude each other. The subjective therefore must supervene to the objective. The conception of nature does not apparently involve the co-presence of an intelligence making an ideal duplicate of it, that is, representing it. This desk for instance would (according to our natural notions) be, though there should exist no sentient being to look at it. This then is the problem of natural philosophy. It assumes the objective or unconscious nature as the first, and as therefore to explain how intelligence can supervene to it, or how itself can grow into intelligence. If it should appear, that all enlightened naturalists, without having distinctly proposed the problem to themselves, have yet constantly moved in the line of its solution, it must afford a strong presumption that the problem itself is founded in nature. For if all knowledge has, as it were, two poles reciprocally required and presupposed, all sciences must proceed from the one or the other, and must tend toward the opposite as far as the equatorial point in which both are reconciled and become identical. The necessary tendency therefore of all natural philosophy is from nature to intelligence; and this, and no other is the true ground and occasion of the instinctive striving to introduce theory into our views of natural phenomena. The highest perfection of natural philosophy would consist in the perfect spiritualization of all the laws of nature into laws of intuition and intellect. The phenomena (the material) most wholly disappear, and the laws alone (the formal) must remain. Thence it comes, that in nature itself the more the principle of law breaks forth, the more does the husk drop off, the phenomena themselves become more spiritual and at length cease altogether in our consciousness. The optical phaenomena are but a geometry, the lines of which are drawn by light, and the materiality of this light itself has already become matter of doubt. In the appearances of magnetism all trace of matter is lost, and of the phenomena of gravitation, which not a few among the most illustrious Newtonians have declared no otherwise comprehensible than as an immediate spiritual influence, there remains nothing but its law, the execution of which on a vast scale is the mechanism of the heavenly motions. The theory of natural philosophy would then be completed, when all nature was demonstrated to be identical in essence with that, which in its highest known power exists in man as intelligence and self-consciousness; when the heavens and the earth shall declare not only the power of their maker, but the glory and the presence of their God, even as he appeared to the great prophet during the vision of the mount in the skirts of his divinity.

This may suffice to show, that even natural science, which commences with the material phenomenon as the reality and substance of things existing, does yet by the necessity of theorizing unconsciously, and as it were instinctively, end in nature as an intelligence; and by this tendency the science of nature becomes finally natural philosophy, the one of the two poles of fundamental science.

2. OR THE SUBJECTIVE IS TAKEN AS THE FIRST, AND THE PROBLEM THEN IS, HOW THERE SUPERVENES TO IT A COINCIDENT OBJECTIVE.

In the pursuit of these sciences, our success in each, depends on an austere and faithful adherence to its own principles, with a careful separation and exclusion of those, which appertain to the opposite science. As the natural philosopher, who directs his views to the objective, avoids above all things the intermixture of the subjective in his knowledge, as for instance, arbitrary suppositions or rather suflictions, occult qualities, spiritual agents, and the substitution of final for efficient causes; so on the other hand, the transcendental or intelligential philosopher is equally anxious to preclude all interpolation of the objective into the subjective principles of his science, as for instance the assumption of impresses or configurations in the brain, correspondent to miniature pictures on the retina painted by rays of light from supposed originals, which are not the immediate and real objects of vision, but deductions from it for the purposes of explanation. This purification of the mind is effected by an absolute and scientific scepticism, to which the mind voluntarily determines itself for the specific purpose of future certainty. Descartes who (in his Meditations) himself first, at least of the moderns, gave a beautiful example of this voluntary doubt, this self-determined indetermination, happily expresses its utter difference from the scepticism of vanity or irreligion: 'Nec tamen in eo scepticos imitabar, qui dubitant tantum ut dubitent, et praeter incertitudinem ipsam nihil quaerunt. Nam contra totus in eo eram ut aliquid certi reperirem. '[1] Descartes, *de Methodo*. Nor is it less distinct in

---

[1] 'Not that I imitated the sceptics, who doubt for the sake of doubting and who seek nothing beyond uncertainty itself. On the contrary, my whole object was to discover certainty' (trans. by H. J. Jackson)—editor's note.

its motives and final aim, than in its proper objects, which are not as in ordinary scepticism the prejudices of education and circumstance, but those original and innate prejudices which nature herself has planted in all men, and which to all but the philosopher are the first principles of knowledge, and the final test of truth.

Now these essential prejudices are all reducible to the one fundamental presumption, that there exist things without us. As this on the one hand originates, neither in grounds nor arguments, and yet on the other hand remains proof against all attempts to remove it by grounds or arguments (*naturam furca expellas tamen usque redibit* [you may drive nature out with a pitchfork, but it will always return]); on the one hand lays claim to immediate certainty as a position at once indemonstrable and irresistible, and yet on the other hand, inasmuch as it refers to something essentially different from ourselves, nay even in opposition to ourselves, leaves it inconceivable how it could possibly become a part of our immediate consciousness; (in other words how that, which *ex hypothesi* [by hypothesis] is and continues to be extrinsic and alien to our being, should become a modification of our being) the philosopher therefore compels himself to treat this faith as nothing more than a prejudice, innate indeed and connatural, but still a prejudice.

The other position, which not only claims but necessitates the admission of its immediate certainty, equally for the scientific reason of the philosopher as for the common sense of mankind at large, namely, I AM, cannot so properly be entitled a prejudice. It is groundless indeed; but then in the very idea it precludes all ground, and separated from the immediate consciousness loses its whole sense and import. It is groundless; but only because it is itself the ground of all other certainty. Now the apparent contradiction, that the former position, namely, the existence of things without us, which from its nature cannot be immediately certain, should be received as blindly and as independently of all grounds as the existence of our own being, the Transcendental philosopher can solve only by the supposition, that the former is unconsciously involved in the latter; that it is not only coherent but identical, and one and the same thing with our own immediate self-consciousness. To demonstrate this identity is the office and object of his philosophy.

If it be said, that this is idealism, let it be remembered that it is only so far idealism, as it is at the same time, and on that very account, the truest and most binding realism. For wherein does the realism of mankind properly consist? In the assertion that there exists a something without them, what, or how, or where they know not, which occasions the objects of their perception? Oh no! This is neither connatural nor universal. It is what a few have taught and learned in the schools, and which the many repeat without asking themselves concerning their own meaning. The realism common to all mankind is far elder and lies infinitely deeper than this hypothetical explanation of the origin of our perceptions, an explanation skimmed from the mere surface of mechanical philosophy. It is the table itself, which the man of common sense believes himself to see, not the phantom of a table, from which he may argumentatively deduce the reality of a table, which he does not see. If to destroy the reality of all, that we actually behold, be idealism, what can be more egregiously so, than the system of modern metaphysics, which banishes us to a land of shadows, surrounds us with apparitions, and distinguishes truth from illusion only by the majority of those who dream the same dream? 'I asserted that the world was mad,' exclaimed poor Lee, 'and the world said, that I was mad, and confound them, they outvoted me.'

It is to the true and original realism, that I would direct the attention. This believes and requires neither more nor less, than the object which it beholds or presents to itself, is the real and very object. In this sense, however much we may strive against it, we are all collectively born idealists, and therefore and only therefore are we at the same time realists. But of this the philosophers of the schools know nothing, or despise the faith as the prejudice of the ignorant vulgar, because they live and move in a crowd of phrases and notions from which human nature has long ago vanished. Oh, ye that reverence yourselves, and walk humbly with the divinity in your own hearts, ye are worthy of a better philosophy! Let the dead bury the dead, but do you preserve your human nature, the depth of which was never yet fathomed by a philosophy made up of notions and mere logical entities.

In the third treatise of my *Logosophia*, announced at the end of this volume,

I shall give (*Deo volente* [God willing]) the demonstrations and constructions of the dynamic philosophy scientifically arranged. It is, according to my conviction, no other than the system of Pythagoras and of Plato revived and purified from impure mixtures. 'Doctrina per tot manus tradita tandem in vappam desiit!'[1] The science of arithmetic furnishes instances, that a rule may be useful in practical application, and for the particular purpose may be sufficiently authenticated by the result, before it has itself been fully demonstrated. It is enough, if only it be rendered intelligible. This will, I trust, have been effected in the following Theses for those of my readers, who are willing to accompany me through the following chapter, in which the results will be applied to the deduction of the Imagination, and with it the principles of production and of genial criticism in the fine arts.

THESIS I

Truth is correlative to being. Knowledge without a correspondent reality is no knowledge; if we know, there must be somewhat known by us. To know is in its very essence a verb active.

THESIS II

All truth is either mediate, that is, derived from some other truth or truths; or immediate and original. The latter is absolute, and its formula A A; the former is of dependent or conditional certainty, and represented in the formula B A. The certainty, which adheres in A, is attributable to B.

Scholium. A chain without a staple, from which all the links derived their stability, or a series without a first, has been not inaptly allegorized, as a string of blind men, each holding the skirt of the man before him, reaching far out of sight, but all moving without the least deviation in one straight line. It would be

---

[1] 'A doctrine passed down through so many hands has ended up as flat wine' (trans. by H. J. Jackson)—editor's note.

naturally taken for granted, that there was a guide at the head of the file: what if it were answered, No! Sir, the men are without number, and infinite blindness supplies the place of sight?

Equally inconceivable is a cycle of equal truths without a common and central principle, which prescribes to each its proper sphere in the system of science. That the absurdity does not so immediately strike us, that it does not seem equally unimaginable, is owing to a surreptitious act of the imagination, which, instinctively and without our noticing the same, not only fills up the intervening spaces, and contemplates the cycle (of B C D E F etc.) as a continuous circle (A) giving to all collectively the unity of their common orbit; but likewise supplies, by a sort of *subintelligitur*, the one central power, which renders the movement harmonious and cyclical.

THESIS III

We are to seek therefore for some absolute truth capable of communicating to other positions a certainty, which it has not itself borrowed; a truth self-grounded, unconditional and known by its own light. In short, we have to find a somewhat which is, simply because it is. In order to be such, it must be one which is its own predicate, so far at least that all other nominal predicates must be modes and repetitions of itself. Its existence too must be such, as to preclude the possibility of requiring a cause or antecedent without an absurdity.

THESIS IV

That there can be but one such principle, may be proved a priori; for were there two or more, each must refer to some other, by which its equality is affirmed; consequently neither would be self-established, as the hypothesis demands. And a posteriori, it will be proved by the principle itself when it is discovered, as involving universal antecedence in its very conception.

Scholium. If we affirm of a board that it is blue, the predicate (blue) is accidental, and not implied in the subject, board. If we affirm of a circle that it is equiradial, the predicate indeed is implied in the definition of the subject; but the existence of the subject itself is contingent, and supposes both a cause and a percipient. The same reasoning will apply to the indefinite number of supposed indemonstrable truths exempted from the profane approach of philosophic investigation by the amiable Beattie, and other less eloquent and not more profound inaugurators of common sense on the throne of philosophy; a fruitless attempt, were it only that it is the two-fold function of philosophy to reconcile reason with common sense, and to elevate common sense into reason.

THESIS V

Such a principle cannot be anything or object. Each thing is what it is in consequence of some other thing. An infinite, independent thing,① is no less a contradiction, than an infinite circle or a sideless triangle. Besides a thing is that, which is capable of being an object which itself is not the sole percipient. But an object is inconceivable without a subject as its antithesis. *Omne perceptum percipientem supponit.*②

But neither can the principle be found in a subject as a subject, contra-distinguished from an object: for *unicuique percipienti aliquid objicitur perceptum.*③ It is to be found therefore neither in object nor subject taken separately, and consequently, as no other third is conceivable, it must be found in that which is neither subject nor object exclusively, but which is the identity of both.

THESIS VI

This principle, and so characterised manifests itself in the SUM or I AM;

---

① The impossibility of an absolute thing (*substantia unica* [unique substance]) as neither genus, species, nor *individuum* [individual]; as well as its utter unfitness for the fundamental position of a philosophic system will be demonstrated in the critique on Spinnozism in the fifth treatise of my Logosophia.
② 'Everything perceived supposes a perceiver' (trans. by H. J. Jackson)—editor's note.
③ 'For every perceiver there is an object perceived' (trans. by H. J. Jackson)—editor's note.

which I shall hereafter indiscriminately express by the words spirit, self, and self-consciousness. In this, and in this alone, object and subject, being and knowing, are identical, each involving and supposing the other. In other words, it is a subject which becomes a subject by the act of constructing itself objectively to itself; but which never is an object except for itself, and only so far as by the very same act it becomes a subject. It may be described therefore as a perpetual self-duplication of one and the same power into object and subject, which presuppose each other, and can exist only as antitheses.

Scholium. If a man be asked how he knows that he is? he can only answer, *sum quia sum* [I am because I am]. But if (the absoluteness of this certainty having been admitted) he be again asked, how he, the individual person, came to be, then in relation to the ground of his existence, not to the ground of his knowledge of that existence, he might reply, *sum quia Deus est* [I am because God is], or still more philosophically, *sum quia in Deo sum* [I am, because I am in God].

But if we elevate our conception to the absolute self, the great eternal I AM, then the principle of being, and of knowledge, of idea, and of reality; the ground of existence, and the ground of the knowledge of existence, are absolutely identical, *Sum quia sum*,① I am, because I affirm myself to be; I affirm myself to be, because I am.

---

① It is most worthy of notice, that in the first revelation of himself, not confined to individuals; indeed in the very first revelation of his absolute being Jehovah at the same time revealed the fundamental truth of all philosophy, which must either commence with the absolute, or have no fixed commencement; i. e. cease to be philosophy. I cannot but express my regret, that in the equivocal use of the word *that,* for *in that,* or *because,* our admirable version has rendered the passage susceptible of a degraded interpretation in the mind of common readers or hearers, as if it were a mere reproof to an impertinent question. I am what I am, which might be equally affirmed of himself by any existent being.

The Cartesian *Cogito, ergo sum* [I think, therefore I am] is objectionable, because either the *Cogito* is used *extra gradum* [absolutely], and then it is involed in the *sum* [I am] and is tautological, or it is taken as a particular modification to the subject modified; and not preordinated as the arguments seem to require. For *Cogito* [I think] is *sum cogitans* [I am, thinking]. This is clear by the inevidence of the converse. *Cogitat, ergo est* [He thinks, therefore he is] is true, because it is a mere application of the logical rule: *Quicquid in*

THESIS VII

If then I know myself only through myself, it is contradictory to require any other predicate of self, but that of self-consciousness. Only in the self-consciousness of a spirit is there the required identity of object and of representation; for herein consists the essence of a spirit, that it is self-representative. If therefore this be the one only immediate truth, in the certainty of which the reality of our collective knowledge is grounded, it must follow that the spirit in all the objects which it views, views only itself. If this could be proved, the immediate reality of all intuitive knowledge would be assured. It has been shown, that a spirit is that, which is its own object, yet not originally an object, but an absolute subject for which all, itself included, may become an object. It must therefore be an act; for every object is, as an object, dead, fixed, incapable in itself of any action, and necessarily finite. Again the spirit (originally the identity of object and subject) must in some sense dissolve this identity, in order to be conscious of it; *fit alter et idem* [it becomes another yet the same]. But this implies an act, and it follows therefore that intelligence or self-consciousness is impossible, except by and in a will. The self-conscious spirit therefore is a will; and freedom

---

genere est, est et in specie [Whatever is in the genus is also in the species]. *Est (cogitans) ergo est* [He is (thinking), therefore he is]. It is a cherry tree; therefore it is a tree. But, *est ergo cogitat* [he is, therefore he thinks], is illogical: for *quod est in specie, non* necessario *in genere est* [what ever is in the species is not *necessarily* in the genus]. It may be true. I hold it to be true, that *quicquid vere est, est per veram sui affirmationem* [whatever truly is, is through the true affirmation of itself]; but it is a derivative, not an immediate truth. Here then we have, by anticipation, the distinction between the conditional finite I (which as known in distinct consciousness by occasion of experience is called by Kant's followers the empirical I) and the absolute I AM, and likewise the dependence or rather the inhererence of the former in the latter; in which 'we live, and move, and have our being,' as St Paul divinely asserts, differing widely from the thesis of the mechanic school (as Sir I. Newton, Locke, etc.) who must say from *whom we had* our being, and with it life and the powers of life.

must be assumed as a ground of philosophy, and can never be deduced from it.

THESIS VIII

Whatever in its origin is objective, is likewise as such necessarily finite. Therefore, since the spirit is not originally an object, and as the subject exists in antithesis to an object, the spirit cannot originally be finite. But neither can it be a subject without becoming an object, and, as it is originally the identity of both, it can be conceived neither as infinite nor finite exclusively, but as the most original union of both. In the existence, in the reconciling, and the recurrence of this contradiction consists the process and mystery of production and life.

THESIS IX

This *principium commune essendi et cognoscendi* [common principle of being and knowing], as subsisting in a will, or primary act of self-duplication, is the mediate or indirect principle of every science; but it is the immediate and direct principle of the ultimate science alone, i. e. of transcendental philosophy alone. For it must be remembered, that all these theses refer solely to one of the two polar sciences, namely, to that which commences with, and rigidly confines itself within, the subjective, leaving the objective (as far as it is exclusively objective) to natural philosophy, which is its opposite pole. In its very idea therefore as a systematic knowledge of our collective knowing, (*scientia scientiae* [knowledge of knowing]) it involves the necessity of some one highest principle of knowing, as at once the source and accompanying form in all particular acts of intellect and perception. This, it has been shown, can be found only in the act and evolution of self-consciousness. We are not investigating an absolute *principium essendi* [principle of being]; for then, I admit, many valid objections might be started against our theory; but an absolute *cog principium noscendi* [principle of knowing]. The result of both the sciences, or their equatorial point, would be the principle of a total and undivided philosophy, as, for prudential reasons, I have chosen to anticipate in the scholium to Thesis VI and the note subjoined. In other words, philosophy would pass into religion, and religion become inclusive of philosophy. We begin with the I KNOW MYSELF, in order to end with the absolute I AM. We proceed from the SELF, in order to lose and find all self in GOD.

THESIS X

The transcendental philosopher does not inquire, what ultimate ground of our knowledge there may lie out of our knowing, but what is the last in our knowing itself, beyond which we cannot pass. The principle of our knowing is sought within the sphere of our knowing. It must be some thing therefore, which can itself be known. It is asserted only, that the act of self-consciousness is for us the source and principle of all our possible knowledge. Whether abstracted from us there exists any thing higher and beyond this primary self-knowing, which is for us the form of all our knowing must be decided by the result.

That the self-consciousness is the fixed point, to which for us all is mortised and annexed, needs no further proof. But that the self-consciousness may be the modification of a higher form of being, perhaps of a higher consciousness, and this again of a yet higher, and so on in an infinite *regressus* [regress]; in short, that self-consciousness may be itself something explicable into something, which must lie beyond the possibility of our knowledge, because the whole synthesis of our intelligence is first formed in and through the self-consciousness, does not at all concern us as transcendental philosophers. For to us, self-consciousness is not a kind of being, but a kind of knowing, and that too the highest and farthest that exists for us. It may however be shown, and has in part already been shown earlier, that even when the objective is assumed as the first, we yet can never pass beyond the principle of self-consciousness. Should we attempt it, we must be driven back from ground to ground, each of which would cease to be a ground the moment we pressed on it. We must be whirled down the gulf of an infinite series. But this would make our reason baffle the end and purpose of all reason, namely, unity and system. Or we must break off the series arbitrarily, and affirm an absolute something that is in and of itself at once cause and effect (*causa sui* [the cause of self]), subject and object, or rather the absolute identity of both. But as this is inconceivable, except in a self-consciousness, it follows, that even as natural philosophers we must arrive at the same principle from which as transcendental philosophers we set out; that is, in a self-consciousness in which the *principium essendi* [principle of being] does not stand to the *principium cognoscende* [principle of knowing] in the relation of cause to effect, but both the one and the other are coinherent and identical. Thus the true system of natural philosophy places the sole reality of things in an absolute, which is at once *causa sui et effectus*, πατηρ αυτοπατωρ, Υιος εαυτου [self-cause and effect, father of himself, Son of himself]—in the absolute identity of subject and object, which it calls nature, and which in its highest power is nothing else than self-conscious will or intelligence. In this sense the position of Malebranche, that we see all things in God, is a *strict* philosophical truth; and equally true is the assertion of Hobbes, of Hartley, and of their masters in ancient Greece, that all real knowledge supposes a prior sensation. For sensation itself is but vision nascent, not the cause of intelligence, but intelligence itself revealed as an earlier power in the process of self-construction.

Μάκαρ, ἰλαθί μοι!
Πάτερ, ἴλαθίμοι
Ει παρὰ, κόσμον,
Ει παρὰ μοῖραν
Τῶν σῶν ἐθιγον! ①

Bearing then this in mind, that intelligence is a self-development, not a quality supervening to a substance, we may abstract from all degree, and for the purpose of philosophic construction reduce it to kind, under the idea of an indestructible power with two opposite and counteracting forces, which by a meta-

---

① 'Be full of goodness unto me, Blessed One, be full of goodness unto me, Father, if beyond what is ordered, beyond what is destined, I touch upon that which is thine' (trans. by H. J. Jackson)—editor's note.

phor borrowed from astronomy, we may call the centrifugal and centripetal forces. The intelligence in the one tends to objectize itself, and in the other to know itself in the object. It will be hereafter my business to construct by a series of intuitions the progressive schemes, that must follow from such a power with such forces, till I arrive at the fulness of the human intelligence. For my present purpose, I assume such a power as my principle, in order to deduce from it a faculty, the generation, agency, and application of which form the contents of the ensuing chapter.

In a preceding page I have justified the use of technical terms in philosophy, whenever they tend to preclude confusion of thought, and when they assist the memory by the exclusive singleness of their meaning more than they may, for a short time, bewilder the attention by their strangeness. I trust, that I have not extended this privilege beyond the grounds on which I have claimed it; namely, the conveniency of the scholastic phrase to distinguish the kind from all degrees, or rather to express the kind with the abstraction of degree, as for instance *multeity* instead of multitude; or secondly, for the sake of correspondence in sound in interdependent or antithetical terms, as subject and object; or lastly, to avoid the wearying recurrence of circumlocutions and definitions. Thus I shall venture to use *potence*, in order to express a specific degree of a power, in imitation of the algebraists. I have even hazarded the new verb *potenziate* with its derivatives, in order to express the combination or transfer of powers. It is with new or unusual terms, as with privileges in courts of justice or legislature; there can be no legitimate privilege, where there already exists a positive law adequate to the purpose; and when there is no law in existence, the privilege is to be justified by its accordance with the end, or final cause, of all law. Unusual and new-coined words are doubtless an evil; but vagueness, confusion, and imperfect conveyance of our thoughts, are a far greater. Every system, which is under the necessity of using terms not familiarized by the metaphysics in fashion, will be described as written in an unintelligible style, and the author must expect the charge of having substituted learned jargon for clear conception; while, according to the creed of our modern philosophers, nothing is deemed a clear conception, but what is representable by a distinct image. Thus the conceivable is reduced within the bounds of the picturable. 'Hinc patet, qui fiat ut, *cum irrepraesentabile* et *impossibile* vulgo ejusdem significatûs habeantur, conceptus tam *Continui*, quam *Infiniti*, a plurimis rejiciantur, quippe quorum, *secundum leges cognitionis intuitivae*, repraesentatio est impossibilis. Quanquam autem harum e non paucis scholis explosarum notionum, praesertim prioris, causam hic non gero, maximi tamen momendi erit monuisse: gravissimo illos errore labi, qui tam perversâ argumentandi ratione utuntur. Quicquid enim *repugnat* legibus intellectûs et rationis, utique est impossibile; quod autem, cum rationis purae sit objectum, legibus cognitionis intuitivae tantummodo *non subest*, non item. Nam hinc dissensus inter facultatem *sensitivam* et *intellectualem*, (quarum indolem mox exponam,) nihil indigitat, nisi, *quas mens ab intellectu acceptas fert ideas abstractas, illas in concreto exsequi, et in Intuitus commutare saepenumero non posse*. Haec autem reluctantia *subjectiva* mentitur, ut plurimum, repugnantiam aliquam *objectivam*, et incautos facile fallit, limitibus, quibus *mens humana* circumscribitur, pro iis habitis, quibus *ipsa rerum essentia* continetur.' ① Kant *de Mundi Sensibilis atque Intelligibilis forma et principiis,* 1770.

    Critics, who are most ready to bring this charge of pedantry and unintelligibility, are the most apt to overlook the important fact, that, besides the language of words, there is a language of spirits (*sermo interior* [inner discourse]) and that

---

①   Translation: 'Hence it is clear, from what cause many reject the notion of the Continuous and the Infinite. They take, namely, the words irrepresentable and impossible in one and the same meaning; and, according to the forms of sensuous evidence, the notion of the Continuous and the Infinite is doubtless impossible. I am not now pleading the cause of these laws, which not a few schools have thought proper to explode, especially the former (the law of contituity). But it is of the highest importance to admonish the reader, that, those, who adopt so perverted a mode of reasoning, are under a grievous error. Whatever opposes the formal principles of the understanding and the reason is confessedly impossible; but not therefore that, which is therefore not amenable to the forms of sensuous evidence, because it is exclusively an object of pure intellect. For this non-coincidence of the sensuous and intellectual (the nature of which I shall presently lay open) proves nothing more, but that the mind cannot always adequately represent in the concrete, and transforms into distinct images, abstract notions derived from the pure intellect. But this contradiction, which is in itsself merely subjective (i. e. an incapacity in the nature of man) too often passes for an incongruity or impossibility in the object (i. e. the notions themselves) and seduces the incautious to mistake the limitations of the human faculties for the limits of things, as they really exist.'

the former is only the vehicle of the latter. Consequently their assurance, that they do not understand the philosophic writer, instead of proving any thing against the philosophy, may furnish an equal, and (*caeteris paribus* [other things being equal]) even a stronger presumption against their own philosophic talent.

Great indeed are the obstacles which an English metaphysician has to encounter. Amongst his most respectable and intelligent judges, there will be many who have devoted their attention exclusively to the concerns and interests of human life, and who bring with them to the perusal of a philosophic system an habitual aversion to all speculations, the utility and application of which are not evident and immediate. To these I would in the first instance merely oppose an authority, which they themselves hold venerable, that of Lord Bacon: 'non inutiles Scientiae existimandae sunt, quarum in se nullus est usus, si ingenia acuant et ordinent.' ①

There are others, whose prejudices are still more formidable, inasmuch as they are grounded in their moral feelings and religious principles, which had been alarmed and shocked by the impious and pernicious tenets defended by Hume, Priestley, and the French fatalists or necessitarians; some of whom had perverted metaphysical reasonings to the denial of the mysteries and indeed of all the peculiar doctrines of Christianity; and others even to the subversion of all distinction between right and wrong. I would request such men to consider what an eminent and successful defender of the Christian faith has observed, that true metaphysics are nothing else but true divinity, and that in fact the writers, who have given them such just offence, were sophists, who had taken advantage of

---

I take this occasion to observe, that here and elsewhere Kant uses the terms intuition, and verb active (*Intueri*, *germanice* Anschauen [to intuit]) for which we have unfortunatly no correspondent word, exclusively for that which can be represented in space and time. He therefore consistently and rightly denies the possiblity of intellectual intuitions. But as I see no adequate reason for this exclusive sense of the term, I have reverted to its wider signification authorized by our elder theologians and metaphysicians, according to whom the term comprehends all truths known to us without a medium.

① 'those sciences ought not to be considered useless that are in themselves without use, if they sharpen and order the wits' (trans. by H. J. Jackson)—editor's note.

the general neglect into which the science of logic has unhappily fallen, rather than metaphysicians, a name indeed which those writers were the first to explode as unmeaning. Secondly, I would remind them, that as long as there are men in the world to whom the Γνῶθι σέαυτον [Know thyself] is an instinct and a command from their own nature, so long will there be metaphysicians and metaphysical speculations; that false metaphysics can be effectually counteracted by true metaphysics alone; and that if the reasoning be clear, solid and pertinent, the truth deduced can never be the less valuable on account of the depth from which it may have been drawn.

A third class profess themselves friendly to metaphysics, and believe that they are themselves metaphysicians. They have no objection to system or terminology, provided it be the method and the nomenclature to which they have been familiarized in the writings of Locke, Hume, Hartley, Condillac, or perhaps Dr Reid, and Professor Stewart. To objections from this cause, it is a sufficient answer, that one main object of my attempt was to demonstrate the vagueness or insufficiency of the terms used in the metaphysical schools of France and Great Britain since the revolution, and that the errors which I propose to attack cannot subsist, except as they are concealed behind the mask of a plausible and indefinite nomenclature.

But the worst and widest impediment still remains. It is the predominance of a popular philosophy, at once the counterfeit and the mortal enemy of all true and manly metaphysical research. It is that corruption, introduced by certain immethodical aphorisming eclectics, who, dismissing not only all system, but all logical connection, pick and choose whatever is most plausible and showy; who select, whatever words can have some semblance of sense attached to them without the least expenditure of thought; in short whatever may enable men to talk of what they do not understand, with a careful avoidance of every thing that might awaken them to a moment's suspicion of their ignorance. This alas! is an irremediable disease, for it brings with it, not so much an indisposition to any particular system, but an utter loss of taste and faculty for all system and for all philosophy. Like echoes that beget each other amongst the mountains, the praise or blame of such men rolls in volleys long after the report from the original blunderbuss. 'Sequacitas est potius et coitio quam consensus: et tamen (quod pessimum est) pusillanimitas ista non sine arrogantia et fastidio se offert.' ① *Novum Organum.*

I shall now proceed to the nature and genesis of the Imagination; but I must first take leave to notice, that after a more accurate perusal of Mr. Wordsworth's remarks on the Imagination, in his preface to the new edition of his poems, I find that my conclusions are not so consentient with his as, I confess, I had taken for granted. In an article contributed by me to Mr. Southey's Omniana, on the soul and its organs of sense, are the following sentences. 'These (the human faculties) I would arrange under the different senses and powers: as the eye, the ear, the touch, etc.; the imitative power, voluntary and automatic; the imagination, or shaping and modifying power; the fancy, or the aggregative and associative power; the understanding, or the regulative, substantiating and realizing power; the speculative reason, *vis theoretica et scientifica* [the capacity for scientific thought], or the power by which we produce or aim to produce unity, necessity, and universality in all our knowledge by means of principles a priori;② the will, or practical reason; the faculty of choice (*Germanice* [in German], Willküehr) and (distinct both from the moral will and the choice,) the *sensation* of volition, which I have found reason to include under the head of single and double touch.' To this, as far as it relates to the subject in question, namely the words 'the aggregative and associative power' Mr Wordsworth's 'only objection is that the definition is too general. To aggregate and to associate, to evoke and to combine, belong as well to the Imagination as to the Fancy.' I reply, that if by the

---

① 'It is a following and going along together rather than a consent; and what is worst of all, this very littleness of spirit comes with a certain air of arrogance and superiority' (trans. by H. J. Jackson)—editor's note.

② This phrase, *a priori*, is in common most grossly misunderstood, and an absurdity burthened on it, which it does not deserve! By knowledge, *a priori*, we do not mean, that we can know anything previously to experience, which would be a contradiction in terms; but that having once known it by occasion of experience (i. e. something acting upon us from without) we then know, that it must have pre-existed, or the experience itself would have been impossible. By experience only I know, that I have eyes; but then my reason convinces me, that I must have had eyes in order to the experience.

power of evoking and combining, Mr W. means the same as, and no more than, I meant by the aggregative and associative, I continue to deny, that it belongs at all to the Imagination; and I am disposed to conjecture, that he has mistaken the co-presence of Fancy with Imagination for the operation of the latter singly. A man may work with two very different tools at the same moment; each has its share in the work, but the work effected by each is distinct and different. But it will probably appear in the next chapter, that deeming it necessary to go back much further than Mr Wordsworth's subject required or permitted, I have attached a meaning to both Fancy and Imagination, which he had not in view, at least while he was writing that preface. He will judge. Would to Heaven, I might meet with many such readers! I will conclude with the words of Bishop Jeremy Taylor: 'He to whom all things are one, who draweth all things to one, and seeth all things in one, may enjoy true peace and rest of spirit. ' (J. Taylor's *Via Pacis.*)

CHAPTER XIII

On the imagination, or esemplastic power.

O Adam! one Almighty is, from whom
All things proceed, and up to him return
If not deprav'd from good: created all
Such to perfection, one first nature all
Indued with various forms, various degrees
Of substance, and, in things that live, of life;
But more refin'd, more spiritous and pure,
As nearer to him plac'd, or nearer tending,
Each in their several active spheres assign'd,
Till body up to spirit work, in bounds
Proportion'd to each kind. So from the root
Springs lighter the green stalk, from thence the leaves
More aery: last the bright consummate flower

Spirits odorous breathes: flowers and their fruit,
Man's nourishment, by gradual scale sublim'd,
To *vital* spirits aspire: to *animal*:
To *intellectual*! —give both life and sense,
Fancy and understanding; whence the soul
Reason receives. And reason is her *being*,
Discursive or intuitive.

Par. Lost, b. v

Sane si res corporales nil nisi materiale continerent, verissime dicerentur in fluxu consistere neque habere substantiale quicquam, quemadmodum et Platonici olim recte agnovere. —Hinc igitur, praeter purè mathematica et phantasiae subjecta, collegi quaedam metaphysica solâque mente perceptibilia, esse admittenda: et massae materiali *principium* quoddam superius et, ut sic dicam, *formale* addendum: quandoquidem omnes veritates rerum corporearum ex solis axiomatibus logisticis et geometricis, nempe de magno et parvo, toto et pârte, figurâ et situ, colligi non possint; sed alia de causâ et effectu, *actioneque* et *passione*, accedere debeant, quibus ordinis rerum rationes salventur. Id principium rerum, an ἐντελεχείαν an vim appellemus, non refert, modó meminerimus, per solam *Virium* notionem intelligibiliter explicari.①

Leibniz: Op. T. II. P. II. P. 53. —T. III. p. 321

---

① If indeed corporeal things contained nothing but matter they might truly be said to consist in flux and to have no substance, as the Platonists once rightly recognized. —And so, apart from the purely mathematical and what is subject to the fancy, I have come to the conclusion that certain metaphysical elements perceptible by the mind alone should be admitted, and that some higher and, so to speak, *formal principle* should be added to the material mass, since all the truths about corporeal things cannot be collected from logistic and geometrical axioms alone, i. e. those concerning great and small, whole and part, shape and position, but others must enter into it, i. e. cause and effect, *action* and *passion*, by which the reasons for the order of things are maintained. It does not matter whether we call this principle of things an entelechy or a power so long as we remember that it is intelligibly to be explained only by the idea of *powers*. (*The Collected Works of Samuel Taylor Coleridge*)

Samuel Taylor Coleridge

Εέβομαι Νοερῶν
Κρυφίαν τάξιν
Χωρει ΤΙ ΜΕΣΟΝ
Ου καταχυθέν.[1]

Synesii, *Hymn*.ɪɪɪ. 1. 231.

Descartes, speaking as a naturalist, and in imitation of Archimedes, said, give me matter and motion and I will construct you the universe. We must of course understand him to have meant; I will render the construction of the universe intelligible. In the same sense the transcendental philosopher says; grant me a nature having two contrary forces, the one of which tends to expand infinitely, while the other strives to apprehend or find itself in this infinity, and I will cause the world of intelllgences with the whole system of their representations to rise up before you. Every other science presupposes intelligence as already existing and complete: the philosopher contemplates it in its growth, and as it were represents its history to the mind from its birth to its maturity.

The venerable sage of Koenigsberg [Kant] has preceded the march of this master-thought as an effective pioneer in his essay on the introduction of negative quantities into philosophy, published 1763. In this he has shown, that instead of assailing the science of mathematics by metaphysics, as Berkeley did in his Analyst, or of sophisticating it, as Wolff did, by the vain attempt of deducing the first principles of geometry from supposed deeper grounds of ontology, it behoved the metaphysician rather to examine whether the only province of knowledge, which man has succeeded in erecting into a pure science, might not furnish materials, or at least hints, for establishing and pacifying the unsettled, warring, and embroiled domain of philosophy. An imitation of the mathematical method had indeed been attempted with no better success than attended the essay of David to wear the armour of Saul. Another use however is possible and of far greater promise, namely, the actual application of the positions which had so wonderful-

---

[1] I venerate the hidden ordering of intellectual things, but there is some medial element that may not be distributed. (*The Collected Works of Samuel Taylor Coleridge*)

ly enlarged the discoveries of geometry, *mutatis mutandis* [changing the things that must be chauged], to philosophical subjects. Kant having briefly illustrated the utility of such an attempt in the questions of space, motion, and infinitely small quantities, as employed by the mathematician, proceeds to the idea of negative quantities and the transfer of them to metaphysical investigation. Opposites, he well observes, are of two kinds, either logical, i. e., such as are absolutely incompatible; or real, without being contradictory. The former he denominates *Nihil negativum irrepraesentabile* [nothing in a negative sense not representable], the connection of which produces nonsense. A body in motion is something—*Aliquid cogitabile* [something conceivable]; but a body, at one and the same time in motion and not in motion, is nothing, or, at most, air articulated into nonsense. But a motory force of a body in one direction, and an equal force of the same body in an opposite direction is not incompatible, and the result, namely, rest, is real and representable. For the purposes of mathematical calculus it is indifferent which force we term negative, and which positive, and consequently we appropriate the latter to that, which happens to be the principal object in our thoughts. Thus if a man's capital be ten and his debts eight, the subtraction will be the same, whether we call the capital negative debt, or the debt negative capital. But in as much as the latter stands practically in reference to the former, we of course represent the sum as 10 - 8. It is equally clear that two equal forces acting in opposite directions, both being finite and each distinguished from the other by its direction only, must neutralize or reduce each other to inaction. Now the transcendental philosophy demands; first, that two forces should be conceived which counteract each other by their essential nature; not only not in consequence of the accidental direction of each, but as prior to all direction, nay, as the primary forces from which the conditions of all possible directions are derivative and deducible: secondly, that these forces should be assumed to be both alike infinite, both alike indestructible. The problem will then be to discover the result or product of two such forces, as distinguished from the result of those forces which are finite, and derive their difference solely from the circumstance of their direction. When we have formed a scheme or outline of these two different kinds of force, and of their different results, by the process of discursive reasoning, it will then remain for us to elevate the thesis from notional to actual, by contemplating intuitively this one power with its two inherent indestructible yet counteracting forces, and the results or generations to which their interpenetration gives existence, in the living principle and in the process of our own self-consciousness. By what instrument this is possible the solution itself will discover, at the same time that it will reveal to and for whom it is possible. *Non omnia possumus omnes* [We are not all capable of everything]. There is a philosophic no less than a poetic genius, which is differenced from the highest perfection of talent, not by degree but by kind.

The counteraction then of the two assumed forces does not depend on their meeting from opposite directions; the power which acts in them is indestructible; it is therefore inexhaustibly re-ebullient; and as something must be the result of these two forces, both alike infinite, and both alike indestructible; and as rest or neutralization cannot be this result; no other conception is possible, but that the product must be a *tertium aliquid* [some third thing], or finite generation. Consequently this conception is necessary. Now this *tertium aliquid* can be no other than an interpenetration of the counteracting powers, partaking of both.

Thus far had the work been transcribed for the press, when I received the following letter from a friend, whose practical judgment I have had ample reason to estimate and revere, and whose taste and sensibility preclude all the excuses which my self-love might possibly have prompted me to set up in plea against the decision of advisers of equal good sense, but with less tact and feeling.

'Dear C.

'You ask my opinion concerning your chapter on the Imagination, both as to the impressions it made on myself, and as to those which I think it will make on the Public, i. e. that part of the public, who, from the title of the work and from its forming a sort of introduction to a volume of poems, are likely to constitute the great majority of your readers.

'As to myself, and stating in the first place the effect on my understanding, your opinions and method of argument were not only so new to me, but so directly the reverse of all I had ever been accustomed to consider as truth, that even if I had comprehended your premises sufficiently to have admitted them, and had seen the necessity of your conclusions, I should still have been in that state of mind, which in your note, p. 196, you have so ingeniously evolved, as the antithesis to that in which a man is, when he makes a bull. In your own words, I should have felt as if I had been standing on my head.

'The effect on my feelings, on the other hand, I cannot better represent, than by supposing myself to have known only our light airy modern chapels of ease, and then for the first time to have been placed, and left alone, in one of our largest Gothic cathedrals in a gusty moonlight night of autumn. "Now in glimmer, and now in gloom"; often in palpable darkness not without a chilly sensation of terror; then suddenly emerging into broad yet visionary lights with coloured shadows of fantastic shapes, yet all decked with holy insignia and mystic symbols; and ever and anon coming out full upon pictures and stone-work images of great men, with whose names I was familiar, but which looked upon me with countenances and an expression, the most dissimilar to all I had been in the habit of connecting with those names. Those whom I had been taught to venerate as almost super-human in magnitude of intellect, I found perched in little fretwork niches, as grotesque dwarfs; while the grotesques, in my hitherto belief, stood guarding the high altar with all the characters of apotheosis. In short, what I had supposed substances were thinned away into shadows, while everywhere shadows were deepened into substances:

If substance might be call'd that shadow seem'd,
For each seem'd either!

Milton

'Yet after all, I could not but repeat the lines which you had quoted from a MS poem of your own in the Friend, and applied to a work of Mr Wordsworth's though with a few of the words altered:

Samuel Taylor Coleridge

...An orphic tale indeed,
A tale *obscure* of high and passionate thoughts
To a *strange* music chaunted!

'Be assured, however, that I look forward anxiously to your great book on the constructive philosophy, which you have promised and announced: and that I will do my best to understand it. Only I will not promise to descend into the dark cave of Trophonius with you, there to rub my own eyes, in order to make the sparks and figured flashes, which I am required to see.

'So much for myself. But as for the Public I do not hesitate a moment in advising and urging you to withdraw the chapter from the present work, and to reserve it for your announced treatises on the Logos or communicative intellect in Man and Deity. First, because imperfectly as I understand the present chapter, I see clearly that you have done too much, and yet not enough. You have been obliged to omit so many links, from the necessity of compression, that what remains, looks (if I may recur to my former illustration) like the fragments of the winding steps of an old ruined tower. Secondly, a still stronger argument (at least one that I am sure will be more forcible with you) is, that your readers will have both right and reason to complain of you. This chapter, which cannot, when it is printed, amount to so little as an hundred pages, will of necessity greatly increase the expense of the work; and every reader who, like myself, is neither prepared nor perhaps calculated for the study of so abstruse a subject so abstrusely treated, will, as I have before hinted, be almost entitled to accuse you of a sort of imposition on him. For who, he might truly observe, could from your title-page, viz. "*My Literary Life and Opinions,*" published too as introductory to a volume of miscellaneous poems, have anticipated, or even conjectured, a long treatise on ideal realism which holds the same relation in abstruseness to Plotinus, as Plotinus does to Plato. It will be well, if already you have not too much of metaphysical disquisition in your work, though as the larger part of the disquisition is historical, it will doubtless be both interesting and instructive to many to whose unprepared minds your speculations on the esemplastic power would be utterly unintelligible. Be assured, if you do publish this chapter in the present work, you will be reminded of Bishop Berkeley's Siris, announced as an Essay on Tar-water, which beginning with Tar ends with the Trinity, the *omne scibile* [everything knowable] forming the interspace. I say in the present work. In that greater work to which you have devoted so many years, and study so intense and various, it will be in its proper place. Your prospectus will have described and announced both its contents and their nature; and if any persons purchase it, who feel no interest in the subjects of which it treats, they will have themselves only to blame.

'I could add to these arguments one derived from pecuniary motives, and particularly from the probable effects on the sale of your present publication; but they would weigh little with you compared with the preceding. Besides, I have long observed, that arguments drawn from your own personal interests more often act on you as narcotics than as stimulants, and that in money concerns you have some small portion of pig-nature in your moral idiosyncrasy, and, like these amiable creatures, must occasionally be pulled backward from the boat in order to make you enter it. All success attend you, for if hard thinking and hard reading are merits, you have deserved it.

Your affectionate, etc. '

In consequence of this very judicious letter, which produced complete conviction on my mind, I shall content myself for the present with stating the main result of the chapter, which I have reserved for that future publication, a detailed prospectus of which the reader will find at the close of the second volume.

The imagination then I consider either as primary, or secondary. The primary Imagination I hold to be the living power and prime agent of all human perception, and as a repetition in the finite mind of the eternal act of creation in the infinite I AM. The secondary Imagination I consider as an echo of the former, co-existing with the conscious will, yet still as identical with the primary in the kind of its agency, and differing only in degree, and in the mode of its operation. It dissolves, diffuses, dissipates, in order to recreate: or where this process is rendered impossible, yet still at all events it struggles to idealize and to unify. It is essentially vital, even as all objects (*as* objects) are essentially fixed and dead.

Fancy, on the contrary, has no other counters to play with, but fixities and definites. The fancy is indeed no other than a mode of memory emancipated from the order of time and space; while it is blended with, and modified by that empirical phaenomenon of the will, which we express by the word choice. But equally with the ordinary memory the Fancy must receive all its materials ready made from the law of association.

Whatever more than this, I shall think it fit to declare concerning the powers and privileges of the imagination in the present work, will be found in the critical essay on the uses of the Supernatural in poetry and the principles that regulate its introduction: which the reader will find prefixed to the poem of The Ancient Mariner.

CHAPTER XIV

Occasion of the Lyrical Ballads, and the objects originally proposed—Preface to the second edition—The ensuing controversy, its causes and acrimony—Philosophic definitions of a poem and poetry with scholia.

During the first year that Mr Wordsworth and I were neighbours, our conversations turned frequently on the two cardinal points of poetry, the power of exciting the sympathy of the reader by a faithful adherence to the truth of nature, and the power of giving the interest of novelty by the modifying colours of imagination. The sudden charm, which accidents of light and shade, which moonlight or sun-set diffused over a known and familiar landscape, appeared to represent the practicability of combining both. These are the poetry of nature. The thought suggested itself (to which of us I do not recollect) that a series of poems might be composed of two sorts. In the one, the incidents and agents were to be, in part at least, supernatural; and the excellence aimed at was to consist in the interesting of the affections by the dramatic truth of such emotions as would naturally accompany such situations, supposing them real. And real in this sense they have been to every human being who, from whatever source of delusion, has at any time believed himself under supernatural agency. For the second class, subjects were to be chosen from ordinary life; the characters and incidents were to be such, as will be found in every village and its vicinity, where there is a meditative and feeling mind to seek after them, or to notice them, when they present themselves.

In this idea originated the plan of the 'Lyrical Ballads'; in which it was agreed, that my endeavours should be directed to persons and characters supernatural, or at least romantic, yet so as to transfer from our inward nature a human interest and a semblance of truth sufficient to procure for these shadows of imagination that willing suspension of disbelief for the moment, which constitutes poetic faith. Mr Wordsworth on the other hand was to propose to himself as his object, to give the charm of novelty to things of every day, and to excite a feeling analogous to the supernatural, by awakening the mind's attention from the lethargy of custom, and directing it to the loveliness and the wonders of the world before us; an inexhaustible treasure, but for which in consequence of the film of familiarity and selfish solicitude we have eyes, yet see not, ears that hear not, and hearts that neither feel nor understand.

With this view I wrote the 'Ancient Mariner,' and was preparing among other poems, the 'Dark Ladie,' and the 'Christabel,' in which I should have more nearly realized my ideal, than I had done in my first attempt. But Mr Wordsworth's industry had proved so much more successful, and the number of his poems so much greater, that my compositions, instead of forming a balance, appeared rather an interpolation of heterogeneous matter. Mr Wordsworth added two or three poems written in his own character, in the impassioned, lofty, and sustained diction, which is characteristic of his genius. In this form the 'Lyrical Ballads' were published; and were presented by him as an experiment, whether subjects, which from their nature rejected the usual ornaments and extra-colloquial style of poems in general, might not be so managed in the language of ordinary life as to produce the pleasurable interest, which it is the peculiar business of poetry to impart. To the second edition he added a preface of considerable length; in which notwithstanding some passages of apparently a contrary import, he was understood to contend for the extension of this style to poetry of all kinds, and to reject as vicious and indefensible all phrases and forms of style that were not included in what he (unfortunately, I think, adopting an equivocal expression) called the language of real life. From this preface, prefixed to poems in which it was impossible to deny the presence of original genius, however mistaken its direction might be deemed, arose the whole long continued controversy. For from the conjunction of perceived power with supposed heresy I explain the inveteracy and in some instances, I grieve to say, the acrimonious passions, with which the controversy has been conducted by the assailants.

Had Mr Wordsworth's poems been the silly, the childish things, which they were for a long time described as being; had they been really distinguished from the compositions of other poets merely by meanness of language and inanity of thought; had they indeed contained nothing more than what is found in the parodies and pretended imitations of them; they must have sunk at once, a dead weight, into the slough of oblivion, and have dragged the preface along with them. But year after year increased the number of Mr Wordsworth's admirers. They were found too not in the lower classes of the reading public, but chiefly among young men of strong ability and meditative minds; and their admiration (inflamed perhaps in some degree by opposition) was distinguished by its intensity, I might almost say, by its *religious* fervour. These facts, and the intellectual energy of the author, which was more or less consciously felt, where it was outwardly and even boisterously denied, meeting with sentiments of aversion to his opinions, and of alarm at their consequences, produced an eddy of criticism, which would of itself have borne up the poems by the violence, with which it whirled them round and round. With many parts of this preface in the sense attributed to them and which the words undoubtedly seem to authorize, I never concurred; but on the contrary objected to them as erroneous in principle, and as contradictory (in appearance at least) both to other parts of the same preface, and to the author's own practice in the greater number of the poems themselves. Mr Wordsworth in his recent collection has, I find, degraded this prefatory disquisition to the end of his second volume, to be read or not at the reader's choice. But he has not, as far as I can discover, announced any change in his poetic creed. At all events, considering it as the source of a controversy, in which I have been honoured more, than I deserve, by the frequent conjunction of my name with his, I think it expedient to declare once for all, in what points I coincide with his opinions, and in what points I altogether differ. But in order to render myself intelligible I must previously, in as few words as possible, explain my ideas, first, of a poem; and secondly, of poetry itself, in kind, and in essence.

The office of philosophical disquisition consists in just distinction; while it is the privilege of the philosopher to preserve himself constantly aware, that distinction is not division. In order to obtain adequate notions of any truth, we must intellectually separate its distinguishable parts; and this is the technical process of philosophy. But having so done, we must then restore them in our conceptions to the unity, in which they actually co-exist; and this is the result of philosophy. A poem contains the same elements as a prose composition; the difference therefore must consist in a different combination of them, in consequence of a different object proposed. According to the difference of the object will be the difference of the combination. It is possible, that the object may be merely to facilitate the recollection of any given facts or observations by artificial arrangement; and the composition will be a poem, merely because it is distinguished from composition in prose by metre, or by rhyme, or by both conjointly. In this, the lowest sense, a man might attribute the name of a poem to the well-known enumeration of the days in the several months;

>   Thirty days hath September,
>   April, June, and November, &c.

and others of the same class and purpose. And as a particular pleasure is found in anticipating the recurrence of sounds and quantities, all compositions that have this charm superadded, whatever be their contents, *may* be entitled poems.

So much for the superficial form. A difference of object and contents supplies an additional ground of distinction. The immediate purpose may be the communication of truths; either of truth absolute and demonstrable, as in works of science; or of facts experienced and recorded, as in history. Pleasure, and that of the highest and most permanent kind, may result from the attainment of the end; but it is not itself the immediate end. In other works the communication of pleasure may be the immediate purpose; and though truth either moral or intellectual, ought to be the ultimate end, yet this will distinguish the character of the author, not the class to which the work belongs. Blessed indeed is that state of society, in which the immediate purpose would be baffled by the perversion of the proper ultimate end; in which no charm of diction or imagery could exempt the Bathyllus even of an Anacreon, or the Alexis of Virgil, from disgust and aversion!

But the communication of pleasure may be the immediate object of a work not metrically composed; and that object may have been in a high degree attained, as in novels and romances. Would then the mere superaddition of metre, with or without rhyme, entitle these to the name of poems? The answer is, that nothing can permanently please, which does not contain in itself the reason why it is so, and not otherwise. If metre be superadded, all other parts must be made consonant with it. They must be such, as to justify the perpetual and distinct attention to each part, which an exact correspondent recurrence of accent and sound are calculated to excite. The final definition then so deduced, may be thus worded. A poem is that species of composition, which is opposed to works of science, by proposing for its immediate object pleasure, not truth; and from all other species (having this object in common with it) it is discriminated by proposing to itself such delight from the whole, as is compatible with a distinct gratification from each component part.

Controversy is not seldom excited in consequence of the disputants attaching each a different meaning to the same word; and in few instances has this been more striking, than in disputes concerning the present subject. If a man chooses to call every composition a poem, which is rhyme, or measure, or both, I must leave his opinion uncontroverted. The distinction is at least competent to characterize the writer's intention. If it were subjoined, that the whole is likewise entertaining or affecting, as a tale, or as a series of interesting reflections, I of course admit this as another fit ingredient of a poem, and an additional merit. But if the definition sought for be that of a legitimate poem, I answer, it must be one, the parts of which mutually support and explain each other; all in their proportion harmonizing with, and supporting the purpose and known influences of metrical arrangement. The philosophic critics of all ages coincide with the ultimate judgement of all countries, in equally denying the praises of a just poem, on the one hand, to a series of striking lines or distichs, each of which absorbing the whole attention of the reader to itself disjoins it from its context, and makes it a separate whole, instead of an harmonizing part; and on the other hand, to an unsustained composition, from which the reader collects rapidly the general result unattracted by the component parts. The reader should be carried forward, not merely or chiefly by the mechanical impulse of curiosity, or by a restless desire to arrive at the final solution; but by the pleasurable activity of mind excited by the attractions of the journey itself. Like the motion of a serpent, which the Egyptians made the emblem of intellectual power; or like the path of sound through the air; at every step he pauses and half recedes, and from the retrogressive movement collects the force which again carries him onward. 'Precipitandus est *liber* spiritus [the *free* spirit must be hurried onward],' says Petronius Arbiter most happily. The epithet, *liber*, here balances the preceding verb; and it is not easy to conceive more meaning condensed in fewer words.

But if this should be admitted as a satisfactory character of a poem, we have still to seek for a definition of poetry. The writings of Plato, and Bishop Taylor, and the Theoria Sacra of Burnet, furnish undeniable proofs that poetry of the highest kind may exist without metre and even without the contradistinguishing objects of a poem. The first chapter of Isaiah (indeed a very large proportion of the whole book) is poetry in the most emphatic sense, yet it would be not less irrational than strange to assert, that pleasure, and not truth, was the immediate object of the prophet. In short, whatever specific import we attach to the word, poetry, there, will be found involved in it, as a necessary consequence, that a poem of any length neither can be, or ought to be, all poetry. Yet if an harmonious whole is to be produced, the remaining parts must be preserved in keeping with the poetry; and this can be no otherwise effected than by such a studied selection and artificial arrangement, as will partake of one, though not a peculiar, property of poetry. And this again can be no other than the property of exciting a more continuous and equal attention, than the language of prose aims at, whether colloquial or written.

My own conclusions on the nature of poetry, in the strictest use of the word, have been in part anticipated in the preceding disquisition on the fancy and imagination. What is poetry? is so nearly the same question with, what is a poem? that the answer to the one is involved in the solution of the other. For it is a distinction resulting from the poetic genius itself, which sustains and modifies the images, thoughts, and emotions of the poet's own mind. A poet, described in ideal perfection, brings the whole soul of man into activity, with the subordination of its faculties to each other, according to their relative worth and dignity. He diffuses a tone, and spirit of unity, that blends, and (as it were) fuses, each into each, by that synthetic and magical power, to which we have exclusively appropriated the name of imagination. This power, first put in action by the will and understanding, and retained under their irremissive, though gentle and unnoticed, control (*laxis effertur habenis* [it is carried onwards with loose reins]) reveals itself in the balance or reconciliation of opposite or discordant qualities: of sameness, with difference; of the general, with the concrete; the idea, with the image; the individual, with the representative; the sense of novelty and freshness, with old and familiar objects; a more than usual state of emotion, with more than usual order; judgement ever awake and steady self-possession, with enthusiasm and feeling profound or vehement; and while it blends and harmonizes the natural and the artificial, still subordinates art to nature; the manner to the matter; and our admiration of the poet to our sympathy with the poetry. 'Doubtless,' as Sir John Davies observes of the soul (and his words may with slight alteration be applied, and even more appropriately to the poetic imagination)

> Doubtless this could not be, but that she turns
> Bodies to spirit by sublimation strange,
> As fire converts to fire the things it burns,
> As we our food into our nature change.

> From their gross matter she abstracts their forms,
> And draws a kind of quintessence from things,
> Which to her proper nature she transforms
> To bear them light, on her celestial wings.
>
> Thus does she, when from individual states
> She doth abstract the universal kinds;
> Which then re-clothed in divers names and fates
> Steal access through our senses to our minds.

Finally, good sense is the body of poetic genius, fancy its drapery, motion its life, and imagination the soul that is everywhere, and in each; and forms all into one graceful and intelligent whole.

CHAPTER XV

The specific symptoms of poetic power elucidated in a critical analysis of Shakespeare's Venus and Adonis, and Lucrece.

In the application of these principles to purposes of practical criticism, as employed in the appraisement of works more or less imperfect, I have endeavoured to discover what the qualities in a poem are, which may be deemed promises and specific symptoms of poetic power, as distinguished from general talent determined to poetic composition by accidental motives, by an act of the will, rather than by the inspiration of a genial and productive nature. In this investigation, I could not, I thought, do better, than keep before me the earliest work of the greatest genius, that perhaps human nature has yet produced, our *myriad-minded* [1] Shakespeare. I mean the 'Venus and Adonis', and the 'Luc-

---

[1] Aνηρ μυριονους, a phrase which I have borrowed from a Greek monk, who applies it to a Patriarch of Constantinople. I might have said, that I have *reclaimed*, rather than borrowed it: for it seems to belong to Shakespeare, *de jure singulari, et ex privilegio naturae* [by a law peculiar to himself, and by privilege of nature].

rece'; works which give at once strong promises of the strength, and yet obvious proofs of the immaturity, of his genius. From these I abstracted the following marks, as characteristics of original poetic genius in general.

1. In the 'Venus and Adonis,' the first and most obvious excellence is the perfect sweetness of the versification; its adaptation to the subject; and the power displayed in varying the march of the words without passing into a loftier and more majestic rhythm than was demanded by the thoughts, or permitted by the propriety of preserving a sense of melody predominant. The delight in richness and sweetness of sound, even to a faulty excess, if it be evidently original, and not the result of an easily imitable mechanism, I regard as a highly favourable promise in the compositions of a young man. 'The man that hath not music in his soul' can indeed never be a genuine poet. Imagery (even taken from nature, much more when transplanted from books, as travels, voyages, and works of natural history), affecting incidents, just thoughts, interesting personal or domestic feelings, and with these the art of their combination or intertexture in the form of a poem; may all by incessant effort be acquired as a trade, by a man of talent and much reading, who, as I once before observed, has mistaken an intense desire of poetic reputation for a natural poetic genius; the love of the arbitrary end for a possession of the peculiar means. But the sense of musical delight, with the power of producing it, is a gift of imagination; and this together with the power of reducing multitude into unity of effect, and modifying a series of thoughts by some one predominant thought or feeling, may be cultivated and improved, but can never be learned. It is in these that 'poeta nascitur non fit [A poet is born, not made].'

2. A second promise of genius is the choice of subjects very remote from the private interests and circumstances of the writer himself. At least I have found, that where the subject is taken immediately from the author's personal sensations and experiences, the excellence of a particular poem is but an equivocal mark, and often a fallacious pledge, of genuine poetic power. We may perhaps remember the tale of the statuary, who had acquired considerable reputation for the legs of his goddesses, though the rest of the statue accorded but indifferently with ideal beauty; till his wife, elated by her husband's praises, mod-

estly acknowledged that she had been his constant model. In the Venus and Adonis, this proof of poetic power exists even to excess. It is throughout as if a superior spirit more intuitive, more intimately conscious, even than the characters themselves, not only of every outward look and act, but of the flux and reflux of the mind in all its subtlest thoughts and feelings, were placing the whole before our view; himself meanwhile unparticipating in the passions, and actuated only by that pleasurable excitement, which had resulted from the energetic fervour of his own spirit in so vividly exhibiting what it had so accurately and profoundly contemplated. I think, I should have conjectured from these poems, that even then the great instinct, which impelled the poet to the drama, was secretly working in him, prompting him by a series and never broken chain of imagery, always vivid and, because unbroken, often minute; by the highest effort of the picturesque in words, of which words are capable, higher perhaps than was ever realized by any other poet, even Dante not excepted; to provide a substitute for that visual language, that constant intervention and running comment by tone, look and gesture, which in his dramatic works he was entitled to expect from the players. His Venus and Adonis seem at once the characters themselves, and the whole representation of those characters by the most consummate actors. You seem to be *told* nothing, but to see and hear everything. Hence it is, from the perpetual activity of attention required on the part of the reader; from the rapid flow, the quick change, and the playful nature of the thoughts and images; and above all from the alienation, and, if I may hazard such an expression, the utter *aloofness* of the poet's own feelings, from those of which he is at once the painter and the analyst; that though the very subject cannot but detract from the pleasure of a delicate mind, yet never was poem less dangerous on a moral account. Instead of doing as Ariosto, and as, still more offensively, Wieland has done, instead of degrading and deforming passion into appetite, the trials of love into the struggles of concupiscence; Shakespeare has here represented the animal impulse itself, so as to preclude all sympathy with it, by dissipating the reader's notice among the thousand outward images, and now beautiful, now fanciful circumstances, which form its dresses and its scenery; or by diverting our attention from the main subject by those frequent witty or profound reflections, which the poet's ever active mind has deduced from, or connected with, the imagery and the incidents. The reader is forced into too much action to sympathize with the merely passive of our nature. As little can a mind thus roused and awakened be brooded on by mean and indistinct emotion, as the low, lazy mist can creep upon the surface of a lake, while a strong gale is driving it onward in waves and billows.

3. It has been before observed, that images however beautiful, though faithfully copied from nature, and as accurately represented in words, do not of themselves characterize the poet. They become proofs of original genius only as far as they are modified by a predominant passion; or by associated thoughts or images awakened by that passion; or when they have the effect of reducing multitude to unity, or succession to an instant; or lastly, when a human and intellectual life is transferred to them from the poet's own spirit,

> Which shoots its being through earth, sea, and air.

In the two following lines for instance, there is nothing objectionable, nothing which would preclude them from forming, in their proper place, part of a descriptive poem:

> Behold yon row of pines, that shorn and bow'd
> Bend from the sea-blast, seen at twilight eve.

But with a small alteration of rhythm, the same words would be equally in their place in a book of topography, or in a descriptive tour. The same image will rise into semblance of poetry if thus conveyed:

> Yon row of bleak and visionary pines,
> By twilight glimpse discerned, mark! how they flee
> From the fierce sea-blast, all their tresses wild
> Streaming before them.

I have given this as an illustration, by no means as an instance, of that particular excellence which I had in view, and in which Shakespeare even in his earliest, as in his latest, works surpasses all other poets. It is by this, that he still gives a dignity and a passion to the objects which he presents. Unaided by any previous excitement, they burst upon us at once in life and in power.

> Full many a glorious morning have I seen
> *Flatter* the mountain tops with sovereign eye.
> Shakespeare's Sonnet 33rd

> Not mine own fears, nor the prophetic soul
> Of the wide world dreaming on things to come—
> * * * * * *
> The mortal moon hath her eclipse endur'd,
> And the sad augurs mock their own presage;
> Incertainties now crown themselves assur'd,
> And Peace proclaims olives of endless age.
> Now with the drops of this most balmy time
> My Love looks fresh, and Death to me subscribes!
> Since spite of him, I'll live in this poor rhyme,
> While he insults o'er dull and speechless tribes.
> And thou in this shalt find thy monument,
> When tyrants' crests, and tombs of brass are spent.
> Sonnet 107

As of higher worth, so doubtless still more characteristic of poetic genius does the imagery become, when it moulds and colours itself to the circumstances, passion, or character, present and foremost in the mind. For unrivalled instances of this excellence, the reader's own memory will refer him to the Lear, Othello, in short to which not of the 'great, ever living, dead man's' dramatic works? *Inopem em copia fecit* [Plenty has made me poor]. How true it is to nature, he has himself finely expressed in the instance of love in his Sonnet 98.

Samuel Taylor Coleridge

> From you have I been absent in the spring,
> When proud-pied April drest in all its trim,
> Hath put a spirit of youth in every thing;
> That heavy Saturn laugh'd and leap'd with him.
> Yet nor the lays of birds, nor the sweet smell
> Of different flowers in odour and in hue,
> Could make me any summer's story tell,
> Or from their proud lap pluck them, where they grew
> Nor did I wonder at the lilies white,
> Nor praise the deep vermilion in the rose;
> They were, tho' sweet, but figures of delight,
> Drawn after you, you pattern of all those.
> Yet seem'd it winter still, and, you away,
> *As with your shadow I with these did play!*

Scarcely less sure, or if a less valuable, not less indispensable mark

> Γονίμου μέν Ποιητου...
> ... οστις ρημα γευναιον λακοι①

will the imagery supply, when, with more than the power of the painter, the poet gives us the liveliest image of succession with the feeling of simultaneousness!

> With this, he breaketh from the sweet embrace
> Of those fair arms, which bound him to her breast,
> And homeward through the dark laund runs apace:
> *Look how a bright star shooteth from the sky!*
> *So glides he in the night from Venus' eye.*

---

① 'of a True Poet, such a one as utters noble words' (trans. by H. J. Jackson)—editor's note.

4. The last character I shall mention, which would prove indeed but little, except as taken conjointly with the former; yet without which the former could scarce exist in a high degree, and (even if this were possible) would give promises only of transitory flashes and a meteoric power; is depth, and energy of thought. No man was ever yet a great poet, without being at the same time a profound philosopher. For poetry is the blossom and the fragrancy of all human knowledge, human thoughts, human passions, emotions, language. In Shakespeare's poems the creative power and the intellectual energy wrestle as in a war embrace. Each in its excess of strength seems to threaten the extinction of the other. At length in the drama they were reconciled, and fought each with its shield before the breast of the other. Or like two rapid streams, that, at their first meeting within narrow and rocky banks, mutually strive to repel each other and intermix reluctantly and in tumult; but soon finding a wider channel and more yielding shores blend, and dilate, and flow on in one current and with one voice. The Venus and Adonis did not perhaps allow the display of the deeper passions. But the story of Lucretia seems to favour and even demand their intensest workings. And yet we find in Shakespeare's management of the tale neither pathos, nor any other dramatic quality. There is the same minute and faithful imagery as in the former poem, in the same vivid colours, inspirited by the same impetuous vigour of thought, and diverging and contracting with the same activity of the assimilative and of the modifying faculties; and with a yet larger display, a yet wider range of knowledge and reflection; and lastly, with the same perfect dominion, often domination, over the whole world of language. What then shall we say? even this; that Shakespeare, no mere child of nature; no automaton of genius; no passive vehicle of inspiration, possessed by the spirit, not possessing it; first studied patiently, meditated deeply, understood minutely, till knowledge, become habitual and intuitive, wedded itself to his habitual feelings, and at length gave birth to that stupendous power, by which he stands alone, with no equal or second in his own class; to that power which seated him on one of the two glory-smitten summits of the poetic mountain, with Milton as his compeer not rival. While the former darts himself forth, and passes into all the forms of human character and passion, the one Proteus of the fire and the flood;

the other attracts all forms and things to himself, into the unity of his own ideal. All things and modes of action shape themselves anew in the being of Milton; while Shakespeare becomes all things, yet for ever remaining himself. O what great men hast thou not produced, England! my country! truly indeed—

> Must *we* be free or die, who speak the tongue,
> Which Shakespeare spake; the faith and morals hold,
> Which Milton held. In every thing we are sprung
> Of earth's first blood, have titles manifold!
>
> Wordsworth

CHAPTER XVII

Examination of the tenets peculiar to Mr Wordsworth—Rustic life (above all, low and rustic life) especially unfavourable to the formation of a human diction—The best parts of language the product of philosophers, not of clowns or shepherds—Poetry essentially ideal and generic—The language of Milton as much the language of real life, yea, incomparably more so than that of the cottager.

As far then as Mr Wordsworth in his preface contended, and most ably contended, for a reformation in our poetic diction, as far as he has evinced the truth of passion, and the dramatic propriety of those figures and metaphors in the original poets, which, stripped of their justifying reasons, and converted into mere artifices of connection or ornament, constitute the characteristic falsity in the poetic style of the moderns; and as far as he has, with equal acuteness and clearness, pointed out the process by which this change was effected, and the resemblances between that state into which the reader's mind is thrown by the pleasurable confusion of thought from an unaccustomed train of words and images; and that state which is induced by the natural language of impassioned feeling; he undertook a useful task, and deserves all praise, both for the attempt and for the execution. The provocations to this remonstrance in behalf of truth and nature were still of perpetual recurrence before and after the publication of this preface. I cannot likewise but add, that the comparison of such poems of merit, as have been given to the public within the last ten or twelve years, with the majority of those produced previously to the appearance of that preface, leave no doubt on my mind, that Mr Wordsworth is fully justified in believing his efforts to have been by no means ineffectual. Not only in the verses of those who have professed their admiration of his genius, but even of those who have distinguished themselves by hostility to his theory, and depreciation of his writings, are the impressions of his principles plainly visible. It is possible, that with these principles others may have been blended, which are not equally evident; and some which are unsteady and subvertible from the narrowness or imperfection of their basis. But it is more than possible, that these errors of defect or exaggeration, by kindling and feeding the controversy, may have conduced not only to the wider propagation of the accompanying truths, but that, by their frequent presentation to the mind in an excited state, they may have won for them a more permanent and practical result. A man will borrow a part from his opponent the more easily, if he feels himself justified in continuing to reject a part. While there remain important points in which he can still feel himself in the right, in which he still finds firm footing for continued resistance, he will gradually adopt those opinions, which were the least remote from his own convictions, as not less congruous with his own theory than with that which he reprobates. In like manner with a kind of instinctive prudence, he will abandon by little and little his weakest posts, till at length he seems to forget that they had ever belonged to him, or affects to consider them at most as accidental and 'petty annexments,' the removal of which leaves the citadel unhurt and unendangered.

My own differences from certain supposed parts of Mr Wordsworth's theory ground themselves on the assumption, that his words had been rightly interpreted, as purporting that the proper diction for poetry in general consists altogether in a language taken, with due exceptions, from the mouths of men in real life, a language which actually constitutes the natural conversation of men under the influence of natural feelings. My objection is, first, that in any sense this rule is applicable only to certain classes of poetry; secondly, that even to these classes it is not applicable, except in such a sense, as hath never by any one (as far as I know or have read) been denied or doubted; and lastly, that as far as, and in that degree in which it is practicable, it is yet as a rule useless, if not injurious, and therefore either need not, or ought not to be practised. The poet informs his reader, that he had generally chosen low and rustic life; but not as low and rustic, or in order to repeat that pleasure of doubtful moral effect, which persons of elevated rank and of superior refinement oftentimes derive from a happy imitation of the rude unpolished manners and discourse of their inferiors. For the pleasure so derived may be traced to three exciting causes. The first is the naturalness, in fact, of the things represented. The second is the apparent naturalness of the representation, as raised and qualified by an imperceptible infusion of the author's own knowledge and talent, which infusion does, indeed, constitute it an imitation as distinguished from a mere copy. The third cause may be found in the reader's conscious feeling of his superiority awakened by the contrast presented to him; even as for the same purpose the kings and great barons of yore retained, sometimes actual clowns and fools, but more frequently shrewd and witty fellows in that character. These, however, were not Mr Wordsworth's objects. He chose low and rustic life, 'because in that condition the essential passions of the heart find a better soil, in which they can attain their maturity, are less under restraint, and speak a plainer and more emphatic language; because in that condition of life our elementary feelings coexist in a state of greater simplicity, and consequently may be more accurately contemplated, and more forcibly communicated; because the manners of rural life germinate from those elementary feelings; and from the necessary character of rural occupations are more easily comprehended, and are more durable; and lastly, because in that condition the passions of men are incorporated with the beautiful and permanent forms of nature.'

Now it is clear to me, that in the most interesting of the poems, in which the author is more or less dramatic, as 'The Brothers,' 'Michael,' 'Ruth,' 'The Mad Mother,' etc. the persons introduced are by no means taken from low or rustic life in the common acceptation of those words! and it is not less clear, that the sentiments and language, as far as they can be conceived to have been really transferred from the minds and conversation of such persons, are attributable to causes and circumstances not necessarily connected with 'their occupations and abode.' The thoughts, feelings, language, and manners of the shepherd-farmers in the vales of Cumberland and Westmoreland, as far as they are actually adopted in those poems, may be accounted for from causes, which will and do produce the same results in every state of life, whether in town or country. As the two principal I rank that independence, which raises a man above servitude, or daily toil for the profit of others, yet not above the necessity of industry and a frugal simplicity of domestic life; and the accompanying unambitious, but solid and religious, education, which has rendered few books familiar, but the Bible, and the liturgy or hymn book. To this latter cause, indeed, which is so far accidental, that it is the blessing of particular countries and a particular age, not the product of particular places or employments, the poet owes the show of probability, that his personages might really feel, think, and talk with any tolerable resemblance to his representation. It is an excellent remark of Dr Henry More's (Enthusiasmus triuphatus, Sec. XXXV) that 'a man of confined education, but of good parts, by constant reading of the Bible will naturally form a more winning and commanding rhetoric than those that are learned: the intermixture of tongues and of artificial phrases debasing their style.'

It is, moreover, to be considered that to the formation of healthy feelings, and a reflecting mind, negations involve impediments not less formidable than sophistication and vicious intermixture. I am convinced, that for the human soul to prosper in rustic life a certain vantage-ground is prerequisite. It is not every man that is likely to be improved by a country life or by country labours. Education, or original sensibility, or both, must pre-exist, if the changes, forms, and incidents of nature are to prove a sufficient stimulant. And where these are not sufficient, the mind contracts and hardens by want of stimulants: and the man becomes selfish, sensual, gross, and hard-hearted. Let the management of the Poor Laws in Liverpool, Manchester, or Bristol be compared with the ordinary dispensation of the poor rates in agricultural villages, where the farmers are the overseers and guardians of the poor. If my own experience have not been particularly unfortunate, as well as that of the many respectable country clergymen with whom I have conversed on the subject, the result would engender more than scepticism concerning the desirable influences of low and rustic life in and for itself. Whatever may be concluded on the other side, from the stronger local attachments and enterprising spirit of the Swiss, and other mountaineers, applies to a particular mode of pastoral life, under forms of property that permit and beget manners truly republican, not to rustic life in general, or to the absence of artificial cultivation. On the contrary the mountaineers, whose manners have been so often eulogized, are in general better educated and greater readers than men of equal rank elsewhere. But where this is not the case, as among the peasantry of North Wales, the ancient mountains, with all their terrors and all their glories, are pictures to the blind, and music to the deaf.

I should not have entered so much into detail upon this passage, but here seems to be the point, to which all the lines of difference converge as to their source and centre. (I mean, as far as, and in whatever respect, my poetic creed does differ from the doctrines promulgated in this preface.) I adopt with full faith, the principle of Aristotle, that poetry, as poetry, is essentially ideal,① that it a-

---

① Say not that I am recommending abstractions, for these class characteristics which constitute the instructiveness of a character, are so modified and particularized in each person of the Shakespearian Drama, that life itself does not excite more distinctly that sense of individuality which belongs to real existence. Parodoxical as it may sound, one of the essential properties of geometry is not less essential to dramatic excellence; and Aristotle has accordingly required of the poet an involution of the universal in the individual. The chief differences are, that in geometry it is the universal truth, which is uppermost in the consciousness; in poetry and individual form, in which the truth is clothed. With the ancients, and not less with the elder dramatists of England and France, both comedy and tragedy were considered as kinds of poetry. They neither sought in comedy to make us laugh merely: much less to make us laugh by wry faces, accidents of jargon, slang phrases for the day, or the clothing of commonplace morals in metaphors drawn from the shops and mechanic occupations of their characters. Nor did they condescend in tragedy to wheedle away the applause of the spectators, by representing before them fascimiles of their own mean selves in all their existing meanness, or to work on their sluggish sympathies by a pathos not a whit more respectable than the maudlin tears of drunkenness. Their tragic scenes were meant to affect us indeed; but yet within the bounds of pleasure, and in union with the activity both of our understanding and imagination. They wished to transport the mind to a sense of possible greatness, and to implant the germs of that greatness, during the temporary oblivion of the worthless 'thing we are,' and of the peculiar state in which each man happens to be, suspending our individual recollections and lulling them to sleep amid the music of nobler thoughts. Friend, Pages 251, 252.

voids and excludes all accident; that its apparent individualities of rank, character, or occupation must be representative of a class; and that the persons of poetry must be clothed with generic attributes, with the common attributes of the class: not with such as one gifted individual might possibly possess, but such as from his situation it is most probable before-hand that he *would* possess. If my premises are right and my deductions legitimate, it follows that there can be no poetic medium between the swains of Theocritus and those of an imaginary Golden Age.

The characters of the vicar and the shepherd-mariner in the poem of 'The Brothers,' and that of the shepherd of Green-head Ghyll in the 'Michael,' have all the verisimilitude and representative quality, that the purposes of poetry can require. They are persons of a known and abiding class, and their manners and sentiments the natural product of circumstances common to the class. Take 'Michael' for instance:

> An old man stout of heart, and strong of limb;
> His bodily frame had been from youth to age
> Of an unusual strength: his mind was keen,
> Intense and frugal, apt for all affairs,
> And in his shepherd's calling he was prompt
> And watchful more than ordinary men.
> Hence he had learned the meaning of all winds,
> Of blasts of every tone, and oftentimes
> When others heeded not, he heard the South
> Make subterraneous music, like the noise
> Of bagpipers on distant highland hills.
> The shepherd, at such warning, of his flock
> Bethought him, and he to himself would say,
> The winds are now devising work for me!
> And truly at all times the storm, that drives
> The traveller to a shelter, summon'd him
> Up to the mountains. He had been alone

> Amid the heart of many thousand mists,
> That came to him and left him on the heights.
> So liv'd he, until his eightieth year was pass'd.
> And grossly that man errs, who should suppose
> That the green valleys, and the streams and rocks,
> Were things indifferent to the shepherd's thoughts.
> Fields, where with cheerful spirits he had breath'd
> The common air; the hills, which he so oft
> Had climb'd with vigorous steps; which had impress'd
> So many incidents upon his mind
> Of hardship, skill or courage, joy or fear;
> Which like a book preserved the memory
> Of the dumb animals, whom he had sav'd,
> Had fed or shelter'd, linking to such acts,
> So grateful in themselves, the certainty
> Of honourable gain; these fields, these hills
> Which were his living being, even more
> Than his own blood—what could they less? had laid
> Strong hold on his affections, were to him
> A pleasurable feeling of blind love,
> The pleasure which there is in life itself.

On the other hand, in the poems which are pitched in a lower key, as the 'Harry Gill,' 'Idiot Boy,' etc. the feelings are those of human nature in general; though the poet has judiciously laid the scene in the country, in order to place himself in the vicinity of interesting images, without the necessity of ascribing a sentimental perception of their beauty to the persons of his drama. In the 'Idiot Boy,' indeed, the mother's character is not so much the real and native product of a 'situation where the essential passions of the heart find a better soil, in which they can attain their maturity and speak a plainer and more emphatic language,' as it is an impersonation of an instinct abandoned by judgment. Hence the two following charges seem to me not wholly groundless: at least, they are the only plausible objections, which I have heard to that fine poem. The one is, that the author has not, in the poem itself, taken sufficient care to preclude from the reader's fancy the disgusting images of ordinary morbid idiocy, which yet it was by no means his intention to represent. He was even by the 'burr, burr, burr, ' uncounteracted by any preceding description of the boy's beauty, assisted in recalling them. The other is, that the idiocy of the boy is so evenly balanced by the folly of the mother, as to present to the general reader rather a laughable burlesque on the blindness of anile dotage, than an analytic display of maternal affection in its ordinary workings.

In the 'Thorn,' the poet himself acknowledges in a note the necessity of an introductory poem, in which he should have portrayed the character of the person from whom the words of the poem are supposed to proceed: a superstitious man moderately imaginative, of slow faculties and deep feelings, 'a captain of a small trading vessel, for example, who, being past the middle age of life, had retired upon an annuity, or small independent income, to some village or country town of which he was not a native, or in which he had not been accustomed to live. Such men having nothing to do become credulous and talkative from indolence. ' But in a poem, still more in a lyric poem (and the Nurse in Shakespeare's Romeo and Juliet alone prevents me from extending the remark even to dramatic poetry, if indeed even the Nurse can be deemed altogether a case in point) it is not possible to imitate truly a dull and garrulous discourser, without repeating the effects of dullness and garrulity. However this may be, I dare assert, that the parts (and these form the far larger portion of the whole) which might as well or still better have proceeded from the poet's own imagination, and have been spoken in his own character, are those which have given, and which will continue to give, universal delight; and that the passages exclusively appropriate to the supposed narrator, such as the last couplet of the third stanza; ① the seven last

---

① I've measured it from side to side;
   'Tis three feet long, and two feet wide.

lines of the tenth;① and the five following stanzas, with the exception of the four

---

① Nay rack your brain—'tis all in vain,
I'll tell you every thing I know;
But to the thorn, and to the pond
Which is a little step beyond,
I wish that you would go:
Perhaps when you are at the place
You something of her tale may trace.

I'll give you the best help I can:
Before you up the mountain go,
Up to the dreary mountain-top,
I'll tell you all I know.
'Tis now some two and twenty years,
Since she (her name is Martha Ray)
Gave with a maiden's true good will
Her company to Stephen Hill;
And she was blithe and gay,
And she was happy, happy still
Whene'er she thought of Stephen Hill.

And they had fix'd the wedding-day,
The morning that must wed them both;
But Stephen to another maid
Had sworn another oath;
And with this other maid to church
Unthinking Stephen went—
Poor Martha! on that woeful day
A pang of pitiless dismay,
Into her soul was sent;
A fire was kindled in her breast,
Which might not burn itself to rest.

They say, full six months after this,
While yet the summer leaves were green,
She to the mountain-top would go,
And there was often seen.
'Tis said, a child was in her womb,
As now to any eye was plain;
She was with child, and she was mad;

admirable lines at the commencement of the fourteenth, are felt by many unprejudiced and unsophisticated hearts, as sudden and unpleasant sinkings from the height to which the poet had previously lifted them, and to which he again re-elevates both himself and his reader.

If then I am compelled to doubt the theory, by which the choice of characters was to be directed, not only a priori, from grounds of reason, but both from the few instances in which the poet himself need be supposed to have been governed by it, and from the comparative inferiority of those instances; still more must I hesitate in my assent to the sentence which immediately follows the former citation; and which I can neither admit as particular fact, nor as general

---

> Yet often she was sober sad
> From her exceeding pain.
> Oh me! ten thousand times I'd rather
> That he had died, that cruel father!
> * * * * *
> Last Christmas when we talked of this,
> Old Farmer Simpson did maintain,
> That in her womb the infant wrought
> About its mother's heart, and brought
> Her senses back again:
> And when at last her time drew near,
> Her looks were calm, her senses clear.
>
> No more I know, I wish I did,
> And I would tell it all to you;
> For what became of this poor child
> There's none that ever knew:
> And if a child was born or no,
> There's no one that could ever tell;
> And if 'twas born alive or dead,
> There's no one knows, as I have said;
> But some remember well,
> That Martha Ray about this time
> Would up the mountain often climb.

rule. 'The language, too, of these men has been adopted (purified indeed from what appear to be its real defects, from all lasting and rational causes of dislike or disgust) because such men hourly communicate with the best objects from which the best part of language is originally derived; and because, from their rank in society and the sameness and narrow circle of their intercourse, being less under the action of social vanity, they convey their feelings and notions in simple and unelaborated expressions. ' To this I reply; that a rustic's language, purified from all provincialism and grossness, and so far reconstructed as to be made consistent with the rules of grammar (which are in essence no other than the laws of universal logic, applied to psychological materials) will not differ from the language of any other man of common sense, however learned or refined he may be, except as far as the notions, which the rustic has to convey, are fewer and more indiscriminate. This will become still clearer, if we add the consideration (equally important though less obvious) that the rustic, from the more imperfect development of his faculties, and from the lower state of their cultivation, aims almost solely to convey insulated facts, either those of his scanty experience or his traditional belief; while the educated man chiefly seeks to discover and express those connections of things, or those relative bearings of fact to fact, from which some more or less general law is deducible. For facts are valuable to a wise man, chiefly as they lead to the discovery of the indwelling law, which is the true being of things, the sole solution of their modes of existence, and in the knowledge of which consists our dignity and our power.

As little can I agree with the assertion, that from the objects with which the rustic hourly communicates the best part of language is formed. For first, if to communicate with an object implies such an acquaintance with it, as renders it capable of being discriminately reflected on, the distinct knowledge of an uneducated rustic would furnish a very scanty vocabulary. The few things and modes of action requisite for his bodily conveniences would alone be individualized; while all the rest of nature would be expressed by a small number of confused general terms. Secondly, I deny that the words and combinations of words derived from the objects, with which the rustic is familiar, whether with distinct or confused knowledge, can be justly said to form the best part of language. It is more than probable, that many classes of the brute creation possess discriminating sounds, by which they can convey to each other notices of such objects as concern their food, shelter, or safety. Yet we hesitate to call the aggregate of such sounds a language, otherwise than metaphorically. The best part of human language, properly so called, is derived from reflection on the acts of the mind itself. It is formed by a voluntary appropriation of fixed symbols to internal acts, to processes and results of imagination, the greater part of which have no place in the consciousness of uneducated man; though in civilized society, by imitation and passive remembrance of what they hear from their religious instructors and other superiors, the most uneducated share in the harvest which they neither sowed, nor reaped. If the history of the phrases in hourly currency among our peasants were traced, a person not previously aware of the fact would be surprised at finding so large a number, which three or four centuries ago were the exclusive property of the universities and the schools; and, at the commencement of the Reformation, had been transferred from the school to the pulpit, and thus gradually passed into common life. The extreme difficulty, and often the impossibility, of finding words for the simplest moral and intellectual processes of the languages of uncivilized tribes has proved perhaps the weightiest obstacle to the progress of our most zealous and adroit missionaries. Yet these tribes are surrounded by the same nature as our peasants are; but in still more impressive forms; and they are, moreover, obliged to particularize many more of them. When, therefore, Mr Wordsworth adds, 'accordingly, such a language' (meaning, as before, the language of rustic life purified from provincialism) 'arising out of repeated experience and regular feelings, is a more permanent, and a far more philosophical language, than that which is frequently substituted for it by poets, who think that they are conferring honour upon themselves and their art in proportion as they indulge in arbitrary and capricious habits of expression;' it may be answered, that the anguage, which he has in view, can be attributed to rustics with no greater right, than the style of Hooker or Bacon to Tom Brown or Sir Roger L'Estrange. Doubtless, if what is peculiar to each were omitted in each, the result must needs be the same. Further, that the poet, who uses an illogical diction, or a style fitted to excite only the low and changeable pleasure of wonder by means of groundless novelty, substitutes a language of folly and vanity, not for that of the rustic, but for that of good sense and natural feeling.

Here let me be permitted to remind the reader, that the positions, which I controvert, are contained in the sentences—'a selection of the real language of men'; —'the language of these men (i. e. men in low and rustic life) I have proposed to myself to imitate, and as far as is possible to adopt the very language of men.' 'Between the language of prose and that of metrical composition, there neither is, nor can be any essential difference.' It is against these exclusively that my opposition is directed.

I object, in the very first instance, to an equivocation in the use of the word 'real.' Every man's language varies, according to the extent of his knowledge, the activity of his faculties, and the depth or quickness of his feelings. Every man's language has, first, its individualities; secondly, the common properties of the class to which he belongs; and thirdly, words and phrases of universal use. The language of Hooker, Bacon, Bishop Taylor, and Burke differs from the common language of the learned class only by the superior number and novelty of the thoughts and relations which they had to convey. The language of Algernon Sidney differs not at all from that, which every well-educated gentleman would wish to write, and (with due allowances for the undeliberateness, and less connected train, of thinking natural and proper to conversation) such as he would wish to talk. Neither one nor the other differ half as much from the general language of cultivated society, as the language of Mr Wordsworth's homeliest composition differs from that of a common peasant. For 'real' therefore, we must substitute ordinary, or *lingua communis* [the common tongue]. And this, we have proved, is no more to be found in the phraseology of low and rustic life than in that of any other class. Omit the peculiarities of each and the result of course must be common to all. And assuredly the omissions and changes to be made in the language of rustics, before it could be transferred to any species of poem, except the drama or other professed imitation, are at least as numerous and weighty, as would be required in adapting to the same purpose the ordinary language of tradesmen and manufacturers. Not to mention, that the language so highly extolled by Mr Wordsworth varies in every county, nay in every village, according to the accidental character of the clergyman, the existence or non-existence of schools; or even, perhaps, as the exciseman, publican, and barber happen to be, or not to be, zealous politicians, and readers of the weekly newspaper *pro bono publico* [for the public good]. Anterior to cultivation the *lingua communis* of every country, as Dante has well observed, exists everywhere in parts, and nowhere as a whole.

Neither is the case rendered at all more tenable by the addition of the words, 'in a state of excitement.' For the nature of a man's words, where he is strongly affected by joy, grief, or anger, must necessarily depend on the number and quality of the general truths, conceptions and images, and of the words expressing them, with which his mind had been previously stored. For the property of passion is not to create; but to set in increased activity. At least, whatever new connections of thoughts or images, or (which is equally, if not more than equally, the appropriate effect of strong excitement) whatever generalizations of truth or experience the heat of passion may produce; yet the terms of their conveyance must have pre-existed in his former conversations, and are only collected and crowded together by the unusual stimulation. It is indeed very possible to adopt in a poem the unmeaning repetitions, habitual phrases, and other blank counters, which an unfurnished or confused understanding interposes at short intervals, in order to keep hold of his subject, which is still slipping from him, and to give him time for recollection; or, in mere aid of vacancy, as in the scanty companies of a country stage the same player pops backwards and forwards, in order to prevent the appearance of empty spaces, in the procession of Macbeth, or Henry VIIIth. But what assistance to the poet, or ornament to the poem, these can supply, I am at a loss to conjecture. Nothing assuredly can differ either in origin or in mode more widely from the apparent tautologies of intense and turbulent feeling, in which the passion is greater and of longer endurance than to be exhausted or satisfied by a single representation of the image or incident exciting it. Such repetitions I admit to be a beauty of the highest kind; as illustrated by Mr Wordsworth himself from the song of Deborah. 'At her feet he bowed, he fell, he lay down; at her feet he bowed, he fell; where he bowed, there he fell down dead.'

CHAPTER XVIII

Language of metrical composition, why and wherein essentially different from that of prose—Origin and elements of metre—Its necessary consequences, and the conditions thereby imposed on the metrical writer in the choice of his diction.

I conclude, therefore, that the attempt is impracticable; and that, were it not impracticable, it would still be useless. For the very power of making the selection implies the previous possession of the language selected. Or where can the poet have lived? And by what rules could he direct his choice, which would not have enabled him to select and arrange his words by the light of his own judgment? We do not adopt the language of a class by the mere adoption of such words exclusively, as that class would use, or at least understand; but likewise by following the order, in which the words of such men are wont to succeed each other. Now this order, in the intercourse of uneducated men, is distinguished from the diction of their superiors in knowledge and power, by the greater disjunction and separation in the component parts of that, whatever it be, which they wish to communicate. There is a want of that prospectiveness of mind, that surview, which enables a man to foresee the whole of what he is to convey, appertaining to any one point; and by this means so to subordinate and arrange the different parts according to their relative importance, as to convey it at once, and as an organized whole.

Now I will take the first stanza, on which I have chanced to open, in the Lyrical Ballads. It is one [of] the most simple and the least peculiar in its language.

> In distant countries have I been,
> And yet I have not often seen
> A healthy man, a man full grown,
> Weep in the public road alone.
> But such a one, on English ground,

> And in the broad highway I met;
> Along the broad highway he came,
> His cheeks with tears were wet.
> Sturdy he seem'd, though he was sad;
> And in his arms a lamb he had.

The words here are doubtless such as are current in all ranks of life; and of course not less so in the hamlet and cottage than in the shop, manufactory, college, or palace. But is this the order, in which the rustic would have placed the words? I am grievously deceived, if the following less compact mode of commencing the same tale be not a far more faithful copy. 'I have been in a many parts, far and near, and I don't know that I ever saw before a man crying by himself in the public road; a grown man I mean, that was neither sick nor hurt,' etc. etc. But when I turn to the following stanza in The Thorn:

> At all times of the day and night
> This wretched woman thither goes;
> And she is known to every star,
> And every wind that blows:
> And there beside the Thorn she sits,
> When the blue day-light's in the skies,
> And when the whirlwind's on the hill,
> Or frosty air is keen and still,
> And to herself she cries,
> Oh misery! Oh misery!
> Oh woe is me! Oh misery!

and compare this with the language of ordinary men; or with that which I can conceive at all likely to proceed, in real life, from such a narrator, as is supposed in the note to the poem; compare it either in the succession of the images or of the sentences; I am reminded of the sublime prayer and hymn of praise, which Milton, in opposition to an established liturgy, presents as a fair specimen of common extemporary devotion, and such as we might expect to hear from every self-inspired minister of a conventicle! And I reflect with delight, how little a mere theory, though of his own workmanship, interferes with the processes of genuine imagination in a man of true poetic genius, who possesses, as Mr Wordsworth, if ever man did, most assuredly does possess,

> The Vision and the Faculty divine.

One point then alone remains, but that the most important; its examination having been, indeed, my chief inducement for the preceding inquisition. 'There neither is nor can be any essential difference between the language of prose and metrical composition.' Such is Mr Wordsworth's assertion. Now prose itself, at least in all argumentative and consecutive works, differs, and ought to differ, from the language of conversation; even as reading① ought to differ from talking. Unless therefore the difference denied be that of the mere words, as materials common to all styles of writing, and not of the style itself in the universally ad-

---

① It is no less an error in teachers, than a torment to the poor children, to enforce the necessary of reading as they would talk. In order to cure them of *singing* as it is called; that is, of too great a difference. The child is made to repeat the words with his eyes from off the book; and then indeed, his tones resemble talking, as far as his fears, tears and trembling will permit. But as soon as the eye is again directed to the printed page, the spell begins anew; for an instinctive sense tells the child's feelings, that to utter its own momentary thoughts, and to recite the written thoughts of another, as of another, and a far wiser than himself, are two widely different things; and as the two acts are accompanied with widely different feelings, so must they justify different modes of enunciation. Joseph Lancaster, among his other sophistications of the excellent Dr Bell's invaluable system, cures this fault of *singing*, by hanging fetters and chains on the child, to the music of which, one of his school fellows who walks before, dolefully chants out the child'd last speech and confession, birth, parentage, and education. And this soul-benumbing ignominy, this unholy and heart-hardening burlesque on the last fearful infliction of outraged law, in pronouncing the sentence to which the stern and ingenious method of remedying—what? and how? —why, one extreme in order to introduce another, scarce less distinct from good sense, and certainly likely to have worse moral effects, by enforcing a semblance of petulant ease and self-sufficiency, in repession, and possible after-perversion of the natural feelings. I have to beg Dr Bell's pardon for his connection of the two names, but he knows that contrast is no less powerful a cause of association than likeness.

mitted sense of the term, it might be naturally presumed that there must exist a still greater between the ordonnance of poetic composition and that of prose, than is expected to distinguish prose from ordinary conversation.

There are not, indeed, examples wanting in the history of literature, of apparent paradoxes that have summoned the public wonder as new and startling truths, but which, on examination, have shrunk into tame and harmless truisms; as the eyes of a cat, seen in the dark, have been mistaken for flames of fire. But Mr Wordsworth is among the last men, to whom a delusion of this kind would be attributed by anyone, who had enjoyed the slightest opportunity of understanding his mind and character. Where an objection has been anticipated by such an author as natural, his answer to it must needs be interpreted in some sense which either is, or has been, or is capable of being controverted. My object then must be to discover some other meaning for the term 'essential difference' in this place, exclusive of the indistinction and community of the words themselves. For whether there ought to exist a class of words in the English, in any degree resembling the poetic dialect of the Greek and Italian, is a question of very subordinate importance. The number of such words would be small indeed, in our language; and even in the Italian and Greek, they consist not so much of different words, as of slight differences in the forms of declining and conjugating the same words; forms, doubtless, which having been, at some period more or less remote, the common grammatic flexions of some tribe or province, had been accidentally appropriated to poetry by the general admiration of certain master intellects, the first established lights of inspiration, to whom that dialect happened to be native.

Essence, in its primary signification, means the principle of individuation, the inmost principle of the possibility of any thing, as that particular thing. It is equivalent to the idea of a thing, whenever we use the word *idea*, with philosophic precision. Existence, on the other hand, is distinguished from essence, by the superinduction of reality. Thus we speak of the essence, and essential properties of a circle; but we do not therefore assert, that any thing, which really *exists*, is mathematically circular. Thus too, without any tautology we contend for the existence of the Supreme Being; that is, for a reality correspondent to the idea. There is, next, a secondary use of the word *essence*, in which it signifies the point or ground of contradistinction between two modifications of the same substance or subject. Thus we should be allowed to say, that the style of architecture of Westminster Abbey is essentially different from that of Saint Paul's, even though both had been built with blocks cut into the same form, and from the same quarry. Only in this latter sense of the term must it have been denied by Mr Wordsworth (for in this sense alone is it affirmed by the general opinion) that the language of poetry (i. e. the formal construction, or architecture, of the words and phrases) is essentially different from that of prose. Now the burden of the proof lies with the oppugner, not with the supporters of the common belief. Mr Wordsworth, in consequence, assigns as the proof of his position, 'that not only the language of a large portion of every good poem, even of the most elevated character, must necessarily, except with reference to the metre, in no respect differ from that of good prose, but likewise that some of the most interesting parts of the best poems will be found to be strictly the language of prose, when prose is well written. The truth of this assertion might be demonstrated by innumerable passages from almost all the poetical writings, even of Milton himself. ' He then quotes Gray's sonnet—

> In vain to me the smiling mornings shine,
> And reddening Phoebus lifts his golden fire;
> The birds in vain their amorous descant join,
> Or cheerful fields resume their green attire.
> These ears, alas! for other notes repine;
> *A different object do these eyes require;*
> *My lonely anguish melts no heart but mine;*
> *And in my breast the imperfect joys expire!*
> Yet morning smiles the busy race to cheer,
> And new-born pleasure brings to happier men:
> The fields to all their wonted tribute bear;
> To warm their little loves the birds complain:
> *I fruitless mourn to him that cannot hear,*
> *And weep the more because I weep in vain;*

and adds the following remark: — 'It will easily be perceived, that the only part of this Sonnet which is of any value, is the lines printed in italics; it is equally obvious, that except in the rhyme, and in the use of the single word "fruitless" for fruitlessly, which is so far a defect, the language of these lines does in no respect differ from that of prose.'

An idealist defending his system by the fact, that when asleep we often believe ourselves awake, was well answered by his plain neighbour, 'Ah, but when awake do we ever believe ourselves asleep?' —Things identical must be convertible. The preceding passage seems to rest on a similar sophism. For the question is not, whether there may not occur in prose an order of words, which would be equally proper in a poem; nor whether there are not beautiful lines and sentences of frequent occurrence in good poems, which would be equally becoming as well as beautiful in good prose; for neither the one nor the other has ever been either denied or doubted by any one. The true question must be, whether there are not modes of expression, a construction, and an order of sentences, which are in their fit and natural place in a serious prose composition, but would be disproportionate and heterogeneous in metrical poetry; and, vice versa, whether in the language of a serious poem there may not be an arrangement both of words and sentences, and a use and selection of (what are called) figures of speech, both as to their kind, their frequency, and their occasions, which on a subject of equal weight would be vicious and alien in correct and manly prose. I contend, that in both cases this unfitness of each for the place of the other frequently will and ought to exist.

And first from the origin of metre. This I would trace to the balance in the mind effected by that spontaneous effort which strives to hold in check the workings of passion. It might be easily explained likewise in what manner this salutary antagonism is assisted by the very state, which it counteracts; and how this balance of antagonists became organized into metre (in the usual acceptation of that term) by a supervening act of the will and judgment, consciously and for the foreseen purpose of pleasure. Assuming these principles, as the data of our argument, we deduce from them two legitimate conditions, which the critic is entitled to expect in every metrical work. First, that as the elements of metre owe their existence to a state of increased excitement, so the metre itself should be accompanied by the natural language of excitement. Secondly, that as these elements are formed into metre artificially, by a voluntary act, with the design and for the purpose of blending delight with emotion, so the traces of present volition should throughout the metrical language be proportionately discernible. Now these two conditions must be reconciled and co-present. There must be not only a partnership, but a union; an interpenetration of passion and of will, of spontaneous impulse and of voluntary purpose. Again, this union can be manifested only in a frequency of forms and figures of speech (originally the offspring of passion, but now the adopted children of power), greater than would be desired or endured, where the emotion is not voluntarily encouraged and kept up for the sake of that pleasure, which such emotion, so tempered and mastered by the will, is found capable of communicating. It not only dictates, but of itself tends to produce, a more frequent employment of picturesque and vivifying language, than would be natural in any other case, in which there did not exist, as there does in the present, a previous and well understood, though tacit, compact between the poet and his reader, that the latter is entitled to expect, and the former bound to supply this species and degree of pleasurable excitement. We may in some measure apply to this union the answer of Polixenes, in the Winter's Tale, to Perdita's neglect of the streaked gilly-flowers, because she had heard it said

> There is an art which, in their piedness shares
> With great creating nature.
>   POL: Say there be:
> Yet nature is made better by no mean,
> But nature makes that mean. So, ev'n that art,
> Which you say adds to nature, is an art,
> That nature makes. You see, sweet maid, we marry
> *A gentler scyon to the wildest stock:*
> And make conceive a bark of ruder kind
> By bud of nobler race. This is an art,
> Which does mend nature—change it rather; but
> The art itself is nature.

Secondly, I argue from the effects of metre. As far as metre acts in and for itself, it tends to increase the vivacity and susceptibility both of the general feelings and of the attention. This effect it produces by the continued excitement of surprise, and by the quick reciprocations of curiosity still gratified and still re-excited, which are too slight indeed to be at any one moment objects of distinct consciousness, yet become considerable in their aggregate influence. As a medicated atmosphere, or as wine during animated conversation, they act powerfully, though themselves unnoticed. Where, therefore, correspondent food and appropriate matter are not provided for the attention and feelings thus roused there must needs be a disappointment felt; like that of leaping in the dark from the last step of a staircase, when we had prepared our muscles for a leap of three or four.

The discussion on the powers of metre in the preface is highly ingenious and touches at all points on truth. But I cannot find any statement of its powers considered abstractly and separately. On the contrary Mr Wordsworth seems always to estimate metre by the powers, which it exerts during (and, as I think, in consequence of) its combination with other elements of poetry. Thus the previous difficulty is left unanswered, what the elements are, with which it must be combined, in order to produce its own effects to any pleasurable purpose. Double and trisyllable rhymes, indeed, form a lower species of wit, and, attended to exclusively for their own sake, may become a source of momentary amusement; as in poor Smart's distich to the Welsh Squire who had promised him a hare:

> Tell me thou son of great Cadwallader!
> Hast sent the hare? or hast thou swallow'd her?

But for any poetic purposes, metre resembles (if the aptness of the simile may excuse its meanness) yeast, worthless or disagreeable by itself, but giving vivacity and spirit to the liquor with which it is proportionally combined.

The reference to the 'Children in the Wood' by no means satisfies my judgment. We all willingly throw ourselves back for awhile into the feelings of our childhood. This ballad, therefore, we read under such recollections of our own childish feelings, as would equally endear to us poems, which Mr Wordsworth himself would regard as faulty in the opposite extreme of gaudy and technical ornament. Before the invention of printing, and in a still greater degree, before the introduction of writing, metre, especially alliterative metre, (whether alliterative at the beginning of the words, as in 'Pierce Plouman,' or at the end, as in rhymes) possessed an independent value as assisting the recollection, and consequently the preservation, of any series of truths or incidents. But I am not convinced by the collation of facts, that the 'Children in the Wood' owes either its preservation, or its popularity, to its metrical form. Mr Marshal's repository affords a number of tales in prose inferior in pathos and general merit, some of as old a date, and many as widely popular. Tom Hickathrift, Jack the Giant-killer, Goody Two-shoes, and Little Red Riding-hood are formidable rivals. And that they have continued in prose, cannot be fairly explained by the assumption, that the comparative meanness of their thoughts and images precluded even the humblest forms of metre. The scene of Goody Two-shoes in the church is perfectly susceptible of metrical narration; and, among the Θαύματα θαυμαστότατα [marvels most marvellous] even of the present age, I do not recollect a more astonishing image than that of the 'whole rookery, that flew out of the giant's beard,' scared by the tremendous voice, with which this monster answered the challenge of the heroic Tom Hickathrift!

If from these we turn to compositions universally, and independently of all early associations, beloved and admired; would the Maria, the Monk, or the Poor Man's Ass of Sterne, be read with more delight, or have a better chance of immortality, had they without any change in the diction been composed in rhyme, than in their present state? If I am not grossly mistaken, the general reply would be in the negative. Nay, I will confess, that, in Mr Wordsworth's own volumes, the Anecdote for Fathers, Simon Lee, Alice Fell, the Beggars, and the Sailor's Mother, notwithstanding the beauties which are to be found in each of them where the poet interposes the music of his own thoughts, would have been more delightful to me in prose, told and managed, as by Mr Wordsworth they would have been, in a moral essay or pedestrian tour.

Metre in itself is simply a stimulant of the attention, and therefore excites the question: Why is the attention to be thus stimulated? Now the question cannot be answered by the pleasure of the metre itself; for this we have shown to be conditional, and dependent on the appropriateness of the thoughts and expressions, to which the metrical form is superadded. Neither can I conceive any other answer that can be rationally given, short of this: I write in metre, because I am about to use a language different from that of prose. Besides, where the language is not such, how interesting soever the reflections are, that are capable of being drawn by a philosophic mind from the thoughts or incidents of the poem, the metre itself must often become feeble. Take the last three stanzas of the Sailor's Mother, for instance. If I could for a moment abstract from the effect produced on the author's feelings, as a man, by the incident at the time of its real occurrence, I would dare appeal to his own judgment, whether in the metre itself he found a sufficient reason for their being written metrically?

>And thus continuing, she said
>I had a son, who many a day
>Sailed on the seas; but he is dead;
>In Denmark he was cast away:
>And I have travelled far as Hull, to see
>What clothes he might have left, or other property.
>
>The bird and cage, they both were his;
>'Twas my son's bird; and neat and trim
>He kept it; many voyages
>This Singing bird hath gone with him;
>When last he sailed he left the bird behind;
>As it might be, perhaps, from bodings of his mind.
>
>He to a fellow-lodger's care
>Had left it, to be watched and fed,
>Till he came back again; and there
>I found it when my son was dead;
>And now, God help me for my little wit!
>I trail it with me, Sir! he took so much delight in it.

If disproportioning the emphasis we read these stanzas so as to make the rhymes perceptible, even trisyllable rhymes could scarcely produce an equal sense of oddity and strangeness, as we feel here in finding rhymes at all in sentences so exclusively colloquial. I would further ask whether, but for that visionary state, into which the figure of the woman and the susceptibility of his own genius had placed the poet's imagination (a state, which spreads its influence and colouring over all, that co-exists with the exciting cause, and in which 'The simplest, and the most familiar things / Gain a strange power of spreading awe around them')① I would ask the poet whether he would not have felt an abrupt downfall in these verses from the preceding stanza?

> The ancient spirit is not dead;
> Old times, thought I, are breathing there!
> Proud was I, that my country bred
> Such strength, a dignity so fair!
> She begged an alms, like one in poor estate;
> I looked at her again, nor did my pride abate.

It must not be omitted, and is besides worthy of notice, that those stanzas furnish the only fair instance that I have been able to discover in all Mr Wordsworth's writings, of an actual adoption, or true imitation, of the real and very language of low and rustic life, freed from provincialisms.

Thirdly, I deduce the position from all the causes elsewhere assigned,

---

① Altered from the description of Night-Mair in the Remorse.
> O Heaven! 'Twas frightful! Now run-down and stared at,
> By hideous shapes that cannot be remembered;
> Now seeing nothing and imagining nothing;
> But only being afraid—stifled with fear!
> While every goodly or familiar form
> Had a strange power of spreading terror round me.

NB. Though Shakespeare has for his own all-justifying purposes introduced the nightmare with her own foals, yet *mair* means a sister or perhaps a hag.

which render metre the proper form of poetry, and poetry imperfect and defective without metre. Metre, therefore, having been connected with poetry most often and by a peculiar fitness, whatever else is combined with metre must, though it be not itself essentially poetic, have nevertheless some property in common with poetry, as an intermedium of affinity, a sort (if I may dare borrow a well-known phrase from technical chemistry) of *mordant* between it and the superadded metre. Now poetry, Mr Wordsworth truly affirms, does always imply passion: which word must be here understood in its most general sense, as an excited state of the feelings and faculties. And as every passion has its proper pulse, so will it likewise have its characteristic modes of expression. But where there exists that degree of genius and talent which entitles a writer to aim at the honours of a poet, the very act of poetic composition itself is, and is allowed to imply and to produce, an unusual state of excitement, which of course justifies and demands a correspondent difference of language, as truly, though not perhaps in as marked a degree, as the excitement of love, fear, rage, or jealousy. The vividness of the descriptions or declamations in Donne or Dryden, is as much and as often derived from the force and fervour of the describer, as from the reflections, forms or incidents, which constitute their subject and materials. The wheels take fire from the mere rapidity of their motion. To what extent, and under what modifications, this may be admitted to act, I shall attempt to define in an after remark on Mr Wordsworth's reply to this objection, or rather on his objection to this reply, as already anticipated in his preface.

Fourthly, and as intimately connected with this, if not the same argument in a more general form, I adduce the high spiritual instinct of the human being impelling us to seek unity by harmonious adjustment, and thus establishing the principle that all the parts of an organized whole must be assimilated to the more important and essential parts. This and the preceding arguments may be strengthened by the reflection, that the composition of a poem is among the imitative arts; and that imitation, as opposed to copying, consists either in the interfusion of the same throughout the radically different, or of the different throughout a base radically the same.

Lastly, I appeal to the practice of the best poets, of all countries and in all ages, as authorizing the opinion, (deduced from all the foregoing) that in every import of the word essential, which would not here involve a mere truism, there may be, is, and ought to be, an *essential* difference between the language of prose and of metrical composition.

In Mr Wordsworth's criticism of Gray's Sonnet, the reader's sympathy with his praise or blame of the different parts is taken for granted rather perhaps too easily. He has not, at least, attempted to win or compel it by argumentative analysis. In my conception at least, the lines rejected as of no value do, with the exception of the two first, differ as much and as little from the language of common life, as those which he has printed in italics as possessing genuine excellence. Of the five lines thus honourably distinguished, two of them differ from prose even more widely, than the lines which either precede or follow, in the position of the words.

> *A different object do these eyes require;*
> My lonely anguish melts no heart but mine;
> *And in my breast the imperfect joys expire.*

But were it otherwise, what would this prove, but a truth, of which no man ever doubted? *Videlicet* [namely], that there are sentences, which would be equally in their place both in verse and prose. Assuredly it does not prove the point, which alone requires proof; namely, that there are not passages, which would suit the one and not suit the other. The first line of this sonnet is distinguished from the ordinary language of men by the epithet to morning. (For we will set aside, at present, the consideration, that the particular word 'smiling' is hackneyed, and, as it involves a sort of personification, not quite congruous with the common and material attribute of 'shining.') And, doubtless, this adjunction of epithets for the purpose of additional description, where no particular attention is demanded for the quality of the thing, would be noticed as giving a poetic cast to a man's conversation. Should the sportsman exclaim, 'Come boys! the rosy morning calls you up,' he will be supposed to have some song in his head. But no one suspects this, when he says, 'A wet morning shall not confine us to our beds.' This then is either a defect in poetry, or it is not. Whoever should decide in the affirmative, I would request him to re-peruse any one poem, of any confessedly great poet from Homer to Milton, or from Aeschylus to Shakespeare; and to strike out (in thought I mean) every instance of this kind. If the number of these fancied erasures did not startle him; or if he continued to deem the work improved by their total omission; he must advance reasons of no ordinary strength and evidence, reasons grounded in the essence of human nature. Otherwise, I should not hesitate to consider him as a man not so much proof against all authority, as dead to it.

The second line,

> And reddening Phoebus lifts his golden fire,

has indeed almost as many faults as words. But then it is a bad line, not because the language is distinct from that of prose; but because it conveys incongruous images; because it confounds the cause and the effect; the real thing with the personified representative of the thing; in short, because it differs from the language of good sense! That the 'Phoebus' is hackneyed, and a school-boy image, is an accidental fault, dependent on the age in which the author wrote, and not deduced from the nature of the thing. That it is part of an exploded mythology, is an objection more deeply grounded. Yet when the torch of ancient learning was rekindled, so cheering were its beams, that our eldest poets, cut off by Christianity from all accredited machinery, and deprived of all acknowledged guardians and symbols of the great objects of nature, were naturally induced to adopt, as a poetic language, those fabulous personages, those forms of the supernatural[1] in nature, which had given them such dear delight in the poems of their great masters. Nay, even at this day what scholar of genial taste will not so far sympathize with them, as to read with pleasure in Petrarch, Chaucer, or Spen-

---

[1] But still more by the mechanical system of philosophy which has needlessly infected our theological opinions, and teaching us to consider the world in its relation to God, as of a building to its mason, leaves the idea of omnipresence a mere abstract notion in the stateroom of our reason.

ser, what he would perhaps condemn as puerile in a modern poet?

I remember no poet, whose writings would safelier stand the test of Mr Wordsworth's theory, than Spenser. Yet will Mr Wordsworth say, that the style of the following stanza is either undistinguished from prose, and the language of ordinary life? Or that it is vicious, and that the stanzas are blots in the Faery Queen?

> By this the northern waggoner had set
> His sevenfold teme behind the stedfast starre,
> That was in ocean waves yet never wet,
> But firme is fixt and sendeth light from farre
> To all that in the wild deep wandering are.
> And chearfull chaunticleer with his note shrill
> Had warned once that Phoebus' fiery carre
> In haste was climbing up the easterne hill,
> Full envious that night so long his room did fill.
> *Book I. Can. 2. St. 2*

> At last the golden orientall gate
> Of greatest heaven gan to open fayre,
> And Phoebus fresh as brydegrome to his mate,
> Came daunceing forth, shaking his deawie hayre,
> And hurl'd his glist'ring beams through gloomy ayre:
> Which when the wakeful elfe perceived, streightway
> He started up, and did him selfe prepayre
> In sun-bright armes, and battailous array;
> For with that pagan proud he combat will that day.
> *Book I. Can. 5. St. 2*

On the contrary to how many passages, both in hymn books and in blank verse poems, could I (were it not invidious) direct the reader's attention, the style of which is most unpoetic, because, and only because, it is the style of prose? He will not suppose me capable of having in my mind such verses, as

> I put my hat upon my head
> And walk'd into the strand;
> And there I met another man,
> Whose hat was in his hand.

To such specimens it would indeed be a fair and full reply, that these lines are not bad, because they are unpoetic; but because they are empty of all sense and feeling; and that it were an idle attempt to prove that an ape is not a Newton, when it is evident that he is not a man. But the sense shall be good and weighty, the language correct and dignified, the subject interesting and treated with feeling; and yet the style shall, notwithstanding all these merits, be justly blamable as prosaic, and solely because the words and the order of the words would find their appropriate place in prose, but are not suitable to metrical composition. The 'Civil Wars' of Daniel is an instructive, and even interesting work; but take the following stanzas (and from the hundred instances which abound I might probably have selected others far more striking):

> And to the end we may with better ease
> Discern the true discourse, vouchsafe to shew
> What were the times foregoing near to these,
> That these we may with better profit know.
> Tell how the world fell into this disease;
> And how so great distemperature did grow;
> So shall we see with what degrees it came;
> How things at full do soon wax out of frame.
>
> Ten kings had from the Norman Conqu'ror reign'd
> With intermix'd and variable fate,
> When England to her greatest height attain'd

> Of power, dominion, glory, wealth, and state;
> After it had with much ado sustain'd
> The violence of princes with debate
> For titles, and the often mutinies
> Of nobles for their ancient liberties.
>
> For first the Norman, conqu'ring all by might,
> By might was forc'd to keep what he had got;
> Mixing our customs and the form of right
> With foreign constitutions, he had brought;
> Mast'ring the mighty, humbling the poorer wight,
> By all severest means that could be wrought;
> And, making the succession doubtful, rent
> His new-got state and left it turbulent.
>
> B. I. St. VII, VIII, and IX

Will it be contended on the one side, that these lines are mean and senseless? Or on the other, that they are not prosaic, and for that reason unpoetic? This poet's well-merited epithet is that of the 'well-languaged Daniel'; but likewise, and by the consent of his contemporaries no less than of all succeeding critics, 'the prosaic Daniel.' Yet those, who thus designate this wise and amiable writer from the frequent incorrespondency of his diction to his metre in the majority of his compositions, not only deem them valuable and interesting on other accounts; but willingly admit, that there are to be found throughout his poems, and especially in his *Epistles* and in his *Hymen's Triumph*, many and exquisite specimens of that style which, as the neutral ground of prose and verse, is common to both. A fine and almost faultless extract, eminent as for other beauties, so for its perfection in this species of diction, may be seen in Lamb's Dramatic Specimens, etc. a work of various interest from the nature of the selections themselves (all from the plays of Shakespeare's contemporaries) and deriving a high additional value from the notes, which are full of just and original criticism, expressed with all the freshness of originality.

Among the possible effects of practical adherence to a theory, that aims to identify the style of prose and verse (if it does not indeed claim for the latter a yet nearer resemblance to the average style of men in the viva voce intercourse of real life) we might anticipate the following as not the least likely to occur. It will happen, as I have indeed before observed, that the metre itself, the sole acknowledged difference, will occasionally become metre to the eye only. The existence of prosaisms, and that they detract from the merit of a poem, must at length be conceded, when a number of successive lines can be rendered, even to the most delicate ear, unrecognizable as verse, or as having even been intended for verse, by simply transcribing them as prose; when if the poem be in blank verse, this can be effected without any alteration, or at most by merely restoring one or two words to their proper places, from which they have been transplanted① for no assignable cause or reason but that of the

---

① As the ingenious gentleman under the influence of the Tragic Muse contrived to dislocate, 'I wish you a good morning, Sir! Thank you, Sir, and I wish you the same,' into two blank verse heroics: —
    To you a morning good, good Sir! I wish.
    You, Sir! I thank: to you the same wish I.

In those parts of Mr Wordsworth's works which I have thoroughly studied, I find fewer instances in which this would be practical than I have met in many poems, where an approximation of prose has been sedulously and on system guarded against. Indeed excepting the stanzas already quoted from the *Sailor's Mother*, I can recollect but one instance: viz. a short passage of four or five lines in The Brothers, that model of English pastoral, which I never yet read with unclouded eye. —'James, pointing to its summit, over which they had all purposed to return together, informed them that he would wait for them there. They parted, and his comrades passed that way some two hours after, but they did not find him at the appointed place, a *circumstance of which they took no heed*: but one of them going by chance into the house, which at this time was James's house, leart *there*, that nobody had seen him all that day.' The only change which has been made is in the position of the little word *there* in two instances, the position in the original being clearly such as is not adopted in ordinary conversation. The other words printed in italics were so marked because, though good and genuine English, they are not the phraseology of common conversation either in the word put in apposition, or in the connection by the genitive pronoun. Men in general would have said, 'but that was a circumstance they paid no attention to, or took no notice of,' and the language is, on the theory of the preface, jutisfied only by the narrator's being the Vicar. Yet if any ear could suspect, that these sentences were ever printed as metre, on those revy words alone could the suspicion have been grounded.

author's convenience; but if it be in rhyme, by the mere exchange of the final word of each line for some other of the same meaning, equally appropriate, dignified and euphonic.

The answer or objection in the preface to the anticipated remark 'that metre paves the way to other distinctions,' is contained in the following words. 'The distinction of rhyme and metre is regular and uniform, and not, like that produced by (what is usually called) poetic diction, arbitrary, and subject to infinite caprices, upon which no calculation whatever can be made. In the one case the reader is utterly at the mercy of the poet respecting what imagery or diction he may choose to connect with the passion.' But is this a poet, of whom a poet is speaking? No surely! rather of a fool or madman: or at best of a vain or ignorant phantast! And might not brains so wild and so deficient make just the same havoc with rhymes and metres, as they are supposed to effect with modes and figures of speech? How is the reader at the mercy of such men? If he continue to read their nonsense, is it not his own fault? The ultimate end of criticism is much more to establish the principles of writing, than to furnish rules how to pass judgment on what has been written by others; if indeed it were possible that the two could be separated. But if it be asked, by what principles the poet is to regulate his own style, if he do not adhere closely to the sort and order of words which he hears in the market, wake, high-road, or plough-field? I reply; by principles, the ignorance or neglect of which would convict him of being no poet, but a silly or presumptuous usurper of the name. By the principles of grammar, logic, psychology. In one word by such a knowledge of the facts, material and spiritual, that most appertain to his art, as, if it have been governed and applied by good sense, and rendered instinctive by habit, becomes the representative and reward of our past conscious reasonings, insights, and conclusions, and acquires the name of Taste. By what rule that does not leave the reader at the poet's mercy, and the poet at his own, is the latter to distinguish between the language suitable to suppressed, and the language, which is characteristic of indulged, anger? Or between that of rage and that of jealousy? Is it obtained by wandering about in search of angry or jealous people in uncultivated society, in order to copy their words? Or not far rather by the power of imagination proceeding upon the *all in each* of human nature? By meditation, rather than by observation? And by the latter in consequence only of the former? As eyes, for which the former has pre-determined their field of vision, and to which, as to its organ, it communicates a microscopic power? There is not, I firmly believe, a man now living, who has, from his own inward experience, a clearer intuition, than Mr Wordsworth himself, that the last mentioned are the true sources of genial discrimination. Through the same process and by the same creative agency will the poet distinguish the degree and kind of the excitement produced by the very act of poetic composition. As intuitively will he know, what differences of style it at once inspires and justifies; what intermixture of conscious volition is natural to that state; and in what instances such figures and colours of speech degenerate into mere creatures of an arbitrary purpose, cold technical artifices of ornament or connection. For, even as truth is its own light and evidence, discovering at once itself and falsehood, so is it the prerogative of poetic genius to distinguish by parental instinct its proper offspring from the changelings, which the gnomes of vanity or the fairies of fashion may have laid in its cradle or called by its names. Could a rule be given from without, poetry would cease to be poetry, and sink into a mechanical art. It would be μορφωσις [shaping], not ποιησσι [creating]. The rules of the Imagination are themselves the very powers of growth and production. The words to which they are reducible, present only the outlines and external appearance of the fruit. A deceptive counterfeit of the superficial form and colours may be elaborated; but the marble peach feels cold and heavy, and children only put it to their mouths. We find no difficulty in admitting as excellent, and the legitimate language of poetic fervour self-impassioned, Donne's apostrophe to the Sun in the second stanza of his 'Progress of the Soul.'

> Thee, eye of heaven! this great soul envies not;
> By thy male force is all, we have, begot.
> In the first East thou now beginn'st to shine,
> Suck'st early balm and island spices there,
> And wilt anon in thy loose-rein'd career
> At Tagus, Po, Seine, Thames, and Danow dine,

> And see at night this western world of mine:
> Yet hast thou not more nations seen than she,
> Who before thee one day began to be,
> And, thy frail light being quench'd, shall long, long outlive thee!

Or the next stanza but one:

> Great Destiny, the commissary of God,
> That hast marked out a path and period
> For ev'ry thing! Who, where we offspring took,
> Our ways and ends see'st at one instant: thou
> Knot of all causes! Thou, whose changeless brow
> Ne'er smiles nor frowns! O! vouchsafe thou to look,
> And shew my story in thy eternal book, etc.

As little difficulty do we find in excluding from the honours of unaffected warmth and elevation the madness prepense of pseudopoesy, or the startling hysteric of weakness over-exerting itself, which bursts on the unprepared reader in sundry odes and apostrophes to abstract terms. Such are the Odes to Jealousy, to Hope, to Oblivion, and the like, in Dodsley's collection and the magazines of that day, which seldom fail to remind me of an Oxford copy of verses on the two Suttons, commencing with

> Inoculation, heavenly maid! descend!

It is not to be denied that men of undoubted talents, and even poets of true, though not of first-rate, genius, have from a mistaken theory deluded both themselves and others in the opposite extreme. I once read to a company of sensible and well-educated women the introductory period of Cowley's preface to his 'Pindaric Odes, written in imitation of the style and manner of the odes of Pindar.' 'If (says Cowley) a man should undertake to translate Pindar, word for word, it would be thought that one madman had translated another as may appear, when he, that understands not the original, reads the verbal traduction of him into Latin prose, than which nothing seems more raving.' I then proceeded with his own free version of the second Olympic, composed for the charitable purpose of rationalizing the Theban Eagle.

> Queen of all harmonious things,
> Dancing words and speaking strings,
> What God, what hero, wilt thou sing?
> What happy man to equal glories bring?
> Begin, begin thy noble choice,
> And let the hills around reflect the image of thy voice.
> Pisa does to Jove belong,
> Jove and Pisa claim thy song.
> The fair first-fruits of war, th' Olympic games,
> Alcides offer'd up to Jove;
> Alcides too thy strings may move!
> But oh! what man to join with these can worthy prove?
> Join Theron boldly to their sacred names;
> Theron the next honour claims;
> Theron to no man gives place,
> Is first in Pisa's and in Virtue's race;
> Theron there, and he alone,
> Ev'n his own swift forefathers has outgone.

One of the company exclaimed, with the full assent of the rest, that if the original were madder than this, it must be incurably mad. I then translated the ode from the Greek, and as nearly as possible, word for word; and the impression was, that in the general movement of the periods, in the form of the connections and transitions, and in the sober majesty of lofty sense, it appeared to them to approach more nearly, than any other poetry they had heard, to the style of our Bible, in the prophetic books. The first strophe will suffice as a specimen:

> Ye harp-controlling hymns! (or) ye hymns the sovereigns of harps!
> What God? what Hero?
> What Man shall we celebrate?
> Truly Pisa indeed is of Jove,
> But the Olympiad (or the Olympic games) did Hercules establish,
> The first-fruits of the spoils of war.
> But Theron for the four-horsed car,
> That bore victory to him,
> It behoves us now to voice aloud:
> The Just, the Hospitable,
> The Bulwark of Agrigentum,
> Of renowned fathers
> The Flower, even him
> Who preserves his native city erect and safe.

But are such rhetorical caprices condemnable only for their deviation from the language of real life? and are they by no other means to be precluded, but by the rejection of all distinctions between prose and verse, save that of metre? Surely good sense, and a moderate insight into the constitution of the human mind, would be amply sufficient to prove, that such language and such combinations are the native product neither of the fancy nor of the imagination; that their operation consists in the excitement of surprise by the juxtaposition and apparent reconciliation of widely different or incompatible things. As when, for instance, the hills are made to reflect the image of a voice. Surely, no unusual taste is requisite to see clearly, that this compulsory juxtaposition is not produced by the presentation of impressive or delightful forms to the inward vision, nor by any sympathy with the modifying powers with which the genius of the poet had united and inspirited all the objects of his thought; that it is therefore a species of wit, a pure work of the will, and implies a leisure and self-possession both of thought and of feeling, incompatible with the steady fervour of a mind possessed and filled with the grandeur of its subject. To sum up the whole in one sentence. When a poem, or a part of a poem, shall be adduced, which is evidently vicious in the figures and contexture of its style, yet for the condemnation of which no reason can be assigned, except that it differs from the style in which men actually converse, then, and not till then, can I hold this theory to be either plausible, or practicable, or capable of furnishing either rule, guidance, or precaution, that might not, more easily and more safely, as well as more naturally, have been deduced in the author's own mind from considerations of grammar, logic, and the truth and nature of things, confirmed by the authority of works, whose fame is not of one country, nor of one age.

On the Principles of Genial Criticism (Essay Third)

I proceed to my promised and more amusing task, that of establishing, illustrating, and exemplifying the distinct powers of the different modes of pleasure excited by the works of nature or of human genius with their exponent and appropriable terms....

Agreeable

We use this word in two senses; in the first for whatever agrees with our nature, for that which is congruous with the primary constitution of our senses. Thus green is naturally agreeable to the eye. In this sense the word expresses, at least involves, a pre-established harmony between the organs and their appointed objects. In the second sense, we convey by the word *agreeable*, that the thing has by force of habit (thence called a second nature) been made to agree with us; or that it has become agreeable to us by its recalling to our minds some one or more things that were dear and pleasing to us; or lastly, on account of some after pleasure or advantage, of which it has been the constant cause or occasion. Thus by force of custom men *make* the taste of tobacco, which was at first hateful to the palate, agreeable to them; thus too, as our Shakespeare observes, 'things base and vile, holding no quality, / Love can transpose to form and dignity—' ① the crutch that had supported a revered parent, after the first anguish of regret, becomes agreeable to the affectionate child; and I once knew a very sensible and accomplished Dutch gentleman, who, spite of his own sense of the ludicrous nature of the feeling, was more delighted by the first grand concert of frogs he heard on this country, than he had been by Catalina singing in the compositions of Cimarosa. The last clause needs no illustrations, as it comprises all the objects that are agreeable to us, only because they are the means by which we gratify our smell, touch, palate, and mere bodily feeling.

Beautiful

The beautiful, contemplated in its essential, that is, in *kind* and not in *degree*, is that in which the *many*, still seen as many, becomes one. Take a familiar instance, one of a thousand sand. The frost on a windowpane has by accident crystallized into a striking resemblance of a tree or a seaweed. With what pleasure we trace the parts, and their relations to each other, and to the whole! Here is the stalk or trunk, and here the branches or sprays—sometimes even the buds or flowers, nor will our pleasure be less, should the caprice of the crystallization represent some object disagreeable to us, provided only we can see or fancy the component parts each in relation to each, and all forming a whole. A lady would see an admirably painted tiger with pleasure, and at once pronounce it beautiful—nay, and owl, a frog, or a toad, who would have shrieked or shuddered at the sight of the things themselves. So far is the beautiful from depending wholly on association, that it is frequently produced by the mere removal of associations. Many a sincere convert to the beauty of various insects, as of the dragonfly, the fangless snake, &c., has natural history made, by exploding the terror or aversion that had been connected with them.

The most general definition of beauty, therefore, is—that I may fulfil my threat of plaguing my readers with hard words—multeity in unity. Now it will

---

① Midsummer Night's Dream, I, i. 232-33. Coleridge substitutes 'quality' for 'quantity'—editor's note.

be always found, that whatever is the definition of the *kind*, independent of degree, becomes likewise the definition of the highest degree of that kind. An old coach wheel lies in the coachmaker's yard, disfigured with tar and dirt (I purposely take the most trivial instances)—if I turn away my attention from these, and regard the *figure* abstractly, 'still, ' I might say to my companion, 'there is beauty in that wheel, and you yourself would not only admit, but would feel it, had you never seen a wheel before. See how the rays proceed from the centre to the circumstances, and how many different images are distinctly comprehended at one glance, as forming one whole, and each part in some harmonious relation to each and to all. ' But imagine the polished golden wheel of the chariot of the sun, as the poets have described it: then the figure, and the real thing so figured, exactly coincide. There is nothing heterogeneous, nothing to abstract from: by its perfect smoothness and circularity in width, each part is (if I may borrow a metaphor from a sister sense) as perfect a melody, as the whole is a complete harmony. This, we should say, is beautiful throughout. Of all 'the many, ' which I actually see, each and all are really reconciled into unity: while the effulgence from the whole coincides with, and seems to represent, the effluence of delight form my own mind in the intuition of it.

It seems evident then, first, that beauty is harmony, and subsists only in composition, and secondly, that the first species of the agreeable can alone be a component part of the beautiful, that namely which is naturally consonant with our senses by the pre-established harmony between nature and the human mind; and thirdly, that even of this species, those objects only can be admitted (according to rule the first) which belong to the eye and ear, because they alone are susceptible of distinction of parts. Should an Englishman gazing on a mass of cloud rich with the rays of the rising sun exclaim, even without distinction of, or reference to its form, or its relation to other objects, 'How beautiful! ' I should have no quarrel with him, first, because by the law of association there is in all visual beholdings at least an indistinct subsumption of form and relation; and, secondly, because even in the coincidence between the sight and the object there is an approximation to the reduction of the many into one. But who, that heard a Frenchman call the flavour of a leg of mutton a beautiful taste would not immediately recognize him for a Frenchman, even though there should be neither grimace or characteristic nasal twang? The result, then, of the whole is that the shapely (i. e. *formosus*) joined with the naturally agreeable, constitutes what, speaking accurately, we mean by the word beautiful (i. e. *pulcher*).

But we are conscious of faculties far superior to the highest impressions of sense; we have life and free will. —What then will be the result, when the beautiful, arising from regular form, is so modified by the perception of life and spontaneous action, as that the latter only shall be the object of our conscious *perception*, while the former merely acts, and yet does effectively act, on our feelings? With pride and pleasure I reply by referring my reader to the group in Mr Allson's grand picture of the *Dead Man Reviving from the Touch of the Bone of the Prophet Elisha*, beginning with the slave at the head of the reviving body, then proceeding to the daughter clasping her swooning mother; to the mother, the wife of the reviving man; then to the soldier behind who supports her; to the two figures eagerly conversing: and lastly, to the exquisitely graceful girl who is behind downward, and whose hand nearly touches the thumb of the slave! You will find, what you had not suspected, that you have here before you a circular group. But by what variety of life, motion, and passion is all the stiffness, that would result from an obvious regular figure swallowed up, and the figure of the group as much concealed by the action and passion, as the skeleton, which gives the form of the human body, is hidden by the flesh and its endless outlines!

In Raphael's admirable *Galatea* (the print of which is doubtless familiar to most of my readers) the circle is perceived at first sight; but with what multiplicity of rays and chords within the area of the circular group, with what elevations and depressions of the circumference, with what an endless variety and sportive wildness in the component figure, and in the junctions of the figures, in the balance, the perfect reconciliation, effected between these two conflicting principles of the free life, and of the confining form! How entirely is the stiffness that would have resulted from the obvious regularity of the later, *fused* and (if I may hazard so bold a metaphor) almost *volatilized* by the interpenetration and electrical flashes of the former.

But I shall recur to this consummate work for more specific illustrations hereafter: and have indeed in some measure offended already against the laws of method, by anticipating materials which rather belong to a more advanced stage of the disquisition. It is time to recapitulate, as briefly as possible, the arguments already advanced, and having summed up the result, to leave behind me this, the only portion of these essays, which, as far as the subject itself is concerned, will demand any *effort* of attention from a reflecting and intelligent reader. And let me be permitted to remind him, that the distinctions, which it is my object to prove and elucidate, have not merely a foundation in nature and the noblest faculties of human mind, but are likewise the very groundwork, nay, an indispensable condition, of all *rational* inquiry concerning the arts. For it is self-evident, that whatever may be judged of differently by different persons, in the very same degree of moral and intellectual cultivation, extolled by one and condemned by another, without any error being assignable to either, can never be an object of general principles: and *vice versa*, that whatever can be brought to the test of general principles presupposes a distinct origin from these pleasures and tastes, which, for the wisest purposes, are made to depend on local and transitory fashions, accidental associations, and the peculiarities of individual temperament: to all which the philosopher, equally with the well-bred man of the world, applies the old adage, *de gustibus non est disputandum* [there is no disputing taste]. Be it, however, observed that *de gustibus* is by no means the same as *de gustu*, nor will it escape the scholar's recollection, that taste, in its metaphorical use, was first adopted by the Romans, and unknown to the less luxurious Greeks, who designed this faculty, sometimes by the word αἴσθησις, and sometimes by Φιλοκαλία—ἀνδρῶν τῶν καο' ἡμᾶς Φιλοκαλώτατος γεγονώς—i. e. 'endowed by nature with the most exquisite taste of any man of our age,' says Porphyry of his friend, Castricius. Still, this metaphor, borrowed from the pregustatores of the old Roman banquets, is singularly happy and appropriate. In the palate, the perception of the object and its qualities is involved in the *sensation*, in the mental taste it is involved in the *sense*. We have a *sensation* of sweetness, in a healthy palate, from honey; a *sense* of beauty, in an uncorrupted taste, from the view of the rising or setting sun.

Samuel Taylor Coleridge

Recapitulation

Principle the First

That which has become, or which has been made agreeable to us, from causes not contained in its own name, or in its original conformity to the human organs and faculties; that which is not pleasing for its own sake, but by connection or association with some other thing, separate or separable from it, is neither *beautiful*, nor capable of being a component part of beauty: though it may greatly increase the sum of our pleasure, when it does not interfere with the beauty of the object, nay, even when it detracts from it. A moss rose, with a spring of myrtle and jasmine, is not more beautiful from having been plucked from the garden, or presented to us by the hand of the woman we love, but is abundantly more delightful. The total pleasure received from one of Mr Bird's finest pictures may, without any impeachment of our taste, be the greater from his having introduced into it the portrait of one of our friends, or from our pride in him as our townsman, or from our knowledge of his personal qualities; but the amiable artist would rightly consider it a coarse compliment, were it affirmed, that the *beauty* of the piece, or its merit as a work of genius, was the more perfect on this account. I am conscious that I look with a stronger and more pleasurable emotion at Mr Allston's large landscape, in the spirit of Swiss scenery, from its having been the occasion of my first acquaintance with him in Rome. This may or may not be a compliment to *him*; but the true compliment to the picture was made by a lady of high rank and cultivated taste, who declared, in my hearing, that she never stood before that landscape without seeming to feel the breeze blow out it upon her. But the most striking instance is afforded by the portrait of a departed or absent friend or parent; which is endeared to us, and more delightful, from some awkward position of the limbs, which had defied the contrivances of art to render it picturesque, but which was the characteristic habit of the original.

Principle the Second

That which is naturally agreeable and consonant to human nature, so that the exceptions may be attributed to disease or defect; that, the pleasure from which is contained in the immediate impression; cannot, indeed, with strict propriety, be called beautiful, exclusive of its relations, but one among the component parts of beauty, in whatever instance it is susceptible of existing as a part of whole. This, of course, excludes the mere objects of the taste, smell, and feeling, though the sensation from these, especially from the latter when organized into touch, may secretly, and without our consciousness, enrich and vivify the perceptions and images of the eye and ear, which alone are true organs of sense, their sensations in a healthy or uninjured state being too faint to be noticed by the mind. We may, indeed, in common conversation, call purple a beautiful colour, or the tone of a single note on an excellent pianoforte a beautiful tone; but if we were questioned, we should agree that a rich or delightful colour, a rich, or sweet, or clear tone; would have been more appropriate—and this with less hesitation in the latter instance than in the former, because the single tone is more manifestly of the nature of a *sensation*, while colour is the medium which seems to blend sensation and perception, so as to hide, as it were, the former in the latter; the direct opposite of which takes place in the lower senses of feeling, smell, and taste. (In strictness, there is even in these an ascending scale. The smell is less sensual and more sentient than mere feeling, the taste than the smell, and the eye than the ear: but between the ear and the taste exists the chasm or break, which divides the beautiful and the elements of beauty from the merely agreeable.) When I reflect on the manner in which smoothness, richness of sound, &c., enter into the formation of the beautiful, I am induced to suspect that they act negatively rather than positively. Something there must be to realize the form, something in and by which the *forma informans* [shaping form] reveals itself: and these, less than any that could be substituted, and in the least possible degree, distract the attention, in the least possible degree obscure the idea, of which they (composed into outline and surface) are the symbol. All illustrative hint may be taken from a pure crystal, as compared with an opaque, semiopaque or clouded mass, on the other hand, and with a perfectly transparent body, such as the air, on the other. The crystal is lost in the light, which yet it contains, embodies, and gives a shape to; but which passes shapeless through the air, and, in the ruder body, is either quenched or dissipated.

Principle the Third

The safest definition, then, of beauty, as well as the oldest, is that of Pythagoras: the reduction of many to one—or, as finely expressed by the sublime discipline of Ammonius, τὸ ἀμερες ὄν, ἐν πολλο ἰξ Φανταζόμενον, of which the following may be offered as both paraphrase and corollary. *The sense of beauty subsists in simultaneous intuition of the relation of parts, each to each, and of all to a whole: exciting an immediate and absolute complacency, without intervenence, therefore, of any interest, sensual or intellectual.* The beautiful is thus at once distinguished both from the agreeable, which is beneath it, and from the good, which is above it: for both these have an interest necessarily attached to them: both act on the will, and excite a desire for the actual existence of the image or idea contemplated: while the sense of beauty rests gratified in the mere contemplation or intuition, regardless whether it be a fictitious Apollo, or a real Antinous.

The Mystics meant the same, when they define beauty as the subjection of matter to spirit so as to be transformed into a symbol, in and through which the spirit reveals itself; and declare *that* the *most* beautiful, where the most obstacles to a full manifestation have been most perfectly overcome.

Scholium

We have sufficiently distinguished the beautiful from the agreeable, by the sure criterion, that, when we find an object agreeable, the *sensation* of pleasure always precedes the judgement, and is its determining cause. We *find* it agreeable. But when we declare an object beautiful, the contemplation or intuition of its beauty precedes the *feeling* of complacency, in order of nature at least: nay, in great depression of spirits may even exist without sensibly producing it.

> A grief without a pang, void, dark, and drear!
> A stifled, drowsy, unimpassioned grief,
>   That finds no natural outlet, no relief,
>   In word, or sigh, or tear!
> O dearest lady! in this heartless mood,
> To other thoughts by yon sweet throstle wooed!
> All this long eve, so balmy and serene,
> Have I been gazing at the western sky.[1]

Now the least reflection convinces us that our sensations, whether of pleasure or of pain, are the incommunicable parts of our nature; such as can be reduced to no universal rule; and in which therefore we have no right to expect that others should agree with us, or to blame them for disagreement. That the Greenlander prefers train oil to olive oil, and even to wine, we explain at once by our knowledge of the climate and productions to which he has been habituated. Were the man as enlightened as Plato, his palate would still find that most agreeable to which it had been most accustomed. But when the Iroquois sachem, after having been led to the most perfect specimens of architecture in Paris, said that he saw nothing so beautiful as the cook's shops, we attribute this without hesitation to savagery of intellect, and infer with certainty that the sense of the beautiful was either altogether dormant in his mind, or at best very imperfect. The beautiful, therefore, not originating in the sensations, must belong to the intellect: and therefore we *declare* an object beautiful, and feel an inward right to *expect* that others should coincide with us. But we feel no right to *demand* it: and this leads us to that, which hitherto we have barely touched upon, and which we shall now attempt to illustrate more fully, namely, to the distinction of the beautiful

---

[1] From Stanza 2 of Coleridge's *Dejection: An Ode*—editor's note.

from the good.

Let us suppose Milton in company with some stern and prejudiced Puritan, contemplating the front of York Cathedral, and at length expressing his admiration of its beauty. We will suppose it too at that time of his life, when his religious opinions, feelings, and prejudices most nearly coincided with those of the rigid antiprelatists. P.: Beauty; I am sure, it is not the beauty of holiness. M.: True; but yet it is beautiful. P.: It delights not me. What is it good for? Is it of any use but to be stared at? M.: Perhaps not! But still it is beautiful. P.: But call to mind the pride and wanton vanity of those cruel shavelings, that wasted the labour and substance of so many thousand poor creatures in the erection of this haughty pile. M.: I do. But still it is very beautiful. P.: Think how many score of places of worship, incomparably better suited both for prayer and preaching, and how many faithful ministers might have been maintained, to the blessing of tens of thousands, to them and their children's children, with the treasures lavished on this worthless mass of stone and cement. M.: Too true! But nevertheless it is *very* beautiful. P.: And it is not merely useless; but it feeds the pride of the prelates, and keeps alive the popish and carnal spirit among the people. M.: Even so! And I presume not to question the wisdom, nor detract from the pious zeal, of the first reformers of Scotland, who for these reasons destroyed so many fabrics, scarce inferior in beauty to this now before our eyes. But I did not call it *good*, nor have I told thee, brother! that if this were levelled with the ground, and existed only in the works of the modeller or engraver, that I should desire to reconstruct it. The good consists in the congruity of a thing with the laws of the reason and the nature of the will, and in its fitness to determine the latter to actualize the former: and it is always discursive. The beautiful arises from the perceived harmony of an object, whether sight or sound, with the inborn and constitutive rules of the judgement and imagination: and it is always intuitive. As light to the eye, even such is beauty to the mind, which cannot but have complacency in whatever is perceived as preconfigured to its living faculties. Hence the Greeks called a beautiful object καλόν quasi καλοῦν, i. e. *calling on* the soul, which receives instantly, and welcomes it as something connatural.

Thomas Love Peacock

The Four Ages of Poetry (1820)

*Qui inter haec nutriuntur non magis sapere possunt,
quam bene olere qui in culina habitant.*
PETRONIUS[1]

POETRY, like the world, may be said to have four ages, but in a different order: the first age of poetry being the age of iron; the second, of gold; the third, of silver; and the fourth, of brass.

The first, or iron age of poetry, is that in which rude bards celebrate in rough numbers the exploits of ruder chiefs, in days when every man is a warrior, and when the great practical maxim of every form of society, 'to keep what we have and to catch what we can,' is not yet disguised under names of justice and forms of law, but is the naked motto of the naked sword, which is the only judge and jury in every question of *meum* and *tuum*.[2] In these days, the only three trades flourishing (besides that of priest which flourishes always) are those of king, thief, and beggar: the beggar being for the most part a king deject, and the thief a king expectant. The first question asked of a stranger is, whether he is a beggar or a thief:[3] The stranger, in reply, usually assumes the first, and awaits a convenient opportunity to prove his claim to the second appellation.

The natural desire of every man to engross to himself as much power and

---

[1] T. Petronius Arbiter, *Satyricon*, II. 'They who are fed on these things can no more be wise than those who dwell in the kitchen can be fragrant.'
[2] 'mine' and 'yours' —editor's note.
[3] See the *Odyssey,* passim: and Thucydides, *History*, I. 5—editor's note.

property as he can acquire by any of the means which might makes right, is accompanied by the no less natural desire of making known to as many people as possible the extent to which he has been a winner in this universal game. The successful warrior becomes a chief; the successful chief becomes a king: his next want is an organ to disseminate the fame of his achievements and the extent of his possessions; and this organ he finds in a bard, who is always ready to celebrate the strength of his arm, being first duly inspired by that of his liquor. This is the origin of poetry, which, like all other trades, takes its rise in the demand for the commodity, and flourishes in proportion to the extent of the market.

Poetry is thus in its origin panegyrical. The first rude songs of all nations appear to be a sort of brief historical notices, in a strain of tumid hyperbole, of the exploits and possessions of a few pre-eminent individuals. They tell us how many battles such a one has fought, how many helmets he has cleft, how many breastplates he has pierced, how many widows he has made, how much land he has appropriated, how many houses he has demolished for other people, what a large one he has built for himself, how much gold he has stowed away in it, and how liberally and plentifully he pays, feeds, and intoxicates the divine and immortal bards, the sons of Jupiter, but for whose everlasting songs the names of heroes would perish.

This is the first stage of poetry before the invention of written letters. The numerical modulation is at once useful as a help to memory, and pleasant to the ears of uncultured men, who are easily caught by sound: and from the exceeding flexibility of the yet unformed language, the poet does no violence to his ideas in subjecting them to the fetters of number. The savage indeed lisps in numbers, and all rude and uncivilized people express themselves in the manner which we call poetical.

The scenery by which he is surrounded, and the superstitions which are the creed of his age, form the poet's mind. Rocks, mountains, seas, unsubdued forests, unnavigable rivers, surround him with forms of power and mystery, which ignorance and fear have peopled with spirits, under multifarious names of gods, goddesses, nymphs, genii, and daemons. Of all these personages marvellous tales are in existence: the nymphs are not indifferent to handsome young men, and the gentlemen-genii are much troubled and very troublesome with a propensity to be rude to pretty maidens: the bard therefore finds no difficulty in tracing the genealogy of his chief to any of the deities in his neighbourhood with whom the said chief may be most desirous of claiming relationship.

In this pursuit, as in all others, some of course will attain a very marked pre-eminence; and these will be held in high honour, like Demodocus in the *Odyssey*, and will be consequently inflated with boundless vanity, like Thamyris in the *Iliad*. Poets are as yet the only historians and chroniclers of their time, and the sole depositories of all the knowledge of their age; and though this knowledge is rather a crude congeries of traditional phantasies than a collection of useful truths, yet, such as it is, they have it to themselves. They are observing and thinking, while others are robbing and fighting: and though their object be nothing more than to secure a share of the spoil, yet they accomplish this end by intellectual, not by physical, power: their success excites emulation to the attainment of intellectual eminence: thus they sharpen their own wits and awaken those of others, at the same time that they gratify vanity and amuse curiosity. A skilful display of the little knowledge they have gains them credit for the possession of much more which they have not. Their familiarity with the secret history of gods and genii obtains for them, without much difficulty, the reputation of inspiration; thus they are not only historians but theologians, moralists, and legislators: delivering their oracles ex cathedra, and being indeed often themselves (as Orpheus and Amphion) regarded as portions and emanations of divinity: building cities with a song, and leading brutes with a symphony; which are only metaphors for the faculty of leading multitudes by the nose.

The golden age of poetry finds its materials in the age of iron. This age begins when poetry begins to be retrospective; when something like a more extended system of civil polity is established; when personal strength and courage avail less to the aggrandizing of their possessor and to the making and marring of kings and kingdoms, and are checked by organized bodies, social institutions, and hereditary successions. Men also live more in the light of truth and within the interchange of observation; and thus perceive that the agency of gods and genii is not so frequent among themselves as, to judge from the songs and legends of the past time, it was among their ancestors. From these two circumstances, really diminished personal power, and apparently diminished familiarity with gods and genii, they very easily and naturally deduce two conclusions: 1st, that men are degenerated, and 2nd, that they are less in favour with the gods. The people of the petty states and colonies, which have now acquired stability and form, which owed their origin and first prosperity to the talents and courage of a single chief, magnify their founder through the mists of distance and tradition, and perceive him achieving wonders with a god or goddess always at his elbow. They find his name and his exploits thus magnified and accompanied in their traditionary songs, which are their only memorials. All that is said of him is in this character. There is nothing to contradict it. The man and his exploits and his tutelary deities are mixed and blended in one invariable association. The marvellous too is very much like a snowball: it grows as it rolls downward, till the little nucleus of truth which began its descent from the summit is hidden in the accumulation of superinduced hyperbole.

When tradition, thus adorned and exaggerated, has surrounded the founders of families and states with so much adventitious power and magnificence, there is no praise which a living poet can, without fear of being kicked for clumsy flattery, address to a living chief, that will not still leave the impression that the latter is not so great a man as his ancestors. The man must in this case be praised through his ancestors. Their greatness must be established, and he must be shown to be their worthy descendant. All the people of a state are interested in the founder of their state. All states that have harmonized into a common form of society, are interested in their respective founders. All men are interested in their ancestors. All men love to look back into the days that are past. In these circumstances traditional national poetry is reconstructed and brought like chaos into order and form. The interest is more universal: understanding is enlarged: passion still has scope and play: character is still various and strong: nature is still unsubdued and existing in all her beauty and magnificence, and men are not yet excluded from her observation by the magnitude of cities or the daily confinement of civic life: poetry is more an art: it requires greater skill in numbers, greater command of language, more extensive and various knowledge, and greater comprehensiveness of mind. It still exists without rivals in any other department of literature; and even the arts, painting and sculpture certainly, and music probably, are comparatively rude and imperfect. The whole field of intellect is its own. It has no rivals in history, nor in philosophy, nor in science. It is cultivated by the greatest intellects of the age, and listened to by all the rest. This is the age of Homer, the golden age of poetry. Poetry has now attained its perfection: it has attained the point which it cannot pass: genius therefore seeks new forms for the treatment of the same subjects: hence the lyric poetry of Pindar and Alcaeus, and the tragic poetry of Aeschylus and Sophocles. The favour of kings, the honour of the Olympic crown, the applause of present multitudes, all that can feed vanity and stimulate rivalry, await the successful cultivator of this art, till its forms become exhausted, and new rivals arise around it in new fields of literature, which gradually acquire more influence as, with the progress of reason and civilization, facts become more interesting than fiction: indeed the maturity of poetry may be considered the infancy of history. The transition from Homer to Herodotus is scarcely more remarkable than that from Herodotus to Thucydides: in the gradual dereliction of fabulous incident and ornamented language, Herodotus is as much a poet in relation to Thucydides as Homer is in relation to Herodotus. The history of Herodotus is half a poem: it was written while the whole field of literature yet belonged to the Muses, and the nine books of which it was composed were therefore of right, as well as of courtesy, superinscribed with their nine names.

Speculations, too, and disputes, on the nature of man and of mind; on moral duties and on good and evil; on the animate and inanimate components of the visible world; begin to share attention with the eggs of Leda and the horns of Io, and to draw off from poetry a portion of its once undivided audience.

Then comes the silver age, or the poetry of civilized life. This poetry is of two kinds, imitative and original. The imitative consists in recasting, and giving an exquisite polish to, the poetry of the age of gold: of this Virgil is the most obvious and striking example. The original is chiefly comic, didactic, or satiric: as in Menander, Aristophanes, Horace, and Juvenal. The poetry of this age is characterized by an exquisite and fastidious selection of words, and a laboured and somewhat monotonous harmony of expression: but its monotony consists in this, that experience having exhausted all the varieties of modulation, the civilized poetry selects the most beautiful, and prefers the repetition of these to ranging through the variety of all. But the best expression being that into which the idea naturally falls, it requires the utmost labour and care so to reconcile the inflexibility of civilized language and the laboured polish of versification with the idea intended to be expressed, that sense may not appear to be sacrificed to sound. Hence numerous efforts and rare success.

This state of poetry is however a step towards its extinction. Feeling and passion are best painted in, and roused by, ornamental and figurative language; but the reason and the understanding are best addressed in the simplest and most unvarnished phrase. Pure reason and dispassionate truth would be perfectly ridiculous in verse, as we may judge by versifying one of Euclid's demonstrations. This will be found true of all dispassionate reasoning whatever, and all reasoning that requires comprehensive views and enlarged combinations. It is only the more tangible points of morality, those which command assent at once, those which have a mirror in every mind, and in which the severity of reason is warmed and rendered palatable by being mixed up with feeling and imagination, that are applicable even to what is called moral poetry: and as the sciences of morals and of mind advance towards perfection, as they become more enlarged and comprehensive in their views, as reason gains the ascendancy in them over imagination and feeling, poetry can no longer accompany them in their progress, but drops into the back ground, and leaves them to advance alone. Thus the empire of thought is withdrawn from poetry, as the empire of facts had been before. In respect of the latter, the poet of the age of iron celebrates the achievements of his contemporaries; the poet of the age of gold celebrates the heroes of the age of iron; the poet of the age of silver recasts the poems of the age of gold: we may here see how very slight a ray of historical truth is sufficient to dissipate all the illusions of poetry. We know no more of the men than of the gods of the *Iliad*, no more of Achilles than we do of Thetis; no more of Hector and Andromache than we do of Vulcan and Venus: these belong altogether to poetry; history has no share in them: but Virgil knew better than to write an epic about Caesar;

he left him to Livy; and travelled out of the confines of truth and history into the old regions of poetry and fiction.

Good sense and elegant learning, conveyed in polished and somewhat monotonous verse, are the perfection of the original and imitative poetry of civilized life. Its range is limited, and when exhausted, nothing remains but the *crambe repetita* [warmed-over cabbage] of common-place, which at length becomes thoroughly wearisome, even to the most indefatigable readers of the newest new nothings.

It is now evident that poetry must either cease to be cultivated, or strike into a new path. The poets of the age of gold have been imitated and repeated till no new imitation will attract notice: the limited range of ethical and didactic poetry is exhausted: the associations of daily life in an advanced state of society are of very dry, methodical, unpoetical matters-of-fact: but there is always a multitude of listless idlers, yawning for amusement, and gaping for novelty: and the poet makes it his glory to be foremost among their purveyors.

Then comes the age of brass, which, by rejecting the polish and the learning of the age of silver, and taking a retrograde stride to the barbarisms and crude traditions of the age of iron, professes to return to nature and revive the age of gold. This is the second childhood of poetry. To the comprehensive energy of the Homeric Muse, which, by giving at once the grand outline of things, presented to the mind a vivid picture in one or two verses, inimitable alike in simplicity and magnificence, is substituted a verbose and minutely-detailed description of thoughts, passions, actions, persons, and things, in that loose rambling style of verse, which any one may write, *stans pede in uno* [standing on one foot], at the rate of two hundred lines in an hour. To this age may be referred all the poets who flourished in the decline of the Roman Empire. The best specimen of it, though not the most generally known, is the *Dionysiaca* of Nonnus, which contains many passages of exceeding beauty in the midst of masses of amplification and repetition.

The iron age of classical poetry may be called the bardic; the golden, the Homeric; the silver, the Virgilian; and the brass, the Nonnic.

Modern poetry has also its four ages: but 'it wears its rue with a difference.' ①

To the age of brass in the ancient world succeeded the dark ages, in which the light of the Gospel began to spread over Europe, and in which, by a mysterious and inscrutable dispensation, the darkness thickened with the progress of the light. The tribes that overran the Roman Empire brought back the days of barbarism, but with this difference, that there were many books in the world, many places in which they were preserved, and occasionally some one by whom they were read, who indeed (if he escaped being burned *pour l'amour de Dieu* [for the love of God],) generally lived an object of mysterious fear, with the reputation of magician, alchymist, and astrologer. The emerging of the nations of Europe from this superinduced barbarism, and their settling into new forms of polity, was accompanied, as the first ages of Greece had been, with a wild spirit of adventure, which, co-operating with new manners and new superstitions, raised up a fresh crop of chimaeras, not less fruitful, though far less beautiful, than those of Greece. The semi-deification of women by the maxims of the age of chivalry, combining with these new fables, produced the romance of the Middle Ages. The founders of the new line of heroes took the place of the demi-gods of Grecian poetry. Charlemagne and his paladins, Arthur and his knights of the round table, the heroes of the iron age of chivalrous poetry, were seen through the same magnifying mist of distance, and their exploits were celebrated with even more extravagant hyperbole. These legends, combined with the exaggerated love that pervades the songs of the troubadours, the reputation of magic that attached to learned men, the infant wonders of natural philosophy, the crazy fanaticism of the crusades, the power and privileges of the great feudal chiefs, and the holy mysteries of monks and nuns, formed a state of society in which no two laymen could meet without fighting, and in which the three staple ingredients of lover, prize-fighter, and fanatic, that composed the basis of the character of every true man, were mixed up and diversified, in different individuals and classes, with so many distinctive excellencies, and under such an infinite motley variety

---

① Hamlet, Ⅳ, v. 183—editor's note.

of costume, as gave the range of a most extensive and picturesque field to the two great constituents of poetry, love and battle.

From these ingredients of the iron age of modern poetry, dispersed in the rhymes of minstrels and the songs of the troubadours, arose the golden age, in which the scattered materials were harmonized and blended about the time of the revival of learning; but with this peculiar difference, that Greek and Roman literature pervaded all the poetry of the golden age of modern poetry, and hence resulted a heterogeneous compound of all ages and nations in one picture; an infinite license, which gave to the poet the free range of the whole field of imagination and memory. This was carried very far by Ariosto, but farthest of all by Shakespeare and his contemporaries, who used time and locality merely because they could not do without them, because every action must have its when and where: but they made no scruple of deposing a Roman Emperor by an Italian Count, and sending him off in the disguise of a French pilgrim to be shot with a blunderbuss by an English archer. This makes the old English drama very picturesque, at any rate, in the variety of costume, and very diversified in action and character; though it is a picture of nothing that ever was seen on earth except a Venetian carnival.

The greatest of English poets, Milton, may be said to stand alone between the ages of gold and silver, combining the excellencies of both; for with all the energy, and power, and freshness of the first, he united all the studied and elaborate magnificence of the second.

The silver age succeeded; beginning with Dryden, coming to perfection with Pope, and ending with Goldsmith, Collins, and Gray.

Cowper divested verse of its exquisite polish; he thought in metre, but paid more attention to his thoughts than his verse. It would be difficult to draw the boundary of prose and blank verse between his letters and his poetry.

The silver age was the reign of authority; but authority now began to be shaken, not only in poetry but in the whole sphere of its dominion. The contemporaries of Gray and Cowper were deep and elaborate thinkers. The subtle scepticism of Hume, the solemn irony of Gibbon, the daring paradoxes of Rousseau, and the biting ridicule of Voltaire, directed the energies of four extraordinary minds to shake every portion of the reign of authority. Enquiry was roused, the activity of intellect was excited, and poetry came in for its share of the general result. The changes had been rung on lovely maid and sylvan shade, summer heat and green retreat, waving trees and sighing breeze, gentle swains and amorous pains, by versifiers who took them on trust, as meaning something very soft and tender, without much caring what: but with this general activity of intellect came a necessity for even poets to appear to know something of what they professed to talk of. Thomson and Cowper looked at the trees and hills which so many ingenious gentlemen had rhymed about so long without looking at them at all, and the effect of the operation on poetry was like the discovery of a new world. Painting shared the influence, and the principles of picturesque beauty were explored by adventurous essayists with indefatigable pertinacity. The success which attended these experiments, and the pleasure which resulted from them, had the usual effect of all new enthusiasms, that of turning the heads of a few unfortunate persons, the patriarchs of the age of brass, who, mistaking the prominent novelty for the all-important totality, seem to have ratiocinated much in the following manner: 'Poetical genius is the finest of all things, and we feel that we have more of it than any one ever had. The way to bring it to perfection is to cultivate poetical impressions exclusively. Poetical impressions can be received only among natural scenes: for all that is artificial is anti-poetical. Society is artificial, therefore we will live out of society. The mountains are natural, therefore we will live in the mountains. There we shall be shining models of purity and virtue, passing the whole day in the innocent and amiable occupation of going up and down hill, receiving poetical impressions, and communicating them in immortal verse to admiring generations.' To some such perversion of intellect we owe that egregious confraternity of rhymesters, known by the name of the Lake Poets; who certainly did receive and communicate to the world some of the most extraordinary poetical impressions that ever were heard of, and ripened into models of public virtue, too splendid to need illustration. They wrote verses on a new principle; saw rocks and rivers in a new light; and remaining studiously ignorant of history, society, and human nature, cultivated the phantasy only at the expence of the memory and the reason; and contrived, though they had retreated from the world for the express purpose of seeing nature as she was, to see her only as she was not, converting the land they lived in into a sort of fairyland, which they peopled with mysticisms and chimaeras. This gave what is called a new tone to poetry, and conjured up a herd of desperate imitators, who have brought the age of brass prematurely to its dotage.

The descriptive poetry of the present day has been called by its cultivators a return to nature. Nothing is more impertinent than this pretension. Poetry cannot travel out of the regions of its birth, the uncultivated lands of semi-civilized men. Mr Wordsworth, the great leader of the returners to nature, cannot describe a scene under his own eyes without putting into it the shadow of a Danish boy or the living ghost of Lucy Gray, or some similar phantastical parturition of the moods of his own mind.

In the origin and perfection of poetry, all the associations of life were composed of poetical materials. With us it is decidedly the reverse. We know too that there are no Dryads in Hyde Park nor Naiads in the Regent's canal. But barbaric manners and supernatural interventions are essential to poetry. Either in the scene, or in the time, or in both, it must be remote from our ordinary perceptions. While the historian and the philosopher are advancing in, and accelerating, the progress of knowledge, the poet is wallowing in the rubbish of departed ignorance, and raking up the ashes of dead savages to find gewgaws and rattles for the grown babies of the age. Mr Scott digs up the poachers and cattle-stealers of the ancient border. Lord Byron cruizes for thieves and pirates on the shores of the Morea and among the Greek Islands. Mr Southey wades through ponderous volumes of travels and old chronicles, from which he carefully selects all that is false, useless, and absurd, as being essentially poetical; and when he has a commonplace book full of monstrosities, strings them into an epic. Mr Wordsworth picks up village legends from old women and sextons; and Mr Coleridge, to the valuable information acquired from similar sources, superadds the dreams of crazy theologians and the mysticisms of German metaphysics, and favours the world with visions in verse, in which the quadruple elements of sexton, old woman, Jeremy Taylor, and Immanuel Kant, are harmonized into a delicious poetical compound. Mr Moore presents us with a Persian, and Mr Campbell with a Pennsylvanian tale, both formed on the same principle as Mr Southey's epics, by extracting from a perfunctory and desultory perusal of a collection of voyages and travels, all that useful investigation would not seek for and that common sense would reject.

These disjointed relics of tradition and fragments of second-hand observation, being woven into a tissue of verse, constructed on what Mr Coleridge calls a new principle (that is, no principle at all), compose a modern-antique compound of frippery and barbarism, in which the puling sentimentality of the present time is grafted on the misrepresented ruggedness of the past into a heterogeneous congeries of unamalgamating manners, sufficient to impose on the common readers of poetry, over whose understandings the poet of this class possesses that commanding advantage, which, in all circumstances and conditions of life, a man who knows something, however little, always possesses over one who knows nothing.

A poet in our times is a semibarbarian in a civilized community. He lives in the days that are past. His ideas, thoughts, feelings, associations, are all with barbarous manners, obsolete customs, and exploded superstitions. The march of his intellect is like that of a crab, backward. The brighter the light diffused around him by the progress of reason, the thicker is the darkness of antiquated barbarism, in which he buries himself like a mole, to throw up the barren hillocks of his Cimmerian labours. The philosophic mental tranquillity which looks round with an equal eye on all external things, collects a store of ideas, discriminates their relative value, assigns to all their proper place, and from the materials of useful knowledge thus collected, appreciated, and arranged, forms new combinations that impress the stamp of their power and utility on the real business of life, is diametrically the reverse of that frame of mind which poetry inspires, or from which poetry can emanate. The highest inspirations of poetry are resolvable into three ingredients: the rant of unregulated passion, the whining of exaggerated feeling, and the cant of factitious sentiment: and can therefore serve only to ripen a splendid lunatic like Alexander, a puling driveller like Werther, or a morbid dreamer like Wordsworth. It can never make a philosopher, nor a statesman, nor in any class of life an useful or rational man. It cannot claim the slightest share in any one of the comforts and utilities of life of which we have witnessed so many and so rapid advances. But though not useful, it may be said it is highly ornamental, and deserves to be cultivated for the pleasure it yields. Even if this be granted, it does not follow that a writer of poetry in the present state of society is not a waster of his own time, and a robber of that of others. Poetry is not one of those arts which, like painting, require repetition and multiplication, in order to be diffused among society. There are more good poems already existing than are sufficient to employ that portion of life which any mere reader and recipient of poetical impressions should devote to them, and these having been produced in poetical times, are far superior in all the characteristics of poetry to the artificial reconstructions of a few morbid ascetics in unpoetical times. To read the promiscuous rubbish of the present time to the exclusion of the select treasures of the past, is to substitute the worse for the better variety of the same mode of enjoyment.

But in whatever degree poetry is cultivated, it must necessarily be to the neglect of some branch of useful study: and it is a lamentable spectacle to see minds, capable of better things, running to seed in the specious indolence of these empty aimless mockeries of intellectual exertion. Poetry was the mental rattle that awakened the attention of intellect in the infancy of civil society: but for the maturity of mind to make a serious business of the playthings of its childhood, is as absurd as for a full-grown man to rub his gums with coral, and cry to be charmed to sleep by the jingle of silver bells.

As to that small portion of our contemporary poetry, which is neither descriptive, nor narrative, nor dramatic, and which, for want of a better name, may be called ethical, the most distinguished portion of it, consisting merely of querulous, egotistical rhapsodies, to express the writer's high dissatisfaction with the world and every thing in it, serves only to confirm what has been said of the semibarbarous character of poets, who from singing dithyrambics and 'Io Triumphe,' while society was savage, grow rabid, and out of their element, as it becomes polished and enlightened.

Now when we consider that it is not the thinking and studious, and scientific and philosophical part of the community, not to those whose minds are bent on the pursuit and promotion of permanently useful ends and aims, that poets must address their minstrelsy, but to that much larger portion of the reading public, whose minds are not awakened to the desire of valuable knowledge, and who are indifferent to any thing beyond being charmed, moved, excited, affected, and exalted: charmed by harmony, moved by sentiment, excited by passion, affected by pathos, and exalted by sublimity: harmony, which is language on the rack of Procrustes; sentiment, which is canting egotism in the mask of refined feeling; passion, which is the commotion of a weak and selfish mind; pathos, which is the whining of an unmanly spirit; and sublimity, which is the inflation of an empty head: when we consider that the great and permanent interests of human society become more and more the main spring of intellectual pursuit; that in proportion as they become so, the subordinacy of the ornamental to the useful will be more and more seen and acknowledged; and that therefore the progress of useful art and science, and of moral and political knowledge, will continue more and more to withdraw attention from frivolous and unconducive, to solid and conducive studies: that therefore the poetical audience will not only continually diminish in the proportion of its number to that of the rest of the reading public, but will also sink lower and lower in the comparison of intellectual acquirement: when we consider that the poet must still please his audience, and must therefore continue to sink to their level, while the rest of the community is rising above it: we may easily conceive that the day is not distant, when the degraded state of every species of poetry will be as generally recognized as that of dramatic poetry has long been: and this not from any decrease either of intellectual power, or intellectual acquisition, but because intellectual power and intellectual acquisition have turned themselves into other and better channels, and have abandoned the cultivation and the fate of poetry to the degenerate fry of modern rhymesters, and their Olympic judges, the magazine critics, who continue to debate and promulgate oracles about poetry, as if it were still what it was in the Homeric age, the all-in-all of intellectual progression, and as if there were no such things in existence as mathematicians, astronomers, chemists, moralists, metaphysicians, historians, politicians, and political economists, who have built into the upper air of intelligence a pyramid, from the summit of which they see the modern Parnassus far beneath them, and, knowing how small a place it occupies in the comprehensiveness of their prospect, smile at the little ambition and the circumscribed perceptions with which the drivellers and mountebanks upon it are contending for the poetical palm and the critical chair.

Percy Bysshe Shelley

A Defence of Poetry;

or, Remarks Suggested by an Essay
Entitled 'The Four Ages of Poetry' (1821)

ACCORDING to one mode of regarding those two classes of mental action, which are called reason and imagination, the former may be considered as mind contemplating the relations borne by one thought to another, however produced, and the latter, as mind acting upon those thoughts so as to colour them with its own light, and composing from them as from elements, other thoughts, each containing within itself the principle of its own integrity. The one is the τὸ ποιειν [making], or the principle of synthesis, and has for its objects those forms which are common to universal nature and existence itself; the other is the τὸ λογιζειν [reasoning], or principle of analysis, and its action regards the relations of things simply as relations; considering thoughts, not in their integral unity, but as the algebraical representations which conduct to certain general results. Reason is the enumeration of qualities already known; imagination is the perception of the value of those qualities, both separately and as a whole. Reason respects the differences, and imagination the similitudes of things. Reason is to imagination as the instrument to the agent, as the body to the spirit, as the shadow to the substance.

Poetry, in a general sense, may be defined to be 'the expression of the imagination': and poetry is connate with the origin of man. Man is an instrument over which a series of external and internal impressions are driven, like the alternations of an ever-changing wind over an Æolian lyre, which move it by their motion to ever-changing melody. But there is a principle within the human being, and perhaps within all sentient beings, which acts otherwise than in the lyre, and produces not melody alone, but harmony, by an internal adjustment of the sounds or motions thus excited to the impressions which excite them. It is as if the lyre could accommodate its chords to the motions of that which strikes them, in a determined proportion of sound; even as the musician can accommodate his voice to the sound of the lyre. A child at play by itself will express its delight by its voice and motions; and every inflexion of tone and every gesture will bear exact relation to a corresponding antitype in the pleasurable impressions which awakened it; it will be the reflected image of that impression; and as the lyre trembles and sounds after the wind has died away; so the child seeks, by prolonging in its voice and motions the duration of the effect, to prolong also a consciousness of the cause. In relation to the objects which delight a child, these expressions are, what Poetry is to higher objects. The savage (for the savage is to ages what the child is to years) expresses the emotions produced in him by surrounding objects in a similar manner; and language and gesture, together with plastic or pictorial imitation, become the image of the combined effect of those objects and of his apprehension of them. Man in society, with all his passions and his pleasures, next becomes the object of the passions and pleasures of man; an additional class of emotions produces an augmented treasure of expressions; and language, gesture, and the imitative arts, become at once the representation and the medium, the pencil and the picture, the chisel and the statute, the chord and the harmony. The social sympathies, or those laws from which as from its elements society results, begin to develop themselves from the moment that two human beings coexist; the future is contained within the present as the plant within the seed; and equality, diversity, unity, contrast, mutual dependence become the principles alone capable of affording the motives according to which the will of a social being is determined to action, inasmuch as he is social; and constitute pleasure in sensation, virtue in sentiment, beauty in art, truth in reasoning, and love in the intercourse of kind. Hence men, even in the infancy of society, observe a certain order in their words and actions, distinct from that of the objects and the impressions represented by them, all expression being subject to the laws of that from which it proceeds. But let us dismiss those more general considerations which might involve an inquiry into the principles of society itself, and restrict our view to the manner in which the imagination is expressed upon its forms.

In the youth of the world, men dance and sing and imitate natural objects, observing in these actions, as in all others, a certain rhythm or order. And, although all men observe a similar, they observe not the same order, in the motions of the dance, in the melody of the song, in the combinations of language, in the series of their imitations of natural objects. For there is a certain order or rhythm belonging to each of these classes of mimetic representation, from which the hearer and the spectator receive an intenser and purer pleasure than from any other: the sense of an approximation to this order has been called taste by modern writers. Every man, in the infancy of art, observes an order which approximates more or less closely to that from which this highest delight results: but the diversity is not sufficiently marked, as that its gradations should be sensible, except in those instances where the predominance of this faculty of approximation to the beautiful (for so we may be permitted to name the relation between this highest pleasure and its cause) is very great. Those in whom it exists in excess are poets, in the most universal sense of the word; and the pleasure resulting from the manner in which they express the influence of society or nature upon their own minds, communicates itself to others, and gathers a sort of reduplication from that community. Their language is vitally metaphorical; that is, it marks the before unapprehended relations of things, and perpetuates their apprehension, until the words which represent them, become through time signs for portions or classes of thoughts instead of pictures of integral thoughts; and then if no new poets should arise to create afresh the associations which have been thus disorganized, language will be dead to all the nobler purposes of human intercourse. These similitudes or relations are finely said by Lord Bacon to be 'the same footsteps of nature impressed upon the various subjects of the world' ["De Augment. Scient.," cap. i, lib. iii—Shelley]—and he considers the faculty which perceives them as the store-house of axioms common to all knowledge. In the infancy of society every author is necessarily a poet, because language itself is poetry; and to be a poet is to apprehend the true and the beautiful, in a word, the good which exists in the relation, subsisting, first between existence and perception, and secondly between perception and expression. Every original language near to its source is in itself the chaos of a cyclic poem: the copiousness of lexicography and the distinctions of grammar are the works of a later age, and are merely the catalogue and the form of the creations of Poetry.

But Poets, or those who imagine and express this indestructible order, are not only the authors of language and of music, of the dance and architecture and statuary and painting: they are the institutors of laws and the founders of civil society and the inventors of the arts of life and the teachers, who draw into a certain propinquity with the beautiful and the true that partial apprehension of the agencies of the invisible world which is called religion. Hence all original religions are allegorical or susceptible of allegory, and like Janus have a double face of false and true. Poets, according to the circumstances of the age and nation in which they appeared, were called in the earlier epochs of the world legislators or prophets: a poet essentially comprises and unites both these characters. For he not only beholds intensely the present as it is, and discovers those laws according to which present things ought to be ordered, but he beholds the future in the present, and his thoughts are the germs of the flower and the fruit of latest time. Not that I assert poets to be prophets in the gross sense of the word, or that they can foretell the form as surely as they foreknow the spirit of events: such is the pretence of superstition, which would make poetry an attribute of prophecy, rather than prophecy an attribute of poetry. A poet participates in the eternal, the infinite and the one; as far as relates to his conceptions, time and place and number are not. The grammatical forms which express the moods of time, and the difference of persons and the distinction of place are convertible with respect to the highest poetry without injuring it as poetry, and the choruses of Aeschylus, and the book of Job, and Dante's 'Paradise' would afford, more than any other writings, examples of this fact, if the limits of this essay did not forbid citation. The creations of sculpture, painting and music are illustrations still more decisive.

Language, color, form, and religious and civil habits of action are all the instruments and materials of poetry; they may be called poetry by that figure of speech which considers the effect as a synonym of the cause. But poetry in a more restricted sense expresses those arrangements of language, and especially metrical language which are created by that imperial faculty, whose throne is curtained within the invisible nature of man. And this springs from the nature itself of language, which is a more direct representation of the actions and passions of our internal being, and is susceptible of more various and delicate combinations, than color, form or motion, and is more plastic and obedient to the control of that faculty of which it is the creation. For language is arbitrarily produced by the Imagination and has relation to thoughts alone; but all other materials, instruments and conditions of art have relations among each other, which limit and interpose between conception and expression. The former is as a mirror which reflects, the latter as a cloud which enfeebles, the light of which both are mediums of communication. Hence the fame of sculptors, painters and musicians, although the intrinsic powers of the great masters of these arts may yield in no degree to that of those who have employed language as the hieroglyphic of their thoughts, has never equalled that of poets in the restricted sense of the term; as two performers of equal skill will produce unequal effects from a guitar and a harp. The fame of legislators and founders of religions, so long as their institutions last, alone seems to exceed that of poets in the restricted sense; but it can scarcely be a question whether, if we deduct the celebrity which their flattery of the gross opinions of the vulgar usually conciliates, together with that which belonged to them in their higher character of poets, any excess will remain.

We have thus circumscribed the word Poetry within the limits of that art which is the most familiar and the most perfect expression of the faculty itself. It is necessary however to make the circle still narrower, and to determine the distinction between measured and unmeasured language; for the popular division into prose and verse is inadmissible in accurate philosophy.

Sounds as well as thoughts have relations, both between each other and towards that which they represent, and a perception of the order of those relations has always been found connected with a perception of the order of the relations of thoughts. Hence the language of poets has ever affected a certain uniform and harmonious recurrence of sound, without which it were not poetry, and which is scarcely less indispensable to the communication of its influence, than the words themselves without reference to that peculiar order. Hence the vanity of translation; it were as wise to cast a violet into a crucible that you might discover the formal principle of its color and odour, as seek to transfuse from one language into another the creations of a poet. The plant must spring again from its seed or it will bear no flower—and this is the burthen of the curse of Babel.

An observation of the regular mode of the recurrence of harmony in the language of poetical minds, together with its relation to music, produced metre, or a certain system of traditional forms of harmony and language. Yet it is by no means essential that a poet should accommodate his language to this traditional form, so that the harmony which is its spirit, be observed. The practice is indeed convenient and popular, and to be preferred, especially in such composition as includes much action: but every great poet must inevitably innovate upon the example of his predecessors in the exact structure of his peculiar versification. The distinction between poets and prose writers is a vulgar error. The distinction between philosophers and poets has been anticipated. Plato was essentially a poet—the truth and splendor of his imagery and the melody of his language is the most intense that it is possible to conceive. He rejected the measure of the epic, dramatic, and lyrical forms, because he sought to kindle a harmony in thoughts divested of shape and action, and he forebore to invent any regular plan of rhythm which would include, under determinate forms, the varied pauses of his style. Cicero sought to imitate the cadence of his periods but with little success. Lord Bacon was a poet.[1] His language has a sweet and majestic rhythm, which satisfies the sense, no less than the almost superhuman wisdom of his philosophy satisfies the intellect; it is a strain which distends, and then bursts the circumference of the hearer's mind,[2] and pours itself forth together with it into the universal element with which it has perpetual sympathy. All the authors of revolutions in opinion are not only necessarily poets as they are inventors, nor even as their

---

[1] See the *Filum Labyrinthi* and the *Essay on Death* particularly.
[2] Shelley wrote 'hearer's' in his fair copy; Mary Shelley changed the word to 'reader's' in her press copy—editor's note.

words unveil the permanent analogy of things by images which participate in the life of truth; but as their periods are harmonious and rhythmical and contain in themselves the elements of verse; being the echo of the eternal music. Nor are those supreme poets, who have employed traditional forms of rhythm on account of the form and action of their subjects, less capable of perceiving and teaching the truth of things, than those who have omitted that form. Shakespeare, Dante and Milton (to confine ourselves to modern writers) are philosophers of the very loftiest power.

A poem is the very image of life expressed in its eternal truth. There is this difference between a story and a poem, that a story is a catalogue of detached facts, which have no other connection than time, place, circumstance, cause and effect; the other is the creation of actions according to the unchangeable forms of human nature, as existing in the mind of the creator, which is itself the image of all other minds. The one is partial, and applies only to a definite period of time, and a certain combination of events which can never again recur; the other is universal, and contains within itself the germ of a relation to whatever motives or actions have place in the possible varieties of human nature. Time, which destroys the beauty and the use of the story of particular facts, stript of the poetry which should invest them, augments that of Poetry, and forever develops new and wonderful applications of the eternal truth which it contains. Hence epitomes have been called the moths of just history; they eat out The poetry of it. The story of particular facts is as a mirror which obscures and distorts that which should be beautiful: Poetry is a mirror which makes beautiful that which is distorted.

The parts of a composition may be poetical, without the composition as a whole being a poem. A single sentence may be considered as a whole though it be found in the midst of a series of unassimilated portions; a single word even may be a spark of inextinguishable thought. And thus all the great historians, Herodotus, Plutarch, Livy, were poets; and although the plan of these writers, especially that of Livy, restrained them from developing this faculty in its highest degree, they made copious and ample amends for their subjection, by filling all the interstices of their subjects with living images.

Having determined what is poetry, and who are poets, let us proceed to estimate its effects upon society.

Poetry is ever accompanied with pleasure: all spirits on which it falls open themselves to receive the wisdom which is mingled with its delight. In the infancy of the world, neither poets themselves nor their auditors are fully aware of the excellence of poetry: for it acts in a divine and unapprehended manner, beyond and above consciousness; and it is reserved for future generations to contemplate and measure the mighty cause and effect in all the strength and splendor of their union. Even in modern times, no living poet ever arrived at the fulness of his fame; the jury which sits in judgment upon a poet, belonging as he does to all time, must be composed of his peers: it must be impanelled by Time from the selectest of the wise of many generations. A Poet is a nightingale, who sits in darkness and sings to cheer its own solitude with sweet sounds; his auditors are as men entranced by the melody of an unseen musician, who feel that they are moved and softened, yet know not whence or why. The poems of Homer and his contemporaries were the delight of infant Greece; they were the elements of that social system which is the column upon which all succeeding civilization has reposed. Homer embodied the ideal perfection of his age in human character; nor can we doubt that those who read his verses were awakened to an ambition of becoming like to Achilles, Hector and Ulysses: the truth and beauty of friendship, patriotism and persevering devotion to an object, were unveiled to the depths in these immortal creations: the sentiments of the auditors must have been refined and enlarged by a sympathy with such great and lovely impersonations, until from admiring they imitated, and from imitation they identified themselves with the objects of their admiration. Nor let it be objected that these characters are remote from moral perfection, and that they can by no means be considered as edifying patterns for general imitation. Every epoch under names more or less specious has deified its peculiar errors; Revenge is the naked idol of the worship of a semibarbarous age: and Self-deceit is the veiled image of unknown evil before which luxury and satiety lie prostrate. But a poet considers the vices of his contemporaries as the temporary dress in which his creations must be arrayed, and which cover without concealing the eternal proportions of their beauty. An epic or dramatic personage is understood to wear them around his soul, as he may the ancient armour or the modern uniform around his body; whilst it is easy to conceive a dress more graceful than either. The beauty of the internal nature cannot be so far concealed by its accidental vesture, but that the spirit of its form shall communicate itself to the very disguise, and indicate the shape it hides from the manner in which it is worn. A majestic form and graceful motions will express themselves through the most barbarous and tasteless costume. Few poets of the highest class have chosen to exhibit the beauty of their conceptions in its naked truth and splendor; and it is doubtful whether the alloy of costume, habit, etc., be not necessary to temper this planetary music for mortal ears.

The whole objection however of the immorality of poetry rests upon a misconception of the manner in which poetry acts to produce the moral improvement of man. Ethical science arranges the elements which poetry has created, and propounds schemes and proposes examples of civil and domestic life: nor is it for want of admirable doctrines that men hate, and despise, and censure, and deceive, and subjugate one another. But Poetry acts in another and diviner manner. It awakens and enlarges the mind itself by rendering it the receptacle of a thousand unapprehended combinations of thought. Poetry lifts the veil from the hidden beauty of the world, and makes familiar objects be as if they were not familiar; it reproduces all that it represents, and the impersonations clothed in its Elysian light stand thenceforward in the minds of those who have once contemplated them, as memorials of that gentle and exalted content which extends itself over all thoughts and actions with which it coexists. The great secret of morals is Love; or a going out of our nature, and an identification of ourselves with the beautiful which exists in thought, action, or person, not our own. A man, to be greatly good, must imagine intensely and comprehensively; he must put himself in the place of another and of many others; the pains and pleasure of his species must become his own. The great instrument of moral good is the imagination; and poetry administers to the effect by acting upon the cause. Poetry enlarges the circumference of the imagination by replenishing it with thoughts of ever new delight, which have the power of attracting and assimilating to their own nature all other thoughts, and which form new intervals and interstices whose void forever craves fresh food. Poetry strengthens the faculty which is the organ of the moral nature of man, in the same manner as exercise strengthens a limb. A poet therefore would do ill to embody his own conceptions of right and wrong, which are usually those of his place and time in his poetical creations, which participate in neither. By this assumption of the inferior office of interpreting the effect, in which perhaps after all he might acquit himself but imperfectly, he would resign a glory in a participation in the cause. There was little danger that Homer, or any of the eternal poets, should have so far misunderstood themselves as to have abdicated this throne of their widest dominion. Those in whom the poetical faculty, though great, is less intense, as Euripides, Lucan, Tasso, Spenser, have frequently affected a moral aim, and the effect of their poetry is diminished in exact proportion to the degree in which they compel us to advert to this purpose.

Homer and the cyclic poets were followed at a certain interval by the dramatic and lyrical poets of Athens, who flourished contemporaneously with all that is most perfect in the kindred expressions of the poetical faculty; architecture, painting, music, the dance, sculpture, philosophy, and we may add the forms of civil life. For although the scheme of Athenian society was deformed by many imperfections which the poetry existing in Chivalry and Christianity has erased from the habits and institutions of modern Europe; yet never at any other period has so much energy, beauty, and virtue been developed; never was blind strength and stubborn form so disciplined and rendered subject to the will of man, or that will less repugnant to the dictates of the beautiful and the true, as during the century which preceded the death of Socrates. Of no other epoch in the history of our species have we records and fragments stamped so visibly with the image of the divinity in man. But it is Poetry alone, in form, in action or in language, which has rendered this epoch memorable above all others, and the storehouse of examples to everlasting time. For written poetry existed at that epoch simultaneously with the other arts, and it is an idle inquiry to demand which gave and which received the light, which all as from a common focus have scattered over the darkest periods of succeeding time. We know no more of cause and effect than a constant conjunction of events: Poetry is ever found to coexist with whatever other arts contribute to the happiness and perfection of man. I appeal to what has already been established to distinguish between the cause and the effect.

It was at the period here adverted to that the drama had its birth; and however a succeeding writer may have equalled or surpassed those few great specimens of the Athenian drama which have been preserved to us, it is indisputable that the art itself never was understood or practised according to the true philosophy of it, as at Athens. For the Athenians employed language, action, music, painting, the dance, and religious institutions to produce a common effect in the representation of the highest idealism of passion and of power; each division in the art was made perfect in its kind of artists of the most consummate skill, and was disciplined into a beautiful proportion and unity one towards the other. On the modern stage a few only of the elements capable of expressing the image of the poet's conception are employed at once. We have tragedy without music and dancing; and music and dancing without the highest impersonations of which they are the fit accompaniment, and both without religion and solemnity. Religious institution has indeed been usually banished from the stage. Our system of divesting the actor's face of a mask, on which the many expressions appropriated to his dramatic character might be moulded into one permanent and unchanging expression, is favorable only to a partial and inharmonious effect; it is fit for nothing but a monologue, where all the attention may be directed to some great master of ideal mimicry. The modern practice of blending comedy with tragedy, though liable to great abuse in point of practice, is undoubtedly an extension of the dramatic circle; but the comedy should be as in *King Lear*, universal, ideal and sublime. It is perhaps the intervention of this principle which determines the balance in favor of *King Lear* against the *Oedipus Tyrannus* or the *Agamemnon*, or, if you will the trilogies with which they are connected; unless the intense power of the choral poetry, especially that of the latter, should be considered as restoring the equilibrium. *King Lear*, if it can sustain this comparison, may be judged to be the most perfect specimen of the dramatic art existing in the world; in spite of the narrow conditions to which the poet was subjected by the ignorance of the philosophy of the drama which has prevailed in modern Europe. Calderon in his religious *Autos* ① has attempted to fulfil some of the high conditions of dramatic representation neglected by Shakespeare; such as the establishing a relation between the drama and religion, and the accommodating them to music and dancing; but he omits the observation of conditions still more important, and more is lost than gained by the substitution of the rigidly defined and ever-repeated idealisms of a distorted superstition for the living impersonations of the truth of human passion.

But we digress. —The Author of the Four Ages of Poetry has prudently omitted to dispute on the effect of the Drama upon life and manners. For, if I know the knight by the device of his shield, I have only to inscribe *Philoctetes* or *Agamemnon* or *Othello* upon mine to put to flight the giant sophisms which have enchanted him, as the mirror of intolerable light, though on the arm of one of the weakest of the Paladins, could blind and scatter whole armies of necromancers and pagans. The connection of scenic exhibitions with the improvement or corruption of the manners of men has been universally recognized: in other words, the presence or absence of poetry in its most perfect and universal form has been found to be connected with good and evil in conduct or habit. The corruption which has been imputed to the drama as an effect begins, when the poetry employed in its constitution ends: I appeal to the history of manners whether the gradations of the growth of the one and the decline of the other have not corresponded with an exactness equal to any example of moral cause and effect.

The drama at Athens or wheresoever else it may have approached to its perfection, coexisted with the moral and intellectual greatness of the age. The tragedies of the Athenian poets are as mirrors in which the spectator beholds himself, under a thin disguise of circumstance, stript of all but that ideal perfection and energy which everyone feels to be the internal type of all that he loves, admires, and would become. The imagination is enlarged by a sympathy with pains and passions so mighty that they distend in their conception the capacity of that by which they are conceived; the good affections are strengthened by pity,

---

① One-act sacramental drama—editor's note.

indignation, terror and sorrow; and an exalted calm is prolonged from the satiety of this high exercise of them into the tumult of familiar life: even crime is disarmed of half its horror and all its contagion by being represented as the fatal consequence of the unfathomable agencies of nature; error is thus divested of its wilfulness; men can no longer cherish it as the creation of their choice. In a drama of the highest order there is little food for censure or hatred; it teaches rather self-knowledge and self-respect. Neither the eye nor the mind can see itself, unless reflected upon that which it resembles. The drama, so long as it continues to express poetry, is as a prismatic and many-sided mirror, which collects the brightest rays of human nature and divides and reproduces them from the simplicity of these elementary forms, and touches them with majesty and beauty, and multiplies all that it reflects, and endows it with the power of propagating its like wherever it may fall.

But in periods of the decay of social life, the drama sympathizes with that decay. Tragedy becomes a cold imitation of the form of the great masterpieces of antiquity, divested of all harmonious accompaniment of the kindred arts; and often the very form misunderstood: or a weak attempt to teach certain doctrines, which the writer considers as moral truths; and which are usually no more than specious flatteries of some gross vice or weakness with which the author in common with his auditors, are infected. Hence what has been called the classical and domestic drama. Addison's *Cato* is a specimen of the one, and would it were not superfluous to cite examples of the other! To such purposes poetry cannot be made subservient. Poetry is a sword of lightning, ever unsheathed, which consumes the scabbard that would contain it. And thus we observe that all dramatic writings of this nature are unimaginative in a singular degree; they affect sentiment and passion, which, divested of imagination, are other names for caprice and appetite. The period in our own history of the grossest degradation of the drama is the reign of Charles II when all forms in which poetry had been accustomed to be expressed became hymns to the triumph of kingly power over liberty and virtue. Milton stood alone illuminating an age unworthy of him. At such periods the calculating principle pervades all the forms of dramatic exhibition, and poetry ceases to be expressed upon them. Comedy loses its ideal universality: wit succeeds to humor; we laugh from self-complacency and triumph, instead of pleasure; malignity, sarcasm and contempt succeed to sympathetic merriment; we hardly laugh, but we smile. Obscenity, which is ever blasphemy against the divine beauty in life, becomes, from the very veil which it assumes, more active if less disgusting: it is a monster for which the corruption of society forever brings forth new food, which it devours in secret.

The drama being that form under which a greater number of modes of expression of poetry are susceptible of being combined than any other, the connection of poetry and social good is more observable in the drama than in whatever other form: and it is indisputable that the highest perfection of human society has ever corresponded with the highest dramatic excellence; and that the corruption or the extinction of the drama in a nation where it has once flourished, is a mark of a corruption of manners, and an extinction of the energies which sustain the soul of social life. But, as Machiavelli says of political institutions, that life may be preserved and renewed, if men should arise capable of bringing back the drama to its principles. And this is true with respect to poetry in its most extended sense: all language, institution and form, require not only to be produced but to be sustained: the office and character of a poet participate in the divine nature as regards providence, no less than as regards creation.

Civil war, the spoils of Asia, and the fatal predominance first of the Macedonian, and then of the Roman arms were so many symbols of the extinction or suspension of the creative faculty in Greece. The bucolic writers, who found patronage under the lettered tyrants of Sicily and Egypt, were the latest representatives of its most glorious reign. Their poetry is intensely melodious; like the odour of the tuberose, it overcomes and sickens the spirit with excess of sweetness; whilst the poetry of the preceding age was as a meadow-gale of June, which mingles the fragrance of all the flowers of the field, and adds a quickening and harmonizing spirit of its own which endows the sense with a power of sustaining its extreme delight. The bucolic and erotic delicacy in written poetry is correlative with that softness in statuary, music, and the kindred arts, and even in manners and institutions which distinguished the epoch to which I now refer. Nor is it the poetical faculty itself, or any misapplication of it, to which this want of harmony is to be imputed. An equal sensibility to the influence of the senses and the affections is to be found in the writings of Homer and Sophocles: the former especially has clothed sensual and pathetic images with irresistible attractions. Their superiority over these succeeding writers consists in the presence of those thoughts which belong to the inner faculties of our nature, not in the absence of those which are connected with the external; their incomparable perfection consists in a harmony of the union of all. It is not what the erotic poets have, but what they have not, in which their imperfection consists. It is not inasmuch as they were Poets, but inasmuch as they were not Poets, that they can be considered with any plausibility as connected with the corruption of their age. Had that corruption availed so as to extinguish in them the sensibility to pleasure, passion and natural scenery, which is imputed to them as an imperfection, the last triumph of evil would have been achieved. For the end of social corruption is to destroy all sensibility to pleasure; and therefore it is corruption. It begins at the imagination and the intellect as at the core, and distributes itself thence as a paralyzing venom, through the affections into the very appetites, until all become a torpid mass in which hardly sense survives. At the approach of such a period, poetry ever addresses itself to those faculties which are the last to be destroyed, and its voice is heard, like the footsteps of Astræa, departing from the world. Poetry ever communicates all the pleasure which men are capable of receiving: it is ever still the light of life; the source of whatever of beautiful or generous or true can have place in an evil time. It will readily be confessed that those among the luxurious citizens of Syracuse and Alexandria, who were delighted with the poems of Theocritus, were less cold, cruel and sensual than the remnant of their tribe. But corruption must utterly have destroyed the fabric of human society before poetry can ever cease. The sacred links of that chain have never been entirely disjoined, which descending through the minds of many men is attached to those great minds, whence as from a magnet the invisible effluence is sent forth, which at once connects, animates and sustains the life of all. It is the faculty which contains within itself the seeds at once of its own and of social renovation. And let us not circumscribe the effects of the bucolic and erotic poetry within the limits of the sensibility of those to whom it was addressed. They may have perceived the beauty of those immortal compositions, simply as fragments and isolated portions: those who are more finely organized, or born in a happier age, may recognize them as episodes to that great poem, which all poets, like the co-operating thoughts of one great mind, have built up since the beginning of the world.

The same revolutions within a narrower sphere had place in ancient Rome; but the actions and forms of its social life never seem to have been perfectly saturated with the poetical element. The Romans appear to have considered the Greeks as the selectest treasuries of the selectest forms of manners and of nature, and to have abstained from creating in measured language, sculpture, music or architecture, anything which might bear a particular relation to their own condition, whilst it should bear a general one to the universal constitution of the world. But we judge from partial evidence, and we judge perhaps partially. Ennius, Varro, Pacuvius, and Accius, all great poets, have been lost. Lucretius is in the highest, and Virgil in a very high sense, a creator. The chosen delicacy of expressions of the latter are as a mist of light which conceal from us the intense and exceeding truth of his conceptions of nature. Livy is instinct with poetry. Yet Horace, Catullus, Ovid, and generally the other great writers of the Vergilian age, saw man and nature in the mirror of Greece. The institutions also, and the religion of Rome, were less poetical than those of Greece, as the shadow is less vivid than the substance. Hence poetry in Rome, seemed to follow rather than accompany the perfection of political and domestic society. The true poetry of Rome lived in its institutions; for whatever of beautiful, true and majestic they contained could have sprung only from the faculty which creates the order in which they consist. The life of Camillus, the death of Regulus; the expectation of the senators, in their godlike state, of the victorious Gauls; the refusal of the Republic to make peace with Hannibal after the battle of Cannæ, were not the consequences of a refined calculation of the probable personal advantage to result from such a rhythm and order in the shows of life, to those who were at once the poets and the actors of these immortal dramas. The imagination beholding the beauty of this order, created it out of itself according to its own idea; the consequence was empire, and the reward ever-living fame. These things are not the less poetry, *quia carent vate sacro* [because they lack a divine poet]. They are the episodes of that cyclic poem written by Time upon the memories of men. The Past, like an inspired rhapsodist, fills the theatre of everlasting generations with their harmony.

At length the ancient system of religion and manners had fulfilled the circle of its revolutions. And the world would have fallen into utter anarchy and darkness, but that there were found poets among the authors of the Christian and Chivalric systems of manners and religion, who created forms of opinion and action never before conceived; which, copied into the imaginations of men, became as generals to the bewildered armies of their thoughts. It is foreign to the present purpose to touch upon the evil produced by these systems: except that we protest, on the ground of the principles already established, that no portion of it can be attributed to the poetry they contain.

It is probable that the poetry of Moses, Job, David, Solomon and Isaiah had produced a great effect upon the mind of Jesus and his disciples. The scattered fragments preserved to us by the biographers of this extraordinary person are all instinct with the most vivid poetry. But his doctrines seem to have been quickly distorted. At a certain period after the prevalence of a system of opinions founded upon those promulgated by him, the three forms into which Plato had distributed the faculties of mind underwent a sort of apotheosis, and became the object of the worship of the civilized world. Here it is to be confessed that 'Light seems to thicken, ' and

> The crow makes wing to the rooky wood,
> Good things of day begin to droop and drowse,
> And night's black agents to their preys do rouze. ①

But mark how beautiful an order has sprung from the dust and blood of this fierce chaos! how the world, as from a resurrection, balancing itself on the golden wings of Knowledge and of Hope, has reassumed its yet unwearied flight into

---

① Shakespeare, *Macbeth*, III. ii. 50-53—editor's note.

the Heaven of time. Listen to the music, unheard by outward ears, which is as a ceaseless and invisible wind, nourishing its everlasting course with strength and swiftness.

The poetry in the doctrines of Jesus Christ, and the mythology and institutions of the Celtic[1] conquerors of the Roman Empire, outlived the darkness and the convulsions connected with their growth and victory, and blended themselves in a new fabric of manners and opinion. It is an error to impute the ignorance of the dark ages to the Christian doctrines or the predominance of the Celtic nations. Whatever of evil their agencies may have contained sprang from the extinction of the poetical principle, connected with the progress of despotism and superstition. Men, from causes too intricate to be here discussed, had become insensible and selfish: their own will had become feeble, and yet they were its slaves, and thence the slaves of the will of others: lust, fear, avarice, cruelty and fraud, characterized a race amongst whom no one was to be found capable of creating in form, language, or institution. The moral anomalies of such a state of society are not justly to be charged upon any class of events immediately connected with them, and those events are most entitled to our approbation which could dissolve it most expeditiously. It is unfortunate for those who cannot distinguish words from thoughts, that many of these anomalies have been incorporated into our popular religion.

It was not until the eleventh century that the effects of the poetry of the Christian and Chivalric systems began to manifest themselves. The principle of equality had been discovered and applied by Plato in his *Republic*, as the theoretical rule of the mode in which the materials of pleasure and of power produced by the common skill and labour of human beings ought to be distributed among them. The limitations of this rule were asserted by him to be determined only by the sensibility of each, or the utility to result to all. Plato, following the doctrines of Timæus and Pythagoras, taught also a moral and intellectual system of doctrine comprehending at once the past, the present, and the future condition

---

[1] Shelley uses the word in its Greek meaning: barbarian tribes to the north of the classical Mediterranean civilization—editor's note.

of man. Jesus Christ divulged the sacred and eternal truths contained in these views to mankind, and Christianity, in its abstract purity, became the exoteric expression of the esoteric doctrines of the poetry and wisdom of antiquity. The incorporation of the Celtic nations with the exhausted population of the South impressed upon it the figure of the poetry existing in their mythology and institutions. The result was a sum of the action and reaction of all the causes included in it; for it may be assumed as a maxim that no nation or religion can supersede any other without incorporating into itself a portion of that which it supersedes. The abolition of personal and domestic slavery, and the emancipation of women from a great part of the degrading restraints of antiquity were among the consequences of these events.

The abolition of personal slavery is the basis of the highest political hope that it can enter into the mind of man to conceive. The freedom of women produced the poetry of sexual love. Love became a religion, the idols of whose worship were ever present. It was as if the statues of Apollo and the Muses had been endowed with life and motion, and had walked forth among their worshippers; so that earth became peopled with the inhabitants of a diviner world. The familiar appearance and proceedings of life became wonderful and heavenly, and a paradise was created as out of the wrecks of Eden. And as this creation itself is poetry, so its creators were poets; and language was the instrument of their art: '*Galeotto fù il libro, e chi lo scrisse*' [Galeotto was the book and the one who wrote it]. The Provençal Trouveurs, or inventors, preceded Petrarch, whose verses are as spells, which unseal the inmost enchanted fountains of the delight which is in the grief of love. It is impossible to feel them without becoming a portion of that beauty which we contemplate: it were superfluous to explain how the gentleness and the elevation of mind connected with these sacred emotions can render men more amiable, more generous and wise, and lift them out of the dull vapours of the little world of self. Dante understood the secret things of love even more than Petrarch. His *Vita Nuova* is an inexhaustible fountain of purity of sentiment and language: it is the idealized history of that period, and those intervals of his life which were dedicated to love. His apotheosis of Beatrice in Paradise and the gradations of his own love and her loveliness, by which as by steps he feigns himself to have ascended to the throne of the Supreme Cause, is the most glorious imagination of modern poetry. The acutest critics have justly reversed the judgment of the vulgar, and the order of the great acts of the *Divine Drama*, in the measure of the admiration which they accord to the Hell, Purgatory and Paradise. The latter is a perpetual hymn of everlasting love. Love, which found a worthy poet in Plato alone of all the ancients, has been celebrated by a chorus of the greatest writers of the renovated world; and the music has penetrated the caverns of society, and its echoes still drown the dissonance of arms and superstition. At successive intervals, Ariosto, Tasso, Shakespeare, Spenser, Calderon, Rousseau, and the great writers of our own age, have celebrated the dominion of love, planting as it were trophies in the human mind of that sublimest victory over sensuality and force. The true relation borne to each other by the sexes into which humankind is distributed has become less misunderstood; and if the error which confounded diversity with inequality of the powers of the two sexes has been partially recognised in the opinions and institutions of modern Europe, we owe this great benefit to the worship of which chivalry was the law, and poets the prophets.

 The poetry of Dante may be considered as the bridge thrown over the stream of time, which unites the modern and ancient world. The distorted notions of invisible things which Dante and his rival Milton have idealized, are merely the mask and the mantle in which these great poets walk through eternity enveloped and disguised. It is a difficult question to determine how far they were conscious of the distinction which must have subsisted in their minds between their own creeds and that of the people. Dante at least appears to wish to mark the full extent of it by placing Rhipæus, whom Vergil calls *justissimus unus* [the one who was most just], in Paradise, and observing a most heretical caprice in his distribution of rewards and punishments. And Milton's poem contains within itself a philosophical refutation of that system of which, by a strange and natural antithesis, it has been a chief popular support. Nothing can exceed the energy and magnificence of the character of Satan as expressed in Paradise Lost. It is a mistake to suppose that he could ever have been intended for the popular personification of evil. Implacable hate, patient cunning, and a sleepless refinement of device to inflict the extremist anguish on an enemy, these things are evil; and although venial in a slave are not to be forgiven in a tyrant; although redeemed by much that ennobles his defeat in one subdued, are marked by all that dishonours his conquest in the victor. Milton's Devil as a moral being is as far superior to his God as one who perseveres in some purpose which he has conceived to be excellent in spite of adversity and torture, is to one who in the cold security of undoubted triumph inflicts the most horrible revenge upon his enemy, not from any mistaken notion of inducing him to repent of a perseverance in enmity, but with the alleged design of exasperating him to deserve new torments. Milton has so far violated the popular creed (if this shall be judged to be a violation) as to have alleged no superiority of moral virtue to his God over his Devil. And this bold neglect of a direct moral purpose is the most decisive proof of the supremacy of Milton's genius. He mingled as it were the elements of human nature as colours upon a single pallet, and arranged them in the composition of his great picture according to the laws of epic truth; that is, according to the laws of that principle by which a series of actions of the external universe and of intelligent and ethical beings is calculated to excite the sympathy of succeeding generations of mankind. The *Divina Commedia* and *Paradise Lost* have conferred upon modern mythology a systematic form; and when change and time shall have added one more superstition to the mass of those which have arisen and decayed upon the earth, commentators will be learnedly employed in elucidating the religion of ancestral Europe, only not utterly forgotten because it will have been stamped with the eternity of genius.

Homer was the first and Dante the second epic poet: that is, the second poet the series of whose creations bore a defined and intelligible relation to the knowledge, and sentiment, and religion, and political conditions of the age in which he lived, and of the ages which followed it, developing itself in correspondence with their development. For Lucretius had limed the wings of his swift spirit in the dregs of the sensible world; and Vergil, with a modesty that ill became his genius, had affected the fame of an imitator, even whilst he created anew all that he copied; and none among the flock of mock-birds, though their notes were sweet, Apollonius Rhodius, Quintus Calaber Smyrnaeus, Nonnus,

Lucan, Statius, or Claudian, have sought even to fulfil a single condition of epic truth. Milton was the third epic poet. For if the title of epic in its highest sense be refused to the *Aeneid,* still less can it be conceded to the *Orlando Furioso,* the *Gerusalemme Liberata,* the *Lusiad,* or the *Faerie Queene.*

Dante and Milton were both deeply penetrated with the ancient religion of the civilized world; and its spirit exists in their poetry probably in the same proportion as its forms survived in the unreformed worship of modern Europe. The one preceded and the other followed the Reformation at almost equal intervals. Dante was the first religious reformer, and Luther surpassed him rather in the rudeness and acrimony than in the boldness of his censures of papal usurpation. Dante was the first awakener of entranced Europe; he created a language in itself music and persuasion out of a chaos of inharmonious barbarians. He was the congregator of those great spirits who presided over the resurrection of learning; the Lucifer of that starry flock which in the thirteenth century shone forth from republican Italy, as from a heaven, into the darkness of the benighted world. His very words are instinct with spirit; each is as a spark, a burning atom of inextinguishable thought; and many yet lie covered in the ashes of their birth, and pregnant with the lightning which has yet found no conductor. All high poetry is infinite; it is as the first acorn, which contained all oaks potentially. Veil after veil may be undrawn, and the inmost naked beauty of the meaning never exposed. A great Poem is a fountain forever overflowing with the waters of wisdom and delight; and after one person and one age has exhausted all its divine effluence which their peculiar relations enable them to share, another and yet another succeeds, and new relations are ever developed, the source of an unforeseen and an unconceived delight.

The age immediately succeeding to that of Dante, Petrarch, and Boccaccio, was characterized by a revival of painting, sculpture, music, and architecture. Chaucer caught the sacred inspiration, and the superstructure of English literature is based upon the materials of Italian invention.

But let us not be betrayed from a defence into a critical history of Poetry and its influence on Society. Be it enough to have pointed out the effects of poets, in the large and true sense of the word, upon their own and all succeeding times and to revert to the partial instances cited as illustrations of an opinion the reverse of that attempted to be established in the Four Ages of Poetry.

But poets have been challenged to resign the civic crown to reasoners and mechanists on another plea. It is admitted that the exercise of the imagination is most delightful, but it is alleged that that of reason is more useful. Let us examine as the grounds of this distinction what is here meant by Utility. Pleasure or good, in a general sense, is that which the consciousness of a sensitive and intelligent being seeks, and in which when found it acquiesces. There are two kinds of pleasure, one durable, universal, and permanent; the other transitory and particular. Utility may either express the means of producing the former or the latter. In the former sense, whatever strengthens and purifies the affections, enlarges the imagination, and adds spirit to sense, is useful. But the meaning in which the Author of the Four Ages of Poetry seems to have employed the word utility is the narrower one of banishing the importunity of the wants of our animal nature, the surrounding men with security of life, the dispersing the grosser delusions of superstitions and the conciliating such a degree of mutual forbearance among men as may consist with the motives of personal advantage.

Undoubtedly the promoters of utility in this limited sense, have their appointed office in society. They follow the footsteps of poets, and copy the sketches of their creations into the book of common life. They make space, and give time. Their exertions are of the highest value so long as they confine their administration of the concerns of the inferior powers of our nature within the limits due to the superior ones. But whilst the sceptic destroys gross superstitions, let him spare to deface, as some of the French writers have defaced, the eternal truths charactered upon the imaginations of men. Whilst the mechanist abridges, and the political economist combines labour, let them beware that their speculations, for want of correspondence with those first principles which belong to the imagination, do not tend, as they have in modern England, to exasperate at once the extremes of luxury and want. They have exemplified the saying, 'To him that hath, more shall be given; and from him that hath not, the little that he hath shall be taken away.' ① The rich have become richer, and the poor have become poorer; and the vessel of the state is driven between the Scylla and Charybdis② of anarchy and despotism. Such are the effects which must ever flow from an unmitigated exercise of the calculating faculty.

It is difficult to define pleasure in its highest sense; the definition involving a number of apparent paradoxes. For, from an inexplicable defect of harmony in the constitution of human nature, the pain of the inferior is frequently connected with the pleasures of the superior portions of our being. Sorrow, terror, anguish, despair itself, are often the chosen expressions of an approximation to the highest good. Our sympathy in tragic fiction depends on this principle; tragedy delights by affording a shadow of the pleasure which exists in pain. This is the source also of the melancholy which is inseparable from the sweetest melody. The pleasure that is in sorrow is sweeter than the pleasure of pleasure itself. And hence the saying, 'It is better to go to the house of mourning than to the house of mirth.'③ Not that this highest species of pleasure is necessarily linked with pain. The delight of love and friendship, the ecstasy of the admiration of nature, the joy of the perception and still more of the creation of poetry is often wholly unalloyed.

The production and assurance of pleasure in this highest sense is true utility. Those who produce and preserve this pleasure are Poets or poetical philosophers.

The exertions of Locke, Hume, Gibbon, Voltaire, Rousseau,④ and their disciples, in favor of oppressed and deluded humanity, are entitled to the gratitude of mankind. Yet it is easy to calculate the degree of moral and intellectual improvement which the world would have exhibited, had they never lived. A little more nonsense would have been talked for a century or two; and perhaps a few more men, women, and children burnt as heretics. We might not at this

---

① Cf. Matthew 25: 29; Mark 4: 25; Luke 8: 18—editor's note.
② Cf. *Odyssey*, XII—editor's note.
③ Cf. Ecclesiastes 7: 2—editor's note.
④ I follow the classification adopted by the author of the Four Ages of Poetry. But Rousseau was essentially a poet. The others, even Voltaire, were mere reasoners.

moment have been congratulating each other on the abolition of the Inquisition in Spain. But it exceeds all imagination to conceive what would have been the moral condition of the world if neither Dante, Petrarch, Boccaccio, Chaucer, Shakespeare, Calderon, Lord Bacon, nor Milton, had ever existed; if Raphael and Michael Angelo had never been born; if the Hebrew poetry had never been translated; if a revival of the study of Greek literature had never taken place; if no monuments of ancient sculpture had been handed down to us; and if the poetry of the religion of the ancient world had been extinguished together with its belief. The human mind could never, except by the intervention of these excitements, have been awakened to the invention of the grosser sciences, and that application of analytical reasoning to the aberrations of society, which it is now attempted to exalt over the direct expression of the inventive and creative faculty itself.

We have more moral, political and historical wisdom than we know how to reduce into practice; we have more scientific and economical knowledge than can be accommodated to the just distribution of the produce which it multiplies. The poetry in these systems of thought is concealed by the accumulation of facts and calculating processes. There is no want of knowledge respecting what is wisest and best in morals, government, and political economy, or at least, what is wiser and better than what men now practise and endure. But we let '*I dare not* wait upon *I would*, like the poor cat i' the adage.' ① We want the creative faculty to imagine that which we know; we want the generous impulse to act that which we imagine; we want the poetry of life; our calculations have outrun conception; we have eaten more than we can digest. The cultivation of those sciences which have enlarged the limits of the empire of man over the external world, has, for want of the poetical faculty, proportionally circumscribed those of the internal world; and man, having enslaved the elements, remains himself a slave. To what but a cultivation of the mechanical arts in a degree disproportioned to the presence of the creative faculty, which is the basis of all knowledge, is to be attributed the abuse of all invention for abridging and combining

---

① Shakespeare, Macbeth, I, vii. 44-45—editor's note.

labour, to the exasperation of the inequality of mankind? From what other cause has it arisen that the discoveries which should have lightened, have added a weight to the curse imposed on Adam? Poetry, and the principle of Self, of which money is the visible incarnation, are the God and Mammon of the world.[1]

The functions of the poetical faculty are two-fold: by one it creates new materials of knowledge, and power, and pleasure; by the other it engenders in the mind a desire to reproduce and arrange them according to a certain rhythm and order which may be called the beautiful and the good. The cultivation of poetry is never more to be desired than at periods when, from an excess of the selfish and calculating principle, the accumulation of the materials of external life exceed the quantity of the power of assimilating them to the internal laws of human nature. The body has then become too unwieldy for that which animates it.

Poetry is indeed something divine. It is at once the centre and circumference of knowledge; it is that which comprehends all science, and that to which all science must be referred. It is at the same time the root and blossom of all other systems of thought; it is that from which all spring, and that which adorns all; and that which, if blighted, denies the fruit and the seed, and withholds from the barren world the nourishment and the succession of the scions of the tree of life. It is the perfect and consummate surface and bloom of all things; it is as the odour and the colour of the rose to the texture of the elements which compose it, as the form and splendor of unfaded beauty to the secrets of anatomy and corruption. What were Virtue, Love, Patriotism, Friendship&c. —what were the scenery of this beautiful Universe which we inhabit; what were our consolations on this side of the grave—and what were our aspirations beyond it, if Poetry did not ascend to bring light and fire from those eternal regions where the owl-winged faculty of calculation dare not ever soar? Poetry is not like reasoning, a power to be exerted according to the determination of the will. A man cannot say, 'I will compose poetry.' The greatest poet even cannot say it; for the mind

---

[1] 'No man can serve two masters ... ye cannot serve God and mammon' (Matthew, 6: 24; see also Luke, 16: 13)—editor's note.

in creation is as a fading coal which some invisible influence, like an inconstant wind, awakens to transitory brightness: this power arises from within, like the colour of a flower which fades and changes as it is developed, and the conscious portions of our natures are unprophetic either of its approach or its departure. Could this influence be durable in its original purity and force, it is impossible to predict the greatness of the results: but when composition begins, inspiration is already on the decline, and the most glorious poetry that has ever been communicated to the world is probably a feeble shadow of the original conceptions of the poet. I appeal to the greatest Poets of the present day, whether it is not an error to assert that the finest passages of poetry are produced by labour and study. The toil and the delay recommended by critics can be justly interpreted to mean no more than a careful observation of the inspired moments, and an artificial connection of the spaces between their suggestions by the intertexture of conventional expressions; a necessity only imposed by the limitedness of the poetical faculty itself; for Milton conceived the *Paradise Lost* as a whole before he executed it in portions. We have his own authority also for the Muse having 'dictated' to him the 'unpremeditated song,' and let this be an answer to those who would allege the fifty-six various readings of the first line of the *Orlando Furioso*. Compositions so produced are to poetry what mosaic is to painting. This instinct and intuition of the poetical faculty are still more observable in the plastic and pictorial arts; a great statue or picture grows under the power of the artis: as a child in a mother's womb, and the very mind which directs the hands in formation is incapable of accounting to itself for the origin, the gradations, or the media of the process.

Poetry is the record of the best and happiest moments of the happiest and best minds. We are aware of evanescent visitations of thought and feeling sometimes associated with place or person, sometimes regarding our own mind alone, and always arising unforeseen and departing unbidden, but elevating and delightful beyond all expression: so that even in the desire and the regret they leave, there cannot but be pleasure, participating as it does in the nature of its object. It is as it were the interpretation of a diviner nature through our own; but its footsteps are like those of a wind over the sea, which the coming calm erases, and whose traces remain only as on the wrinkled sand which paves it. These and corresponding conditions of being are experienced principally by those of the most delicate sensibility and the most enlarged imagination; and the state of mind produced by them is at war with every base desire. The enthusiasm of virtue, love, patriotism, and friendship is essentially linked with such emotions; and whilst they last, self appears as what it is, an atom to a universe. Poets are not only subject to these experiences as spirits of the most refined organization, but they can colour all that they combine with the evanescent hues of this ethereal world; a word, a trait in the representation of a scene or a passion will touch the enchanted chord, and reanimate, in those who have ever experienced these emotions, the sleeping, the cold, the buried image of the past. Poetry thus makes immortal all that is best and most beautiful in the world; it arrests the vanishing apparitions which haunt the interlunations of life, and veiling them, or in language or in form, sends them forth among mankind, bearing sweet news of kindred joy to those with whom their sisters abide—abide, because there is no portal of expression from the caverns of the spirit which they inhabit into the universe of things. Poetry redeems from decay the visitations of the divinity in man.

Poetry turns all things to loveliness; it exalts the beauty of that which is most beautiful, and it adds beauty to that which is most deformed; it marries exultation and horror, grief and pleasure, eternity and change; it subdues to union under its light yoke all irreconcilable things. It transmutes all that it touches, and every form moving within the radiance of its presence is changed by wondrous sympathy to an incarnation of the spirit which it breathes: its secret alchemy turns to potable gold the poisonous waters which flow from death through life; it strips the veil of familiarity from the world, and lays bare the naked and sleeping beauty which is the spirit of its forms.

All things exist as they are perceived: at least in relation to the percipient. 'The mind is its own place, and of itself can make a heaven of hell, a hell of heaven.'[1] But poetry defeats the curse which binds us to be subjected to the accident of surrounding impressions. And whether it spreads its own figured cur-

---

[1] Milton, *Paradise Lost*, I. 254-55—editor's note.

tain, or withdraws life's dark veil from before the scene of things, it equally creates for us a being within our being. It makes us the inhabitants of a world to which the familiar world is a chaos. It reproduces the common universe of which we are portions and percipients, and it purges from our inward sight the film of familiarity which obscures from us the wonder of our being. It compels us to feel that which we perceive, and to imagine that which we know. It creates anew the universe after it has been annihilated in our minds by the recurrence of impressions blunted by reiteration. It justifies the bold and true words of Tasso—*Non merita nome di creatore, se non Iddio ed il Poeta* [No one but God and the Poet deserve the name of Creator].

A poet, as he is the author to others of the highest wisdom, pleasure, virtue and glory, so he ought personally to be the happiest, the best, the wisest, and the most illustrious of men. As to his glory, let Time be challenged to declare whether the fame of any other institutor of human life be comparable to that of a poet. That he is the wisest, the happiest, and the best, inasmuch as he is a poet, is equally incontrovertible: the greatest poets have been men of the most spotless virtue, of the most consummate prudence, and, if we would look into the interior of their lives, the most fortunate of men: and the exceptions, as they regard those who possessed the poetic faculty in a high yet inferior degree, will be found on consideration to confine rather than destroy the rule. Let us for a moment stoop to the arbitration of popular breath, and usurping and uniting in our own persons the incompatible characters of accuser, witness, judge, and executioner, let us decide without trial, testimony, or form, that certain motives of those who are 'there sitting where we dare not soar' ① are reprehensible. Let us assume that Homer was a drunkard, that Vergil was a flatterer, that Horace was a coward, that Tasso was a madman, that Lord Bacon was a peculator, that Raphael was a libertine, that Spenser was a poet laureate. It is inconsistent with this division of our subject to cite living poets, but posterity has done ample justice to the great names now referred to. Their errors have been weighed and found to have been dust in the balance; if their sins 'were as scarlet, they are now white as

---

① Milton, *Paradise Lost*, IV. 829—editor's note.

snow';[1] they have been washed in the blood of the mediator and redeemer, Time. Observe in what a ludicrous chaos the imputations of real or fictitious crime have been confused in the contemporary calumnies against poetry and poets; consider how little is as it appears—or appears as it is; look to your own motives, and judge not, lest ye be judged.

Poetry, as has been said, differs in this respect from logic, that it is not subject to the control of the active powers of the mind, and that its birth and recurrence have no necessary connection with the consciousness or will. It is presumptuous to determine that these are the necessary conditions of all mental causation, when mental effects are experienced unsusceptible of being referred to them. The frequent recurrence of the poetical power, it is obvious to suppose, may produce in the mind a habit of order and harmony correlative with its own nature and with its effects upon other minds. But in the intervals of inspiration, and they may be frequent without being durable, a poet becomes a man, and is abandoned to the sudden reflux of the influences under which others habitually live. But as he is more delicately organized than other men, and sensible to pain and pleasure, both his own and that of others, in a degree unknown to them, he will avoid the one and pursue the other with an ardour proportioned to this difference. And he renders himself obnoxious to calumny, when he neglects to observe the circumstances under which these objects of universal pursuit and flight have disguised themselves in one another's garments.

But there is nothing necessarily evil in this error, and thus cruelty, envy, revenge, avarice, and the passions purely evil, have never formed any portion of the popular imputations on the lives of poets.

I have thought it most favorable to the cause of truth to set down these remarks according to the order in which they were suggested to my mind, by a consideration of the subject itself, instead of following that of the treatise that excited me to make them public. Thus although devoid of the formality of a polemical reply; if the views which they contain be just, they will be found to involve a refutation of the Four Ages of Poetry, so far at least as regards the first

---

[1] Isaiah 1: 18—editor's note.

division of the subject. I can readily conjecture what should have moved the gall of the learned and intelligent author of that paper; I confess myself like them unwilling to be stunned by the Theseids of the hoarse Codri of the day. Bavius and Mævius undoubtedly are, as they ever were, insufferable persons. But it belongs to a philosophical critic to distinguish rather than confound.[1]

The first part of these remarks has related to poetry in its elements and principles; and it has been shown, as well as the narrow limits assigned them would permit, that what is called Poetry, in a restricted sense, has a common source with all other forms of order and of beauty, according to which the materials of human life are susceptible of being arranged, and which is Poetry in an universal sense.

The second part will have for its object an application of these principles to the present state of the cultivation of Poetry, and a defence of the attempt to idealize the modern forms of manners and opinions, and compel them into a subordination to the imaginative and creative faculty. For the literature of England, an energetic development of which has ever preceded or accompanied a great and free development of the national will, has arisen as it were from a new birth. In spite of the low-thoughted envy which would undervalue contemporary merit, our own will be a memorable age in intellectual achievements, and we live among such philosophers and poets as surpass beyond comparison any who have appeared since the last national struggle for civil and religious liberty. The most unfailing herald, companion, and follower of the awakening of a great people to work a beneficial change in opinion or institution, is Poetry. At such periods there is an accumulation of the power of communicating and receiving intense and impassioned conceptions respecting man and nature. The person in whom this power resides, may often, as far as regards many portions of their nature, have little apparent correspondence with that spirit of good of which they are the ministers. But even whilst they deny and abjure, they are yet compelled to serve, the Power which is seated on the throne of their own soul. It is impos-

---

[1] Codrus, Bavius, and Maevius were inferior Latin poets castigated by Juvenal, Virgil, and Horace—editor's note.

sible to read the compositions of the most celebrated writers of the present day without being startled with the electric life which burns within their words. They measure the circumference and sound the depths of human nature with a comprehensive and all-penetrating spirit, and they are themselves perhaps the most sincerely astonished at its manifestations, for it is less their spirit than the spirit of the age. Poets are the hierophants of an unapprehended inspiration, the mirrors of the gigantic shadows which futurity casts upon the present, the words which express what they understand not, the trumpets which sing to battle and feel not what they inspire: the influence which is moved not, but moves. Poets are the unacknowledged legislators of the World.

John Keats

Letters

To Benjamin Bailey, 22nd November 1817

I will get over the first part of this Letter as soon as possible for it relates to the affair of poor Crips—To a Man of your nature such a Letter as Haydon's must have been extremely cutting— What occasions the greater part of the World's Quarrels? Simply this, two Minds meet and do not understand each other time enough to prevent any shock or surprise at the conduct of either party — As soon as I had known Haydon three days I had got enough of his character not to have been surprised at such a Letter as he has hurt you with. Nor when I knew it was it a principle with me to drop his acquaintance although with you it would have been an imperious feeling. I wish you knew all that I think about Genius and the Heart—and yet I think you are thoroughly acquainted with my innermost breast in that respect, or you could not have known me even thus long and still hold me worthy to be your dear friend. In passing however I must say of one thing that has pressed upon me lately and encreased my Humility and capability of submission and that is this truth— Men of Genius are great as certain ethereal Chemicals operating on the Mass of neutral intellect— but they have not any individuality, any determined Character—I would call the top and head of those who have a proper self Men of Power.

But I am running my head into a Subject which I am certain I could not do justice to under five years Study and 3 vols octavo—and moreover long to be talking about the Imagination—so my dear Bailey do not think of this unpleasant affair if possible—do not—I defy any harm to come of it—I defy. I shall write to Crips this Week and request him to tell me all his going on from time to time by Letter wherever I may be—it will all go on well so don't because you have suddenly discover'd a Coldness in Haydon suffer yourself to be teased. Do not my dear fellow. O I wish I was as certain of the end of all your troubles as that of your momentary start about the authenticity of the Imagination. I am certain of nothing but of the holiness of the Heart's affections and the truth of Imagination—What the imagination seizes as Beauty must be truth—whether it existed before or not—for I have the same idea of all our passions as of love: they are all, in their sublime, creative of essential beauty. In a word, you may know my favorite speculation by my first book, and the little song I send in my last, which is a representation from the fancy of the probable mode of operating in these matters. The imagination may be compared to Adam's dream, —he awoke and found it truth. I am more zealous in this affair because I have never yet been able to perceive how anything can be known for truth by consecutive reasoning— and yet it must be. Can it be that even the greatest philosopher ever arrived at his goal without putting aside numerous objections? However it may be, O for a life of sensation rather than of thoughts! It is a 'Vision in the form of Youth, ' a shadow of reality to come. And this consideration has further convinced me, — for it has come as auxiliary to another favorite speculation of mine, —that we shall enjoy ourselves hereafter by having what we called happiness on earth repeated in a finer tone and so repeated. And yet such a fate can only befall those who delight in sensation, rather than hunger as you do after truth. Adam's dream will do here, and seems to be a conviction that imagination and its empyreal reflection is the same as human life and its spiritual repetition. But, as I was saying, the simple imaginative mind may have its rewards in the repetition of its own silent working coming continually on the spirit with a fine suddenness—to compare great things with small—have you never by being Surprised with an old Melody—in a delicious place—by a delicious voice, felt over again your very Speculations and Surmises at the time it first operated on your Soul—do you not remember forming to yourself the singer's face more beautiful than it was possible and yet with the elevation of the Moment you did not think so—even then you were mounted on the Wings of Imagination so high—that the Protrotype must be hereafter—that delicious face you will see. What a time! I am continually running away from the subject—sure this cannot be exactly the case with a complex Mind—one that is imaginative and at the same time careful of its fruits—who would exist partly on Sensation partly on thought—to whom it is necessary that years should bring the philosophic Mind—such a one I consider your's and therefore it is necessary to your eternal Happiness that you not only drink this old Wine of Heaven, which I shall call the redigestion of our most ethereal Musings on Earth; but also increase in knowledge and know all things. I am glad to hear you are in a fair way for Easter—you will soon get through your unpleasent reading and then! —but the world is full of troubles and I have not much reason to think myself pesterd with many—I think Jane or Marianne has a better opinion of me than I deserve—for really and truly I do not think my Brother's illness connected with mine—you know more of the real Cause than they do nor have I any chance of being rack'd as you have been—You perhaps at one time thought there was such a thing as worldly happiness to be arrived at, at certain periods of time marked out, —you have of necessity from your disposition been thus led away—I scarcely remember counting upon any happiness—I look for it if it be not in the present hour, —nothing startles me beyond the moment. The setting sun will always set me to rights, or if a sparrow come before my window, I take part in its existence and pick about the gravel. The first thing that strikes me on hearing a misfortune having befallen another is this— 'Well, it cannot be helped: he will have the pleasure of trying the resources of his spirit' —and I beg now, my dear Bailey, that hereafter should you observe anything cold in me not to put it to the account of heartlessness, but abstraction—for I assure you I sometimes feel not the influence of a passion or affection during a whole week—and so long this sometimes continues, I begin to suspect myself, and the genuineness of my feelings at other times—thinking them a few barren tragedy tears.

To George and Tom Keats, 21st December 1817

I must crave your pardon for not having written ere this. I have had two very pleasant evenings with Dilke yesterday & today; and I am at this moment just come from him and feel in the humour to go on with this, began in the morning. I spent Friday evening with Wells and went the next morning to see *Death on the Pale Horse*. It is a wonderful picture, when West's age is considered. But there is nothing to be intense upon; no women one feels mad to kiss; no face swelling into reality. The excellence of every Art is its intensity, capable of making all disagreeables evaporate, from their being in close relationship with Beauty and Truth—Examine *King Lear* and you will find this exemplified throughout; but in this picture we have unpleasantness without any momentous depth of speculation excited, in which to bury its repulsiveness ...

Brown and Dilke walked with me and back from the Christmas pantomime. I had not a dispute but a disquisition with Dilke, on various subjects; several things dovetailed in my mind, and at once it struck me, what quality went to form a Man of Achievement especially in literature and which Shakespeare possessed so enormously—I mean Negative Capability, that is when man is capable of being in uncertainties, Mysteries, doubts, without any irritable reaching after fact and reason—Coleridge, for instance, would let go by a fine isolated verisimilitude caught from the Penetralium of mystery, from being incapable of remaining content with half knowledge. This pursued through Volumes would perhaps take us no further than this, that with a great poet the sense of Beauty overcomes every other consideration, or rather obliterates all consideration.

Write soon to your most sincere friend and affectionate brother.

To John Hamilton Reynolds, 3rd Februrary 1818

What I complain of is that I have been in so an uneasy state of Mind as not to be fit to write to an invalid. I cannot write to any length under a disguised feeling. I should have loaded you with an addition of gloom, which I am sure you do not want. I am now thank God in a humour to give you a good groat's worth—for Tom, after a Night without a Wink of sleep, and overburdened with fever, has got up after a refreshing fay sleep and is better than he has been for a long time; and you I trust have been again round the Common without any effect but refreshment. —As to the Matter I hope I can say with Sir Andrew 'I have matter enough in my head' in your favor. And now, in the second place, for I reckon that I have finished my Imprimis, I am glad you blow up the weather— all through your letter there is a leaning towards a climate-curse, and you know what a delicate satisfaction there is in having a vexation anathematized: one would think there has been growing up for these last four thousand years, a grandchild Scion of the old forbidden tree, and that some modern Eve had just violated it; and that there was come with double charge, 'Notus and Afer black with thunderous clouds from Sierra-leona' ①—I shall breathe worsted stockings sooner than I thought for. Tom wants to be in Town—we will have some such days upon the heath like that of last summer and why not with the same book or what say you to a black Letter Chaucer printed in 1596: aye I've got one huzza! I shall have it bounden gothique, a nice sombre binding—it will go a little way to unmodernize. And also I see no reason, because I have been away this last month, why I should not have a peep at your Spencerian—notwithstanding you speak of your office, in my thought a little too early, for I do not see why a Mind like yours is not capable of harbouring and digesting the whole Mystery of Law as easily as Parson Hugh does Pepins—which did not hinder him from his poetic Canary—Were I to study physic or rather Medicine again, —I feel it would not make the least difference in my Poetry; when the Mind is in its infancy a Bias is in reality a Bias, but when we have acquired more strength, a Bias becomes no Bias. Every department of knowledge we see excellent and calculated towards a great whole. I am so convinced of this, that I am glad at not having given away my medical Books, which I shall again look over to keep alive the little I know thitherwards; and moreover intend through you and Rice to become a sort of Pip-civilian. An extensive knowledge is needful to thinking people—it takes away the heat and fever; and helps, by widening speculation, to ease the

---

① Milton, *Paradise Lost*, X. 702-03—editor's note.

Burden of the Mystery: a thing I begin to understand a little, and which weighed upon you in the most gloomy and true sentence in your Letter. The difference of high Sensations with and without knowledge appears to me this—in the latter case we are falling continually ten thousand fathoms deep and being blown up again without wings and with all horror of a bare shouldered Creature—in the former case, our shoulders are fledge, and we go thro' the same air and space without fear. This is running one's rigs on the score of abstracted benefit—when we come to human Life and the affections it is impossible how a parallel of breast and head can be drawn—(you will forgive me for thus privately treading out [of] my depth and take it for treading as schoolboys tread the water)—it is impossible to know how far knowledge will console us for the death of a friend and the ill 'that flesh is heir to' ①—With respect to the affections and Poetry you must know by a sympathy my thoughts that way; and I dare say these few lines will be but a ratification: I wrote them on May-day—and intend to finish the ode all in good time. —

> Mother of Hermes! and still youthful Maia!
> May I sing to thee
> As thou was hymned on the shores of Baiæ?
> Or may I woo thee
> In earlier Sicilian? or thy smiles
> Seek as they once were sought, in Grecian isles,
> By Bards who died content in pleasant sward,
> Leaving great verse unto a little clan?
> O give me their old vigour, and unheard,
> Save of the quiet Primrose, and the span
> Of Heave, and few ears
> Rounded by thee my song should die away
> Content as theirs
> Rich in the simple worship of a day. —

---

① *Hamlet*, III. i. 63—editor's note.

You may be anxious to know for fact to what sentence in your Letter I allude. You say 'I fear there is little chance of any thing else in this life.' You seem by that to have been going through with a more painful and acute zest the same labyrinth that I have—I have come to the same conclusion thus far. My Branchings out therefrom have been numerous: one of them is the consideration of Wordsworth's genius and as a help, in the manner of gold being the meridian Line of worldly wealth, —how he differs from Milton. —And here I have nothing but surmises, from an uncertainty whether Milton's apparently less anxiety for Humanity proceeds from his seeing further or no than Wordsworth: And whether Wordsworth has in truth epic passion, and martyrs himself to the human heart, the main region of his song—In regard to his genius alone—we find what he says true as far as we have experienced and we can judge no further but by larger experience—for axioms in philosophy are not axioms until they are proved upon our pulses: We have read fine things but never feel them to the full until we have gone the same steps as the Author. —I know this is not plain; you will know exactly my meaning when I say, that now I shall relish *Hamlet* more than I ever have done—Or, better—You are sensible no man can set down Venery as a bestial or joyless thing until he is sick of it and therefore all philosophizing in it would be mere wording. Until we are sick, we understand not; — in fine, as Byron says, 'Knowledge is Sorrow'; and I go on to say that 'Sorrow is Wisdom'—and further for aught we can know for certainty! 'Wisdom is folly'—So you see how I have run away from Wordsworth and Milton; and shall still run away from what was in my head, to observe, that some kind of letters are good squares others handsome ovals, and others some orbicular, others spheroid—and why should there not be another species with two rough edges like a Rat-trap? I hope you will find all my long letters of that species, and all will be well; for by merely touching the spring delicately and etherially, the rough edged will fly immediately into a proper compactness, and thus you may make a good wholesome load, with your own leven in it, of my fragments—If you cannot find this said Rat-trap sufficiently tractable—alas for me, it being an impossibility in grain for my ink to stain otherwise: If I scribble long letters I must play my vagaries. I must be too heavy, or too light, for whole pages—I must be quaint and free of Tropes and figures—I must play my draughts as I please, and for my advantage and your erudition, crown a white with a black, or a black with a white, and move into black or white, far and near as I please—I must go from Hazlitt to Patmore, and make Wordsworth and Coleman play at leap-frog—or keep one of them down a whole half holiday at fly the garter—'From Gray to Gay, from Little to Shakespeare'—Also as a long cause requires two or more sittings of the Court, so a long letter will require two or more sittings of the Breech wherefore I shall resume after dinner.

Have you not seen a Gull, an orc, a sea Mew, or any thing to bring this Line to a proper length, and also fill up this clear part; that like the Gull I may dip—I hope, not out of sight, and also, like a Gull, I hope to be lucky in a good sized fish—This crossing a letter is not without its association —for chequer work leads us naturally to a Milkmaid, a Milkmaid to Hogarth, Hogarth to Shakespeare, Shakespear to Hazlitt—Hazlitt to Shakespeare and thus by merely pulling an apron string we set a pretty peal of Chimes at work—Let them chime on while, with your patience, —I will return to Wordsworth—whether or no he has an extended vision or a circumscribed grandeur —whether he is an eagle in his nest, or on the wing—And to be more explicit and to show you how tall I stand by the giant, I will put down a simile of human life as far as I now perceive it; that is, to the point to which I say we both have arrived at—Well—I compare human life to a large Mansion of Many Apartments, two of which I can only describe, the doors of the rest being yet shut upon me—The first we step into we call the infant or thoughtless Chamber, in which we remain as long as we do not think—We remain there a long while, and notwithstanding the doors of the second Chamber remain wide open, showing a bright appearance, we care not to hasten to it; but are at length imperceptibly impelled by the awakening of the thinking principle—within us— we no sooner get into the second Chamber, which I shall call the Chamber of Maiden-Thought, than we become intoxicated with the light and the atmosphere, we see nothing but pleasant wonders, and think of delaying there for ever in delight: However among the effects this breathing is father of is that tremendous one of sharpening one's vision into the heart and nature of Man—of convincing ones nerves that the

World is full of Misery and Heartbreak, Pain, Sickness and oppression—whereby This Chamber of Maiden Thought become gradually darken'd and at the same time on all sides of it many doors are set open—but all dark—all leading to dark passages— We see not the ballance of good and evil. We are in a Mist—We are now in that state—We feel the 'burden of the Mystery.' To this point was Wordsworth come, as far as I can conceive when he wrote 'Tintern Abbey' and it seems to me that his Genius is explorative of those dark Passages. Now if we live, and go on thinking, we too shall explore them. He is a Genius and superior [to] us, in so far as he can, more than we, make discoveries, and shed a light in them—Here I must think Wordsworth is deeper than Milton—though I think it has depended more upon the general and gregarious advance of intellect, than individual greatness of Mind—From the *Paradise Lost* and the other Works of Milton, I hope it is not too presuming, even between ourselves to say, his Philosophy, human and divine, may be tolerably understood by one not much advanced in years. In his time englishmen were just emancipated form a great superstition—and Men had got hold of certain points and resting places in reasoning which were too newly born to be doubted, and too much opposed by the Mass of Europe not to be thought etherial and authentically divine—who could gainsay his ideas on virtue, vice, and Chastity in *Comus*, just at the time of the dismissal of Cod-pieces and a hundred other disgraces? who would not rest satisfied with his hintings at good and evil in the *Paradise Lost*, when just free form the inquisition and burning in Smithfield? The Reformation produced such immediate and great benefits, that Protestantism was considered under the immediate eye of heaven, and its own remaining Dogmas and superstition, then, as it were, regenerated, constituted those resting places and seeming sure points of Reasoning—from that I have mentioned, Milton, whatever he may have thought in the sequel, appears to have been content with these by his writings—He did not think into the human heart, as Wordsworth has done—Yet Milton as a Philosopher, had sure as great powers as Wordsworth—What is then to be inferr'd? O many things—It proves there is really a grand march of intellect—it proves that a mighty providence subdues the mightiest Minds to the service of the time being, whether it be in human Knowledge or Religion—I have often pitied a Tutor who has to hear 'Nom: Musa'—so often dinn'd into his ears—I hope you may not have the same pain in this scribbling—I may have read these things before, but I never had even a thus dim perception of them: and moreover I like to say my lesson to one who will endure my tediousness for my own sake—After all there is certainly something real in the World—Moore's present to Hazlitt is real—I like that Moore, and am glad I saw him at the Theatre just before I left Town. Tom has spit a leetle blood this afternoon, and that is rather a damper, —but I know—the truth is there is something real in the World Your third Chamber of Life shall be a lucky and a gentle one—stores with the wine of love—and the Bread of Friendship—When you see George if he should not have recēd a letter form me tell him he will find one at home most likely—tell Bailey I hope soon to see him—Remember me to all. The leaves have been out here, for MONY a day—I have written to George for the first stanzas of my Isabel—I shall have them soon and will copy the whole out for you..

To John Hamilton Reynolds, 19th February 1818

I had an idea that a Man might pass a very pleasant life in this manner— Let him on a certain day read a certain page of full Poesy or distilled Prose, and let him wander upon it, and bring home to it, and prophesy upon it, and dream upon it: until it becomes stale—But when will it do so? Never —When Man has arrived at a certain ripeness in intellect any one grand and spiritual passage serves him as a starting-post towards all 'the two-and-thirty Palaces.' How happy is such a voyage of concentration, what delicious diligent Indolence! ... Nor will this sparing touch of noble Books be any irreverence to their Writers— for perhaps the honors paid by Man to Man are trifles in comparison to the Benefit done by great works to the 'spirit and pulse of good' by their mere passive existence. Memory should not be called Knowledge—Many have original minds who do not think it—they are led away by Custom. Now it appears to me that almost any Man may like the spider spin from his own inwards his own airy Citadel—the points of leaves and twigs on which the spider begins her work are few, and she fills the air with a beautiful circuiting. Man should be content with as few points to tip with the fine Web of his Soul, and weave a tapestry empyrean full of symbols for his spiritual eye, of softness for his spiritual touch, of space for his wandering, of distinctness for his luxury. But the Minds of Mortals are so different and bent on such diverse journeys that it may at first appear impossible for any common taste and fellowship to exist between two or three under these suppositions. It is however quite the contrary. Minds would leave each other in contrary directions, traverse each other in numberless points, and at last greet each other at the journey's end. An old Man and a child would talk together and the old Man be led on his path and the child left thinking. Man should not dispute or assert but whisper results to his neighbour and thus by every germ of spirit sucking the sap from mould ethereal every human might become great, and Humanity instead of being a wide heath of Furze and Briars with here and there a remote Oak or Pine, would become a grand democracy of Forest Trees! It has been an old comparison for our urging on—the Beehive; however, it seems to me that we should rather be the flower than the Bee—for it is a false notion that more is gained by receiving than giving—no, the receiver and the giver are equal in their benefits. The flower, I doubt not, receives a fair guerdon from the Bee—its leaves blush deeper in the next spring—and who shall say between man and woman which is the most delighted? Now it is more noble to sit like Jove than to fly like Mercury—let us not therefore go hurrying about and collecting honey, bee-like buzzing here and there impatiently from a knowledge of what is to be aimed at; but let us open our leaves like a flower and be passive and receptive—budding patiently under the eye of Apollo and taking hints from every noble insect that favours us with a visit—sap will be given us for meat and dew for drink. I was led into these thoughts, my dear Reynolds, by the beauty of the morning operating on a sense of Idleness—I have not read any books—the Morning said I was right—I had no idea but of the morning, and the thrush said I was right—seeming to say,

> O thou whose face hath felt the Winter's wind,
> Whose eye has seen the snow-clouds hung in mist,
> And the black elm-tops 'mong the freezing stars,

> To thee the Spring will be a harvest-time.
> O thou, whose only book has been the light
> Of supreme darkness which thou feddest on
> Night after night when Phoebus was away,
> To thee the Spring shall be a triple morn.
> O fret not after knowledge—I have none,
> And yet my song comes native with the warmth.
> O fret not after knowledge—I have none,
> And yet the Evening listens. He who saddens
> At thought of idleness cannot be idle,
> And he's awake who thinks himself asleep.

Now I am sensible all this is a mere sophistication (however it may neighbour to any truths), to excuse my own indolence—so I will not deceive myself that man should be equal with Jove—but think himself very well off as a sort of scullion-Mercury, or even a humble Bee. It is no matter whether I am right or wrong, either one way or another, if there is sufficient to lift a little time from your shoulders.

To James Augustus Hessey, 9th October 1818

My dear Hessey—You are very good in sending me the letters from the Chronicle—and I am very bad in not acknowledging such a kindness sooner— pray forgive me. It has so chanced that I have had that paper every day—I have seen to-day's. I cannot but feel indebted to those Gentlemen who have taken my part—As for the rest, I begin to get a little acquainted with my own strength and weakness. —Praise or blame has but a momentary effect on the man whose love of beauty in the abstract makes him a severe critic on his own Works. My own domestic criticism has given me pain without comparison beyond what Blackwood or the Quarterly could possibly inflict—and also when I feel I am right, no external praise can give me such a glow as my own solitary reperception and ratification of what is fine. J. S. is perfectly right in regard to the slip-shod *Endymion*. That it is so is no fault of mine. No! —though it may sound a little paradoxical. It is as good as I had power to make it—by myself— Had I been nervous about its being a perfect piece, and with that view asked advice, and trembled over every page, it would not have been written; for it is not in my nature to fumble—I will write independently. —I have written independently without Judgment. I may write independently, and with Judgment, hereafter. The Genius of Poetry must work out its own salvation in a man: It cannot be matured by law and precept, but by sensation and watchfulness in itself—That which is creative must create itself—In *Endymion*, I leaped headlong into the sea, and thereby have become better acquainted with the Soundings, the quicksands, and the rocks, than if I had stayed upon the green shore, and piped a silly pipe, and took tea and comfortable advice. I was never afraid of failure; for I would sooner fail than not be among the greatest—But I am nigh getting into a rant. So, with remembrances to Taylor and Woodhouse etc. I am

Yours very sincerely

To Richard Woodhouse, 27th October 1818

Your letter gave me a great satisfaction; more on account of its friendliness, than any relish of that matter in it which is accounted so acceptable in the 'genus irritable.' The best answer I can give you is in a clerk-like manner to make some observations on two principle points, which seem to point like indices into the midst of the whole pro and con, about genius, and views and achievements and ambition and cetera. 1st. As to the poetical Character itself (I mean that sort of which, if I am any thing, I am a Member; that sort distinguished from the Wordsworthian or egotistical sublime; which is a thing per se and stands alone) it is not itself—it has no self—it is every thing and nothing—It has no character—it enjoys light and shade; it lives in gusto, be it foul or fair, high or low, rich or poor, mean or elevated—It has as much delight in conceiving an Iago as an Imogen. What shocks the virtuous philosopher, delights the camelion Poet. It does no harm from its relish of the dark side of things any more than from its taste for the bright one; because they both end in speculation. A Poet is the most unpoetical of any thing in existence; because he has no Identity—he is continually in for—and filling some other Body—The Sun, the Moon, the Sea and Men and Women who are creatures of impulse are poetical and have about them an unchangeable attribute—the poet has none; no identity—he is certainly the most unpoetical of all God's Creatures. If then he has no self, and if I am a Poet, where is the Wonder that I should say I would write no more? Might I not at that very instant have been cogitating on the Characters of Saturn and Ops? It is a wretched thing to confess; but is a very fact that not one word I ever utter can be taken for granted as an opinion growing out of my identical nature—how can it, when I have no nature? When I am in a room with People if ever am free from speculating on creations of my own brain, then not myself goes home to myself: but the identity of everyone in the room begins to press upom me that, I am in a very little time an[ni]hilated—not only among Men; but it would be the same in a Nursery of children: I know not whether I make myself wholly understood: I hope enough so to let you see that no dependence is to be placed on what I said that day.

In the second place I will speak of my views, and of the life I purpose to myself—I am ambitious of doing the world some good: if I should be spared that may the the work of maturer years—in the interval I will assay to reach as high a summit in Poetry as the nerve bestowed upon me will suffer. The faint conceptions I have of Poems to come brings the blood frequently into my forehead—All I hope is that I may not lose all interest in human affairs—that the solitary indifference I feel for applause even from the finest Spirits, will not blunt my acuteness of vision I may have. I do not think it will—I feel assured I should write from the mere yearning and fondness I have for the Beautiful even if my night's labours should be burnt every morning and no eye ever shine upon them. But even now I am perhaps not speaking from myself, but from some character in whose soul I now live. I am sure however that this next sentence is from myself. I feel your anxiety, good opinion and friendliness in the highest degree, and am

Your's most sincerely

To George and Georgiana Keats, 16th December 1818

You will be prepared, before this reaches you for the worst news you could have, nay if Haslam's letter arrives in proper time, I have a consolation in thinking the first shock will be past before you receive this. The last days of poor Tom were of the most distressing nature; but his last moments were not so painful, and his very last was without a pang—I will not enter into any parsonic comments on death—yet the common observations of the commonest people on death are as true as their proverbs. I have scarce a doubt of immortality of some nature of other—neither had Tom. My friends have been exceedingly kind to me every one of them—Brown detained me at his house. I suppose no one could have had their time made smoother than mine has been. During poor Tom's illness I was not able to write and since his death the task of beginning has been a hindrance to me.

Mrs. Browne who took Brown's house for the summer, still resides in Hampstead—she is a very nice woman—and her daughter is I think beautiful and elegant, graceful, silly, fashionable and strange we have a little tiff now and then—and she behaves a little better, o[r] I must have sheered off.

Shall I give you Miss Browne? She is about my height—with a fine style of countenance of the lengthened sort—she wants sentiment in every feature—she manages to make her hair look well—her nostrils are fine—though a little painful—her mouth is bad and good—her profil is better than her full-face which indeed is not full put pale and thin without showing any bone—her shape is very graceful and so are her movements—her arms are good her hand badish—her feet tolerable—she is not seventeen—but she is ignorant—monstrous in her behaviour flying out in all directions, calling people such names—that I was forced lately to make use of the term Minx—this is I think not from any innate vice but from a penchant she has for acting stylishly. I am however tired of such style and shall decline any more of it. But I will go no further—I may be speaking sacrilegiously—and on my word I have thought so little that I have not one opinion upon any thing except in matters of taste—I never can feel certain of any truth but from a clear perception of its Beauty—and I find myself very young minded even in that perceptive power—which I hope will encrease—A year ago I could not understand in the slightest degree Raphael's cartoons—now I begin to read them a little.

When I was last at Haydon's I looked over a book of prints taken from the fresco of the church at Milan the name of which I forget—in it are comprised Specimens of the first and second age of art in Italy—I do not think I ever had a greater treat out of Shakespeare—Full of Romance and the most tender feeling—magnificence of draperies beyond any I ever saw not excepting Raphael's— But Grotesque to a curious pitch—yet still making up a fine whole—even finer to me than more accomplished works—as there was left so much room for imagination.

To George and Georgiana Keats, 19th March 1819

I have been reading lately two very different books Robertson's America and Voltaire's Siecle De Louis XIV. It is like walking arm and arm between Pizarro and the great-little Monarch. In How lamentable a case do we see the great body of the people in both instances: in the first, where Men might seem to inherit quiet of Mind from unsophisticated senses; from uncontamination of civilization; and especially from their being as it were estranged from the mutual helps of Soceity and its mutual injuries—and thereby more immediately under the Protections of Providence—even there they had mortal pains to bear as bad or even worse than Baliffs, Debts and Poverties of civilized life—The whole appears to resolve into this—that Man is originally 'a poor forked creature' subject to the same mischances as the beasts of the forest, destined to hardships and disquietude of some kind or other. If he improves by degrees his bodily accommodations and comforts—at each stage, at each accent there are waiting for him a fresh set of annoyances—he is mortal and there is still a heaven with its stars above his head. The most interesting question that can come before us is, how far by the persevering endearvours of a seldom appearing Socrates. Mankind may be made happy—I can imagine such happiness carried to an extreme—but what must it end in? —Death—and who could in such a case bear with death—the whole troubles of life which are now frittered away in a series of years, would then be accumulated for the last days of a being who instead of hailing its approach, would leave this world as Eve left Paradise—But in truth I do not at all believe in this sort of perfectibility—the nature of the world will not admit of it—the inhabitants of the world will correspond to itself—Let the fish philosophies the ice away from the Rivers in winter time and they shall be at continual play in the tepid delight of summer. Look at the Poles and at the sands of Africa, Whirlpools and volcanoes—let men exterminates them and I will say that they may arrive at earthly Happiness—The point at which Man may arrive is as far as the parallel state in inanimate nature and no further—For instance suppose a rose to have sensation, it blooms on a beautiful morning it enjoys itself—but there comes a cold wind, a hot sun—it cannot escape it, it cannot destroy its annoyances—they are as native to the world as itself: No more can man be happy in spite, the worldly elements will prey upon his nature—The common cognomen of this world among the misguided and superstitious is 'a vale of tears' from which we are to be redeemed by a certain arbitary interposition of God and taken to Heaven—What a little circumscribed straightened notion! Call the world if you Please — The vale of Soul-making.

Then you will find out the use of the world (I am speaking now in the highest terms for human nature admitting it to be immortal which I will here take for granted for the purpose of showing a thought which has struck me concerning it) I say — soul making—soul as distinguished from an Intelligence—There may be intelligences or sparkles of the divinity in millions—but they are not Souls till they acquire identities, till each one is personally itself. Intelligences are atoms of perception—they know and they see and they are pure, in short they are God—how then are Souls to be made? How then are these sparks which are God to have identity given them—so as ever to possess a bliss peculiar to each one's individual existence? How, but by the medium of a world like this? This point I sincerely wish to consider because I think it a grand system of salvation than the chrystian religion—or rather it is a system of Spirit-creation—This is effected by there grand materials acting the one upon the other for a series of years—These three Materials are the Intelligence—the human heart (as distinguished from intelligence or mind) and the world of elemental space suited for the proper action of mind and heart on each other for the purpose of forming the soul for intelligence destined to possess the sense of identity. I can scarcely express what I but dimly perceive—and yet I think I perceive it—that you may judge the more clearly I will put it in the most homely form possible—I will call the world a school instituted for the purpose of teaching little children to read—I will call the human heart the horn book used in that school—and I will call the child able to read, the soul made from that school and its hornbook. Do you not see how necessary a world of pains and troubles is to school an intelligence and make it a soul? A place where the heart must feel and suffer in a thousand diverse ways. Not merely is the Heart a Hornbook. It is the mind's Bible, it is the minds experience, it is the teat from which the mind or intelligence sucks its identity—As various as the Lives of Men are—so various become identical souls of the sparks of his own essence—This appears to me a faint sketch of a system of Salvation which does not affront our reason and humanity—I am convinced that many difficulties which Christians labour under would vanish before it.

If what I have said should not be plain enough, as I fear it may not be, I will but you in the place where I began in this series of thoughts—I mean, I began by seeing how man was formed by circumstances—and what are circumstances? —but touchstones of his heart—? And what are touch stones? —but provings of his heart? —and what are provings of his heart but fortifiers or alterers of his nature? And what is his altered nature but his soul? —and what was his soul before it came into the world and had these provings and alterations and perfectionings? —an intelligence—without Identity—and how is this Identity to be made? Through the medium of the heart? And how is the heart to become this Medium but in a world of Circumstances?

To Percy Bysshe Shelley, 16th August 1820

I am very much gratified that you, in a foreign country, and with a mind almost over-occupied, should write to me in the strain of the letter beside me. If I do not take advantage of your invitation, it will be prevented by a circumstance I have very much at heart to prophesy. There is no doubt that an English winter would put an end to me, and do so in a lingering hateful manner. Therefore, I must either voyage or journey to Italy, as a soldier marches up to a battery. My nerves at present are the worst part of me, yet they feel soothed that, come what extreme may, I shall not be destined to remain in one spot long enough to take a hatred of any four particular bedposts. I am glad you take any pleasure in my poor poem, which I would willingly take the trouble to unwrite, if possible, did I care so much as I have done about reputation. I received a copy of the *Cenci*, as from yourself, from Hunt. There is only one part of it I am judge of—the poetry and dramatic effect, which by many spirits nowadays is considered the Mammon. A modern work, it is said, must have a purpose, which may be the God. An artist must serve Mammon; he must have 'self-concentration'—selfishness, perhaps. You, I am sure, will forgive me for sincerely remarking that you might curb your magnanimity, and be more of an artist, and load every rift of your subject with ore. The thought of such discipline must fall like cold chains upon you, who perhaps never sat with your wings furled for six months together. And is this not extraordinary talk for the writer of *Endymion*, whose mind was like a pack of scattered cards? I am picked up and sorted to a pip. My imagination is a monastery, and I am its monk. You must explain my metaphors to yourself. I am in expectation of *Prometheus* every day. Could I have my own wish effected, you would have it still in manuscript, or be but now putting an end to the second act. I remember you advising me not to publish my first-blights, on Hampstead Heath. I am returning advice upon your hands. Most of the poems in the volume I send you have been written above two years, and would never have been published but from a hope of gain; so you see I am inclined enough to take your advice now. I must express once more my deep sense of your kindness, adding my sincere thanks and respects for Mrs Shelley.

In the hope of soon seeing you, I remain

                                                                    most sincerely yours

William Hazlitt

The Spirit of the Age or Contemporary Portraits

Mr Coleridge

The present is an age of talkers, and not of doers; and the reason is, that the world is growing old. We are so far advanced in the Arts and Sciences, that we live in retrospect, and doat on past achievements. The accumulation of knowledge has been so great, that we are lost in wonder at the height it has reached, instead of attempting to climb or add to it: while the variety of objects distracts and dazzles the looker-on. What niche remains unoccupied? What path untried? What is the use of doing anything, unless we could do better than all those who have gone before us? What hope is there of this? We are like those who have been to see some noble monument of art, who are content to admire without thinking of rivalling it; or like guests after a feast, who praise the hospitality of the donor 'and thank the bounteous Pan'—perhaps carrying away some trifling fragments; or like the spectators of a mighty battle, who still hear its sound afar off, and the clashing of armour and the neighing of the war-horse and the shout of victory is in their ears, like the rushing of innumerable waters!

Mr Coleridge has 'a mind reflecting ages past': his voice is like the echo of the congregated roar of the 'dark rearward and abyss' of thought. He who has seen a mouldering tower by the side of a crystal lake, hid by the mist, but glittering in the wave below, may conceive the dim, gleaming, uncertain intelligence of his eye: he who has marked the evening clouds uprolled (a world of vapours) has seen the picture of his mind, unearthly, unsubstantial, with gorgeous tints and ever-varying forms—

> That which was now a horse, even with a thought
> The rack dislimns, and makes it indistinct
> As water is in water.

Our author's mind is (as he himself might express it) tangential. There is no subject on which he has not touched, none on which he has rested. With an understanding fertile, subtle, expansive, 'quick, forgetive, apprehensive,' beyond all living precedent, few traces of it perhaps remain, he lends himself to all impressions alike; he gives up his mind and liberty of thought to none. He is a general lover of art and science, and wedded to no one in particular. He pursues knowledge as a mistress, with outstretched hands and winged speed; but as he is about to embrace her, his Daphne turns—alas! not to a laurel! Hardly a speculation has been left on record from the earliest time, but it is loosely folded up in Mr Coleridge's memory, like a rich, but somewhat tattered piece of tapestry: we might add (with more seeming than real extravagance) that scarce a thought can pass through the mind of man, but its sound has at some time or other passed over his head with rustling pinions.

On whatever question or author you speak, he is prepared to take up the theme with advantage—from Peter Abelard down to Thomas Moore, from the subtlest metaphysics to the politics of the Courier. There is no man of genius, in whose praise he descants, but the critic seems to stand above the author, and 'what in him is weak, to strengthen, what is low, to raise and support': nor is there any work of genius that does not come out of his hands like an illuminated Missal, sparkling even in its defects. If Mr Coleridge had not been the most impressive talker of his age, he would probably have been the finest writer; but he lays down his pen to make sure of an auditor, and mortgages the admiration of posterity for the stare of an idler. If he had not been a poet, he would have been a powerful logician; if he had not dipped his wing in the Unitarian controversy, he might have soared to the very summit of fancy. But, in writing verse, he is trying to subject the Muse to transcendental theories: in his abstract reasoning, he misses his way by strewing it with flowers.

All that he has done of moment, he had done twenty years ago: since then, he may be said to have lived on the sound of his own voice. Mr Coleridge is too rich in intellectual wealth, to need to task himself to any drudgery: he has only to draw the sliders of his imagination, and a thousand subjects expand before him, startling him with their brilliancy, or losing themselves in endless obscurity—

> And by the force of blear illusion,
> They draw him on to his confusion.

What is the little he could add to the stock, compared with the countless stores that lie about him, that he should stoop to pick up a name, or to polish an idle fancy? He walks abroad in the majesty of an universal understanding, eyeing the 'rich strond,' or golden sky above him, and 'goes sounding on his way,' in eloquent accents, uncompelled and free!

Persons of the greatest capacity are often those, who for this reason do the least; for surveying themselves from the highest point of view, amidst the infinite variety of the universe, their own share in it seems trifling, and scarce worth a thought; and they prefer the contemplation of all that is, or has been, or can be, to the making a coil about doing what, when done, is no better than vanity. It is hard to concentrate all our attention and efforts on one pursuit, except from ignorance of others; and without this concentration of our faculties no great progress can be made in any one thing. It is not merely that the mind is not capable of the effort; it does not think the effort worth making. Action is one; but thought is manifold. He whose restless eye glances through the wide compass of nature and art, will not consent to have 'his own nothings monstered'; but he must do this before he can give his whole soul to them. The mind, after 'letting contemplation have its fill,' or

> Sailing with supreme dominion
> Through the azure deep of air,

sinks down on the ground, breathless, exhausted, powerless, inactive; or if it must have some vent to its feelings, seeks the most easy and obvious; is soothed by friendly flattery, lulled by the murmur of immediate applause: thinks, as it were, aloud, and babbles in its dreams!

A scholar (so to speak) is a more disinterested and abstracted character than a mere author. The first looks at the numberless volumes of a library, and says, 'All these are mine': the other points to a single volume (perhaps it may be an immortal one) and says, 'My name is written on the back of it.' This is a puny and grovelling ambition, beneath the lofty amplitude of Mr Coleridge's mind. No, he revolves in his wayward soul, or utters to the passing wind, or discourses to his own shadow, things mightier and more various! —Let us draw the curtain, and unlock the shrine.

Learning rocked him in his cradle, and while yet a child,

> He lisped in numbers, for the numbers came.

At sixteen he wrote his Ode on Chatterton, and he still reverts to that period with delight, not so much as it relates to himself (for that string of his own early promise of fame rather jars than otherwise) but as exemplifying the youth of a poet. Mr Coleridge talks of himself without being an egotist; for in him the individual is always merged in the abstract and general. He distinguished himself at school and at the University by his knowledge of the classics, and gained several prizes for Greek epigrams. How many men are there (great scholars, celebrated names in literature) who, having done the same thing in their youth, have no other idea all the rest of their lives but of this achievement, of a fellowship and dinner, and who, installed in academic honours, would look down on our author as a mere strolling bard! At Christ's Hospital, where he was brought up, he was the idol of those among his schoolfellows, who mingled with their bookish studies the music of thought and of humanity; and he was usually attended round the cloisters by a group of these (inspiring and inspired) whose hearts even then burnt within them as he talked, and where the sounds yet linger to mock ELIA on his way, still turning pensive to the past!

One of the finest and rarest parts of Mr Coleridge's conversation is, when he expatiates on the Greek tragedians (not that he is not well acquainted, when he pleases, with the epic poets, or the philosophers, or orators, or historians of antiquity)—on the subtle reasonings and melting pathos of Euripides, on the harmonious gracefulness of Sophocles, tuning his love-laboured song, like sweetest warblings from a sacred grove; on the high-wrought, trumpet-tongued eloquence of Æschylus, whose Prometheus, above all, is like an Ode to Fate and a pleading with Providence, his thoughts being let loose as his body is chained on his solitary rock, and his afflicted will (the emblem of mortality)

Struggling in vain with ruthless destiny.

As the impassioned critic speaks and rises in his theme, you would think you heard the voice of the Man hated by the Gods, contending with the wild winds as they roar; and his eye glitters with the spirit of Antiquity!

Next, he was engaged with Hartley's tribes of mind, 'etherial braid, thought-woven,'—and he busied himself for a year or two with vibrations and vibratiuncles, and the great law of association that binds all things in its mystic chain, and the doctrine of Necessity (the mild teacher of Charity) and the Millennium, anticipative of a life to come; and he plunged deep into the controversy on Matter and Spirit, and, as an escape from Dr Priestley's Materialism, where he felt himself imprisoned by the logician's spell, like Ariel in the cloven pine-tree, he became suddenly enamoured of Bishop Berkeley's fairy-world, and used in all companies to build the universe, like a brave, poetical fiction, of fine words. And he was deep-read in Malebranche, and in Cudworth's Intellectual System (a huge pile of learning, unwieldy, enormous) and in Lord Brook's hieroglyphic theories, and in Bishop Butler's Sermons, and in the Duchess of Newcastle's fantastic folios, and in Clarke and South, and Tillotson, and all the fine thinkers and masculine reasoners of that age; and Leibnitz's Pre-established Harmony reared its arch above his head, like the rainbow in the cloud, covenanting with the hopes of man.

And then he fell plumb, ten thousand fathoms down (but his wings saved him harmless) into the hortus siccus of Dissent, where he pared religion down to the standard of reason, and stripped faith of mystery, and preached Christ crucified and the Unity of the Godhead, and so dwelt for a while in the spirit with John Buss and Jerome of Prague and Socinus and old John Zisca, and ran through Neal's History of the Puritans and Calamys Non-Conformists' Memorial, having like thoughts and passions with them. But then Spinoza became his God, and he took up the vast chain of being in his hand, and the round world became the centre and the soul of all things in some shadowy sense, forlorn of meaning, and around him he beheld the living traces and the sky-pointing proportions of the mighty Pan; but poetry redeemed him from this spectral philosophy, and he bathed his heart in beauty, and gazed at the golden light of heaven, and drank of the spirit of the universe, and wandered at eve by fairy-stream or fountain,

> —When he saw nought but beauty,
> When be heard the voice of that Almighty One
> In every breeze that blew, or wave that murmured—

and wedded with truth in Plato's shade, and in the writings of Proclus and Plotinus saw the ideas of things in the eternal mind, and unfolded all mysteries with the Schoolmen and fathomed the depths of Duns Scotus and Thomas Aquinas, and entered the third heaven with Jacob Behmen, and walked hand in hand with Swedenborg through the pavilions of the New Jerusalem, and sang his faith in the promise and in the word in his Religious Musings.

And lowering himself from that dizzy height [he] poised himself on Milton's wings, and spread out his thoughts in charity with the glad prose of Jeremy Taylor, and wept over Bowles's Sonnets, and studied Cowper's blank verse, and betook himself to Thomson's Castle of Indolence, and sported with the wits of Charles the Second's days and of Queen Anne, and relished Swift's style and that of the John Bull (Arbuthnot's we mean, not Mr Croker's), and dallied with the British Essayists and Novelists, and knew all qualities of more modern writers with a learned spirit: Johnson, and Goldsmith, and Junius, and Burke, and Godwin, and the Sorrows of Werther, and Jean Jacques Rousseau, and Voltaire, and Marivaux, and Crebillon, and thousands more: now 'laughed with Rabelais in his easy chair' or pointed to Hogarth, or afterwards dwelt on Claude's classic scenes, or spoke with rapture of Raphael, and compared the women at Rome to figures that had walked out of his pictures, or visited the Oratory of Pisa, and described the works of Giotto and Ghirlandaio and Massaccio, and gave the moral of the picture of the Triumph of Death, where the beggars and the wretched invoke his dreadful dart, but the rich and mighty of the earth quail and shrink before it; and in that land of siren sights and sounds, saw a dance of peasant girls, and was charmed with lutes and gondolas, —or wandered into Germany and lost himself in the labyrinths of the Hartz Forest and of the Kantean philosophy, and amongst the cabalistic names of Fichtè amid Schelling and Lessing, and God knows who. This was long after; but all the former while he had nerved his heart and filled his eyes with tears, as he hailed the rising orb of liberty, since quenched in darkness and in blood, and had kindled his affections at the blaze of the French Revolution, and sang for joy, when the towers of the Bastille and the proud places of the insolent and the oppressor fell, and would have floated his bark, freighted with fondest fancies, across the Atlantic wave with Southey and others to seek for peace and freedom—

> In Philarmonia's undivided dale!

Alas! 'Frailty, thy name is Genius!' —What is become of all this mighty heap of hope, of thought, of learning and humanity? It has ended in swallowing doses of oblivion and in writing paragraphs in the Courier. Such and so little is the mind of man.

It was not to be supposed that Mr Coleridge could keep on at the rate he set off. He could not realize all he knew or thought, and less could not fix his desultory ambition. Other stimulants supplied the place, and kept up the intoxicating dream, the fever and the madness of his early impressions. Liberty (the philosopher's and the poet's bride) had fallen a victim, meanwhile, to the murderous practices of the hag Legitimacy. Proscribed by court hirelings, too romantic for the herd of vulgar politicians, our enthusiast stood at bay, and at last tur ned on the pivot of a subtle casuistry to the unclean side: but his discursive reason would not let him trammel himself into a poet-laureate or stamp-distributor; and he stopped, ere he had quite passed that well-known 'bourne from whence no traveller returns' —and so has sunk into torpid, uneasy repose, tantalized by useless resources, haunted by vain imaginings, his lips idly moving, but his heart for ever still, or, as the shattered chords vibrate of themselves, making melancholy music to the ear of memory! Such is the fate of genius in an age when, in the unequal contest with sovereign wrong, every man is ground to powder who is not either a born slave, or who does not willingly and at once offer up the yearnings of humanity and the dictates of reason as a welcome sacrifice to besotted prejudice and loathsome power.

Of all Mr Coleridge's productions, the Ancient Mariner is the only one that we could with confidence put into any person's hands, on whom we wished to impress a favourable idea of his extraordinary powers. Let whatever other objections be made to it, it is unquestionably a work of genius—of wild, irregular, overwhelming imagination, and has that rich, varied movement in the verse, which gives a distant idea of the lofty or changeful tones of Mr Coleridge's voice. In the Christobel, there is one splendid passage on divided friendship. The Translation of Schiller's Wallenstein is also a masterly production in its kind, faithful and spirited. Among his smaller pieces there are occasional bursts of pathos and fancy, equal to what we might expect from him; but these form the exception, and not the rule. Such, for instance, is his affecting Sonnet to the author of the Robbers.

> Schiller! that hour I would have wish'd to die,
> If through the shudd'ring midnight I had sent
> From the dark dungeon of the tower time-rent,
> That fearful voice, a famish'd father's cry—
> That in no after-moment aught less vast
> Might stamp me mortal! A triumphant shout
> Black horror scream'd, and all her goblin rout

> From the more with'ring scene diminish'd pass'd.
>
> Ah! Bard tremendous in sublimity!
> Could I behold thee in thy loftier mood,
> Wand'ring at eve, with finely frenzied eye,
> Beneath some vast old tempest-swinging wood !
> Awhile, with mute awe gazing, I would brood,
> Then weep aloud in a wild ecstasy.

His Tragedy, entitled *Remorse*, is full of beautiful and striking passages; but it does not place the author in the first rank of dramatic writers. But if Mr Coleridge's works do not place him in that rank, they injure instead of conveying a just idea of the man; for he himself is certainly in the first class of general intellect.

If our author's poetry is inferior to his conversation, his prose is utterly abortive. Hardly a gleam is to be found in it of the brilliancy and richness of those stores of thought and language that he pours out incessantly, when they are lost like drops of water in the ground. The principal work, in which he has attempted to embody his general views of things, is the *Friend*, of which, though it contains some noble passages and fine trains of thought, prolixity and obscurity are the most frequent characteristics.

No two persons can be conceived more opposite in character or genius than the subject of the present and of the preceding sketch. Mr Godwin,① with less natural capacity and with fewer acquired advantages, by concentrating his mind on some given object, and doing what he had to do with all his might, has accomplished much, and will leave more than one monument of a powerful intellect behind him; Mr Coleridge, by dissipating his, and dallying with every subject by turns, has done little or nothing to justify to the world or to posterity the high opinion which all who have ever heard him converse, or known him intimately, with one accord entertain of him. Mr Godwin's faculties have kept at home, and plied their task in the workshop of the brain, diligently and effectual-

---

① The preceding chapter talks about Godwin—editor's note.

ly: Mr Coleridge's have gossipped away their time, and gadded about from house to house, as if life's business were to melt the hours in listless talk. Mr. Godwin is intent on a subject, only as it concerns himself and his reputation; he works it out as a matter of duty, and discards from his mind whatever does not forward his main object as impertinent and vain.

Mr Coleridge, on the other hand, delights in nothing but episodes and digressions, neglects whatever he undertakes to perform, and can act only on spontaneous impulses without object or method. 'He cannot be constrained by mastery.' While he should be occupied with a given pursuit, he is thinking of a thousand other things: a thousand tastes, a thousand objects tempt him, and distract his mind, which keeps open house, and entertains all comers; and after being fatigued and amused with morning calls from idle visitors finds the day consumed and its business unconcluded. Mr Godwin, on the contrary, is somewhat exclusive and unsocial in his habits of mind, entertains no company but what he gives his whole time and attention to, and wisely writes over the doors of his understanding, his fancy, and his senses—'No admittance except on business.' He has none of that fastidious refinement and false delicacy, which might lead him to balance between the endless variety of modern attainments. He does not throw away his life (nor a single half hour of it) in adjusting the claims of different accomplishments, and in choosing between them or making himself master of them all. He sets about his task (whatever it may be), and goes through it with spirit and fortitude. He has the happiness to think an author the greatest character in the world, and himself the greatest author in it.

Mr Coleridge, in writing an harmonious stanza, would stop to consider whether there was not more grace and beauty in a *Pas de trois* [three-person dance], and would not proceed till he had resolved this question by a chain of metaphysical reasoning without end. Not so Mr Godwin. That is best to him, which he can do best. He does not waste himself in vain aspirations and effeminate sympathies. He is blind, deaf, insensible to all but the trump of Fame. Plays, operas, painting, music, ball-rooms, wealth, fashion, titles, lords, ladies, touch him not. All these are no more to him than to the magician in his cell, and he writes on to the end of the chapter through good report and evil report.

'Pingo in eternitatem' is his motto. He neither envies nor admires what others are, but is contented to be what he is, and strives to do the utmost he can. Mr Coleridge has flirted with the Muses as with a set of mistresses: Mr Godwin has been married twice, to Reason and to Fancy, and has to boast no short-lived progeny by each.

So to speak, he has valves belonging to his mind, to regulate the quantity of gas admitted into it, so that like the bare, unsightly, but well-compacted steam-vessel, it cuts its liquid way, and arrives at its promised end: while Mr Coleridge's bark, 'taught with the little nautilus to sail,' the sport of every breath, dancing to every wave,

> Youth at its prow, and Pleasure at its helm,

flutters its gaudy pennons in the air, glitters in the sun, but we wait in vain to hear of its arrival in the destined harbour. Mr Godwin, with less variety and vividness, with less subtlety and susceptibility both of thought and feeling, has had firmer nerves, a more determined purpose, a more comprehensive grasp of his subject; and the results are as we find them. Each has met with his reward: for justice has, after all, been done to the pretensions of each: and we must, in all cases, use means to ends!

It was a misfortune to any man of talent to be born in the latter end of the last century. Genius stopped the way of Legitimacy, and therefore it was to be abated, crushed, or set aside as a nuisance. The spirit of the monarchy was at variance with the spirit of the age. The flame of liberty, the light of intellect, was to be extinguished with the sword—or with slander, whose edge is sharper than the sword. The war between power and reason was carried on by the first of these abroad, by the last at home. No quarter was given (then or now) by the Government-critics, the authorized censors of the press, to those who followed the dictates of independence, who listened to the voice of the tempter Fancy. Instead of gathering fruits and flowers, immortal fruits and amaranthine flowers, they soon found themselves beset not only by a host of prejudices, but assailed with all the engines of power: by nicknames, by lies, by all the arts of malice, interest and hypocrisy, without the possibility of their defending themselves 'from the pelting of the pitiless storm,' that poured down upon them from the strongholds of corruption and authority.

The philosophers, the dry abstract reasoners, submitted to this reverse pretty well, and armed themselves with patience 'as with triple steel,' to bear discomfiture, persecution, and disgrace. But the poets, the creatures of sympathy, could not stand the frowns both of king and people. They did not like to be shut out when places and pensions, when the critic's praises, and the laurel wreath were about to be distributed. They did not stomach being sent to Coventry, and Mr Coleridge sounded a retreat for them by the help of casuistry and a musical voice. —'His words were hollow, but they pleased the ear' of his friends of the Lake School, who turned back disgusted and panic-struck—from the dry desert of unpopularity, like Hassan the camel-driver,

> And curs'd the hour, and curs'd the luckless day,
> When first from Shiraz' walls they bent their way.

They are safely inclosed there. But Mr Coleridge did not enter with them; pitching his tent upon the barren waste without, and having no abiding place nor city of refuge!

Sir Walter Scott

Sir Walter Scott is undoubtedly the most popular writer of the age, the 'lord of the ascendant' for the time being. He is just half what the human intellect is capable of being: if you take the universe, and divide it into two parts, he knows all that it has been; all that it is to be is nothing to him. His is a mind brooding over antiquity—scorning 'the present ignorant time.' He is '*laudator temporis acti*' —a 'prophesier of things past.' The old world is to him a crowded map; the new one a dull, hateful blank. He dotes on all well-authenticated superstitions; he shudders at the shadow of innovation. His retentiveness of memory, his accumulated weight of interested prejudice or romantic association have overlaid his other faculties. The cells of his memory are vast, various, full even to bursting with life and motion; his speculative understanding is empty, flaccid, poor, and dead. His mind receives and treasures up every thing brought to it by tradition or custom—it does not project itself beyond this into the world unknown, but mechanically shrinks back as from the edge of a precipice. The land of pure reason is to his apprehension like Van Diemen's Land—barren, miserable, distant, a place of exile, the dreary abode of savages, convicts, and adventurers. Sir Walter would make a bad hand of a description of the Millennium, unless he could lay the scene in Scotland five hundred years ago, and then he would want facts and worm-eaten parchments to support his drooping style. Our historical novelist firmly thinks that nothing is but what has been, that the moral world stands still, as the material one was supposed to do of old, and that we can never get beyond the point where we actually are without utter destruction, though everything changes and will change from what it was three hundred years ago to what it is now—from what it is now to all that the bigoted admirer of the good old times most dreads and hates!

It is long since we read, and long since we thought of our author's poetry. It would probably have gone out of date with the immediate occasion, even if he himself had not contrived to banish it from our recollection. It is not to be denied that it had great merit, both of an obvious and intrinsic kind. It abounded in vivid descriptions, in spirited action, in smooth and flowing versification. But it wanted character. It was 'poetry of no mark or likelihood. ' It slid out of the mind as soon as read, like a river; and would have been forgotten, but that the public curiosity was fed with ever new supplies from the same teeming liquid source. It is not every man that can write six quarto volumes in verse, that are caught up with avidity, even by fastidious judges. But what a difference between their popularity and that of the Scotch Novels! It is true, the public read and admired the *Lay of the Last Minstrel, Marmion,* and so on, and each individual was contented to read and admire because the public did so but with regard to the proseworks of the same (supposed) author, it is quite another-guess sort of thing. Here every one stands forward to applaud on his own ground, would be thought to go before the public opinion: is eager to extol his favourite characters louder, to understand them better, than everybody else, and has his own scale of comparative excellence for each work, supported by nothing but his own enthusiastic and fearless convictions.

It must be amusing to the Author of Waverley to hear his readers and admirers (and are not these the same thing?) quarrelling which of his novels is the best, opposing character to character, quoting passage against passage, striving to surpass each other in the extravagance of their encomiums, and yet unable to settle the precedence, or to do the author's writings justice—so various, so equal, so transcendant are their merits! His volumes of poetry were received as fashionable and well-dressed acquaintances: we are ready to tear the others in pieces as old friends. There was something meretricious in Sir Walter's ballad-rhymes; and like those who keep opera figurantes, we were willing to have our admiration shared, and our taste confirmed by the town. But the Novels are like the betrothed of our hearts, bone of our bone, and flesh of our flesh, and we are jealous that any one should be as much delighted or as thoroughly acquainted with their beauties as ourselves. For which of his poetical heroines would the reader break a lance so soon as for Jeanie Deans? What Lady of the Lake can compare with the beautiful Rebecca? We believe the late Mr John Scott went to his death-bed (though a painful and premature one) with some degree of satisfaction, inasmuch as be had penned the most elaborate panegyric on the Scotch Novels that had as yet appeared!

The Epics are not poems, so much as metrical romances. There is a glittering veil of verse thrown over the features of nature and of old romance. The deep incisions into character are 'skinned and filmed over'; the details are lost or shaped into flimsy and insipid decorum; and the truth of feeling and of circumstance is translated into a tinkling sound, a tinsel common-place. It must be owned, there is a power in true poetry that lifts the mind from the ground of reality to a higher sphere, that penetrates the inert, scattered, incoherent materials presented to it, and by a force and inspiration of its own, melts and moulds them into sublimity and beauty. But Sir Walter (we contend, under correction) has not this creative impulse, this plastic power, this capacity of reacting on his first impressions. He is a learned, a literal, a matter-of-fact expounder of truth or fable:

he does not soar above and look down upon his subject, imparting his own lofty views and feelings to his descriptions of nature—he relies upon it, is raised by it, is one with it, or he is nothing. A poet is essentially a maker; that is, he must atone for what he loses in individuality and local resemblance by the energies and resources of his own mind.

The writer of whom we speak is deficient in these last. He has either not the faculty or not the will to impregnate his subject by an effort of pure invention. The execution also is much upon a par with the more ephemeral effusions of the press. It is light, agreeable, effeminate, diffuse. Sir Walter's Muse is a Modern Antique. The smooth, glossy texture of his verse contrasts happily with the quaint, uncouth, rugged materials of which it is composed, and takes away any appearance of heaviness or harshness from the body of local traditions and obsolete costume. We see grim knights and iron armour; but then they are woven in silk with a careless, delicate hand, and have the softness of flowers. The poet's figures might be compared to old tapestries copied on the finest velvet: —they are not like Raphael's Cartoons; but they are very like Mr Westall's drawings which accompany, and are intended to illustrate, them.

This facility and grace of execution is the more remarkable, as a story goes that not long before the appearance of the *Lay of the Last Minstrel*, Sir Walter (then Mr) Scott, having, in the company of a friend, to cross the Frith of Forth in a ferry-boat, they proposed to beguile the time by writing a number of verses on a given subject, and that, at the end of an hour's hard study, they found they had produced only six lines between them. 'It is plain, ' said the unconscious author to his fellow-labourer, 'that you and I need never think of getting our living by writing poetry! ' In a year or so after this, he set to work, and poured out quarto upon quarto, as if they had been drops of water. As to the rest, and compared with true and great poets, our Scottish Minstrel is but 'a metre ballad-monger. ' We would rather have written one song of Burns, or a single passage in Lord Byron's Heaven and Earth, or one of Wordsworth's 'fancies and good-nights, ' than all his epics. What is he to Spenser, over whose immortal, ever-amiable verse beauty hovers and trembles, and who has shed the purple light of Fancy from his ambrosial wings over all nature? What is there of the might of Milton, whose head is canopied in the blue serene, and who takes us to sit with him there? What is there in his ambling rhymes of the deep pathos of Chaucer? Or of the o'er-informing power of Shakespear, whose eye, watching alike the minutest traces of character and the strongest movements of passion, 'glances from heaven to earth, from earth to heaven,' and with the lambent flame of genius, playing round each object, lights up the universe in a robe of its own radiance? Sir Walter has no voluntary power of combination: all his associations (as we said before) are those of habit or of tradition. He is a mere narrative and descriptive poet, garrulous of the old time. The definition of his poetry is a pleasing superficiality.

Not so of his novels and romances. There we turn over a new leaf—another and the same—the same in matter, but in form, in power how different! The author of *Waverley* has got rid of the tagging of rhymes, the eking out of syllables, the supplying of epithets, the colours of style, the grouping of his characters, and the regular march of events, and comes to the point at once, and strikes at the heart of his subject, without dismay and without disguise. His poetry was a lady's waiting-maid, dressed out in cast-off finery: his prose is a beautiful, rustic nymph, that, like Dorothea in *Don Quixote*, when she is surprised with dishevelled tresses bathing her naked feet in the brook, looks round her, abashed at the admiration her charms have excited! The grand secret of the author's success in these latter productions is that he has completely got rid of the trammels of authorship, and torn off at one rent (as Jack got rid of so many yards of lace in the *Tale of a Tub*) all the ornaments of fine writing and worn-out sentimentality.

All is fresh, as from the hand of nature: by going a century or two back and laying the scene in a remote and uncultivated district, all becomes new and startling in the present advanced period. Highland manners, characters, scenery, superstitions: Northern dialect and costume: the wars, the religion, and politics of the sixteenth and seventeenth centuries, give a charming and wholesome relief to the fastidious refinement and 'over-laboured lassitude' of modern readers, like the effect of plunging a nervous valetudinarian into a cold bath.

The Scotch Novels, for this reason, are not so much admired in Scotland as in England. The contrast, the transition is less striking. From the top of the Calton Hill, the inhabitants of 'Auld Reekie' can descry, or fancy they descry, the peaks of Ben Lomond and the waving outline of Rob Roy's country: we who live at the southern extremity of the island can only catch a glimpse of the billowy scene in the descriptions of the Author of *Waverley*. The mountain air is most bracing to our languid nerves, and it is brought us in ship-loads from the neighbourhood of Abbot's-Ford. There is another circumstance to be taken into the account. In Edinburgh there is a little opposition and something of the spirit of cabal between the partisans of works proceeding from Mr Constable's and Mr Blackwood's shops. Mr Constable gives the highest prices; but, being the Whig bookseller, it is grudged that he should do so. An attempt is therefore made to transfer a certain share of popularity to the second-rate Scotch novels, 'the embryo fry, the little aëry of ricketty children,' issuing through Mr Blackwood's shop-door. This operates a diversion, which does not affect us here.

The Author of *Waverley* wears the palm of legendary lore alone. Sir Walter may, indeed, surfeit us: his imitators make us sick! It may be asked, it has been asked, 'Have we no materials for romance in England? Must we look to Scotland for a supply of whatever is original and striking in this kind?' And we answer 'Yes!' Every foot of soil is with us worked up: nearly every movement of the social machine is calculable. We have no room left for violent catastrophes, for grotesque quaintnesses, for wizard spells. The last skirts of ignorance and barbarism are seen hovering (in Sir Walter's pages) over the Border. We have, it is true, gipsies in this country as well as at the Cairn of Der ncleugh: but they live under clipped hedges and repose in camp-beds, and do not perch on crags, like eagles, or take shelter, like sea-mews, in basaltic subterranean caverns. We have heaths with rude heaps of stones upon them: but no existing superstition converts them into the Geese of Micklestane-Moor, or sees a Black Dwarf groping among them. We have sects in religion: but the only thing sublime or ridiculous in that way is Mr Irving, the Caledonian preacher, who 'comes like a satyr staring from the woods, and yet speaks like an orator!'

We had a Parson Adams not quite a hundred years ago, a Sir Roger de Coverley rather more than a hundred! Even Sir Walter is ordinarily obliged to pitch his angle (strong as the hook is) a hundred miles to the North of the 'Modern Athens' or a century back. His last work indeed is mystical, is romantic in nothing but the title-page. Instead of a holy-water sprinkle dipped in dew, ' he has given us a fashionable watering-place; and we see what he has made of it. He must not come down from his fastnesses in traditional barbarism and native rusticity: the level, the littleness, the frippery of modern civilization will undo him, as it has undone us.

Sir Walter has found out (O rare discovery) that facts are better than fiction, that there is no romance like the romance of real life, and that, if we can but arrive at what men feel, do, and say in striking and singular situations, the result will be 'more lively, audible, and full of vent, ' than the fine-spun cobwebs of the brain. With reverence be it spoken, he is like the man who, having to imitate the squeaking of a pig upon the stage, brought the animal under his coat with him. Our author has conjured up the actual people he has to deal with, or as much as he could get of them, in 'their habits as they lived. ' He has ransacked old chronicles, and poured the contents upon his page; he has squeezed out musty records; he has consulted wayfaring pilgrims, bed-rid sybils. He has invoked the spirits of the air; he has conversed with the living and the dead, and let them tell their story their own way; and by borrowing of others has enriched his own genius with everlasting variety, truth, and freedom. He has taken his materials from the original, authentic sources in large concrete masses, and not tampered with or too much frittered them away.

He is only the amanuensis of truth and history. It is impossible to say how fine his writings in consequence are, unless we could describe how fine nature is. All that portion of the history of his country that he has touched upon (wide as the scope is)—the manners, the personages, the events, the scenery, lives over again in his volumes. Nothing is wanting—the illusion is complete. There is a hurtling in the air, a trampling of feet upon the ground, as these perfect representations of human character or fanciful belief come thronging back upon our imaginations. We will merely recall a few of the subjects of his pencil to the reader's recollection; for nothing we could add, by way of note or commendation, could make the impression more vivid.

There is (first and foremost, because the earliest of our acquaintance) the

Baron of Bradwardine, stately, kind-hearted, whimsical, pedantic: and Flora MacIvor (whom even we forgive for her Jacobitism), the fierce Vich Ian Vohr, and Evan Dhu, constant in death, and Davie Gellatly roasting his eggs or turning his rhymes with restless volubility, and the two stag-hounds that met Waverley, as fine as ever Titian painted, or Paul Veronese. Then there is old Balfour of Burley, brandishing his sword and his Bible with fire-eyed fury, trying a fall with the insolent, gigantic Bothwell at the Change-house, and vanquishing him at the noble battle of Loudon-hill; there is Bothwell himself, drawn to the life: proud, cruel, selfish, profligate, but with the love-letters of the gentle Agnes (written thirty years before) and his verses to her memory found in his pocket after his death. In the same volume of *Old Mortality* is that lone figure, like a figure in Scripture, of the woman sitting on the stone at the turning to the mountain, to warn Burley that there is a lion in his path; and the fawning Claverhouse, beautiful as a panther, smooth-looking, blood-spotted; and the fanatics, Macbriar and Mucklewrath, crazed with zeal and sufferings; and the inflexible Morton and the faithful Edith, who refused to 'give her hand to another while her heart was with her lover in the deep and dead sea.'

And in the *Heart of Mid-Lothian* we have Effie Deans (that sweet, faded flower) and Jeanie, her more than sister, and old David Deans, the patriarch of St Leonard's Crags, and Butler, and Dumbiedikes, eloquent in his silence, and Mr Bartoline Saddle-tree and his prudent helpmate, and Porteous swinging in the wind, and Madge Wildfire, full of finery and madness, and her ghastly mother. Again, there is Meg Merrilies, standing on her rock, stretched on her bier with 'her head to the east,' and Dirk Hatterick (equal to Shakespear's Master Barnardine), and Glossin, the soul of an attorney, and Dandie Dinmont, with his terrier-pack and his pony Dumple, and the fiery Colonel Mannering, and the modish old counsellor Pleydell, and Dominie Sampson, and Rob Roy (like the eagle in his eyry), and Baillie Nicol Jarvie, and the inimitable Major Galbraith, and Rashleigh Osbaldistone, and Die Vernon, the best of secret-keepers. And in the Antiquary, the ingenious and abstruse Mr Jonathan Oldbuck, and the old beadsman Edie Ochiltree, and that preternatural figure of old Edith Elspeith, a living shadow, in whom the lamp of life had been long extinguished, had it not been fed by remorse and 'thick-coming' recollections; and that striking picture of the effects of feudal tyranny and fiendish pride, the unhappy Earl of Glenallan; and the Black Dwarf and his friend Habbie of the Heughfoot (the cheerful hunter), and his cousin Grace Armstrong, fresh and laughing like the morning; and the Children of the Mist, and the baying of the blood-hound that tracks their steps at a distance (the hollow echoes are in our ears now), and Amy and her hapless love, and the villain Varney, and the deep voice of George of Douglas—and the immovable Balafre, and Master Oliver the Barber in *Quentin Durward*—and the quaint humour of the Fortunes of Nigel, and the comic spirit of Peveril of the Peak—and the fine old English romance of *Ivanhoe.*

What a list of names! What a host of associations! What a thing is human life! What a power is that of genius! What a world of thought and feeling is thus rescued from oblivion! How many hours of heartfelt satisfaction has our author given to the gay and thoughtless! How many sad hearts has he soothed in pain and solitude! It is no wonder that the public repay with lengthened applause and gratitude the pleasure they receive. He writes as fast as they can read, and he does not write himself down. He is always in the public eye, and we do not tire of him. His worst is better than any other person's best. His back-grounds (and his later works are little else but back-grounds capitally made out) are more attractive than the principal figures and most complicated actions of other writers. His works (taken together) are almost like a new edition of human nature. This is indeed to be an author!

The political bearing of the Scotch Novels has been a considerable recommendation to them. They are a relief to the mind, rarefied as it has been with modern philosophy, and heated with ultra-radicalism. At a time also, when we bid fair to revive the principles of the Stuarts, it is interesting to bring us acquainted with their persons and misfortunes. The candour of Sir Walter's historic pen levels our bristling prejudices on this score, and sees fair play between Roundheads and Cavaliers, between Protestant and Papist. He is a writer reconciling all the diversities of human nature to the reader. He does not enter into the distinctions of hostile sects or parties, but treats of the strength or the infirmity of the human mind, of the virtues or vices of the human breast, as they are to be found blended in the whole race of mankind. Nothing can show more handsomely or be more gallantly executed. There was a talk at one time that our author was about to take Guy Faux for the subject of one of his novels, in order to put a more liberal and humane construction on the Gunpowder Plot than our 'No Popery' prejudices have hitherto permitted.

Sir Walter is a professed clarifier of the age from the vulgar and still lurking old-English antipathy to Popery and Slavery. Through some odd process of servile logic, it should seem, that in restoring the claims of the Stuarts by the courtesy of romance, the House of Brunswick are more firmly seated in point of fact, and the Bourbons, by collateral reasoning, become legitimate! In any other point of view, we cannot possibly conceive how Sir Walter imagines 'he has done something to revive the declining spirit of loyalty' by these novels. His loyalty is founded on would-be treason: he props the actual throne by the shadow of rebellion. Does he really think of making us enamoured of the 'good old times' by the faithful and harrowing portraits he has drawn of them? Would he carry us back to the early stages of barbarism, of clanship, of the feudal system, as 'a consummation devoutly to be wished'? Is he infatuated enough, or does he so doat and drivel over his own slothful and self-willed prejudices, as to believe that he will make a single convert to the beauty of Legitimacy, that is, of lawless power and savage bigotry, when he himself is obliged to apologize for the horrors he describes, and even render his descriptions credible to the modern reader by referring to the authentic history of these delectable times?

He is indeed so besotted as to the moral of his own story, that he has even the blindness to go out of his way to have a fling at flints and dungs (the contemptible ingredients, as he would have us believe, of a modern rabble) at the very time when he is describing a mob of the twelfth century—a mob (one should think) after the writer's own heart, without one particle of modern philosophy or revolutionary politics in their composition, who were to a man, to a hair, just what priests, and kings, and nobles let them be, and who were collected to witness (a spectacle proper to the times) the burning of the lovely Rebecca at a stake for a sorceress, because she was a Jewess, beautiful and innocent, and the consequent victim of insane bigotry and unbridled profligacy. And it is at this moment (when the heart is kindled and bursting with indignation at the revolting abuses of self-constituted power) that Sir Walter stops the press to have a sneer at the people, and to put a spoke (as he thinks) in the wheel of upstart innovation! This is what he 'calls backing his friends'; it is thus he administers charms and philtres to our love of Legitimacy, makes us conceive a horror of all reform, civil, political or religious, and would fain put down the Spirit of the Age.

The author of *Waverley* might just as well get up and make a speech at a dinner at Edinburgh, abusing Mr Mac-Adam for his improvements in the roads, on the ground that they were nearly impassable in many places 'sixty years since'; or object to Mr Peel's Police-Bill, by insisting that Hounslow-Heath was formerly a scene of greater interest and terror to highwaymen and travellers, and cut a greater figure in the Newgate Calendar than it does at present. O Wickliff, Luther, Hampden, Sidney, Somers, mistaken Whigs and thoughtless Reformers in religion and politics, and all ye, whether poets or philosophers, heroes or sages, inventors of arts or sciences, patriots, benefactors of the human race, enlighteners and civilisers of the world, who have (so far) reduced opinion to reason and power to law, who are the cause that we no longer burn witches and heretics at slow fires, that the thumb-screws are no longer applied by ghastly, smiling judges, to extort confession of imputed crimes from sufferers for conscience sake: that men are no longer strung up like acorns on trees without judge or jury, or hunted like wild beasts through thickets and glens: who have abated the cruelty of priests, the pride of nobles, the divinity of kings in former times; to whom we owe it that we no longer wear round our necks the collar of Garth the swineherd and of Wamba the jester, that the castles of great lords are no longer the dens of banditti, whence they issue with fire and sword to lay waste the land: that we no longer expire in loathsome dungeons without knowing the cause, or have our right hands struck off for raising them in self-defence against wanton insult, that we can sleep without fear of being burnt in our beds, or travel without making our wills: that no Amy Robsarts are thrown down trap-doors by Richard Varneys with impunity, that no Red Reiver of Westburn-Flat sets fire to peaceful cottages, that no Claverhouse signs cold-blooded death-warrants in Sport, that we have no Tristan L'Hermite or Petit-Andre, crawling near us like spiders, and making our flesh creep, and our hearts sicken within us at every moment of our lives—ye, who have produced this change in the face of nature and society, return to earth once more, and beg pardon of Sir Walter and his patrons, who sigh at not being able to undo all that you have done!

Leaving this question, there are two other remarks which we wished to make on the Novels. The one was, to express our admiration of the good nature of the mottos, in which the author has taken occasion to remember and quote almost every living author (whether illustrious or obscure) but himself—an indirect argument in favour of the general opinion as to the source from which they spring; and the other was, to hint our astonishment at the innumerable and incessant instances of bad and slovenly English in them—more, we believe, than in any other works now printed. We should think the writer could not possibly read the manuscript after he has once written it, or overlook the press.

If there were a writer, who 'born for the universe' —

—Narrow'd his mind,
And to party gave up what was meant for mankind—

who, from the height of his genius looking abroad into nature, and scanning the recesses of the human heart, 'winked and shut his apprehension up' to every thought or purpose that tended to the future good of mankind—who, raised by affluence, the reward of successful industry, and by the voice of fame above the want of any but the most honourable patronage, stooped to the unworthy arts of adulation, and abetted the views of the great with the pettifogging feelings of the meanest dependant on office—who, having secured the admiration of the public (with the probable reversion of immortality), showed no respect for himself, for that genius that had raised him to distinction, for that nature which he trampled under foot—who, amiable, frank, friendly, manly in private life, was seized with the dotage of age and the fury of a woman the instant politics were concerned—who reserved all his candour and comprehensiveness of view for history, and vented his littleness, pique, resentment, bigotry and intolerance on his contemporaries—who took the wrong side, and defended it by unfair means—who, the moment his own interest or the prejudices of others interfered, seemed to forget all that was due to the pride of intellect, to the sense of manhood—who, praised, admired by men of all parties alike, repaid the public liberality by striking a secret and envenomed blow at the reputation of every one who was not the ready tool of power—who strewed the slime of rankling malice and mercenary scorn over the bud and promise of genius, because it was not fostered in the hot-bed of corruption, or warped by the trammels of servility—who supported the worst abuses of authority in the worst spirit—who joined a gang of desperadoes to spread calumny, contempt, infamy, wherever they were merited by honesty or talent on a different side—who officiously undertook to decide public questions by private insinuations, to prop the throne by nicknames and the altar by lies—who being (by common consent) the finest, the most humane and accomplished writer of his age, associated himself with and encouraged the lowest panders of a venal press: deluging, nauseating the public mind with the offal and garbage of Billingsgate abuse and vulgar slang: showing no remorse, no relenting or compassion towards the victims of this nefarious and organized system of party-proscription, carried on under the mask of literary criticism and fair discussion, insulting the misfortunes of some, and trampling on the early grave of others—

> Who would not grieve if such a man there be?
> Who would not weep if Atticus were he?

But we believe there is no other age or country of the world (but ours), in which such genius could have been so degraded!

Lord Byron

Lord Byron and Sir Walter Scott are among writers now living, the two, who would carry away a majority of suffrages as the greatest geniuses of the age. The former would, perhaps, obtain the preference with the fine gentlemen and ladies (squeamishness apart), the latter with the critics and the vulgar. We shall treat of them in the same connection, partly on account of their distinguished pre-eminence, and partly because they afford a complete contrast to each other. In their poetry, in their prose, in their politics, and in their tempers, no two men can be more unlike.

If Sir Walter Scott may be thought by some to have been

> Born universal heir to all humanity,

it is plain Lord Byron can set up no such pretension. He is, in a striking degree, the creature of his own will. He holds no communion with his kind, but stands alone without mate or fellow—

> As if a man were author of himself,
> And owned no other kin.

He is like a solitary peak, all access to which is cut off not more by elevation than distance. He is seated on a lofty eminence, 'cloud-capt,' or reflecting the last rays of setting suns, and in his poetical moods reminds us of the fabled Titans, retired to a ridgy steep, playing on their Pan's-pipes, and taking up ordinary men and things in their hands with haughty indifference. He raises his subject to himself, or tramples on it; he neither stoops to, nor loses himself in it. He exists not by sympathy, but by antipathy. He scorns all things, even himself. Nature must come to him to sit for her picture: he does not go to her. She must consult his time, his convenience and his humour, and wear a sombre or a fantastic garb, or his Lordship turns his back upon her. There is no ease, no unaffected simplicity of manner, no 'golden mean.' All is strained, or petulant in the extreme. His thoughts are sphered and crystalline; his style 'prouder than when blue Iris bends'; his spirit fiery, impatient, wayward, indefatigable. Instead of taking his impressions from without, in entire and almost unimpaired masses, he moulds them according to his own temperament, and heats the materials of his imagination in the furnace of his passions. Lord Byron's verse glows like a flame, consuming every thing in its way; Sir Walter Scott's glides like a river: clear, gentle, harmless. The poetry of the first scorches, that of the last scarcely warms. The light of the one proceeds from an internal source, ensanguined, sullen, fixed; the other reflects the hues of Heaven or the face of nature, glancing, vivid and various.

The productions of the Northern Bard have the rust and the freshness of antiquity about them; those of the Noble Poet cease to startle from their extreme ambition of novelty, both in style and matter. Sir Walter's rhymes are 'silly sooth' —

> And dally with the innocence of thought,
> Like the old age—

his Lordship's Muse spurns the olden time, and affects all the supercilious airs of a modern fine lady and an upstart. The object of the one writer is to restore us to truth and nature: the other chiefly thinks how he shall display his own power, or vent his spleen, or astonish the reader either by starting new subjects and trains of speculation, or by expressing old ones in a more striking and emphatic manner than they have been expressed before. He cares little what it is he says, so that he can say it differently from others. This may account for the charges of plagiarism which have been repeatedly brought against the Noble Poet. If he can borrow an image or sentiment from another, and heighten it by an epithet or an allusion of greater force and beauty than is to be found in the original passage, he thinks he shows his superiority of execution in this in a more marked manner than if the first suggestion had been his own. It is not the value of the observation itself he is solicitous about; but he wishes to shine by contrast—even nature only serves as a foil to set off his style. He therefore takes the thoughts of others (whether contemporaries or not) out of their mouths, and is content to make them his own, to set his stamp upon them, by imparting to them a more meretricious gloss, a higher relief, a greater loftiness of tone, and a characteristic inveteracy of purpose.

Even in those collateral ornaments of modern style, slovenliness, abruptness and eccentricity (as well as in terseness and significance), Lord Byron, when he pleases, defies competition and surpasses all his contemporaries. Whatever he does, he must do in a more decided and daring manner than any one else; he lounges with extravagance, and yawns so as to alarm the reader! Self-will, passion, the love of singularity, a disdain of himself and of others (with a conscious sense that this is among the ways and means of procuring admiration) are the proper categories of his mind: he is a lordly writer, is above his own reputation, and condescends to the Muses with a scornful grace!

Lord Byron, who in his politics is a liberal, in his genius is haughty and aristocratic: Walter Scott, who is an aristocrat in principle, is popular in his writings, and is (as it were) equally servile to nature and to opinion. The genius of Sir Walter is essentially imitative, or 'denotes a foregone conclusion' : that of Lord Byron is self-dependent or at least requires no aid, is governed by no law but the impulses of its own will. We confess, however much we may admire independence of feeling and erectness of spirit in general or practical questions, yet in works of genius we prefer him who bows to the authority of nature, who appeals to actual objects, to mouldering superstitions, to history, observation and tradition, before him who only consults the pragmatical and restless workings of his own breast, and gives them out as oracles to the world. We like a writer (whether poet or prose writer) who takes in (or is willing to take in) the range of half the universe in feeling, character, description, much better than we do one who obstinately and invariably shuts himself up in the Bastille of his own ruling passions. In short, we had rather be Sir Walter Scott (meaning thereby the Author of *Waverley*) than Lord Byron a hundred times over, and for the reason just given, namely, that he casts his descriptions in the mould of nature, ever-varying, never tiresome, always interesting and always instructive, instead of casting them constantly in the mould of his own individual impressions.

He gives us man as he is, or as he was, in almost every variety of situation, action and feeling. Lord Byron makes man after his own image, woman after his own heart; the one is a capricious tyrant, the other a yielding slave; he gives us the misanthrope and the voluptuary by turns; and with these two characters, burning or melting in their own fires, he makes out everlasting centos of himself. He hangs the cloud, the film of his existence over all outward things, sits in the centre of his thoughts, and enjoys dark night, bright day, the glitter and the gloom 'in cell monastic. ' We see the mournful pall, the crucifix, the death's heads, the faded chaplet of flowers, the gleaming tapers, the agonized brow of genius, the wasted form of beauty; but we are still imprisoned in a dungeon; a curtain intercepts our view; we do not breathe freely the air of nature or of our own thoughts. The other admired author draws aside the curtain, and the veil of egotism is rent; and he shows us the crowd of living men and women, the endless groups, the landscape background, the cloud and the rainbow, and enriches our imaginations and relieves one passion by another, and expands and lightens reflection, and takes away that tightness at the breast which arises from thinking or wishing to think that there is nothing in the world out of a man's self!

In this point of view, the Author of *Waverley* is one of the greatest teachers of morality that ever lived, by emancipating the mind from petty, narrow, and bigoted prejudices: Lord Byron is the greatest pamperer of those prejudices, by seeming to think there is nothing else worth encouraging but the seeds or the full luxuriant growth of dogmatism and self-conceit. In reading the Scotch Novels, we never think about the author, except from a feeling of curiosity respecting our unknown benefactor: in reading Lord Byron's works, he himself is never absent from our minds. The colouring of Lord Byron's style, however rich and dipped in Tyrian dyes, is nevertheless opaque, is in itself an object of delight and wonder: Sir Walter Scott's is perfectly transparent. In studying the one, you seem to gaze at the figures cut in stained glass, which exclude the view beyond, and where the pure light of Heaven is only a means of setting off the gorgeousness of art: in reading the other, you look through a noble window at the clear and varied landscape without. Or to sum up the distinction in one word, Sir Walter Scott is the most dramatic writer now living, and Lord Byron is the least so.

It would be difficult to imagine that the Author of *Waverley* is in the smallest degree a pedant, as it would be hard to persuade ourselves that the author of *Childe Harold* and *Don Juan* is not a coxcomb, though a provoking and sublime one. In this decided preference given to Sir Walter Scott over Lord Byron, we distinctly include the proseworks of the former; for we do not think his poetry alone by any means entitles him to that precedence. Sir Walter in his poetry, though pleasing and natural, is a comparative trifler: it is in his anonymous productions that he has shown himself for what he is.

Intensity is the great and prominent distinction of Lord Byron's writings. He seldom gets beyond force of style, nor has he produced any regular work or masterly whole. He does not prepare any plan beforehand, nor revise and retouch what he has written with polished accuracy. His only object seems to be to stimulate himself and his readers for the moment—to keep both alive, to drive away ennui, to substitute a feverish and irritable state of excitement for listless indolence or even calm enjoyment. For this purpose he pitches on any subject at random without much thought or delicacy. He is only impatient to begin, and takes care to adorn and enrich it as he proceeds with 'thoughts that breathe and words that burn.' He composes (as he himself has said) whether he is in the bath, in his study, or on horseback; he writes as habitually as others talk or think; and whether we have the inspiration of the Muse or not, we always find the spirit of the man of genius breathing from his verse. He grapples with his subject, and moves, penetrates and animates it by the electric force of his own feelings. He is often monotonous, extravagant, offensive; but he is never dull or tedious, but when he writes prose.

Lord Byron does not exhibit a new view of nature, or raise insignificant objects into importance by the romantic associations with which he surrounds them, but generally (at least) takes common-place thoughts and events, and endeavours to express them in stronger and statelier language than others. His poetry stands like a Martello tower by the side of his subject. He does not, like Mr Wordsworth, lift poetry from the ground, or create a sentiment out of nothing. He does not describe a daisy or a periwinkle, but the cedar or the cypress: not 'poor men's cottages, but princes' palaces.' His *Childe Harold* contains a lofty and impassioned review of the great events of history, of the mighty objects left as wrecks of time; but he dwells chiefly on what is familiar to the mind of every school-boy, has brought out few new traits of feeling or thought, and has done no more than justice to the reader's preconceptions by the sustained force and brilliancy of his style and imagery.

Lord Byron's earlier productions, Lara, the Corsair, etc., were wild and gloomy romances, put into rapid and shining verse. They discover the madness of poetry, together with the inspiration: sullen, moody, capricious, fierce, inexorable: gloating on beauty, thirsting for revenge: hurrying from the extremes of pleasure to pain, but with nothing permanent, nothing healthy or natural. The gaudy decorations and the morbid sentiments remind one of flowers strewed over the face of death! In his *Childe Harold* (as has been just observed) he assumes a lofty and philosophic tone, and 'reasons high of providence, fore-knowledge, will, and fate.' He takes the highest points in the history of the world, and comments on them from a more commanding eminence. He shows us the crumbling monuments of time; he invokes the great names, the mighty spirit of antiquity. The universe is changed into a stately mausoleum: in solemn measures he chaunts a hymn to fame. Lord Byron has strength and elevation enough to fill up the moulds of our classical and time-hallowed recollections, and to rekindle the earliest aspirations of the mind after greatness and true glory with a pen of fire. The names of Tasso, of Ariosto, of Dante, of Cincinnatus, of Cæsar, of Scipio, lose nothing of their pomp or their lustre in his hands, and when he begins and continues a strain of panegyric on such subjects, we indeed sit down with him to a banquet of rich praise, brooding over imperishable glories,

> Till Contemplation has her fill.

Lord Byron seems to cast himself indignantly from 'this bank and shoal of time,' or the frail tottering bark that bears up modern reputation, into the huge sea of ancient renown, and to revel there with untired, outspread plume. Even this in him is spleen; his contempt of his contemporaries makes him turn back to the lustrous past, or project himself forward to the dim future! Lord Byron's tragedies, *Faliero, Sardanapalus*, etc., are not equal to his other works. They want the essence of the drama. They abound in speeches and descriptions, such as he himself might make either to himself or others, lolling on his couch of a morning, but do not carry the reader out of the poet's mind to the scenes and events recorded. They have neither action, character, nor interest, but are a sort of gossamer tragedies, spun out and glittering, and spreading a flimsy veil over the face of nature. Yet he spins them on. Of all that he has done in this way the Heaven and Earth (the same subject as Mr Moore's *Loves of the Angels*) is the best. We prefer it even to *Manfred.* Manfred is merely himself with a fancy-drapery on. But, in the dramatic fragment published in the Liberal, the space between heaven and earth, the stage on which his characters have to pass to and fro, seems to fill his Lordship's imagination; and the Deluge, which he has so finely described, may be said to have drowned all his own idle humours.

We must say we think little of our author's turn for satire. His *English Bards and Scotch Reviewers* is dogmatical and insolent, but without refinement or point. He calls people names, and tries to transfix a character with an epithet, which does not stick, because it has no other foundation than his own petulance and spite; or he endeavours to degrade by alluding to some circumstance of external situation. He says of Mr Wordsworth's poetry, that 'it is his aversion. ' That may be: but whose fault is it? This is the satire of a lord, who is accustomed to have all his whims or dislikes taken for gospel, and who cannot be at the pains to do more than signify his contempt or displeasure. If a great man meets with a rebuff which he does not like, he turns on his heel, and this passes for a repartee. The Noble Author says of a celebrated barrister and critic, that he was 'born in a garret sixteen stories high. ' The insinuation is not true, or, if it were, it is low. The allusion degrades the person who makes it, not him to whom it is applied. This is also the satire of a person of birth and quality, who measures all merit by external rank, that is, by his own standard. So his Lordship, in a 'Letter to the Editor of my Grandmother's Review, ' addresses him fifty times as 'my dear Robarts' ; nor is there any other wit in the article. This is surely a mere assumption of superiority from his Lordship's rank, and is the sort of quizzing he might use to a person who came to hire himself as a valet to him at Long's. The waiters might laugh; the public will not. in like manner, in the controversy about Pope, he claps Mr Bowles on the back with a coarse facetious familiarity, as if he were his chaplain whom he had invited to dine with him, or was about to present to a benefice. The reverend divine might submit to the obligation; but he has no occasion to subscribe to the jest. If it is a jest that Mr Bowles should be a parson and Lord Byron a peer, the world knew this before; there was no need to write a pamphlet to prove it.

The *Don Juan* indeed has great power; hut its power is owing to the force of the serious writing, and to the contrast between that and the flashy passages with which it is interlarded. From the sublime to the ridiculous there is but one step. You laugh and are surprised that any one should turn round and travestie himself: the drollery is in the utter discontinuity of ideas and feelings. He makes virtue serve as a foil to vice; dandyism is (for want of any other) a variety of genius. A classical intoxication is followed by the splashing of sodawater, by frothy effusions of ordinary bile. After the lightning and the hurricane, we are introduced to the interior of the cabin and the contents of the wash-hand basins. The solemn hero of tragedy plays Scrub in the farce. This is 'very tolerable and not to be endured. '

The noble Lord is almost the only writer who has prostituted his talents in this way. He hallows in order to desecrate, takes a pleasure in defacing the images of beauty his hands have wrought, and raises our hopes and our belief in goodness to Heaven only to dash them to the earth again, and break them in pieces the more effectually from the very height they have fallen. Our enthusiasm for genius or virtue is thus turned into a jest by the very person who has kindled it, and who thus fatally quenches the spark of both. It is not that Lord Byron is sometimes serious and sometimes trifling, sometimes profligate and sometimes moral; but when he is most serious and most moral, he is only preparing to mortify the unsuspecting reader by putting a pitiful hoax upon him. This is a most unaccountable anomaly. It is as if the eagle were to build its eyry in a common sewer, or the owl were seen soaring to the mid-day sun. Such a sight might make one laugh, but one would not wish or expect it to occur more than once!

In fact, Lord Byron is the spoiled child of fame as well as fortune. He has taken a surfeit of popularity, and is not contented to delight, unless he can shock, the public. He would force them to admire in spite of decency and common sense; he would have them read what they would read in no one but himself, or he would not give a rush for their applause. He is to be 'a chartered libertine, ' from whom insults are favours, whose contempt is to be a new incentive to admiration. His Lordship is hard to please: he is equally averse to notice or neglect, enraged at censure and scorning praise. He tries the patience of the town to the very utmost, and when they show signs of weariness or disgust, threatens to discard them. He says he will write on, whether he is read or not. He would never write another page, if it were not to court popular applause, or to affect a superiority over it. In this respect also, Lord Byron presents a striking contrast to Sir Walter Scott. The latter takes what part of the public favour falls to his share, without grumbling (to be sure, he has no reason to complain); the former is always quarrelling with the world about his modicum of applause, the spolia opima of vanity, and ungraciously throwing the offerings of incense heaped on his shrine back in the faces of his admirers.

Again, there is no taint in the writings of the Author of *Waverley*; all is fair and natural and above-board; he never outrages the public mind. He introduces no anomalous character, broaches no staggering opinion. If he goes back to old prejudices and superstitions as a relief to the modern reader, while Lord Byron floats on swelling paradoxes—

> Like proud seas under him;

if the one defers too much to the spirit of antiquity, the other panders to the spirit of the age, goes to the very edge of extreme and licentious speculation, and breaks his neck over it. Grossness and levity are the playthings of his pen. It is a ludicrous circumstance that he should have dedicated his Cain to the worthy Baronet! Did the latter ever acknowledge the obligation? We are not nice, not very nice; but we do not particularly approve those subjects that shine chiefly from their rottenness: nor do we wish to see the Muses drest out in the flounces of a false or questionable philosophy, like Portia and Nerissa in the garb of Doctors of Law. We like metaphysics as well as Lord Byron but not to see them making flowery speeches, nor dancing a measure in the fetters of verse. We have as good as hinted, that his Lordship's poetry consists mostly of a tissue of superb common-places; even his paradoxes are common-place. They are familiar in the schools: they are only new and striking in his dramas and stanzas by being out of place. In a word, we think that poetry moves best within the circle of nature and received opinion: speculative theory and subtle casuistry are forbidden ground to it.

But Lord Byron often wanders into this ground wantonly, wilfully, and unwarrantably. The only apology we can conceive for the spirit of some of Lord Byron's writings, is the spirit of some of those opposed to him. They would provoke a man to write anything. 'Farthest from them is best.' The extravagance and license of the one seems a proper antidote to the bigotry and narrowness of the other. The first Vision of Judgment was a set-off to the second, though

> None but itself could be its parallel.

Perhaps the chief cause of most of Lord Byron's errors is, that he is that anomaly in letters and in society, a Noble Poet. It is a double privilege, almost too much for humanity. He has all the pride of birth and genius. The strength of his imagination leads him to indulge in fantastic opinions; the elevation of his rank sets censure at defiance. He becomes a pampered egotist. He has a seat in the House of Lords, a niche in the Temple of Fame. Every-day mortals, opinions, things are not good enough for him to touch or think of. A mere nobleman is, in his estimation, but 'the tenth transmitter of a foolish face': a mere man of genius is no better than a worm. His Muse is also a lady of quality. The people are not polite enough for him; the Court is not sufficiently intellectual. He hates the one and despises the other. By hating and despising others, he does not learn to be satisfied with himself. A fastidious man soon grows querulous and splenetic. If there is nobody but ourselves to come up to our idea of fancied perfection, we easily get tired of our idol.

When a man is tired of what he is, by a natural perversity he sets up for what he is not. If he is a poet, he pretends to be a metaphysician: if he is a patrician in rank and feeling, he would fain be one of the people. His ruling motive is not the love of the people, but of distinction: not of truth, but of singularity. He patronizes men of letters out of vanity, and deserts them from caprice or from the advice of friends. He embarks in an obnoxious publication to provoke censure, and leaves it to shift for itself for fear of scandal. We do not like Sir Walter's gratuitous servility: we like Lord Byron's preposterous liberalism little better. He may affect the principles of equality, but he resumes his privilege of peerage, upon occasion. His Lordship has made great offers of service to the Greeks—money and horses. He is at present in Cephalonia, waiting the event!

We had written thus far when news came of the death of Lord Byron, and put an end at once to a strain of somewhat peevish invective, which was intended to meet his eye, not to insult his memory. Had we known that we were writing his epitaph, we must have done it with a different feeling. As it is, we think it better and more like himself, to let what we had written stand, than to take up our leaden shafts, and try to melt them into 'tears of sensibility,' or mould them into dull praise and an affected show of candour. We were not silent during the author's life-time, either for his reproof or encouragement (such as we could give, and he did not disdain to accept) nor can we now turn undertakers' men to fix the glittering plate upon his coffin, or fall into the procession of popular woe. Death cancels every thing but truth, and strips a man of every thing but genius and virtue. It is a sort of natural canonization. It makes the meanest of us sacred; it installs the poet in his immortality, arid lifts him to the skies. Death is the great assayer of the sterling ore of talent. At his touch the drossy particles fall off, the irritable, the personal, the gross, and mingle with the dust—the finer and more ethereal part mounts with the winged spirit to watch over our latest memory, and protect our bones from insult. We consign the least worthy qualities to oblivion, and cherish the nobler and imperishable nature with double pride and fondness.

Nothing could show the real superiority of genius in a more striking point of view than the idle contests and the public indifference about the place of Lord Byron's interment, whether in Westminster Abbey or his own family vault. A king must have a coronation—a nobleman a funeral-procession. The man is nothing without the pageant. The poet's cemetery is the human mind, in which he sows the seeds of never-ending thought—his monument is to be found in his works:

> Nothing can cover his high fame but Heaven;
> No pyramids set off his memory,
> But the eternal substance of his greatness.

Lord Byron is dead: he also died a martyr to his zeal in the cause of freedom, for the last, best hopes of man. Let that be his excuse and his epitaph!

Mr Southey

Mr Southey, as we formerly remember to have seen him, had a hectic flush upon his cheek, a roving fire in his eye, a falcon glance, a look at once aspiring and dejected. it was the look that had been impressed upon his face by the events that marked the outset of his life. It was the dawn of Liberty that still tinged his cheek, a smile betwixt hope and sadness that still played upon his quivering lip. Mr Southey's mind is essentially sanguine, even to overweeningness. It is prophetic of good; it cordially embraces it; it casts a longing, lingering look after it, even when it is gone for ever. He cannot bear to give up the thought of happiness, his confidence in his fellow-man, when all else despair. It is the very element, 'where he must live or have no life at all.' While he supposed it possible that a better form of society could be introduced than any that had hitherto existed, while the light of the French Revolution beamed into his soul (and long after, it was seen reflected on his brow, like the light of setting suns on the peak of some high mountain, or lonely range of clouds, floating in purer ether!)—while he had this hope, this faith in man left, he cherished it with child-like simplicity, he clung to it with the fondness of a lover. He was an enthusiast, a fanatic, a leveller; he stuck at nothing that he thought would banish all pain and misery from the world; in his impatience of the smallest error or injustice, he would have sacrificed himself and the existing generation (a holocaust) to his devotion to the right cause. But when he once believed after many staggering doubts and painful struggles, that this was no longer possible, when his chimeras and golden dreams of human perfectibility vanished from him, he turned suddenly round, and maintained that 'whatever is, is right.'

Mr Southey has not fortitude of mind, has not patience to think that evil is inseparable from the nature of things. His irritable sense rejects the alternative altogether, as a weak stomach rejects the food that is distasteful to it. He hopes on against hope: he believes in all unbelief. He must either repose on actual or on imaginary good. He missed his way in Utopia: he has found it at Old Sarum—

> His generous ardour no cold medium knows;

his eagerness admits of no doubt or delay. He is ever in extremes, and ever in the wrong!

The reason is, that not truth, but self-opinion is the ruling principle of Mr Southey's mind. The charm of novelty, the applause of the multitude, the sanction of power, the venerableness of antiquity: pique, resentment, the spirit of contradiction, have a good deal to do with his preferences. His inquiries are partial and hasty, his conclusions raw and unconcocted, and with a considerable infusion of whim and humour and a monkish spleen. His opinions are like certain wines, warm and generous when new; but they will not keep, and soon turn flat or sour, for want of a stronger spirit of the understanding to give a body to them. He wooed Liberty as a youthful lover, but it was perhaps more as a mistress than a bride; and he has since wedded with an elderly and not very reputable lady, called Legitimacy.

A wilful man, according to the Scotch proverb, must have his way. If it were the cause to which he was sincerely attached, he would adhere to it through good report and evil report; but it is himself to whom he does homage, and would have others do so; and he therefore changes sides, rather than submit to apparent defeat or temporary mortification. Abstract principle has no rule but the understood distinction between right and wrong; the indulgence of vanity, of caprice, or prejudice is regulated by the convenience or bias of the moment. The temperament of our politician's mind is poetical, not philosophical. He is more the creature of impulse, than he is of reflection. He invents the unreal; he embellishes the false with the glosses of fancy, but pays little attention to 'the words of truth and soberness. ' His impressions are accidental, immediate, personal, instead of being permanent and universal. Of all mortals he is surely the most impatient of contradiction, even when he has completely turned the tables on himself. Is not this very inconsistency the reason? Is he not tenacious of his opinions, in proportion as they are brittle and hastily formed? Is he not jealous of the grounds of his belief, because he fears they will not bear inspection, or is conscious he has shifted them? Does he not confine others to the strict line of orthodoxy, because he has himself taken every liberty? Is he not afraid to look to the right or the left, lest he should see the ghosts of his former extravagances staring him in the face? Does he not refuse to tolerate the smallest shade of difference in others, because he feels that he wants the utmost latitude of construction for differing so widely from himself? Is he not captious, dogmatical, petulant in delivering his sentiments, according as he has been inconsistent, rash, and fanciful in adopting them? He maintains that there can be no possible ground for differing from him, because he looks only at his own side of the question! He sets up his own favourite notions as the standard of reason and honesty, because he has changed from one extreme to another! He treats his opponents with contempt, because he is himself afraid of meeting with disrespect! He says that 'a Reformer is a worse character than a housebreaker, ' in order to stifle the recollection that he himself once was one! We must say that 'we relish Mr Southey more in the Reformer' than in his lately acquired, but by no means natural or becoming character of poet-laureat and courtier. He may rest assured that a garland of wild flowers suits him better than the laureat-wreath: that his pastoral odes and popular inscriptions were far more adapted to his genius than his presentation-poems. He is nothing akin to birth-day suits and drawing-room fopperies. 'He is nothing if not fantastical. ' In his figure, in his movements, in his sentiments, he is sharp and angular, quaint and eccentric. Mr Southey is not of the court, courtly. Every thing of him and about him is from the people. He is not classical: he is not legitimate. He is not a man cast in the mould of other men's opinions: he is not shaped on any model: he bows to no authority: he yields only to his own wayward peculiarities. He is wild, irregular, singular, extreme. He is no formalist, not he! All is crude and chaotic, self-opinionated, vain. He wants proportion, keeping, system, standard rules. He is not teres et rotundus. Mr Southey walks with his chin erect through the streets of London, and with an umbrella sticking out under his arm, in the finest weather. He has not sacrificed to the Graces, nor studied decorum. With him every thing is projecting, starting from its place, an episode, a digression, a poetic license. He does not move in any given orbit, but, like a falling star, shoots from his sphere. He is pragmatical, restless, unfixed, full of experiments, beginning every thing anew, wiser than his betters, judging for himself, dictating to others. He is decidedly revolutionary. He may have given up the reform of the State: but depend upon it, he has some other hobby of the same kind.

Does he not dedicate to his present Majesty that extraordinary poem on the death of his father, called *The Vision of Judgment*, as a specimen of what might be done in English hexameters? In a court-poem all should be trite and on an approved model. He might as well have presented himself at the levee in a fancy or masquerade dress. Mr Southey was not to try conclusions with Majesty—still less on such an occasion. The extreme freedoms with departed greatness, the party-petulance carried to the Throne of Grace, the unchecked indulgence of private humour, the assumption of infallibility and even of the voice of Heaven in this poem, are pointed instances of what I have said. They show the singular state of over-excitement of Mr Southey's mind, and the force of old habits of independent and unbridled thinking, which cannot be kept down even in addressing his Sovereign! Look at Mr Southey's larger poems, his *Kehama*, his *Thalaba*, his *Madoc*, his *Roderic*.

Who will deny the spirit, the scope, the splendid imagery, the hurried and startling interest that pervades them? Who will say that they are not sustained on fictions wilder than his own Glendoveer, that they are not the daring creations of a mind curbed by no law, tamed by no fear: that they are not rather like the trances than the waking dreams of genius, that they are not the very paradoxes of poetry? All this is very well, very intelligible, and very harmless, if we regard the rank excrescences of Mr Southey's poetry, like the red and blue flowers in corn, as the unweeded growth of a luxuriant and wandering fancy; or if we allow the yeasty workings of an ardent spirit to ferment and boil over—the variety, the boldness, the lively stimulus given to the mind may then atone for the violation of rules and the offences to bed-rid authority; but not if our poetic libertine sets up for a law-giver and judge, or an apprehender of vagrants in the regions either of taste or opinion. Our motley gentleman deserves the strait-waistcoat, if he is for setting others in the stocks of servility, or condemning them to the pillory for a new mode of rhyme or reason. Or if a composer of sacred Dramas on classic models, or a translator of an old Latin author (that will hardly bear translation), or a vamper-up of vapid cantos and Odes set to music, were to turn pander to prescription and palliator of every dull, incorrigible abuse, it would not be much to be wondered at or even regretted.

But in Mr Southey it was a lamentable falling-off. It is indeed to be deplored; it is a stain on genius, a blow to humanity, that the author of Joan of Arc—that work in which the love of Liberty is exhaled like the breath of spring—mild, balmy, heaven-born, —that is full of tears and virgin-sighs and yearnings of affection after truth and good, gushing warm and crimson from the heart, should ever after turn to folly, or become the advocate of a rotten cause. After giving up his heart to that subject, he ought not (whatever others might do) ever to have set his foot within the threshold of a court. He might be sure that he would not gain forgiveness or favour by it, nor obtain a single cordial smile from greatness. All that Mr Southey is or that he does best, is independent, spontaneous, free as the vital air he draws. When he affects the courtier or the sophist, he is obliged to put a constraint upon himself, to hold his breath: he loses his genius, and offers a violence to his nature. His characteristic faults are the excess of a lively, unguarded temperament: —oh! let them not degenerate into cold-blooded, heartless vices! If we speak or have ever spoken of Mr Southey with severity, it is with 'the malice of old friends,' for we count ourselves among his sincerest and heartiest well-wishers. But while he himself is anomalous, incalculable, eccentric, from youth to age (the *Wat Tyler* and the *Vision of Judgment* are the Alpha and Omega of his disjointed career): full of sallies of humour, of ebullitions of spleen, making jets d'eaux, cascades, fountains, and waterworks of his idle opinions, he would shut up the wits of others in leaden cisterns, to stagnate and corrupt, or bury them under ground—

> ...from the sun and summer gale!

He would suppress the freedom of wit and humour, of which he has set the example, and claim a privilege for playing antics. He would introduce an uniformity of intellectual weights and measures, of irregular metres and settled opinions, and enforce it with a high hand.

This has been judged hard by some, and has brought down a severity of recrimination, perhaps disproportioned to the injury done. 'Because he is virtuous ' (it has been asked), 'are there to be no more cakes and ale? ' Because he is loyal, are we to take all our notions from the *Quarterly Review*? Because he is orthodox, are we to do nothing but read the Book of the Church? We declare we think his former poetical scepticism was not only more amiable, but had more the spirit of religion in it, implied a more heartfelt trust in nature and providence than his present bigotry. We are at the same time free to declare that we think his articles in the *Quarterly* Review, notwithstanding their virulence and the talent they display, have a tendency to qualify its most pernicious effects. They have redeeming traits in them. 'A little leaven leaveneth the whole lump'; and the spirit of humanity (thanks to Mr Southey) is not quite expelled from the *Quarterly Review*. At the corner of his pen, 'there hangs a vapourous drop profound' of independence and liberality, which falls upon its pages, and oozes out through the pores of the public mind. There is a fortunate difference between writers whose hearts are naturally callous to truth, and whose understandings are hermetically sealed against all impressions but those of self-interest, and a man like Mr Southey. Once a philanthropist and always a philanthropist. No man can entirely baulk his nature: it breaks out in spite of him. In all those questions, where the spirit of contradiction does not interfere, on which he is not sore from old bruises, or sick from the extravagance of youthful intoxication, as from a last night's debauch, our laureate is still bold, free, candid, open to conviction, a reformist without knowing it. He does not advocate the slave-trade, he does not arm Mr Malthus's revolting ratios with his authority, he does not strain hard to deluge Ireland with blood. On such points, where humanity has not become obnoxious, where liberty has not passed into a by-word, Mr Southey is still liberal and humane. The elasticity of his spirit is unbroken: the bow recoils to its old position. He still stands convicted of his early passion for inquiry and improvement. He was not regularly articled as a government-tool!

Perhaps the most pleasing and striking of all Mr Southey's poems are not his triumphant taunts hurled against oppression, are not his glowing effusions to Liberty, but those in which, with a mild melancholy, he seems conscious of his own infirmities of temper, and to feel a wish to correct by thought and time the precocity and sharpness of his disposition. May the quaint but affecting aspiration expressed in one of these be fulfilled, that, as he mellows into maturer age, all such asperities may wear off, and he himself become

        Like the high leaves upon the holly-tree!

Mr. Southey's prose style can scarcely be too much praised. It is plain, clear, pointed, familiar: perfectly modern in its texture, but with a grave and sparkling admixture of archaisms in its ornaments and occasional phraseology. He is the best and most natural prose-writer of any poet of the day; we mean that he is far better than Lord Byron, Mr Wordsworth, or Mr Coleridge, for instance. The manner is perhaps superior to the matter—that is, in his Essays and Reviews. There is rather a want of originality and even of impetus: but there is no want of playful or biting satire, of ingenuity, of casuistry, of learning and of information. He is 'full of wise saws and modern' (as well as ancient) 'instances.' Mr Southey may not always convince his opponents; but he seldom fails to stagger, never to gall them. In a word, we may describe his style by saying that it has not the body or thickness of port wine, but is like clear sherry with kernels of old authors thrown into it!

He also excels as an historian and prose translator. His histories abound in information, and exhibit proofs of the most indefatigable patience and industry. By no uncommon process of the mind, Mr Southey seems willing to steady the extreme levity of his opinions and feelings by an appeal to facts. His translations of the Spanish and French romances are also executed con amore, and with the literal fidelity and care of a mere linguist. That of the *Cid*, in particular, is a masterpiece. Not a word could be altered for the better in the old scriptural style which it adopts in conformity to the original. It is no less interesting in itself, or as a record of high and chivalrous feelings and manners, than it is worthy of perusal as a literary curiosity.

Mr Southey's conversation has a little resemblance to a common-place book, his habitual deportment to a piece of clock-work. He is not remarkable either as a reasoner or an observer: but he is quick, unaffected, replete with anecdote, various and retentive in his reading, and exceedingly happy in his play upon words, as most scholars are who give their minds this sportive turn. We have chiefly seen Mr Southey in company where few people appear to advantage, we mean in that of Mr Coleridge. He has not certainly the same range of speculation, nor the same flow of sounding words; but he makes up by the details of knowledge and by a scrupulous correctness of statement for what he wants in originality of thought or impetuous declamation. The tones of Mr Coleridge's voice are [of] ence: those of Mr Southey are meagre, shrill, and dry. Mr Coleridge's forte is conversation, and he is conscious of this: Mr Southey evidently considers writing as his stronghold, and if gravelled in an argument, or at a loss for an explanation, refers to something he has written on the subject, or brings out his port-folio, doubled down in dog-ears, in confirmation of some fact.

He is scholastic and professional in his ideas. He sets more value on what he writes than on what he says: he is perhaps prouder of his library than of his own productions—themselves a library! He is more simple in his manners than his friend Mr Coleridge, but at the same time less cordial or conciliating. He is less vain, or has less hope of pleasing, and therefore lays himself less out to please. There is an air of condescension in his civility. With a tall, loose figure, a peaked austerity of countenance, and no inclination to embonpoint, you would say he has something puritanical, something ascetic in his appearance. He answers to Mandeville's description of Addison, 'a parson in a tye-wig. ' He is not a boon companion, nor does he indulge in the pleasures of the table, nor in any other vice; nor are we aware that Mr Southey is chargeable with any human frailty but want of charity! Having fewer errors to plead guilty to, he is less lenient to those of others. He was born an age too late. Had he lived a century or two ago, he would have been a happy as well as blameless character. But the distraction of the time has unsettled him, and the multiplicity of his pretensions have jostled with each other. No man in our day (at least no man of genius) has led so uniformly and entirely the life of a scholar from boyhood to the present hour, devoting himself to learning with the enthusiasm of an early love, with the severity and constancy of a religious vow; and well would it have been for him if he had confined himself to this, and not undertaken to pull down or to patch up the State! However irregular in his opinions, Mr Southey is constant, unremitting, mechanical in his studies and the performance of his duties. There is nothing Pindaric or Shandean here. In all the relations and charities of private life, he is correct, exemplary, generous, just. We never heard a single impropriety laid to his charge; and if he has many enemies, few men can boast more numerous or stauncher friends.

The variety and piquancy of his writings form a striking contrast to the mode in which they are produced. He rises early, and writes or reads till breakfast time. He writes or reads after breakfast till dinner, after dinner till tea, and from tea till bedtime—

> And follows so the ever-running year
> With profitable labour to his grave—

on Derwent's banks, beneath the foot of Skiddaw. Study serves him for business, exercise, recreation. He passes from verse to prose, from history to poetry, from reading to writing, by a stop-watch. He writes a fair hand without blots, sitting upright in his chair, leaves off when he comes to the bottom of the page, and changes the subject for another, as opposite as the Antipodes. His mind is after all rather the recipient and transmitter of knowledge, than the originator of it. He has hardly grasp of thought enough to arrive at any great leading truth. His passions do not amount to more than irritability. With some gall in his pen and coldness in his manner, he has a great deal of kindness in his heart. Rash in his opinions, he is steady in his attachments, and is a man, in many particulars admirable, in all respectable—his political inconsistency alone excepted!

Mr Wordsworth

Mr Wordsworth's genius is a pure emanation of the Spirit of the Age. Had he lived in any other period of the world, he would never have been heard of. As it is, he has some difficulty to contend with the hebetude of his intellect and the meanness of his subject. With him 'lowliness is young ambition's ladder': but he finds it a toil to climb in this way the steep of Fame. His homely Muse can hardly raise her wing from the ground, nor spread her hidden glories to the sun. He has 'no figures nor no fantasies, which busy passion draws in the brains of men': neither the gorgeous machinery of mythologic lore, nor the splendid colours of poetic diction. His style is vernacular: he delivers household truths. He sees nothing loftier than human hopes, nothing deeper than the human heart. This he probes, this he tampers with, this he poises, with all its incalculable weight of thought and feeling, in his hands, and at the same time calms the throbbing pulses of his own heart by keeping his eye ever fixed on the face of nature. If he can make the life-blood flow from the wounded breast, this is the living colouring with which he paints his verse: if he can assuage the pain or close up the wound with the balm of solitary musing, or the healing power of plants and herbs and 'skyey influences,' this is the sole triumph of his art. He takes the simplest elements of nature and of the human mind, the mere abstract conditions inseparable from our being, and tries to compound a new system of poetry from them; and has perhaps succeeded as well as any one could. 'Nihil humani a me alienum puto [nothing human do I regard as foreign to me]' is the motto of his works. He thinks nothing low or indifferent of which this can be affirmed: every thing that professes to be more than this, that is not an absolute essence of truth and feeling, he holds to be vitiated, false and spurious. In a word, his poetry is founded on setting up an opposition (and pushing it to the utmost length) between the natural and the artificial, between the spirit of humanity and the spirit of fashion and of the world.

It is one of the innovations of the time. It partakes of, and is carried along with, the revolutionary movement of our age: the political changes of the day were the model on which he formed and conducted his poetical experiments. His Muse (it cannot be denied, and without this we cannot explain its character at all) is a levelling one. It proceeds on a principle of equality, and strives to reduce all things to the same standard. It is distinguished by a proud humility. It relies upon its own resources, and disdains external show and relief. It takes the commonest events and objects, as a test to prove that nature is always interesting from its inherent truth and beauty, without any of the ornaments of dress or pomp of circumstances to set it off. Hence the unaccountable mixture of seeming simplicity and real abstruseness in the *Lyrical Ballads*. Fools have laughed at, wise men scarcely understand, them. He takes a subject or a story merely as pegs or loops to hang thought and feeling on; the incidents are trifling, in proportion to his contempt for imposing appearances; the reflections are profound, according to the gravity and aspiring pretensions of his mind.

His popular, inartificial style gets rid (at a blow) of all the trappings of verse, of all the high places of poetry: 'the cloud-capt towers, the solemn temples, the gorgeous palaces, ' are swept to the ground, and 'like the baseless fabric of a vision, leave not a wreck behind. ' All the traditions of learning, all the superstitions of age, are obliterated and effaced. We begin *de novo* [over again] on a *tabula rasa* [empty place] of poetry. The purple pall, the nodding plume of tragedy are exploded as mere pantomime and trick, to return to the simplicity of truth and nature. Kings, queens, priests, nobles, the altar and the throne, the distinctions of rank, birth, wealth, power, 'the judge's robe, the marshal's truncheon, the ceremony that to great ones' longs, ' are not to be found here. The author tramples on the pride of art with greater pride. The Ode and Epode, the Strophe and the Antistrophe, he laughs to scorn. The harp of Homer, the trump of Pindar and of Alcæus, are still. The decencies of costume, the decorations of vanity are stripped off without mercy as barbarous, idle, and Gothic. The jewels in the crisped hair, the diadem on the polished brow, are thought meretricious, theatrical, vulgar; and nothing contents his fastidious taste beyond a simple garland of flowers. Neither does he avail himself of the advantages which nature or accident holds out to him. He chooses to have his subject a foil to his invention, to owe nothing but to himself.

He gathers manna in the wilderness; he strikes the barren rock for the gushing moisture. He elevates the mean by the strength of his own aspirations; he clothes the naked with beauty and grandeur from the stores of his own recollections. No cypress grove loads his verse with funeral pomp: but his imagination lends a sense of joy

> To the bare trees and mountains bare,
> And grass in the green field..

No storm, no shipwreck startles us by its horrors: but the rainbow lifts its head in the cloud, and the breeze sighs through the withered fern. No sad vicissitude of fate, no overwhelming catastrophe in nature deforms his page: but the dewdrop glitters on the bending flower, the tear collects in the glistening eye.

> Beneath the hills, along the flowery vales,
> The generations are prepared; the pangs,
> The internal pangs are ready; the dread strife
> Of poor humanity's afflicted will,
> Struggling in vain with ruthless destiny.

As the lark ascends from its low bed on fluttering wing, and salutes the morning skies, so Mr Wordsworth's unpretending Muse in russet guise scales the summits of reflection, while it makes the round earth its footstool and its home!

Possibly a good deal of this may be regarded as the effect of disappointed views and an inverted ambition. Prevented by native pride and indolence from climbing the ascent of learning or greatness, taught by political opinions to say to the vain pomp and glory of the world, 'I hate ye,' seeing the path of classical and artificial poetry blocked up by the cumbrous ornaments of style and turgid common-places, so that nothing more could be achieved in that direction but by the most ridiculous bombast or the tamest servility, he has turned back, partly from the bias of his mind, partly perhaps from a judicious policy—has struck into the sequestered vale of humble life, sought out the Muse among sheep-cotes and hamlets, and the peasant's mountain-haunts, has discarded all the tinsel pageantry of verse, and endeavoured (not in vain) to aggrandise the trivial, and add the charm of novelty to the familiar. No one has shown the same imagination in raising trifles into importance: no one has displayed the same pathos in treating of the simplest feelings of the heart. Reserved, yet haughty, having no unruly or violent passions (or those passions having been early suppressed), Mr Wordsworth has passed his life in solitary musing or in daily converse with the face of nature. He exemplifies in an eminent degree the association; for his poetry has no other source or character. He has dwelt among pastoral scenes, till each object has become connected with a thousand feelings, a link in the chain of thought, a fibre of his own heart. Every one is by habit and familiarity strongly attached to the place of his birth, or to objects that recall the most pleasing and eventful circumstances of his life.

But to the author of the *Lyrical Ballads* nature is a kind of home; and he may be said to take a personal interest in the universe. There is no image so insignificant that it has not in some mood or other found the way into his heart: no sound that does not awaken the memory of other years. —

> To him the meanest flower that blows can give
> Thoughts that do often lie too deep for tears.

The daisy looks up to him with sparkling eye as an old acquaintance: the cuckoo haunts him with sounds of early youth not to be expressed: a linnet's nest startles him with boyish delight: an old withered thorn is weighed down with a heap of recollections: a grey cloak, seen on some wild moor, torn by the wind or drenched in the rain, afterwards becomes an object of imagination to him: even the lichens on the rock have a life and being in his thoughts. He has described all these objects in a way and with an intensity of feeling that no one else had done before him, and has given a new view or aspect of nature. He is in this sense the most original poet now living, and the one whose writings could the least be spared: for they have no substitute elsewhere. The vulgar do not read them; the learned, who see all things through books, do not understand them; the great despise. The fashionable may ridicule them: but the author has created himself an interest in the heart of the retired and lonely student of nature, which can never die.

Persons of this class will still continue to feel what he has felt: he has expressed what they might in vain wish to express, except with glistening eye and faltering tongue! There is a lofty philosophic tone, a thoughtful humanity, infused into his pastoral vein. Remote from the passions and events of the great world, he has communicated interest and dignity to the primal movements of the heart of man, and in-grafted his own conscious reflections on the casual thoughts of hinds and shepherds. Nursed amidst the grandeur of mountain scenery, he has stooped to have a nearer view of the daisy under his feet, or plucked a branch of white-thorn from the spray: but, in describing it, his mind seems imbued with the majesty and solemnity of the objects around him. The tall rock lifts its head in the erectness of his spirit; the cataract roars in the sound of his verse; and in its dim and mysterious meaning the mists seem to gather in the hollows of Helvellyn, and the forked Skiddaw hovers in the distance. There is little mention of mountainous scenery in Mr Wordsworth's poetry; but by internal evidence one might be almost sure that it was written in a mountainous country, from its bareness, its simplicity, its loftiness and its depth!

His later philosophic productions have a somewhat different character. They are a departure from, a dereliction of, his first principles. They are classical and courtly. They are polished in style without being gaudy, dignified in subject without affectation. They seem to have been composed not in a cottage at Grasmere, but among the half-inspired groves and stately recollections of Cole-Orton. We might allude in particular, for examples of what we mean, to the lines on a Picture by Claude Lorraine and to the exquisite poem, entitled Laodamia. The last of these breathes the pure spirit of the finest fragments of antiquity—the sweetness, the gravity, the strength, the beauty and the languor of death—

> Calm contemplation and majestic pains.

Its glossy brilliancy arises from the perfection of the finishing, like that of a careful sculpture, not from gaudy colouring. The texture of the thoughts has the smoothness and solidity of marble. It is a poem that might be read aloud in Elysium, and the spirits of departed heroes and sages would gather round to listen to it!

Mr Wordsworth's philosophic poetry, with a less glowing aspect and less tumult in the veins than Lord Byron's on similar occasions, bends a calmer and keener eye on mortality; the impression, if less vivid, is more pleasing and permanent; and we confess it (perhaps it is a want of taste and proper feeling) that there are lines and poems of our author's, that we think of ten times for once that we recur to any of Lord Byron's. Or if there are any of the latter's writings, that we can dwell upon in the same way, that is, as lasting and heart-felt sentiments, it is when laying aside his usual pomp and pretension, he descends with Mr Wordsworth to the common ground of a disinterested humanity. It may be considered as characteristic of our poet's writings, that they either make no impression on the mind at all, seem mere nonsense-verses, or that they leave a mark behind them that never wears out. They either

Fall blunted from the indurated breast—

without any perceptible result, or they absorb it like a passion. To one class of readers he appears sublime, to another (and we fear the largest) ridiculous. He has probably realised Milton's wish, —'and fit audience found, though few': but we suspect he is not reconciled to the alternative.

There are delightful passages in the *Excursion*, both of natural description and of inspired reflection (passages of the latter kind that in the sound of the thoughts and of the swelling language resemble heavenly symphonies, mournful requiems over the grave of human hopes); but we must add, in justice and in sincerity, that we think it impossible that this work should ever become popular, even in the same degree as the *Lyrical Ballads*. It affects a system without having any intelligible clue to one, and, instead of unfolding a principle in various and striking lights, repeats the same conclusions till they become flat and insipid. Mr Wordsworth's mind is obtuse, except as it is the organ and the receptacle of accumulated feelings: it is not analytic, but synthetic; it is reflecting, rather than theoretical. The *Excursion*, we believe, fell still-born from the press. There was something abortive, and clumsy, and ill-judged in the attempt. It was long and laboured. The personages, for the most part, were low, the fare rustic; the plan raised expectations which were not fulfilled; and the effect was like being ushered into a stately hail and invited to sit down to a splendid banquet in the company of clowns, and with nothing but successive courses of apple-dumplings served up. It was not even toujours perdrix!

Mr Wordsworth, in his person, is above the middle size, with marked features and an air somewhat stately and quixotic. He reminds one of some of Holbein's heads: grave, saturnine, with a slight indication of sly humour, kept under by the manners of the age or by the pretensions of the person. He has a peculiar sweetness in his smile, and great depth and manliness and a rugged harmony in the tones of his voice. His manner of reading his own poetry is particularly imposing; and in his favourite passages his eye beams with preternatural lustre, and the meaning labours slowly up from his swelling breast. No one who has seen him at these moments could go away with an impression that he was a 'man of no mark or likelihood.' Perhaps the comment of his face and voice is necessary to convey a full idea of his poetry. His language may not be intelligible; but his manner is not to be mistaken. It is clear that he is either mad or inspired. In company, even in a *tête-à-tête* [private conversation between two persons], Mr Wordsworth is often silent, indolent and reserved. If he has become verbose and oracular of late years, he was not so in his better days. He threw out a bold or an indifferent remark without either effort or pretension, and relapsed into musing again. He shone most (because he seemed most roused and animated) in reciting his own poetry, or in talking about it. He sometimes gave striking views of his feelings and trains of association in composing certain passages; or if one did not always understand his distinctions, still there was no want of interest: there was a latent meaning worth inquiring into, like a vein of ore that one cannot exactly hit upon at the moment, but of which there are sure indications. His standard of poetry is high and severe, almost to exclusiveness. He admits of nothing below, scarcely of anything above, himself. It is fine to hear him talk of the way in which certain subjects should have been treated by eminent poets, according to his notions of the art. Thus he finds fault with Dryden's description of Bacchus in the *Alexander's Feast*, as if he were a mere good-looking youth or boon companion—

> Flushed with a purple grace,
> He shows his honest face—

instead of representing the God returning from the conquest of India, crowned with vine-leaves and drawn by panthers, and followed by troops of satyrs, of wild men and animals that he had tamed. You would think, in hearing him speak on this subject, that you saw Titian's picture of the meeting of Bacchus and Ariadne—so classic were his conceptions, so glowing his style.

Milton is his great idol, and he sometimes dares to compare himself with him. His Sonnets, indeed, have something of the same high-raised tone and prophetic spirit. Chaucer is another prime favourite of his, and he has been at the pains to modernize some of the *Canterbury Tales*. Those persons, who look upon Mr Wordsworth as a merely puerile writer, must be rather at a loss to account for his strong predilection for such geniuses as Dante and Michael Angelo. We do not think our author has any very cordial sympathy with Shakespeare. How should he? Shakespeare was the least of an egotist of any body in the world. He does not much relish the variety and scope of dramatic composition. 'He hates those interlocutions between Lucius and Caius.' Yet Mr Wordsworth himself wrote a tragedy when he was young; and we have heard the following energetic lines quoted from it, as put into the mouth of a person smit with remorse for some rash crime:

> —Action is momentary,
> The motion of a muscle this way or that;
> Suffering is long, obscure and infinite!

Perhaps for want of light and shade, and the unshackled spirit of the drama, this performance was never brought forward. Our critic has a great dislike to Gray, and a fondness for Thomson and Collins. It is mortifying to hear him speak of Pope and Dryden whom, because they have been supposed to have all the possible excellences of poetry, he will allow to have none.

Nothing, however, can be fairer, or more amusing than the way in which he sometimes exposes the unmeaning verbiage of modern poetry. Thus, in the beginning of Dr Johnson's *Vanity of Human Wishes*—

> Let observation with extensive view
> Survey mankind from China to Peru—

he says there is a total want of imagination accompanying the words; the same idea is repeated three times under the disguise of a different phraseology. It comes to this: 'let observation with extensive observation observe mankind'; or take away the first line, and the second,

> Survey mankind from China to Peru,

literally conveys the whole. Mr Wordsworth is, we must say, a perfect Drawcansir as to prose writers. He complains of the dry reasoners and matter-of-fact people for their want of passion; and he is jealous of the rhetorical declaimers and rhapsodists as trenching on the province of poetry. He condemns all French writers (as well of poetry as prose) in the lump. His list in this way is indeed small. He approves of Walton's Angler, Paley, and some other writers of an inoffensive modesty of pretension. He also likes books of voyages and travels, and *Robinson Crusoe*. In art, he greatly esteems Bewick's woodcuts and Waterloo's sylvan etchings. But he sometimes takes a higher tone, and gives his mind fair play. We have known him enlarge with a noble intelligence and enthusiasm on Nicolas Poussin's fine landscape compositions, pointing out the unity of design that pervades them, the superintending mind, the imaginative principle that brings all to bear on the same end; and declaring he would not give a rush for any landscape that did not express the time of day, the climate, the period of the world it was meant to illustrate, or had not this character of wholeness in it.

His eye also does justice to Rembrandt's fine and masterly effects. In the way in which that artist works something out of nothing, and transforms the stump of a tree, a common figure, into an ideal object by the gorgeous light and shade thrown upon it, he perceives an analogy to his own mode of investing the minute details of nature with an atmosphere of sentiment, and in pronouncing Rembrandt to be a man of genius, feels that he strengthens his own claim to the title. It has been said of Mr Wordsworth, that 'he hates conchology, that he hates the Venus of Medicis.' But these, we hope, are mere epigrams and jeux-d'esprit [witty comments], as far from truth as they are free from malice: a sort of running satire or critical clenches—

> Where one for sense and one for rhyme
> Is quite sufficient at one time.

We think, however, that if Mr Wordsworth had been a more liberal and candid critic, he would have been a more sterling writer. If a greater number of sources of pleasure had been open to him, he would have communicated pleasure to the world more frequently. Had he been less fastidious in pronouncing sentence on the works of others, his own would have been received more favourably, and treated more leniently. The current of his feelings is deep, but narrow; the range of his understanding is lofty and aspiring rather than discursive. The force, the originality, the absolute truth and identity, with which he feels some things, make him indifferent to so many others. The simplicity and enthusiasm of his feelings, with respect to nature, render him bigoted and intolerant in his judgments of men and things. But it happens to him, as to others, that his strength lies in his weakness; and perhaps we have no right to complain. We might get rid of the cynic and the egotist, and find in his stead a common-place man. We should 'take the good the Gods provide us': a fine and original vein of poetry is not one of their most contemptible gifts; and the rest is scarcely worth thinking of, except as it may be a mortification to those who expect perfection from human nature, or who have been idle enough at some period of their lives to deify men of genius as possessing claims above it. But this is a chord that jars, and we shall not dwell upon it.

Lord Byron we have called, according to the old proverb, 'the spoiled child of fortune': Mr Wordsworth might plead, in mitigation of some peculiarities, that he is the spoiled child of disappointment. We are convinced, if he had been early a popular poet, he would have borne his honours meekly, and would have been a person of great bonhomie and frankness of disposition. But the sense of injustice and of undeserved ridicule sours the temper and narrows the views. To have produced works of genius, and to find them neglected or treated with scorn, is one of the heaviest trials of human patience. We exaggerate our own merits when they are denied by others, and are apt to grudge and cavil at every particle of praise bestowed on those to whom we feel a conscious superiority. In mere self-defence we turn against the world when it turns against us, brood over the undeserved slights we receive; and thus the genial current of the soul is stopped, or vents itself in effusions of petulance and self-conceit. Mr Wordsworth has thought too much of contemporary critics and criticism, and less than he ought of the award of posterity and of the opinion, we do not say of private friends, but of those who were made so by their admiration of his genius.

He did not court popularity by a conformity to established models, and he ought not to have been surprised that his originality was not understood as a matter of course. He has gnawed too much on the bridle, and has often thrown out crusts to the critics, in mere defiance or as a point of honour when he was challenged, which otherwise his own good sense would have withheld. We suspect that Mr Wordsworth's feelings are a little morbid in this respect, or that he resents censure more than he is gratified by praise. Otherwise, the tide has turned much in his favour of late years. He has a large body of determined partisans, and is at present sufficiently in request with the public to save or relieve him from the last necessity to which a man of genius can be reduced—that of becoming the God of his own idolatry!